HOBO JINGO

Also by Jeff Dennis:

The Wisdom of Loons (2009)

King of the Hobos (2012)

Daydreams and Night Screams (2013)

To Touch Infinity (2015)

HOBO JINGO

The thrilling sequel to *KING OF THE HOBOS*

J E F F   D E N N I S

This is a work of fiction. The events described are imaginary. The characters and settings are fictitious. Any references to real persons or places are included only to lend authenticity to the story.

HOBO JINGO

FIRST EDITION

All rights reserved.
Copyright © 2017 by Jeff Dennis

Cover & Title Page Art: Carole Mauge-Lewis

This book may not be reproduced in whole or in part, without permission of the author, except in the case of brief quotations embodied in critical articles or reviews.

ISBN: 978-0-9911871-5-7

Nightbird Publishing
An imprint of WordCraft Resources, Inc.
www.wordcraft_resources@yahoo.com

Author website: www.jeffdennisauthor.com

Author e-mail : jeff@jeffdennisauthor.com

PRINTED IN THE UNITED STATES OF AMERICA

First Printing: July 2017

10 9 8 7 6 5 4 3 2 1

HOBO JINGO

by Jeff Dennis

PART 1: Return to Lost Horizon……… 1
PART 2: The Posse Rides …………… 95
PART 3: Kingdom of Puppets ………… 177
PART 4: Flashpoint ……………………… 249
PART 5: Aftermath: Five Years Later   363

HOBO JINGO 1

Part 1:
RETURN TO LOST HORIZON

Howl at the Moon
East of Nogales
Lost Horizon
Moonlight Madness
Worship at the Altar of Mother Nature
A Palette of Fury
Big Rock Candy Mountain
The Sedona Express
Costa Rican Blues
In Search of the Lost Swedes
All Dressed Up and Nowhere to Go
Follow the Money Trail
Down and Out in Monterrey
The Killing Barn
Mexican Jumping Beans
Home on the Range
Shrink Wrapped Elaine
Breezers and Bloodweed
Showdown at Shangri-La

Howl at the Moon

Costa Rica

Three years after Parnell's escape from the United States . . .

JUST BEFORE DAWN, the jungle erupted in frenzied growls and agitated barks.

The clamorous racket brought Parnell out of a deep sleep. Howler monkeys rampaged through the treetops, bellowing deep-throated shrieks. The cacophony reminded him of hunting dogs hot on the scent.

Extremely bad karma.

He sat up in bed, fluffing the pillows with angry punches.

Elaine stirred beside him, yawning. She propped herself on an elbow, looked at him in the dim glow of the nightlight.

"They're really bad tonight," she said, her voice husky with sleep.

"Yeah," he said. *Damned monkeys! It's an omen, and not a good one.*

"What has them so worked up?"

"No idea."

She slid next to him, her naked body warm, her skin soft. He felt her fingers tracing feathery patterns across his belly.

Her warm breath tickled his ear as she whispered, "Maybe it's a chimp orgy."

"They're *monkeys*, Lainey. They have *tails*. Chimps don't have tails."

"Damnit, Derek!" She pulled away from him, retreating to her side of the bed. "I didn't realize we were playing *Jeopardy* for Chrissakes!"

He sighed, in no mood for her petulance. This scenario had been playing out with more frequency lately, he rejecting her advances and Elaine going into her snappish, *you-have-done-me-*

wrong act. It had become tiresome, irritating. Predictable.

His cell phone erupted, the locomotive air-horn ringtone urgent and demanding. Heart racing, he reached out blindly, hand fumbling across the nightstand, grabbed the phone and squinted at the caller ID.

RITA MILLER.

"It's Jenny," he said, an uneasy feeling dropping into the pit of his stomach. No word from his daughter for several months and now a call at 4:30 in the morning? His anxiety gear clicked into overdrive.

"Hello, sweets," he said. "Long time no hear. To what do I owe—?"

"Russell's dead, Poppy. They shot him! Gunned him down! Oh my gawd, I'm so—"

"Slow down, sweetie," he said, his heart hammering. "I can barely understand you. Is it safe to talk on this line?"

"Of *course* it's safe. It's my WITSEC phone. What's wrong with you?"

"I, um . . . I'm still half asleep," he said, trying to collect his wits. The howler monkey pandemonium wasn't helping.

Russell Holt, Jennifer's lover the past couple of years, dared to testify against a connected Las Vegas kingpin. He'd had to go into the witness protection program along with Jennifer shortly after the trial.

Jennifer's voice in his ear, "Sorry to call you at this ungodly hour but they're after me, Daddy. I'm scared! *Really* freakin' terrified!"

She called him *Daddy*. His twenty-two-year-old daughter rarely addressed him that way anymore. *Poppy* was her preferred name for him now.

"Wait, slow down, Jenny," he said, trying to keep his voice steady. "Who are the '*they*' you're referring to?"

"The two assholes who made you run for your life."

Parnell sat up on his side of the bed, planted his bare feet on the floor. His heartbeat thudded in his throat. "Dobkin and Miles?"

"Yes."

Parnell had lived the past few years fearing this kind of reprisal. John Dobkin and Blanton Miles had finally struck. In their trademark fashion, they bided their time before going after Russell Holt, a high-ranking ex-employee of Dobkin's. Holt had testified against him in a grand jury trial, and Dobkin, using his money and connections, had skated clean away.

"When did this happen?"

"A week ago . . . maybe two. I don't know. I'm so confused right now," she said, her voice shaky. "I've been runnin' around, thinkin' what to do. Afraid. I didn't want to call you because I knew how—"

"Tell me what happened," he said. "Who shot Russell? Were you there?"

"Oh, was I ever! Russ and I were eating at an Italian restaurant. This big albino goon with spiked platinum hair and scary robot eyes approached our table and opened fire right in the middle of the dinner hour. Like something out of one of those freakin' *Godfather* movies you like . . ."

Big albino goon. His insides turned to ice. Had to be Lars. There weren't many men who creeped Derek Parnell, but Lars certainly did, with his empty laser stare, huge side-of-beef body, and blinding-white fluorescent skin.

". . . Russ never had a chance. I hightailed it out of there before the law arrived. I'm really scared! I can't handle this alone anymore."

"Where are you?"

"Hooked me a southbound on the run."

"You're riding the rails?"

"Best way to travel when the heat is on. Surely I don't have to tell *you* that."

Parnell listened for a beat. "Doesn't sound like you're on the move."

"I'm not. I'm sitting in a switching yard waitin' to be coupled to another teapot."

She's using hobo lingo?

"Where would I meet you?" he inquired. "That is, if in fact, I make the trip," he added, looking across the bed at a frowning Elaine.

"We could meet at one of the camps."

"Camps? One of the *hobo* camps?"

"Exactly."

Parnell felt things slipping away from him. "Sweetness, do you have any idea how dangerous it is for me to enter the U.S.? Don't you know how unsafe it is for *you* to be in the States?"

"I *do* know that, yes. But I'm already in the States. That's a big part of the problem."

Jennifer's words shocked him. "You're not in Canada?"

"No."

He nearly dropped the phone. He thought she had more smarts than this. "What the hell are you *thinking*?"

"Please, I don't need a lecture. I need you here with me . . ."

Parnell held the phone to his ear, listening to his frantic daughter. He watched Lainey run her hand through her shoulder-length hair, the patch covering her blind eye darkening the left side of her face. She didn't look happy.

His Jenny had been so good the past year, working under federal witness protection as an assistant manager in a Vancouver, British Columbia book shop as Rita Miller, the wife of James Miller (Russell Holt). She and Holt had been model WITSEC clients, playing their married roles quietly and to perfection. Parnell knew his daughter loved Holt and would never intentionally do anything to jeopardize his safety. He knew Jennifer could be spontaneous and headstrong, but he never dreamed she would do something this reckless. She had to be following Russell Holt's lead.

Holt had done his best to bring down John Dobkin for his role in orchestrating the bombing of a fringe militia group's munitions bunker in the Rocky Mountains. Forty-seven people had died there, nearly half of them innocent underage girls being held captive as part of a lucrative human sex-trafficking ring, managed and controlled by none other than John Dobkin. Jennifer had been part of that twisted harem, had been a sex slave for the Liberty Dog soldiers for seven long years. Those animals had done their damnedest to ruin her. Holt had been there, working undercover for four months before the big bang occurred.

". . . You still there, Poppy?"

"Yeah, I am. But I've gotta say, I'm extremely disappointed in—"

"Don't even go there," she said. "I know we screwed up. I'm paying for it dearly. I lost my Russ and I need you here with me. Please come!"

"I, um . . . I just don't know, honey," he said, thinking about the long trip (3,000+ miles to Arizona). The FBI bounty on his head prevented him from flying; he was on all the no-fly lists. The feds would scope him in a heartbeat if he set foot on a commercial flight. But he could arrange for a private flight. His Costa Rican fishing buddy, Vance Toohey, had a friend in San Jose who was a flight instructor and owned a twin-prop plane. Vance always said his pilot friend could fly him wherever he wanted to go for the right price. He could fly into Mexico, avoiding the risky border crossings of Nicaragua, Honduras, and Guatemala. He could then hook onto a freighter in the Mexico City Yards and ride the rails to the U.S. border. He wanted to go in the worst way. He had unfinished business to attend to. Still, all those miles. All that time. It would be a hard trip. And he had to consider Elaine's reaction should he elect to leave her again.

He heard Jennifer in his ear. "Did I lose you, Poppy?"

"No, no . . . I'm still here."

"Quit spacing out on me."

"I'm, uh, I'm just—I guess I'm having a tough time processing all this, Jenny."

"What is there to process? Russ was murdered. I'm all alone trying to dodge people who want me dead. I need you here. *Please!*"

The naked, desperate need in her voice got to him, threw a noose around his heart and strangled the shit out of it.

"Okay," he heard himself say. "But it'll take me a few days."

"Please hurry!"

The howler monkeys continued to rant outside, chaotic and feverish. He snuck a glance at Elaine, who glared at him through her good eye. Parnell knew her stance on returning to the States. *Over my dead body* she had said many times before. She had no use for the States anymore. Costa Rica was her adopted country now. This stilt house on the deserted stretch of Caribbean beach just north of the Panama border was Elaine Leibrandt's little paradise. She saw it as her reward for the hell she had been through with Parnell in the recent past—riding the rails, barely escaping with their lives, leaving behind a trail of death and destruction. Lainey felt she had earned this quiet life they enjoyed here. The resolute stare she gave him now said all that and more.

"I've got a better idea," Parnell said, eyes still on Elaine. "Why don't you come *here*? You haven't been back since you left."

"I can't. The feds are tracking me. Can't get *out* of the country right now. I can't even return to Canada."

He thought about that. "So tell me one thing," he said evenly. "Why did you leave Vancouver? You were safe up there."

"No, we weren't. Look," she said impatiently, "I'll tell you everything when you get here. Please hurry!"

"Shit, Jenny," he said, conflicted. "You're really putting me in a difficult position here."

"I'm sorry about that. I *really* am."

Parnell shook his head in consternation. This was a mess on so many levels. "All right. Tell me where you want to meet. Which camp?" On the far side of the bed Elaine slumped her shoulders, shook her head in disgust.

"Shangri-La."

Hearing the long-unspoken name of the Winslow, Arizona hobo camp trip off his daughter's tongue surprised him. "Okay. It'll take me a few days to get up there."

"Oh, thank you, Daddy! I love you."

"I love you, too, sweetness," he said before disconnecting.

"So you're going, then," Elaine said, intruding on his dark thoughts. A statement, not a question.

He nodded. "I have to. It's Jennifer."

Silently, she rose from the bed and went to the closet, grabbed her robe from a hangar and put it on. She walked around the bed, never looking at him, never speaking, then exited the bedroom and closed the door behind her.

The monkey caterwaul rose to a frightening roar.

Definitely an omen. Very black karma, indeed.

What does it mean?

He considered the possibilities and felt a strong urge to howl along with them.

East of Nogales

FROM WHERE HE SAT inside the covered hopper car, Parnell heard the loud hiss of air brakes, the metallic screech of wheels against steel rails. The train decelerated, then pulled to a dead stop.

Twenty-five hours from Mexico City riding this Ferromex grain hopper. And now this unscheduled stop.

Something's wrong. This freighter should have been cleared for entry into the States.

He had to get a look.

He fought his way across the heap of livestock feed in which he was mired. Each movement through the barley and alfalfa pellets sucked him down with the pull of a quicksand bog. Swirling barley dust and a sauna-like heat made breathing difficult. Sweat dripped into his eyes and soaked his shirt. His legs screamed in pain as he tried to advance through the grainy quagmire. With great difficulty, he moved under a ceiling hatch and popped it open, cautiously stuck his head out and scanned the line of railcars hitched to the twin locomotives a hundred yards up the tracks.

He squinted against the blinding early afternoon sun, spying a group of uniformed men getting out of official government vehicles. Car doors slammed. Jumbled voices carried on the hot desert breeze.

A small parade of men approached the lead locomotive. U.S. Customs and Mexican Border Patrol agents. The conductor stepped down and turned to face his visitors. A second man, the engineer, followed. The knot of *federales* surrounded the two Ferromex trainmen. The body language of the authorities and the way everyone talked at once told Parnell there was confusion.

He wondered why U.S. Customs would be concerned about this nondescript freighter entering the States. The cargo consisted primarily of farm animal feed and fertilizer. This border crossing should be slam-dunk safe, being in the wide-open no-man's land east of the official crossing point at Nogales. He counted a total of seven agents.

Overkill.

What makes this train so special?

Border agencies had been crippled by budget cutbacks in this long-running Great Depression 2.0. Following the disastrous Wall Street Crash of several years back, the payrolls of the American Border Patrol and ICE (Immigration and Customs Enforcement) had been slashed considerably, and so it was surprising to see so many agents congregated in one place. Especially a place as desolate as this.

Two more cars approached from the American side, throwing up rooster tails of dust behind them—a U.S. Customs and Border Protection Ford Explorer followed by a Department of Homeland Security Chrysler.

Serious shit.

Are they looking for me? Is that possible? Has someone ratted me out?

Impossible. No one knew he'd planned to enter the States by riding the rails through Mexico. The private pilot he'd paid to fly him from Costa Rica to Mexico only knew him by his alias (Samuel Cooper) and had no idea of his plans after dropping him off at the Mexico City airport. *Vance Toohey, maybe? Now you're really letting your paranoia get the best of you, Derek old boy. Your angler friend couldn't care less what you are doing in Mexico.*

He watched as the authorities moved down the line, ordering the train engineers to inspect every railcar. The trainmen grunted as they slid back heavy steel doors on enclosed cars and pulled open hatches and trapdoors on intermodal containers. Two inspectors followed along, scanning each interior with large flashlights.

Soon they would get to the covered hoppers. Surely they would inspect his grain car.

His mind raced. He could bury himself deep under the barley and alfalfa, but the hopper was a dry-heat sauna and he would run the very real risk of suffocating. In fact, the heat and dust and stink in the enclosed hopper car had become so overwhelming on the long haul from Mexico City he'd had to ride on the roof for long stretches.

Can't hide on the roof now. Time to jump off this iron horse.

Parnell dropped back through the open hatch, arms and legs spread wide to prevent being sucked into the pile of animal feed. He retrieved his backpack and checked his gun, making sure he had a full clip, then struggled back up, poking his head out the opening.

Snow-capped mountains to the west toward Nogales. Rolling plains of arid desert dotted by giant saguaro cactus and scrub brush to the north and east. Minimal concealment.

Nowhere to run. Nowhere to hide. The feds would spot him in a second if he made a run for it. He'd be captured, or worse, before he made it fifty yards.

An idea came to him as he noticed the agents ignoring the undercarriages of the railcars. Safety regulations required that tanker cars hauling combustible fuels have a higher clearance and shield plates as precaution against explosions from rail sparks. As always, before catching this freighter, he'd scoped its configuration. Several tanker cars pulled up the rear.

He had his escape plan.

Time for some axle swinging.

He pulled himself up through the open hatch and slithered on his belly across the roof, dropping down on the far side of the train. He moved stealthily along the tracks to the second tanker in line, ensuring his backpack was secure and his gun strapped tight with the safety on. He then ducked underneath and pulled himself up into a network of steel braces supporting the mammoth cylinder above. He squeezed in under the thick steel endplate and nestled into a mesh of crisscrossed struts. This position supported his back and took the strain off his arms. He was careful not to touch or block the computerized sensors he knew would report any fault conditions immediately to the locomotive engineer.

Waiting, suspended, the curved floor of the tank inches above his face, the cool support bars dug into his calves and shoulders. Muffled voices, the squeak and clank of boxcar doors and container hatches opened and shut, the noxious creosote stench coming up from the tracks.

He waited, his discomfort increasing. Each minute spent jammed up in this precarious, claustrophobic position gave Elaine's parting words more credibility:

"You're fifty-two, Derek. A little long in the tooth for riding the rails. It's been three years since you slept in railcars and ate roadkill. You can't ignore your age. I think deep down you know there are young tigers out there who could eat you alive. Your survival skills are rusty. Too much of the good life here in Costa Rica, babe . . ."

Lainey had spoken the truth. He felt the toll of the years and miles in his arms and legs, the arthritic ache in his joints and back. Yes, he *was* older now. No denying that. But he was still strong enough and tough enough to do what had to be done. Jennifer needed him. Dangerous people wanted her dead. He had to help her. However, he also had mercenary reasons for making this risky trip—an opportunity to nail John Dobkin and Blanton Miles. Perhaps his last opportunity. And he'd get Lady Thor and Lars while he was at it.

Justice will be served. The four of them have eaten away at my soul the past three years. Oh how I'll make them pay!

Lainey's voice filled his head: "And in case you forgot, you are very much a wanted man, Derek. Once word gets out you are alive and back in the States, every two-bit loser will be stalking you for the reward money. I'm worried sick about this. I'll miss you like crazy and think about you every minute you're gone. But try as I might, I can't go with you. I can't go through that hell again, babe."

She had ended her goodbye speech in convulsive tears, saying: "I pray the next time I see you I won't be looking down at you in the bottom of a coffin."

That had been when he left, three days ago. Everything she said to him was from her heart and it nearly broke him to have to walk out on her like that. Elaine loved him in spite of his restless nature. His hobo hotfoot had once again intruded on their relationship. They had been through so many tearful partings, but this one especially tore him apart. This time he wasn't sure whether there would be a sweet reunion at the end of the trail. He had never loved anyone as much as he loved Elaine Leibrandt.

He'd taken a bus to San Jose and the Toboas Bolanos Aeropuerto, where, through his fishing buddy, Vance Toohey, he'd arranged for a flight instructor to fly him to Mexico City. His fake identification got him through Mexican Customs. He'd then hiked to the Ferrovalle switching yards and broke into the Ferromex hopper car.

And now he was faced with this difficult border crossing.

He listened as the border agents got closer, their boots scuffing through the trackside gravel. The swirl of English and Spanish conversation increased in volume.

A tapping sound, a knocking against the tanker in front of him, each knock producing a sonar-like echo.

"Full?" one of the inspectors asked.

"*Si.*"

"What are these tankers hauling?"

"*Liquido de hidrógeno.*" Liquid hydrogen.

One of the Americans responded, "It's here in the shipping manifest. Three DOT113 cryogenic liquid tankers. All full. Seventeen thousand pounds, pressurized to the standard twenty-five PSI."

More shuffling feet. Four taps against the shell of his tanker, each followed by high-pitched watery echoes.

The engineer mumbled something indecipherable in Spanish, and one of the Americans said, "I ain't crawlin' under there."

More garbled Spanish, then footfalls shuffling down the line.

He waited for what seemed an eternity, nestled in the steel ribs of the tanker's undercarriage. Finally, doors slammed and car engines roared. Sand and gravel pinged the undersides of departing vehicles. The authorities were leaving.

He waited until the train was moving, the metallic clanking of couplers pulling against one another, then shifting into a slow roll. He climbed out from under the tanker and jogged back to the grain hopper, scaling the ladder up the far sidewall where he couldn't be seen. Once atop the roof, he stretched out, face down, keeping his body flat as the massive iron horse gained momentum. The roof burned his skin and the scorching desert wind whipped at him, but he much preferred this mode of travel to dropping back down into that hot, malodorous hopper.

Riding the rails, the sun baking his back, he pondered why the authorities had ripped this train apart.

Standard operating procedure or something else?

Suspected terrorist attack? Illegal immigration? Attempted drug cartel crossing?

Surely he alone wasn't enough to get border agents from two countries out in force in one of the more isolated places in the Sonoran desert.

Five minutes later, he lifted his head to see the sign rush past:
ARIZONA U.S.A.

Derek Parnell was back in the United States for the first time in three years.

Two hours to Tucson.

Hot wind whipped against his face. He squinted into the bright sky.

Are the FBI and NSA satellites tracking me?

Lost Horizon

JENN MADE IT TO THE CAMP by late afternoon. She stood atop a bluff overlooking a grassy vale, taking in the clutter of tumbledown shacks, ragged tents, and rickety hovels. Disappointment dogged her. This couldn't possibly be Shangri-La.

To hear Poppy tell it, this hobo village was the Land of Oz. Emerald City at the end of the Yellow Brick Road. A gleaming, majestic place where dreams came true. Spread out before her was something closer to a third-world refugee camp.

The camp's exotic name had led her to James Hilton's novel, *Lost Horizon*. The fictional Shangri-La was a mystical, earthly paradise isolated from the outside world. Hilton's world was a Himalayan utopia promising peace and harmony.

The sight of this ugly shanty village made her reluctant to venture down the hill and make contact. She sat, her back against a tree. Pulled a canteen from her backpack and slaked her thirst. An enormous metal cross towered over a plywood stage, gleaming in the afternoon sun and dwarfing the rest of the village. A sign painted in bright blue calligraphy hung from the edge:

FINNEGAN'S HOUSE OF WORSHIP.

A breeze brought cooking smells. She hadn't eaten since yesterday afternoon, before hopping a Union Pacific cannonball far north at the Pocatello train yards. Oh how she needed some grub!

She sensed movement behind her, heard a growly voice address her.

"Who are you and what's your business here?"

She scrambled to her feet. Two disheveled men pointed rifles at her.

"Uh," she stammered, dropping the canteen and raising her hands over her head. "I'm a fellow breezer. Just a bo-ette on the run," she said, using hobo terms Poppy had taught her. "I was told I could find sanctuary here."

"Who tol' you that?" said the younger man, stepping closer.

"My father. He's well known in these parts."

"Yeah? Who might that be?"

"King Midas. He told me I'd be safe here."

The two men exchanged glances.

"*There's* a name outta the past," the older man said, keeping his rifle trained on her chest. "Thought that crazy sumbitch was long dead and gone. You claimin' to be his kin?"

"That's right. I'm his daughter."

"Got any identification on ya, sweetheart?"

Her only ID was from WITSEC, showing her to be Rita Miller of Vancouver.

"I don't have ID proving I'm related to Derek Parnell. But I can tell you some of the things he's told me about this place. Stuff that went on when he traveled through these parts."

"Okay, try me out," the older man said.

Jenn tried an endearing smile. "Sure, but could you please lower your weapons? Those things scare me."

"You sure are a polite li'l twist. Suppose I gotta cooperate when you ask nice like that." He lowered his rifle and the younger man followed his lead. "Go ahead, tell us what you know."

She dropped her arms and scoured her memory, dredging up every detail she could recall from Poppy's stories. "Well, I know you call this place Shangri-La," she began.

Jenn told them what she knew about Nurse Annie from Albuquerque, who had tended to one of Poppy's employees, Kevin Spottswood, after he had been mortally wounded in a shootout with the Colorado State Police. She mentioned Poppy's good friend, Greg Bethea, a man they called Weasel. She told them that a musician, Fingers Johnston, used to play his battered guitar and sing, leading the camp in protest songs against the government. She told them about Alice the camp cook, who served squirrel and rabbit dishes on shiny hubcaps while wearing an *Alice's Restaurant* apron. She related what she knew about the resident drug dealer, Buttonhead Murphy, with his trademark porkpie hat and his expertise in harvesting psilocybin peyote button.

"That's some recall you got goin' for you, woman," the older man said, giving her an uneven grin. "No way anybody but Derek Parnell's kin could know all that." He stepped forward, extending a grubby hand, still cradling his rifle in the crook of his arm. "You already know me. I'm Greg Bethea and this is Ollie McKellar. We're camp security."

Jenn said, "*You're* Greg Bethea? The one they call Weasel?"

"As I live and breathe."

Jenn clasped his hand firmly. She should have known this was Poppy's old friend. Her father had described him so vividly. The narrow face, slender torso, long prairie dog neck, black predatory eyes and stringy silver mustache that extended from his face like catfish whiskers.

"So good to meet you, Mister Bethea. I've heard some great stories about you from my dad."

Weasel smiled, showing tiny, worn-down teeth. "I'm sure they're all tall tales. Derek was always bigger than life and so were his stories." He studied her. "I hate to ask this, but is he still alive?"

"Oh yeah, very much so. At least he was earlier in the week when we talked on the phone."

"Well, whaddaya know," Weasel said, shaking his head, "I just assumed the law finally caught up with him. Thought he'd taken the westbound to the great beyond." He turned to the younger man. "What's it been, Ollie? A coupla years since we seen King Midas?"

"Try *three* years," Jenn interjected.

"Where's he been hidin' all this time?" Weasel asked.

"In exile."

Weasel continued to stare at her with his dark beady eyes, making her uncomfortable. Finally a look of something remembered relaxed his stare, and he said, "I'll be damned. You're the long-lost daughter Parnell was searchin' for all those years. He finally found you."

"Yeah, he did. In Colorado." She flashed a magnanimous smile.

"You're Ginger? No that's not right. Help me out here, Ollie."

"I'm Jennifer. I go by Jenn these days. Jenn, with two *n's*"

"Howdy, Jenn with two *n's*," Weasel said. "Welcome to Shangri-La."

"Thank you."

"Comes with an apology 'cause I should never have doubted Derek," Weasel said. "Parnell always was a determined son of a bitch. How did he find you?"

"It's a long and painful story. Maybe he'll tell it to you when he gets here."

A flash of excitement crossed Weasel's lean face. "The King's comin' home, here to Winslow?"

"Yep. He's on his way as we speak."

Ollie McKellar looked at her doubtfully. "You said you talked to him on the phone?"

"I did, yes."

"So how about we call him and see where he's at."

Jenn turned to face the one named Ollie. Stared at him until he blinked. "He only uses burner phones," she said. "Once and done."

"How convenient," McKellar said with contempt. "Sounds like a big pile of hoo-ha to me."

"Lay off her, Ollie," Weasel said. "This pretty gal is descended royalty. She's our guest and we need to treat her with respect."

McKellar grunted in disgust. "Yeah? Well I don't believe a word she says. And even if she *is* Parnell's daughter, that ain't no royalty in my book. The man was a lyin', murderin' piece of shit. Derek Parnell always waltzed into camp like he was the second coming or somethin'. All high an' mighty, like he was better than us. Just cuz he had money. I was hopin' somebody'd finally put a bullet in him. He wasn't nothin' but trouble."

Weasel glared at his young accomplice. "Give it a rest, Mick. You're way outta line. Derek Parnell did all of us a lot of good over the years."

Ollie McKellar's tone became more submissive. "Well shit, Greg. Come on. You're always preachin' we need to be hyper-vigilant out here. Hell, you've seen the kinda people been driftin' through here lately. Desperate losers. Most of 'em lookin' to cash in on Parnell's bounty."

Weasel turned to her. "Boy's right, missy. Hate to say it, but as much as I would like to see your father again, this place ain't safe for him. And by association, it ain't safe for you either."

"It don't matter," McKellar said. "Parnell ain't stupid enough to come here."

But Poppy *was* coming here. At least she hoped he made it here.

"Come on," Weasel Bethea said to her. "I'll take you to meet some of the folks who knew your father. Reverend Ann sure will be pleased to meet you."

"You mean Nurse Annie? Annie Finnegan?"

"Yes. *Doctor* Finnegan. She's also Reverend Ann. She gives us good health and hope."

McKellar made a sound of disgust deep in his throat.

"What the hell's *your* problem?" Weasel asked him.

"Nothin'. Let's escort little miss liar down the hill."

"*I'll* take her," Weasel said, shaking his head. "You stay up here and walk the perimeter."

As they moved down the slope, Jenn saw Ollie McKellar spit into the dust and glare at Weasel Bethea with contempt.

Weasel held her steady at the elbow as they negotiated the rocky terrain down the hillside.

"Shangri-La sure isn't what I expected," she told him as they walked.

"How so?"

"Well, my dad made this place sound like paradise."

Weasel laughed. "As I said, your father is one helluva storyteller!"

Moonlight Madness

THE DESERT SUN LOWERED over Mobley Yards, casting shadowy fingers across the network of tracks, switching stations, and decoupled railcars waiting to be redeployed. Parnell had arrived at the Phoenix Burlington Northern Santa Fe yards after catching a graffiti-tagged side-car Pullman (boxcar) from Tucson. It had been a short two-hour jaunt here, passing through scenic Saguaro National Park, the little burg of Marana, and finally through the Gila Indian Reservation, home of the Pima and Maricopa tribes.

Mobley Yards was an important hub on the BNSF rail system. Parnell had been through here many times during his rail-hopping days when Elaine lived in Flagstaff. It was a major switching station on the western line, and from here he could catch a freighter going almost any direction. But though he knew the yard's layout, and ebb and flow of railway car knockers (train assemblers), eagle eyes (engineers), and snakes (switchmen), he had to exercise caution. At this busy terminus the bulls (rail cops), were some of the most merciless and vicious in the western states. His drifter friends had been roughed up here by overzealous bulls in years past. With the large bounty on his head, he couldn't afford to get sloppy.

He hunched between two covered hoppers, watching a pair of bulls walk the line several tracks over. A K-9 unit. The harnessed German shepherd led two beefy cops down the sidewalk overlooking Track 5. Fortunately, the breeze was in his face, carrying his scent away from the dog. He watched the bulls strut their stuff, feeling some of his younger self surface. It would give him great pleasure to confront them and pummel them. Rail yard bulls had become public enemy number one to the hobo community. The Great Depression 2.0 had shifted the class structure dramatically. The American hobo sat at the bottom of the food chain and that wasn't going to change anytime soon.

Exhaustion sapped him. His body ached. Maybe Lainey had been right. Maybe he *was* too old for this nomadic lifestyle now. This trip was one of the longest he had ever logged. And after such a grueling journey he had no guarantee that Jennifer would be waiting for him at Shangri-La.

The things we do for family!

He shook his head, marveling at the sway his daughter had over him.

He watched the dog lead the bulls around the corner of the east switching house and disappear, then made his move. He walked briskly along Track 9, ever on the alert, darting between decoupled rail cars. His creaky joints protested with each step. The straps of his overloaded backpack cut into his shoulders. The firearms in his pockets weighed him down as he moved away from the stacked-up rail cars and out into the open. The going was slow over the numerous raised switchbacks and the primary turntable, but no one spotted him. Soon he was through the switching yards and out on 19th Avenue.

First stop: Walmart, the only one still open in Phoenix. He purchased two burner cell phones with the cash he'd pulled from his Costa Rica stash. From there he took a taxi to a small roadside motel on the outskirts of Phoenix, the Moonlight Inn, an hourly-rate fleabag that was home for drug dealers, prostitutes, and transient drifters who could afford the twenty-five-dollar-a-night fee. The Moonlight was cash-only and the management never asked questions. The kind of place hobos called a no-tell. Even though the place was a certifiable dump, it afforded him a decent night's sleep in a real bed before the three-hour train ride over to Winslow and the hike into Shangri-La tomorrow.

Parnell checked into his room, little more than a glorified closet really. The smell of lilac air freshener hit him in the face, a cloying scent that failed to cover up the stench of pesticide spray. He flicked on the lights. Two plump cockroaches scuttled along the baseboards and darted into a crack in the woodwork. The tiny bed sat lopsided, a missing leg causing it to slant precariously to one side. The bedspread was stained. A framed print of Jesus, who wore a forlorn look, as if disapproving of the accommodations, hung crookedly on the wall.

"I know what you mean, big guy," he said, tossing his backpack and guns on the bed.

He pulled the burner phones from the pack and sat in the wobbly desk chair, checked for connectivity, then punched in Jennifer's number.

She answered on the second ring. "Hello? Who is this?"

"It's me, sweetie."

"Oh my gawd. It really *is* you. Where have you been? I've been worried."

"I didn't have the greatest travel arrangements. It's a long way from the banana republic. You at the camp?"

"Yes. Been here two days."

"Have my friends been good to you?"

"Well, yeah . . . most of them, anyway."

"Listen, we need to keep this short. I'm close. I'll be coming in tomorrow."

"Tomorrow? Can't you make it tonight?"

"Are you okay?"

"Yeah, but—"

"I need to get some rest," he said. "Haven't had much shuteye the past forty-eight hours. Just hold tight. I'll be there. Don't call me back. This phone is toast after I sign off. I love you and I'll see you soon."

"Okay," she said. "I love you, too."

Parnell disconnected the call, then dropped the phone on the floor and stomped it into plastic shards.

No sense in helping the feds track me.

He picked up the second phone and punched in Elaine's cell number. Nothing but empty rings on the other end. Finally, Lainey's voice: "Hi, we're not available right now. You know the routine."

Beep.

Parnell hesitated before speaking. "Hey, E, it's me. Wanted to let you know I made it. I'll be hooking up with you-know-who tomorrow. I just talked with her and she's fine. She made it to the camp. I'll be in touch again soon. I love you and miss you."

He disconnected.

He sat there, thinking. Where could Lainey be at this early-evening hour? Why didn't she pick up?

He punched in her number a second time. Same result. He didn't leave a message.

Mystified, the sound of her voice worked on him like a sad song. Only three days out and already he was getting sentimental.

Against his better judgment, he didn't destroy the second burner phone. He'd try her again later.

He needed to rustle up some food. He snatched his Mauser semiautomatic from the bed and stuck it in his waistband, then took all his cash from the backpack. Donned an Arizona Diamondbacks baseball cap and slung it low over his forehead, then walked a couple of blocks to a greasy burger joint. There he enjoyed a veritable feast of three double cheeseburgers, two large fries, and a chocolate shake, all the while keeping an eye out for people showing any interest in him.

Sated for the first time in three days, Parnell returned to the room and crashed on the bed after securing the three dead-bolt locks. He slept on his back, the Mauser at his side, and dreamed pleasantly of Elaine and Jennifer.

At five in the morning, his beautiful dream turned ugly.

A smoky fire surrounded the three of them. Jennifer screamed, "Help us! Help us!" The far wall went up in flames, collapsing on Elaine, her hair catching fire before she disappeared beneath the burning rubble. A curtain of blinding smoke rolled over him. He gasped for air, his lungs scorching with each painful breath. Losing sight of Jennifer, he heard her screaming out to him "Please, Daddy! Help me! Hurry, Daddy!"

He awoke coughing and gasping, drenched in a cold sweat. Disoriented and confused, he grabbed the Mauser and flicked the safety off, jumped to his feet, fired off a round of shots in a bewildered fury, peppering the far wall, smashing the mirror over the dresser and blowing out the TV screen.

Parnell slumped to the floor amid the glass debris, shaking. *The horrible fire nightmare. Almost forgot how bad they are.*

Another premonition?

A voice called to him from behind. He turned to look. Jesus stared down at him. Bullet holes pocked the wall around the framed print.

Jesus moved his mouth: "I understand your pain, my son, but you need to work on your aim."

Holy shit! The hallucinations are back!

He scrambled to gather his things and made it out the door as sirens wailed in the distance.

Worship at the Altar of Mother Nature

THE LITTLE COLORADO RIVER held Jenn spellbound. Crystalline greenish-blue water flowed over blood-red boulders in a rhythmic rush. This location, a short walk from camp, had become her refuge the two days she'd been at Shangri-La. So peaceful. Such gorgeous land. Ann Finnegan told her this part of the river channeled the main drainage from the Painted Desert. *Of course, where else could this vivid kaleidoscope of color come from?*

The trickle and hiss of the river lulled her into a meditative state. She thought about Poppy's phone call. He said he would be here soon. He'd told her he loved her. His words had warmed her, calmed her. But still, she had never felt so alone and vulnerable. She needed him here with her.

"There you are, Jenny. Is everything okay?"

Ann Finnegan again. Jenn just couldn't seem to get away from the woman.

She turned to see Ann approaching, gave her a fleeting smile, then looked back across the river. "No worries, I'm fine."

"Mind if I join you?"

"Pull up a rock," Jenn said dully, focusing on twin crimson buttes that lined the far side of the river.

Ann positioned herself cross-legged on the ground next to her. Long minutes went by in silence. They stared across the broad stretch of waterway, the sun reflecting off the rushing pools and eddies in sparkly diamond flashes.

Ann broke the silence. "It's gorgeous, isn't it?"

Jenn, in a contemplative mood, didn't want to make conversation. She nodded in agreement. The river flowed a striking aquamarine, the kind of clean, clear cerulean hue she'd known of the Caribbean waters that lapped the beach in Costa Rica where she'd lived with Poppy and Elaine.

As if reading her mind, Ann said, "You know how the Little Colorado gets that stunning color?"

"No."

"From the dissolved travertine and limestone. There are healing properties in this river that are simply amazing. My people bathe in it daily. It's a gift from God."

Jenn looked at her. "*Your* people?"

"My congregation. My patients. The camp breezers. They all depend on me. They all need me."

Jenn thought this just a bit over-the-top egotistical, but she held her tongue. After all, Ann had given her a cot in her own luxurious abode the past two nights (luxurious at least compared to other crude Shangri-La accommodations).

"I've always found this river to be therapeutic," Ann continued, a dreaminess in her voice, her expression blissful. "The water rushing downstream . . . so eternal and life affirming. It's a wonder how it keeps flowing, day after day, month after month, year after year. So much water. Millions of gallons. Makes you wonder where it all comes from. It's a miracle."

"It's no miracle," Jenn said, feeling the need to debate this woman. Poppy had called Ann pretentious. "It comes down from the Big Colorado."

"And how does the main Colorado River get so much water?"

Jenn turned to her. "From rain and the runoff of melting snow high in the mountains. Nothing but simple science."

Ann smiled at her, a hint of exasperation in her glance. "You have all the answers, don't you?"

"I've learned a lot in my twenty-two years."

"Maybe so," Ann said, maintaining a knowing smile. "But one thing you haven't learned is how to dive deeper into the questions. The eternal questions of life and death. Who we are and where we are going. What purpose the Lord has for us in this journey. You need to examine those things before you can arrive at answers, Jenny."

Jenn turned back to the rushing river. She wanted to tell Ann she *had* examined those things and they freaked her out. Jenn had learned to shuffle those thoughts to a back corner of her mind, out of sight. It's the only way she could survive.

She heard Ann going on. ". . . God created all the mountains and rivers. God created what we know as science. God lives in every drop of that river that flows before us. The Lord gives us sustenance and good health in these cobalt waters. This river is proof that a higher power is at work." Ann touched Jenn's hand

and her voice became more solemn. "Allow me to recite from the book of John: '. . . but whoever drinks the water I give them will never thirst. Indeed, the water I give them will become in them a spring of water welling up to eternal life.' "

Here she goes again, reciting scripture, whether she has her damn Bible or not.

Jenn couldn't take any more. She pulled her hand back and raised her voice. "Look, I don't need any more of your preaching, Ann. I spent seven years in the bowels of a cave abused by some of the nastiest men you could ever imagine. There wasn't any higher power down in those catacombs. God was AWOL, plain and simple. Pure evil was all I knew in those caves."

"I see. Do you want to talk about it?"

"No, I don't. I just thought maybe you should know that."

"Well thanks for sharing that with me, Jenny. You're a hard person to get to know."

"Maybe I wouldn't be if you didn't come on so strong. I have a problem with people who try to push themselves on me."

Ann frowned. "And you think that's what I'm doing? Pushing myself on you?"

"What would you call it? Ever since I got here you've hardly let me out of your sight. You've been interrogating me. You've been drowning me in your religious bullshit. You're trying too hard. Just back off a little, would you?"

Ann gave her a wounded look. "I'm sorry. It's just that I sense you are greatly troubled, that you're searching for something. I think it's something I can help you find, if you'll let me."

"I have everything I need, thank you very much."

"Do you, Jenny?"

She answered with a silent, contemptible stare.

Ann pointed at the cell phone cradled in her lap. "What did your father have to say?"

"How do you know it was him I was talking to? Were you spying on me?"

"I would *never* do that to you, Jenny. I'm just interested. I always liked your father. I'm pleased he's still alive. Overjoyed, in fact."

"He told me how you stalked him. How you caught the same freighter as him and followed him from Albuquerque. How he finally ditched you here."

Ann emitted a tiny snort. "Is that what he said? That I *stalked* him?"

Jenn nodded. "His exact words."

"I didn't stalk your father. I *followed* him."

"Why?"

"Because he represented all the things I thought I wanted back then. All the things that weren't available to me in Albuquerque."

"Like what?"

Ann got a pensive, faraway look on her face. "Excitement, danger . . . wanderlust. When Derek Parnell came into my clinic, I knew God had sent him to me. Your dad was worldly. He'd been around. I wanted that and it was obvious he needed me. Or so I thought. I was young and naive then."

"That was only three years ago, Ann."

"True. But I've grown quite a bit since then. Yes, your father abandoned me here after he left for Sedona and Flagstaff. I was angry at first. But then, as I got to know the people at Shangri-La and I fell in love with the land out here, I realized God had brought me here. It was His plan for me. This is my promised land, Jenny."

Ann closed her eyes. After a long reflective moment, she said, "You know, you remind me a lot of him."

"Oh yeah? How?"

"Not in looks. Those must have come from your mother. But I see the Parnell in you through your defiance, your rebelliousness. You're obstinate and very much your own person, just like he was—"

"Is," Jenn corrected.

"What?"

"You said just like he *was*. Past tense. Poppy is still very much alive and well."

Ann smiled. "That's what you call him? Poppy?"

"Yeah."

"I understand your Poppy is on his way here, that he'll be here tomorrow. Is that true?"

Jenn eyed her warily. "Maybe. Why do you need to know?"

"Well, you've told others in the camp this. I don't understand why you feel like you can't confide in me. I offer my home to you, make sure you get the best of our food. I protect you from dangers. I'm sure you know there are folks here in the village who don't appreciate your father the way I do."

"Yeah, I've run into Ollie McKellar a few times. He's a punk and a coward."

"Ollie does have his challenges. But he's not the only one, Jenny. There are a few here who have scores to settle with your Poppy. Most folks here are good souls. They look forward to seeing your father again. They are grateful for all the good things he did for them over the years. But there's a small group of malcontents that worry me. That's why I've taken you under my wing. That's why I've been looking out for you."

"Look, I really appreciate you letting me crash at your pad and all you've done for me. But I don't need any protection. I can handle things myself."

Ann looked at her doubtfully. "Can you? It can be a hard world out here."

Jenn thought back to her turbulent childhood in upstate New York, with Poppy trying to care for her while her wild-assed partying mother beat her down emotionally. She remembered the violent fights her parents had, explosive cussing and dishes thrown and furniture broken while she cowered in her locked bedroom. Being abducted at age eleven by her mother's first husband and whisked off to the high mountains of Colorado where she was sold into a human trafficking network. Poppy finding her and coming to her rescue and their bold and dangerous escape from Mount Zirkel. Hopping trains through Colorado, Utah, and Arizona with feds in hot pursuit via helicopter. The deaths on the train trestle over the Yampa River. The tense crossing at the border in Nogales. More recently, the murder of her Russell.

She said, "All I've ever known are hard worlds."

Ann studied her for an endless moment, then took Jenn's hand in hers again. "Yes, I see that. And that's why you need me, Jenny. I want to help you."

Jenn was about to protest when she heard a commotion up on the hill behind them. Startled, both of them sprung from where they sat. Weasel Bethea approached in a slow trot, his ever-present rifle out in front of him.

"Come quick, Ann," he shouted. "We've got visitors. They're asking for you."

"What do they want, Greg?" she said, making her way up the knoll.

"They want Derek Parnell."

"Well, obviously he's not here."

"That's what I told them." Jenn saw Bethea stop halfway

down the hill and look in her direction. "They know Derek's daughter is here."

His words iced Jenn's heart.

Ann maintained her cool, kept her voice steady. "Tell them to wait for me, Greg. I'll see them momentarily."

To Jenn she said, "You wait down here until I return." She took Jenn's hands in hers, stared into her eyes, the look conveying sincere compassion. "I'll take care of it, Jenny. You just stay out of sight."

Jenn watched Ann go up the hill with Greg Bethea. Heart racing, she looked at the cell phone in her hand, wishing there was some way to warn Poppy. She decided to try his burner phone. Maybe he hadn't destroyed it yet.

Hoping for some much needed luck, fingers trembling, she punched the call-back option, held the phone to her ear.

No connection. No voicemail.

A crushing loneliness overwhelmed her.

She dropped to her knees and began to cry. Guilt consumed her.

Once again, I have led Poppy into extreme danger.

A Palette of Fury

ELAINE STOOD IN FRONT OF HER EASEL, brush in hand. She had no idea what she was trying to create, but slapping blobs of paint on the canvas felt wonderfully cathartic.

Therapy to soften the hard edges of her resentment.

She stepped back and checked her work. A complete mess. Like Jackson Pollock strung out on hallucinogens. She would name this piece *My Fury*.

Derek was the subject of her wrath. After hearing nothing from him for three days, he called twice last night. As much as she wanted to speak with him, she'd let voicemail answer. The sound of his voice soothed her and she was relieved he was safe. But her anger over his leaving had heated to a boil during the three days of silence.

Splat, slop, splash . . . she smothered the canvas with another layer of paint.

So many things about Derek ratcheted up the crazy in her: his uncontrollable desire to ride the rails, his obsessive need to travel incommunicado, his goddamned selfishness.

She had fallen for him ten years before. Derek Parnell, the roving wanderer. The ultimate nomad. He was her Don Quixote, the Man of La Mancha, her knight in rusted armor, always rushing off on some twisted quest, always looking for dragons to slay.

Why isn't my love for him enough? After all we went through three years ago, narrowly escaping death, and he prefers danger over me?

She shook her head. Loving such a man presented real challenges and she couldn't find it in her heart to forgive him.

Splash, slap, plop . . . Elaine was so angry her hands shook as she hurled paint at the canvas.

Paint streaked the wall behind the easel—vivid blues and yellows and greens—resembling the aftermath of an intense paintball shootout. Sticky-slippery puddles smeared the floor. She was creating a huge mess that would be difficult to clean up, but she didn't care.

She tried to calm herself by recollecting how wonderful things had been between them for most of the three years they'd been here in Costa Rica. After Jennifer left it was just the two of them. Best period of her life. He made her feel wanted, needed, *adored.* The kick and spark of romance had reignited their relationship. He'd focused on her, made her feel special again. He brought her beautiful bouquets of parrot flowers and bamboo orchids after his trips into the village. He gave her trays of *bolitas de coco,* the sweet Costa Rican coconut balls she loved. He left her passionate notes before his walks down the beach, carefully penned in his bold handwriting, professing his deep and undying love for her. Derek seemed happy with his new station in life, and he filled her with the same euphoria.

But life had a habit of giving her the middle finger.

Four months ago Derek changed. He became moody, quick to snap at her. He spent more time out on Vance Toohey's fishing boat and invented excuses to stay away. Her attempts at conversation brought silent nods. He was there physically, but his mind was focused on things he elected to keep private. She feared he was getting the hobo hotfoot again, that he was hearing the mournful blast of the locomotive whistle that had always worked on him like a wakeup call. She feared he was plotting revenge against the men who had wronged him.

Her fears had been spot on.

He had left her again. Don Quixote had ridden the iron horse north on another quest.

Bastard!

Splash, slap, smack, smack, smack . . . she squeezed a full tube of Napthol Scarlet on the canvas and used her palette knife to smear it around.

She examined the swirl of colors. The canvas resembled a bleeding tornado. She smiled. The painting symbolized her life. Elaine had certainly seen a lot of bloodshed. And her past was as chaotic and fierce as a category five twister.

She grabbed a thin brush and swabbed a dab of Perylene Black from her palette, leaned in and titled the work: *My Fury.* Added her signature underneath. *Not my best work by any stretch.* But then, she hadn't painted since they relocated here. Seemed just like yesterday she was a highly sought-after artist, showcasing her paintings, pen-and-ink drawings, and charcoal sketches in prestigious galleries around Flagstaff and Sedona.

What's happened to me?

She recalled her last professional painting, a chillingly lifelike portrait of the crossbow hunter who attempted to rape her in the hunting shack north of Chinle. She had captured every frightening detail of the man: his deranged face, his malicious empty stare, the lethal crossbow broadhead jutting out in front of him that would have decapitated her had he launched it.

Suddenly she experienced being back in that grungy shack: his horrendous breath in her face, pants down around his ankles, right hand waving the big blade of his hunting knife near her good eye, left hand squeezing her throat in a choke hold.

The Rorschach paint blots morphed into his face. His husky voice boomed, "Time fer me to fuck yer other eye out, bitch!"

She yelled out, "Oh, dear God, no! *Please* don't hurt me!"

Her face was slick with sweat.

Her anxiety raged.

Her body trembled.

She screamed and threw her palette knife at the easel, piercing the canvas with a scarlet slash. Heart hammering, she grabbed a plastic bottle of linseed oil, unscrewed the cap and wildly doused the canvas.

The yellowish oil splattering the painting took her back to another ghastly hell. Jessie Waltham, appearing at the door of her Los Angeles apartment a month after she had broken it off with him. She opens the door to confront him, to remind him of the restraining order she has taken out on him. Sees him teetering side to side, drunk, his mouth set in a determined slash. She spots the glass jar in his hand containing a pale yellow liquid. Sees his arm move, the jar come up, the sulfuric acid splashing the left side of her face. Intense burning-melting. The detestable smell of burnt hair and scalded skin. Intolerable pain. Unconsciousness.

She screamed again and jumped back from the easel, slipping on the slick floor and going down hard on her tailbone, a shower of linseed oil drenching her. She lay on the paint-slimed floor, her ass throbbing, her mind jumbled. Frustrated, she threw the bottle at the wall and it bounced back, hitting her in the forehead.

"Shit!" she groaned, rubbing her head.

Goddamn you, Derek Parnell, this is all your fault!

And then she realized the ridiculousness of her situation and burst into insane laughter. Her mad hoots and cackles filled the small room. She was sprawled on the sticky floor, her clothes spattered with oil paints every color of the rainbow, the biting stench of turpentine and linseed oil stinging her nasal passages, her ass bone bruised and her self-esteem humiliated. She was bitching out Derek, who was thousands of miles away.

How absurd is this?

You're a hot mess, Lainey old girl.

She glanced up at her painting, which seemed to mock her with its slapdash mix of colors, chaotic movement, and punctured canvas. She studied it, beginning to see the brilliance of it. Something about the bold brush strokes and the phantasmagoric blend of colors.

Slowly she got to her feet, massaging her sore backside. She retrieved her brush and painted over *My Fury*, then dabbed in the new title above her signature.

My Life With Derek.

Big Rock Candy Mountain

PARNELL MADE IT TO THE CAMP ahead of the storm. He no sooner made it through the entrance aqueduct when the leaden skies opened up, pelting the area with driving rain and tiny hailstones.

Weasel Bethea, brandishing a tattered umbrella in his left hand and a rifle in his right, had intercepted him on his way in. They hugged enthusiastically as the rain soaked them. Parnell didn't know what to expect after being away for three years, but running into Greg Bethea was a good sign. He wondered how many other old timers were still here.

Parnell inquired about Jenny, and Weasel told him Jenn was doing fine. "She's staying with Ann Finnegan."

"Nurse Annie's still here?"

"Yep."

Parnell gave him a sour look.

"She's changed, bro," Bethea hollered over the lashing rain. "Ann's not the pain-in-the-ass you knew back when. She's been lookin' out for your daughter. Yesterday she saved Jenny's ass."

"How so?"

Sleety rain pinged the canopy of the umbrella as they walked. "Some people showed up lookin' for you. And Jenn."

Parnell pulled up short, stopping Bethea. "Were they feds?"

"No. Civilians. Bounty hunters. Looking for the reward money."

"Give me the scoop," Parnell said, anxiety fluttering in his stomach.

The rain dripped from the brim of the umbrella onto Bethea's yellow slicker. Drops of condensation nestled in his catfish whiskers.

"There were three of 'em. Real aggressive. Somehow they knew Jenn was here and that you were on the way. Thought they'd stumbled onto the big score. You could almost see the dollar signs in their eyes. But Ann cut 'em off at the knees. Convinced 'em that neither of the Parnells were here and that you hadn't been seen in these parts for many years. They refused to leave so Ann threatened 'em. She put the fear of the almighty in 'em. Told 'em she was a Santa Muerte priestess who practiced Day of the Dead occult rituals. Told 'em she was in need of a human sacrifice and they looked like good candidates. It was somethin' to see."

Parnell processed this. "And they bought that bullshit?"

"Did they ever. You should've seen 'em turn tail and run. Ann was on stage, givin' a Tony-winning performance."

A flash of lightning lit up the camp. A clap of thunder shook the ground.

"C'mon, bro," Weasel yelled over the downpour. "We'll get zapped if we keep chattin' out here."

Bethea led him through rows of ragged tents, crude wooden huts, and tin-roofed lean-tos, glommed together like a refugee settlement. They passed two rusted-out port-o-lets converted into cramped living accommodations. The tents were bed sheets stretched over rickety two-by-four frames, struggling to hold their own against the relentless deluge. Dilapidated huts lined the woods on the southern side. Parnell couldn't believe the squalor and shabbiness of the place. The camp had a desperate, hopeless feel to it, the breezers living on top of each other. The decline over three years troubled him.

He shouted into Bethea's ear as they slogged through the mud under the umbrella. "This place has grown. How many are here now?"

"Usually around one-fifty."

Parnell whistled. "The times are bad, eh?"

"You ain't lyin', compadre."

Bethea ushered him out to an open field. Their boots squished through the muck in loud sucking noises. *Suck-slurp ... suck-slurp.* Like walking on a giant sponge.

The stormy late-morning soup hampered visibility, but Parnell was able to make out a large dwelling in the distance. As they moved closer, he saw a house built of stones and mortared with what looked like roofing tar. Gabled copper roof. Cement foundation with concrete load-bearing beams. Solid oak door bearing a large metallic cross. A plastic-sheeted bay window. Compared to the rest of the camp, the structure was a castle.

"Don't tell me," Parnell said as they crossed the field. "Nurse Annie's place, right?"

"Yep. This is where your Jenny's been staying."

Parnell had hoped Annie Finnegan would have moved on by

now, but no such luck. He dreaded a reunion with the clingy, Bible-thumping nurse he'd met at the Albuquerque clinic three years ago. *Santa Muerte priestess? Day of the Dead occult rituals? What has this woman become?*

The front door squeaked open. Ann Finnegan greeted them.

"You two look like a pair of drowned river rats," she yelled into the stormy morning. Her familiar voice ate holes in Parnell's psyche. "Come, enter my humble abode."

Not so humble, Parnell thought as Bethea steered him closer to the door.

Greg Bethea announced in a bold orator voice, "Ann, the great King Midas has returned to us."

"Cut the crap, Weasel," Parnell said.

"Greg's just giving you your due respect," Ann said. "You'll always be known around here as King Midas. Come here and give me a big hug. C'mon, Derek, don't get all bashful on me," she said, arms wide open, raindrops pockmarking her blouse.

Reluctantly, Parnell stepped out from beneath the umbrella and moved forward, gave Ann a half-hearted hug.

She surprised him with a chaste kiss on the cheek and whispered words: "I've missed you so much. I've prayed for you these past years. God has answered my prayers. He brought you back to me."

They broke the embrace, Parnell embarrassed by her awkward display of affection.

A muffled cry came from inside the house. "Poppy! You made it!"

Jenn was a blur as she leaped into his arms. "Oh gawd, I'm so glad you're here!" she said, hugging him close.

Weasel Bethea and Ann stood inside the doorway, observing the wet family reunion, smiling at each other.

Ann said, "Goodness, Jenny dear, don't kill your Poppy." She glanced skyward, checking out the storm. "God created this slop for pigs and duck hunters. Not us. Let's all get inside where it's dry."

Twenty minutes later, dry and relaxed, they sat in the cavernous main room. Ann said, "Make yourselves at home while I rustle up some coffee."

Ann disappeared into the kitchen and Parnell took in his surroundings. A pleasant fragrance perfumed the air, a mix of sandalwood and jasmine that overlaid a hint of mossy grit and mortar cement. The stone walls reached high overhead to an expansive ceiling of brushed copper. Colorful Persian rugs covered much of the cement flooring. The furniture looked like it had been constructed with indigenous woods: cushioned chairs of black walnut; long sofa on which he and Jenn sat built with sturdy red oak; the coffee table and end tables made of what looked like ash. Parnell had long been amazed that the residents of Shangri-La had been able to live off this beautiful land without interference from the government. Probably because his fellow hobos were squatting in a remote corner of Homolovi State Park, on the opposite side of the Little Colorado River from the Hopi reservation. Secluded. Difficult to reach on foot. With ample tree cover making it nearly impossible to spot from the air.

"Poppy, are you awake?"

Jenn's voice brought him back. "Yeah."

"I asked if you ran into any snags getting here."

"Well, yeah. Had a spot of trouble at the border. Had to do a little axle swinging."

"You rode the belly of a drag?" Bethea asked.

"Yeah," he said, declining to mention that he only hid under the tanker and didn't actually ride the underbelly.

"That's hard core, my friend. Glad you made it through."

Jenn snuggled next to him and squeezed his hand. "I've been so worried about you."

He squeezed back, but said nothing. He was still irked at her for her stupidity. Neither of them should be here in this mess. He should be back in Costa Rica with Elaine. Jenn should be in Vancouver in her safe house. He couldn't let go of that troubling fact. They had a lot to discuss, did father and daughter, but this wasn't the appropriate time or place.

"Here we are," Ann said, entering the room with a tea set on a tray.

She poured coffee for everyone. Parnell noticed the cups and saucers were fine bone china. The spoons were high quality stainless steel with fancy floral detailing. *Annie certainly has developed expensive tastes.*

Ann took a seat to the left of Bethea, facing Parnell and Jenn. An awkward silence ensued as they sipped their coffee. Rain pelted the roof. Thunder boomed in the distance. A clock on the wall ticked. Parnell could hear the faint rumble of generators out back.

Ann's voice broke through the silence. "So how's Elaine, Derek?"

"Lainey's great," he said. He didn't want to discuss Elaine, so he redirected the conversation back to her. "Quite a nice place you have here, Annie."

"Thank you."

"You've come a long way since I saw you last. I have to ask. How'd you get such plush accommodations when the rest of the camp is living in a cesspool?"

"Poppy!" Jenn said. "How rude!"

"It's okay, Jenny," Ann said, looking at Parnell. "It's an honest question. No one here has money to pay for my medical services. So my patients do work for me. They hauled these stones from the river for the walls. They crafted this furniture from trees in the grove. Barry Burtelson used to be a contractor. He had a line on some cheap concrete and the knowledge to lay the foundation. This place went up pretty fast."

"So they're your servants, in other words," Parnell said, giving her an uninviting smile. "I mean, how much could your medical services be worth? Certainly not this much," he said, waving his arm around the spacious room.

Greg Bethea came to her defense. "Come on, Derek, give Ann a break. She's been a blessing to us out here. She's performed major surgeries. She's set broken bones and healed folks with snakebites and strange viruses. Delivered babies. She's saved lives, for Chrissakes."

She didn't save Kevin Spottswood's life, he thought. *She read him scripture from the big black book of fairy tales and let him die a horrible death.*

Aloud, he said, "Okay, so my fellow jungle breezers out there aren't your servants. Got it." Parnell took a sip of coffee and looked up at the expansive ceiling. "What about that copper roofing? Brushed copper like that is hugely expensive. Not to mention rare these days."

"Poppy, please. You're embarrassing me."

"Think about it, Jenny," he snapped. "Here she is, living like the Queen of England when another hundred-and-forty-plus sad souls are struggling out there like rats in a sewer. It doesn't seem right to me."

Jenn shook her head, gave Ann an apologetic look.

"You're correct, Derek. It *isn't* right," Ann said. "I guess you didn't see the east meadow on your way in."

"No. I came in through the aqueduct."

"We're building homes for our folks. Same kind of construction as my place. We've just begun laying the groundwork. These houses will be deeded to those with seniority and those who do the work. It's all a part of improving our community. God is our architect."

"I see," Parnell said, taking another sip of coffee. "And I suppose God sent you the copper."

"Poppy, please."

Bethea said, "If you must know, I'm the one who got the copper for Ann's roof. I've got a friend in Winslow who does reclamation work on foreclosed businesses. He got a truckload of copper sheeting from a hotel that went belly up. He donated it to our church here. All I had to do was help him get it here."

His old friend taking sides with the Bible thumper? Outrageous! "Greg, Greg, Greg," he said. "I didn't just fall off the ass end of a bobtail freighter. That much copper is worth a small fortune. No one in their right mind would donate it to a bunch of hobos."

Ann cleared her throat, then said, "You know, Derek, you haven't changed a bit. You're still the same hard-bitten cynic. The same misanthropic loner I knew back when. You don't trust anybody and you question everything. To you everyone is guilty before they have a chance to prove their innocence. You live by a very strange Wild West code of justice."

Parnell set his cup on the coffee table and clapped his hands sarcastically. "Very observant, Annie. And thanks to my—what was that again?—*strange Wild West code of justice,* I'm still alive today."

Bethea said, "You know, Derek, it's not safe here for you and Jenn. We're gettin' more and more people coming here every week looking for you. People with dollar signs in their eyes."

"I'm aware of that. Me and Jenn won't be staying long. Soon as the weather clears, we're heading to Sedona."

"We are?" Jenn said.

"Yeah. We've got unfinished business to take care of. And you're going to help us, Weasel."

"I am?"

"You are indeed." Parnell looked at his old friend. "I'm recruiting you as my deputy."

Bethea studied him for a long moment, then said, "And you're the sheriff?"

Parnell smiled. "I'm the sheriff, judge, jury, and executioner."

"And just what is this mission all about?"

"It's about putting a posse together to—"

"A posse?"

"Yeah. We're going to bring down four criminals, one by one. This posse will see that justice is served." He eyed Ann. "Using my strange, Wild West kind of justice."

Parnell rose from the sofa and patted Bethea on the shoulder. "Your first task as deputy is to recruit two more guys and get them trained while Jenn and I are gone. Men you can trust. Guys who know how to ride the rails. Men who can shoot and aren't afraid of a little rough and tumble. They need to be smart, quick on their feet. I don't want any dopes or Caspar milquetoasts."

Bethea stood. "I've got a few candidates in mind."

"Excellent. Jenn and I will be back in a few days. Be ready to roll."

Ann spoke up. "You know, Derek, if you really have to do this it might be helpful to have a medic along. Just in case."

Parnell laughed. "You?"

She stood. "Why not me?"

"Because you're too used to the soft life here at your Big Rock Candy Mountain," he said, invoking the breezer term for a hobo's paradise. "You'd only slow us down . . . hold us back."

Ann looked befuddled. "Big Rock Candy Mountain?"

"The fact you don't know what that means tells me all I need to know, Annie."

She regarded him, shaking her head. A melancholy sadness softened her face. "I'll be praying for you, Derek. I'll be praying very hard."

The Sedona Express

THE STORM CLEARED BY EARLY AFTERNOON. The sun baked the high desert. After a refreshing dip in the river, Jenn and Parnell hiked to Winslow Yard and broke into an insulated boxcar containing bagged flour and canned goods.

First stop: Sedona. Poppy told her they would start with a fortuneteller working under the name of Madame Crystal. The gypsy woman had been his connection to Genevieve Thorssen, whose bodyguard was the albino assassin, Lars.

The train chugged through stretches of arid desert scrubland, gaining altitude as it entered thick forests of Arizona cypress, pinion pine, and juniper. The steel wheels thumped the tracks with a metronomic *clickety-clack, clickety-clack* rhythm. The boxcar rattled and trundled as the freighter negotiated twists and turns. She sat propped against a pallet of chicken soup cans, staring out the open doors at the verdant scenery flashing past. The sweet coniferous fragrance gave Jenn a buzz, bringing back pleasant memories of her childhood when Poppy brought home freshly-cut Christmas trees.

His voice pulled her from her trance.

"What?" she said, looking at him hunched in the corner.

"I said give me your cell phone."

"Why?"

"I wanna make a call."

"You should've kept your burner phone if you wanted to make calls," she said, digging into her backpack, retrieving her cell and looking at the display, then scooting across the floor and handing it to him.

He removed the back cover and yanked out the battery.

"What are you doing, Poppy?"

"What I should have done back at the camp." He hurled the battery and the phone from the train.

"Hey!" she yelled. "You can't just . . . shit, that phone has my whole life on it."

"Exactly. In case you forgot, young lady, there're a lot of people looking for us. Those things are nothing but Big Brother tracking devices."

That phone had cost her dearly back in Vancouver. Try as she might, she couldn't harness her wrath. "You're such an asshole sometimes."

"*I'm* the asshole? You've got that *so* wrong, sweetheart. You'd best watch your mouth."

"No, I *won't* watch my mouth!" she said petulantly. "You *are* an asshole. A rude, arrogant asswipe."

"Wow," Parnell said. "All this because I trashed your phone?"

She remained silent, thinking it wasn't just the phone. It was just as much about the way he had treated Ann Finnegan.

"You seem to have forgotten that I've come more than three thousand miles to help you."

She knew he was right, and she felt a blush of shame. But that phone contained her only photos of Russ. And of Luanne Solton. The two loves of her life.

"You were rude as hell to Ann Finnegan today," she said. "You treated Greg Bethea like shit, too. It embarrassed me."

"Embarrassed you?"

"Yeah. They're good people. They watched out for me while you were in transit."

"Listen to me, oh sweet naive daughter of mine. Annie Finnegan is a fraud and a con artist extraordinaire. Not to mention greedy and self-absorbed. She calls herself a reverend, but far as I know, she isn't an ordained preacher. She refers to herself as a doctor, but I know she doesn't have a medical degree. And yet she has everybody at Shangri-La fawning over her, kissing her ass like she's some kind of savior."

"And you, dearest Poppy, are not a sheriff. Nor are you a judge and jury like you told Weasel. By your definition, that makes you a fraud and con artist, too, doesn't it?"

Silence from his corner, then, "Damn, you're impossible, Jenny."

"All I know is that Ann took me in and treated me nice. Fed me well. Kept those bounty hunters away from me. You should be thanking her."

"You're way too trusting and accepting of what folks *seem* to be, sweets. You're with this woman for what, a few days? You think you know her, but you don't. You don't know Annie at all. You're too young to know much about people and their agendas."

"I know *plenty* about people!" she boomed. "Don't treat me

like a child."

"How else am I supposed to treat you, Jenny? It's because of your carelessness that we're here at all. What possessed you and Russ to venture back into the States? You were all set up and tucked into Vancouver nice and neat. Out of the country and safe."

Here it is, she thought. She wondered when they would get to this. "You don't know the whole story," she said, the anger burning in her throat. "You always think you know what's going on, but you don't. You don't have a clue what happened."

"Well maybe if you'd kept in better touch, I would—"

"Oh, don't give me that crap, Poppy. It was you who said it was dangerous for us to correspond much. The few phone conversations we've had, you couldn't wait to disconnect. It's your own fault you're not informed, not mine."

"So educate me, then."

And she did, letting Parnell know everything that made Jenn and Russ flee British Columbia and return to the States. She told him about that first year following the widely-publicized trial. The U.S. Marshals Service had been vigilant in their protection of the young couple, providing them with fresh identities and setting them up with a home and jobs in Vancouver. They provided round-the-clock security. She and Russ attended regular meetings with their WITSEC agent. All was good that first year. But as the trial faded into the past, and further cutbacks in the U.S. Marshals program occurred, their protection became more threadbare. They were shuffled from one deputy to the next. The meetings occurred less frequently. And the past six months had become scary.

"Russ began noticing questionable people following him," she continued over the roll and clatter of the train. "We started getting threatening phone calls in the middle of the night. Gruff voices saying things like *'We know who you are'* and *'You'll pay for what you've done.'* Shit like that. Strangely, for the first time, we couldn't get in touch with our agent. He'd vanished. Then, a month ago, around midnight, a brick crashes through our front window. A note was attached. It said, *JD says hello. The next time you hear from him will be the last.* The signature was a crude drawing of a skull and crossbones."

"JD? John Dobkin?"

"Yeah. Scared the freakin' shit outta me. But Russ, he was real ticked off. After all he'd tried to do to bring down Dobkin and his organization, and the guy was still out, roaming around free, threatening him . . . bullying us."

"So that's when you took off?"

"No. Not right away. We kept trying to get in touch with WITSEC through our encrypted devices, but got no response. It finally dawned on us that someone had infiltrated the witness protection program . . . bought their way in."

"Dobkin."

"Yeah, I'm sure it's Dobkin. You know as well as I do that bribes open doors and John Dobkin has enough money and influence to open very big doors. A big payoff from a moneybags like him could buy a lot of cooperation. I believe that's what happened. Anyway, Russ knew it was just a matter of time before they got to us. He said it was time to get out."

"But why head back into the States? Why not get far away? Someplace in Europe. The Australian Outback or New Zealand."

"Because Russ wanted to go after Dobkin, to put him down once and for all so he'd never be able to threaten us again. We knew he was still operating out of Las Vegas and we went there. But it was dangerous for us because Dobkin and his people knew both of us on sight. We couldn't penetrate his fortress without some outside help."

"Okay, I get that. But why eat in a public restaurant in Denver, of all places? You might as well have been on stage, with spotlights shining on you. Christ!"

"Russ arranged a meet in Denver with someone he knew in Dobkin's organization. A man named Oscar who had infiltrated the Liberty Dogs' compound. Russ worked there with Oscar a couple of months. Said the guy was cool, that Dobkin had thrown him under the bus and screwed him over several times before firing him. He wanted to help us put his old boss down. Russ met with him alone and came back from the meeting saying he trusted him. Said Oscar not only could help us eliminate Dobkin but also knew where Blanton Miles was."

"Unbelievable, Jennifer. You two fell for the oldest trick in the confidence game. You should've called me before you left Canada, let me know all this was going on. I would've taken care of it."

"Russ didn't want to drag you back into our mess. He thought he could take care of things himself. And you and I weren't exactly regular correspondents."

"He took care of things, all right. Damned fool. He led you to them. And you followed that idiot like he was the Pied Piper or something. Like two lambs in a slaughterhouse. Christ, Jennifer. What happened to your good sense?"

Poppy's venom tore at her heart. She couldn't believe the cruelty behind the barb. He had wounded her, stung her. Emotion swelled in her chest, building, blooming, bursting. Memories of Russ brutally gunned down in the restaurant as she and other diners looked on in horror came flooding back. And now, insults from Poppy. Too much for her to handle this soon after.

Her chest heaved in great sobs. Her shoulders collapsed. Tears collected in her eyes, then spilled freely down her cheeks. She tasted the saltiness on her lips as she cried out over the shaking and knocking of the train car. "How can you say such a thing, you bastard! About the man I loved." She crab-walked across the dirty floor, sobbing, flailing her arms at him, landing weak blows against his thighs and stomach. "How could you say that, you piece of shit!" screaming in his face, pounding his chest, "How could you even *think* that? You're nothing but a cold-hearted son of a bitch! I despise you! I HATE YOU!"

Finally, her energy expended, her emotional well drained, she collapsed into his arms, quaking, shivering, weeping, her tears wetting his shoulder. He took her in, held her close, cocooning her, rocking her gently back and forth as she sobbed into his shirt.

He whispered into her ear as he rocked her and rubbed her arms. "I'm so sorry, Jenny. I wasn't thinking. You've been through a lot and here I am being an asshole. So, so sorry, honey. I'd give anything to be able to take those words back . . ."

She lay against his chest, listening to the pounding of his heart and the hitch in his voice as he continued to comfort her.

Is he crying?

After a time he stopped whispering and she pulled back from him, glancing up, seeing the transformation in his weather-beaten face. His expression took her back to when she was a little girl, when he read her bedtime stories. When he was completely devoted to her.

He's crying. Weeping freely in fact.

She reached up and wiped a runaway tear from his cheek, then kissed his forehead. "I know you have my back, Daddy. I'm sorry, too. For so many things."

She dropped back into his arms and he cradled her, all the way to Sedona.

Costa Rican Blues

DAY FOUR OF HER SOLITARY CONFINEMENT at the beach house. Trying to cope without Derek was proving impossible.

Loneliness pressed down on Elaine with a crushing gravity. The silence in the stilt house was immense, penetrated only by the chirpy calls of white-collared manakins and quetzals. Ordinarily she loved the bird species that populated this Caribbean side of Costa Rica. She liked the splashes of color they added to the surrounding jungle, enjoyed their warbling tunes that filled the rainforest with music. But without Derek here, their bright, trilling calls only added to her growing depression.

How can they be so happy and vivacious when I'm so sad?

Nothing she did could obliterate the chronic ache of this forced, alien solitude, a pain that throbbed under her ribs like some undiagnosed cancer. Drinking didn't work. Dipping into her stash of Royal Highness weed only made her groggy and weepy. Painting and sketching worked for a while, but soon lost its allure. Long walks along the deserted beach did little other than make her legs and feet sore. Listening to Calypso music didn't lift her mood the way it usually did. Nothing seemed to pull her out of this morass of tangled emotions.

All because of Derek.

He had left her once again.

Elaine rarely experienced this kind of loneliness when she lived in Flagstaff. She reminisced about her beautiful home on the perimeter of the Coconino National Forest, the five-acre spread that skirted the snowcapped San Francisco Peaks. Spacious three-bedroom house in an upscale gated community. Thicket of white birch lining the rolling meadow of heather out back. Her artist's studio with the panoramic view. Her sister Gina lived in that house now, with her husband Frank. Derek had often gone off and left her there, too. But she'd had friends in Flagstaff to keep her company.

Elaine had no real friends here. At least not now. She'd had friends back when they'd first settled here, when she did volunteer work for the Sea Turtle Conservation program. She had befriended a group of women involved in that turtle rescue operation. Two American retirees, Martha Turnbull and Denise Allicotti, and a Costa Rican girl named Ioma, whose sing-song broken-English intonation charmed her. They had walked the beach on night patrol together, collecting eggs from leatherback and hawksbill turtle nests and taking them to the hatchery so poachers and natural predators wouldn't get them. They had also worked with professional marine conservationists, tagging mature turtles with GPS devices to track their migratory habits. Those were heady, purposeful times. She regretted losing touch with her old friends. She missed the camaraderie and laughter she'd shared with those women.

Derek was the reason she had stopped her volunteer work. He'd been against her making the long trek up the coast to Tortuguero, reasoning it wasn't smart for her to be that exposed twice a week when they were wanted by American authorities. He said he worried about her, and reminded her that the U.S. Department of Justice had a long reach. And she, frustrated with his constant harping on the subject, accused him of being a paranoid drama king, which hadn't gone over well. After weeks of head-butting arguments, she surrendered to his wishes and quit the group.

Difficult though he could be, Derek Parnell was the love of her life. His absence carved out an emptiness in her she couldn't seem to fill.

She sat now, nestled in a wicker chair in the glassed-in sunroom that overlooked the Caribbean, a Mai Tai in one hand, a freshly rolled joint in the other. Her recent attempts at art surrounded her. Two charcoal sketches that she thought were hideous. A pencil sketch of Derek that wasn't bad. A slapdash oil painting she had titled *My Life with Derek*.

She took a deep drag on the joint, held the smoke in. The buzz hit her immediately. A welcoming dreaminess came over her. Her aching muscles relaxed. Her mind melted into euphoric bliss. She exhaled, and became mesmerized by the sunlight that stitched golden threads through the swirling smoke.

She took a sip of her citrusy rum. She'd been too hard on Derek. Sure, he had left her without much warning. But he was doing the noble thing, going after his daughter when Jennifer needed him. Elaine couldn't blame him for that. *But I did blame him. Blamed him for leaving me. Called him self-centered and many things worse.* Thinking only of herself. She had been the selfish one. She certainly could have made the trip with him. But she hadn't.

A great shame washed over her. Derek Parnell had done so much for her. Without even knowing who she was, he'd come to her aid as she lay in the Torrance Memorial Burn Center, shrouded like a mummy after her third round of surgery following the acid-hurling attack that claimed her left eye. He had sweetened those endless days of pain in the burn ward. She would peer through the bandages with her good right eye at this mysterious and wonderful man who kept coming to visit her. This man with the big heart and even bigger wallet. She didn't understand how it was that Fate smiled down upon her in that hospital bed, what she'd done to deserve such a thing. But she had known that something life-changing had happened with his arrival.

He'd paid all her medical bills and stayed by her side until she was released. Afterward, while she recuperated in her Los Angeles apartment, he had purchased the Flagstaff house for her, then helped her relocate. He didn't have to do any of that. He didn't know her from Eve. And later, after she had set up housekeeping in Flagstaff and redirected her career from the catalog model she had been to the popular artist she became, he came clean with her. Told her who he was. Never lied about it. Said though he was wealthy, he rode the rails masquerading as a hobo, looking for his long-missing daughter. Said he wouldn't stop until he found her and that meant he'd have to leave Elaine for long periods to continue his search. It was all incredibly exciting to her, this dashing mystery man who professed his love for her in so many ways, running off to fight the good fight and returning to her with affection in his heart and lust in his loins.

She absently fingered her eye patch. Had it not been for the attack from a sociopathic ex-boyfriend, she and Derek probably never would have met. Destiny and Chance had come together in that Los Angeles burn ward. The result was kismet. Or as Derek called it, *karma.*

Elaine stubbed out the joint and set her drink aside. She had convinced herself there was only one thing to do.

Go to him, a commanding internal voice said to her. *You belong by his side. Go join him. He needs you.*

She reached for her cell, found the number of the burn phone he'd called her from. Hoped for the best.

In Search of the Lost Swedes

PARNELL AND JENN WATCHED Madame Crystal enter the waiting area.

She took a hard look at them. A snide smile crossed her face. "Well whaddaya know. Our conquering hero has finally returned to pay his debts."

Parnell rose from his seat. "What're you talking about?"

The gypsy woman peered at him from behind tinted granny glasses, tiny dark dots perched on either side of her hooked nose. "You know damn well what I mean. You only gave me five-hundred last time you were here, what was it? Two years ago?"

"More than three, actually."

"My how time flies. You still owe me forty-five-hundred. And that's before the accrued interest."

Parnell looked at Jenn and laughed. "Didn't I tell you, sweets? This is one ballsy little lady we're dealing with here." He turned back to the fortuneteller. "Your information last time wasn't worth shit."

"I gave you a connection to Thor, which eventually led to finding your daughter. I'd say that's pretty solid. Well worth the price tag."

"Solid? It led Elaine and me into a trap. Almost got us killed."

She waved it off, her turquoise bracelets jangling, the crystal rings adorning her fingers flashing in the sunlight that filtered through the front blinds. "Not my problem, Mister Parnell. I'm not responsible for how you handle my intel." She tugged on the sleeve of her lacy renaissance blouse, impatient. "Look, you're interrupting my session with a *paying* client. So unless you fork over what you owe me, we're done here."

Parnell turned back to Jenn. "Madame Cuckoo here thinks she's calling the shots." He went to his backpack, unzipped a side pocket and pulled out his Mauser, pointed it at the gypsy woman. "I believe *we're* the ones calling the shots."

The fortuneteller gasped, took a step back. "Um, okay, let's be reasonable here." She eyed the gun, pulled her lavender sequined shawl tighter around her shoulders. "What is it you want?"

"Same thing as last time. I want Lady Thor and her bodyguard, Lars."

"I don't know anyone named Lars."

"Maybe you don't. But you *do* know Thor. Genevieve Thorssen to be precise. And where there's Thor, there's usually Lars."

"I, um . . . I don't work with her any more. You've been away a long time. A lot has changed."

"So people keep telling me. But I'm betting you could still contact Thorssen if you were properly motivated."

Madame Crystal shuffled backward, toward the receptionist desk.

"Stop right there," he barked. He took a step forward and waved the gun in her face. "Stay away from that desk."

"If you don't leave immediately, I'll call the police."

Parnell smiled. "Be my guest. I'm sure the Sedona cops would love to book you on murder conspiracy charges. At the very least, accessory to multiple murders or obstruction of justice."

"You're being ridiculous."

"Am I? I'm sure the authorities would love to know about your association with the two Swedes. You've been pimping murders for them for years."

Madame Crystal's olive complexion darkened. "You have no idea what you're talking about."

"Oh, but I do. In fact, I know the Swedes pulled off a brutal murder just a month ago up in Denver. I believe you had a connection to that one."

She faced Parnell with a defensive posture. "You can't prove anything."

"I beg to differ," Parnell said. "I think maybe if we tear this place apart, we'll find a lot of damning evidence connecting you with them."

The Madame contemplated this, then seemed to regain a bit of confidence as she said, "You know what? Forget the Sedona Police. I think a call to the FBI might get me whole lot more than what you owe me. I believe there is a bounty on your head for a hundred grand?"

He snorted. "And I believe you have forgotten that I'm the one holding the gun. That makes me the guy in charge. Now we can do this nice and quiet, with your cooperation. Or, you can be difficult and I will blow your head off and stuff your body deep in the dumpster out back and we'll search this place on our own. Which way do you want to go with this?"

For a long minute, it looked as if the fortuneteller was about to scream out. His trigger finger tensed. But then he saw her expression soften, her body relax. Parnell could see it in her eyes. She realized he was a hard-case killer and there was no way out.

"Okay," she said in a defeated tone. "Tell me what you need me to do."

He grinned. "Good choice," he said, amazed at how easy it was to get people to snitch on others to save their own asses. "Jenn," he said, never taking his eyes or aim off the gypsy woman, "please escort Madame into the back room and have her tell her client that today's session is over."

The Madame said, "But he's already paid for today's session."

"Then give him a refund."

Jenn rummaged through her pack, pulled out the snub-nose pistol she had purchased in a pawn shop before she and Russ left Vancouver. "Let's go," she said to the fortuneteller, taking charge.

Madame Crystal said, "I have two more appointments scheduled this afternoon."

"Not anymore. Jenn, please assist her in canceling those appointments."

"Sure thing, Poppy."

They disappeared into the back area of the shop and weren't gone more than thirty seconds when Parnell heard a strange chirping coming from his backpack. *What the hell?* He stuck the Mauser in his waistband and went to it, unzipped, dug deep. *Ah, the cell phone.* He checked the incoming number.

Lainey.

He couldn't let Jenn see him chatting on his cell after he'd trashed hers. With one hand he hoisted his pack over his shoulder and stepped outside into the blistering heat. Accepted the call.

"Hi, babe," he said, glancing up and down Inspirational Drive, the hot, dusty breeze making his eyes water.

"Derek? Is this really you?"

"I told you. No names on the phone."

"Sorry. It's just that I've been worried about you. I thought you said this was a burner phone."

"It is."

"Well, why do you still have it?"

"I threw it in my bindle and forgot about it." His answer was partially true.

"Good, I'm glad," she said. "It's really wonderful to hear your voice."

Parnell thought she sounded tired, weepy. "Are you okay, babe? Something wrong?"

"No, no . . . not really. Just that I miss you like crazy."

"I miss you, too. But look, we're going to have to keep this short. We're working on something here."

"You and J?"

"Yeah."

"Where are you?"

"You know I can't tell you that over the phone. In fact I need to destroy this thing now."

"I understand. Listen, I just want to say that I never should have let you make this trip solo. I should've come with you."

"No you should *not* have."

"Yes, I *should*," she said adamantly. "And I have decided to come join you."

"You've decided *what*?"

"I'm coming there. I'm leaving the day after tomorrow."

"No you're *not*! You stay there where you're safe."

"I'm going out of my gourd. I can't stay here all alone. It's driving me insane . . . short drive, I know, ha-ha. But I'm not used to you being away. It's killing me. I'm coming to join you and that's final."

This call reminded Parnell of how difficult Elaine could be once she got something in her head. "No you're *not*," he nearly shouted.

"Yes I *am*. Buy another burn phone and text me a coded message telling me when and where to meet you. I love you and hope to see you soon. Bye."

Parnell started to give her a piece of his mind, but realized she had disconnected. Quickly, he punched the recall button, but the call went directly to voicemail. He left a curt, angry message: *"You stay the hell at home, E. It's too dangerous for you to make that trip alone. This has to be one of your craziest ideas ever!"*

Just as he clicked off, Madame Crystal and Jenn led the customer out the front door and into the heat.

"Okay then, Mister Gradney," Madame said, "sorry it didn't work out today, but I'll see you Friday."

Jenn spotted Parnell with the cell phone in his hand and said,

"What the hell is that?"

"What, *this*?" Parnell felt like a kid caught with his hand in the cookie jar.

"Yeah, *that*," Jenn said, eyeing him suspiciously.

He watched Madame's customer go to his car parked in the oversized driveway. "It's a throw-away."

"Give it to me, you hypocrite," Jenn demanded.

He handed the phone to her and she dismantled it, first removing the battery from the back, then smashing it on Madame Crystal's front porch.

As she knelt to pick up the plastic fragments, she squinted at him and said, "Now we're even, Poppy."

All Dressed Up and Nowhere to Go

ELAINE STEPPED OFF THE INTERBUS shuttle at San Jose's Juan Santamaría International Airport. The pneumatic doors of the bus swished shut behind her and she started her trek to the terminal. She had booked an AeroMéxico flight to Monterrey with a stopover in Mexico City.

Derek no longer controlled her from afar.

A carefree buoyancy lightened her step.

She entered the cool womb of the terminal and her excitement gave way to an encroaching panic. She was headed north and still no communication from him. *What if he doesn't text me a meet location? Where will I go? What will I do?* Her only recourse would be to go to her house in Flagstaff and stay with her sister Gina. But that wouldn't be safe. The feds still kept an eye on Gina.

As she jostled through the ranks of swarming bodies on her way to the ticket counter, she realized maybe this wasn't such a good idea. She had impulsively left the stilt house without much of a plan.

A sense of isolation enveloped her. She couldn't catch her breath. The faces of strangers toting luggage mutated into terrifying demons as they passed. A cold sweat dampened her blouse. Sounds of chattering travelers and flight announcements broadcast over a booming PA ricocheted through her head.

Lightheaded, she went to a taxi lounge and dropped into a chair, the heavy backpack forcing her to sit awkwardly. She attempted to get her breathing under control, tried to keep from puking up breakfast.

Derek would never leave me stranded, would he?

She felt weak and shaky, gripped by the palsied hand of anxiety.

If he does abandon me, can I survive on my own?

She couldn't answer that. She had no experience being on the run alone, no idea where the friendly hobo camps other than Shangri-La were located. She had no weapon; she left her gun and pepper spray behind due to her decision to take public transportation. She felt unprepared and unprotected.

She took in deep gulps of air, tried to regulate her erratic heartbeat.

You're an idiot, Leibrandt. A blue chip fool. Did you really think someone like Derek Parnell would bend to your will?

She thought about canceling her flight and getting back on the bus to head home. Back to the beach house. Back to the barking howler monkeys and screeching birds and intense loneliness. At least she would be safe there.

She pulled out her phone and listened to Derek's last voicemail: *"You stay the hell at home, E. It's too dangerous for you to make that trip alone. This has to be one of your craziest ideas ever!"*

She wanted to curl up in the chair and die. What had she done? Had her loneliness overruled her rationality?

She sat for a while, watching travelers lug baggage to check-in stations and hurry to gates to catch flights. Gradually her breathing returned to normal. Her heart rate slowed. Her strength and determination returned. *You have started this journey, and you are going to finish it.*

She had to keep the faith that Derek would text her with a meet location. Surely, the delay tactic was to teach her a lesson. He was a stubborn and prideful man, but he'd always come through for her.

She checked the time. Three hours until departure. She stood, made her way to AeroMéxico ticketing and checked in. She paid cash in Costa Rican colónes for a one-way flight. The price was higher than she expected, and when she inquired about it, the ticketing clerk informed her that a departure tax had been added. She checked no luggage, keeping her backpack as a carry-on. This fed the clerk's suspicions. He studied her Karen Cooper driver's license and passport, repeatedly looking up at her then back at the photo IDs.

Time slowed.

She felt the shakes return. *What's the holdup? Should I have paid for a round trip with a credit card? Would it have been better to check fake baggage?*

The clerk laid Elaine's identification on the counter and went back to the keyboard, his fingers tapping at the keys, a look of concentration crossing his narrow face as he stared at the monitor.

Hurry up, hurry up, hurry up.

She felt weak in the knees, woozy. This was taking too long. People in line behind her stamped their feet and shuffled around impatiently. *Is he checking some international database to see if I'm on a no-fly list? Is it possible that Costa Rican authorities know who I am? Should I say something?*

She was about to speak up when the clerk handed her a ticket, boarding pass, and her identification. "Your flight is on time, Mizz Cooper," he said with a smile. "You'll be boarding at Gate 5 in the Main terminal. Thank you for choosing AeroMéxico. Have a pleasant flight."

Elaine collected her documents. She let out a breath she wasn't aware she'd been holding as she headed to the gate entry.

She waited twenty minutes in the Customs queue. When she arrived at the front of the line, an agent with a surly demeanor and pock-marked complexion questioned her as to why she was going to Monterrey and how long she planned to be there. She had a well rehearsed spiel prepared, telling him she was an artist who had business to conduct with several galleries there, didn't know how long she would have to stay.

The agent stared at her as though trying to figure something out. *What the hell is he looking at? Did he not buy my story? Have I been made?* Loud static blared from the walkie-talkie clipped to his belt. Worry soured her stomach. She was sure he could read into her uptight demeanor and know she was lying.

Finally he said, "What's wrong with your eye?"

"Oh, this?" she said, pointing to her left eye. "I lost it in an accident. It's glass. Actually it's hard acrylic. I just say it's glass so I don't have to explain what acrylic is." Her nerves were making her ramble.

"It looks weird. Your face is lopsided," he said, handing back her paperwork and waving her through with a flinty smile.

What an absolutely rude asshole! She stewed as she headed to the security checkpoint. She wanted to turn around and tell him off, but held it in check. *I've got to keep walking . . . can't afford to make a scene.*

Still flustered as she arrived at the Security queue, she angrily removed her shoes and placed them on the conveyor belt along with her backpack, watched them slide through the x-ray machine, then walked through the metal detector without incident. Emerging on the other side, she stopped abruptly. Three airport agents ripped through her backpack, chattering in Spanish, throwing the contents out on the table, taking great delight in handling her bras and panties. One of them found Elaine's eye patch and, using the elastic band, shot it at another agent slingshot style. The second man caught it, strapped it on, and pretended to brandish a sword, laughing, shouting out something in Spanish. Elaine could only make out the words *Blackbeard* and *pirate* amid the three agents' uproarious laughter.

Unbelievable!

Stunned onlookers stood with her and watched the spectacle. Elaine's rage grew as she observed the airport employees play with her things and blatantly steal items from other travelers' carry-ons. She looked around, hoping to see someone from airport management come put a stop to it, but no one showed. Apparently this was a common occurrence. Her indignation grew.

She went to the table, nudging one of the agents out of her way with her hip. She gathered her things and hastily stuffed them in her pack, got the hell out of there before she did something stupid.

Her nerves were frayed, her emotions frazzled. Her face flushed with humiliation. Her back ached as she walked. She tried to forget the brazen airport security agents, but couldn't. She passed a sign that made her shake her head:

WELCOME TO THE HAPPIEST COUNTRY IN THE WORLD.

Of course they're happy. They steal what they want without consequence.

What she had just been through was surreal. Was this horrible airport experience an omen of things to come? Derek was always going on about omens and portents and how they were usually accurate signposts predicting the near future. He'd claimed that being able to read and understand them had saved him from bad outcomes on numerous occasions.

She stopped in a restaurant near her departure gate and picked a table well away from the horseshoe bar. The waitress came and she ordered a chili guaro liqueur and ensalada palmito. She pulled out her cell phone, thankful those offensive security agents hadn't confiscated it. She tried Derek's burn phone without success. She tried Jennifer's cell. No connection there either. Finally she tried her sister Gina, who answered immediately.

"Hello?"

Elaine smiled, relishing the sound of Gina's high tenor. "Jeen! It's me. How are you?"

Slight pause, then, "Oh, wow. I'm, uh . . . I'm fine, I guess. How about you?"

"I'm okay," she lied. "Just getting ready to catch a flight and wanted to say hi before I board."

"You're not coming here are you?"

The cynicism in her sister's voice wounded her. "You sound like you don't want to see me, Gina."

"Um, no. It's not that. You sound tired."

"I've had a rough day. Long bus ride and a difficult time with airport security. You wouldn't believe—"

"You can't come here, Elaine," Gina said abruptly, fear creeping into her voice. "You shouldn't be calling. It's not safe."

The waitress brought her drink and Elaine took a tentative sip of the reddish liqueur, the *cacicón* blending nicely with the tomato juice and Tabasco. She squeezed the mandarin lime in to sweeten the concoction as she listened to Gina go on.

". . . just had visitors here today looking for you. Rough looking pair. Very determined to find you."

"Were they feds?"

"No. Private bounty hunters. They're worse than the paparazzi. Even had a bunch of them camping out under the aspens last week. Frank ran them off with a few shotgun blasts. But their types keep coming back. They're like a plague, I'm telling you. They come at all hours of the day and night, no concern for us or the property. I worry about you, li'l sis. Someday they're going to catch up with you. Please tell me you're not on your way here."

She took another sip of her drink, thought about responding that she might be forced to come to her Flagstaff house, but then thought better of it, held back. "No, no I'm not coming there, Jeen."

"Good. Is Derek with you?"

"No. Have you heard from him?"

Gina said, "Why would *I* hear from Derek? Are you two having problems?"

The waitress brought her salad, and Elaine stared at the humongous serving overflowing the rosewood bowl. "No, not problems, really," she said. "Just distance."

"He left you again? Jesus H. He's finally come back to the States and you're following him."

"No, now listen—"

"I *knew* it was just a matter of time, Elaine. That man of yours is so predictable."

She wanted to tell her big sister that Derek Parnell was anything but predictable. Instead she said, "Look, Gina, my food just came and I need to eat before I catch my flight."

"Well, before you go, there's something you should know."

"What's that?"

"Frank and I really appreciate you letting us stay here rent free, but things are getting out of hand. We can't take much more. We're thinking of moving back east where we can get a little privacy. No telling what these maniac bounty seekers will do to your place if it's empty."

"Don't worry about it. Just lock it up good and tight when you leave. I'll take care of things there eventually. Gotta run, now. Love you."

"Okay. You be careful, Elaine. You don't sound so good."

They disconnected and she dug into her salad. Big sister Gina had always been able to read her perfectly. Even on the phone more than three thousand miles apart.

Follow the Money Trail

THEY TORE MADAME CRYSTAL'S shop apart looking for evidence that would implicate her in Russ Holt's murder. Parnell was becoming exasperated with the search. The gypsy woman refused to cooperate. Her recordkeeping was sloppy and disorganized. She didn't believe in computers, saying they were "the devil's dark conscience," and elected to keep her financial records in leather-bound ledger books that were scattered everywhere.

The past twelve hours saw Parnell and Jenn thumbing through the ledgers, squinting at the Madame's tiny, oftentimes illegible, ink scrawls, making their own notes, coming up with theories that Madame Crystal neither confessed to nor denied.

They had uncovered a lot about the secretive fortuneteller. Her birth name was Loretta Pesky. She had purchased this residential home on Inspirational Drive in Sedona seventeen years ago for a price of $320,000, and paid it off in five years. Shortly before she paid off the loan in full, the area was rezoned commercial, and she opened her business on the ground floor. This was probably the beginning of Pesky's crooked ways. Surely no smalltime psychic could afford a place like this from fortunetelling revenues alone. There had to be other sources of income. And sure enough, they found it. Jenn stumbled across several bank books rubber-banded together and buried deep in a credenza in the back room where sessions took place. Dozens of large deposits, increasing in size and regularity in recent years. The first, registered almost two years before the start of her business, through the last deposit entry six weeks ago for $70,000.

Parnell was well versed in offshore banking practices from his days running Locomotion Enterprises. He recognized the 8-character transit formats for two banks as being BIC/SWIFT codes, identifying them as foreign accounts (the US banking system used 9-digit ABA routing numbers). These transactions suggested she had set up the fortunetelling gig as a front to launder money. The date six weeks ago also lined up with the hit on Russell Holt. A debit entry for a $50,000 wire transfer payment appeared a week later. *The payout for Holt's murder?* There was no notation indicating the recipient of the payment.

They found lots of other odds and ends—old photographs of Loretta Pesky before she became Madame Crystal, handwritten letters, many from some guy named Aurelio, vet bills for numerous cats, registration for two expensive automobiles (a Rolls and a Maserati GranTurismo), lists of client names with contact information, lists of personal contacts—but nothing pertaining to Genevieve Thorssen or her deadly sidekick Lars.

Finally, somewhere around five in the morning, their persistence paid off. The Madame, exhausted from being kept up all night, relented. She told them she couldn't take any more of this invasion of her privacy and if it was the two Swedes they were interested in, she could deliver them.

"Is this your confession that you have a working relationship with Lady Thor and Lars?" Parnell asked.

"No. No confession," she said bitchily. "I just want you two out of my life so I can get on with my business."

"Business?" Jenn said. "You mean murdering people?"

The Madame huffed. "I've never killed a soul in my life. I *help* people."

"Sure you do," Parnell said. "Keep telling yourself that. One thing I'm sure of. You've *arranged* a few murders. That's conspiracy if nothing else."

"Think what you want. You have no proof."

Jenn said, "Oh, I believe we do. The authorities would be very interested in those offshore bank accounts of yours."

"You and your lunatic father are the last two who would go to the authorities, darlin'."

Parnell ignored the barb, said, "So how do you set up meets with the Swedes?"

"I just call Thorssen and she meets me. Usually within a day or two."

"Where? Here at your shop?"

The Madame's tired, baggy eyes bore holes into Parnell. "Do you take me for a clueless fool? Of *course* not here in the shop."

"Where, then?" Jenn said.

"Somewhere private, out in the open. Away from public places."

"Like the desert?"

"Sometimes. More often at an abandoned warehouse. Plenty of those around after The Crash."

"And what about Lars?"

"What about him?"

Parnell nodded. "You said you meet with Thorssen. Does Lars ever accompany her?"

"No, not on initial consults. Thorssen handles all the business arrangements. Lars is just dumb muscle. In fact, I've never laid eyes on him."

Parnell looked at Jenn. Her expression told him she thought the Madame was lying. He thought a moment, then said, "What would it take to get Lars at one of these consults?"

A flash of fear crossed the gypsy woman's face, quick but noticeable. "Oh no, that won't happen. Thorssen would never allow that. Too easy for her to be implicated."

"And you," Jenn said.

"And me, what?"

"Too easy for *you* to be implicated along with Lady Thor."

"You're putting words in my mouth."

"Am I? Tell me to my face you had nothing to do with my Russell's murder."

"I don't have to tell you a damn thing!" The Madame smiled at her thinly.

Jenn started to go after her, but Parnell held her back. "Let's keep our emotions out of this," he said calmly. To the Madame he said, "Go ahead and set up the meet with Thorssen. Strongly request that Lars come along. Tell her this is a special assignment that requires his attendance. Let her know this will be their biggest payoff yet. Genevieve Thorssen dances to the tune of U.S. currency. I'm sure she'll comply."

"No, she won't. She's not stupid."

Parnell pondered this. "You're right," he said. "She's very smart. And we don't want to set off alarms by asking for something outside the normal protocol. Set up the meet with Thorssen the way you normally do."

"Now? It's not even dawn yet."

"I don't care. Do it. Here's your phone," he said, handing back her cell that he'd confiscated. "And if you pull any tricks, well, my trigger finger is mighty itchy."

Loretta Pesky punched in a number and connected with Genevieve Thorssen. Parnell had her keep it on speakerphone so they could all hear the conversation. The two women negotiated a meet in two days at an abandoned barn near Cottonwood. Parnell got the impression it was a common meeting place for them. He felt his blood pressure spike as he listened to Genevieve Thorssen talk; her familiar English-Swedish tongue irritated him. Her tone was transparently obsequious, the big money offered by Madame Crystal for the fictional hit making her delirious. She fawned all over the gypsy woman. Best of friends, they were. Everything would go well, both agreed.

Madame Crystal clicked off and looked at Parnell. "There. You happy now?"

He shook his head. "No, I'm not."

"I've done everything you asked me to do."

"We're just getting started, Loretta. I need a few more things from you."

"Like what?"

He took his time answering, thinking the setup for this meet was ideal, but that he would need help to pull it off. With just the two of them, it would be difficult to monitor the two women while trying to root out Lars who, as Lady Thor's trusted bodyguard, would surely be lurking nearby. Too many moving parts to this thing. He hoped Weasel Bethea had done his recruiting and had his posse ready for action.

Finally he answered the Madame. "You're our ride this week. You're driving us to Winslow."

"The *hell* I am! I've got clients booked solid the next few days."

"My heart bleeds for you, dear. Your marks can live without you for a while."

"They aren't *marks*," she protested. "They're my esteemed *clients*. Look, haven't you already done enough damage to my business?"

He laughed. "I'd say judging by your bank ledgers, your business is doing quite well. But you'll have to leave it behind. This week you're our esteemed chauffeur. Get your shit together. We leave for Winslow in an hour. You can leave that ridiculous gypsy getup here. Pack some outdoor clothes and comfortable walking shoes. We'll be doing some hiking."

Down and Out in Monterrey

ELAINE CAME AWAKE WITH A WIDE YAWN as her plane touched down at Monterrey International Airport. The three-hour flight from San Jose to Mexico City, followed by a two-hour layover, then the final 90-minute leg to Monterrey, had drained her.

She watched passengers gather their things from the overhead bins and file down the aisle. Her next stop was the Monterrey train yard. She questioned whether she had the strength and resolve to hop a freighter that would take her to the U.S. border. She had traveled 2,200 miles but the toughest part of the trip still remained—another four hours by train to Piedras Negras, then a crossing of the Rio Grande into Eagle Pass, Texas.

She checked her cell phone. Still no text from Derek. It made her crazy. If only he had left her some way to contact him.

Terminal A was mostly deserted at this late hour in the middle of the week. She followed signs to ground transportation, planning to take a cab to the rail yard. She walked through the North Concourse, passing a few people waiting to depart, others waiting for arrivals. As she turned the corner and headed for the taxi stand, she suspected she was being followed. Two Hispanic men. They stayed well back, but kept with her through the terminal.

Quickly, she ducked into a restroom and washed her face and hands at the sinks. She stared at her reflection in the mirror. Her face looked haggard. Thin and gaunt. She dried off with a paper towel and entered one of the stalls. Locking herself in, she checked her cell phone again. Nothing from Derek. She was four hours from the U.S. border and she still had no idea where she would go after the crossing. Elaine wanted to cry. She had never felt this aimless and alone.

Ten minutes passed. Fifteen. She heard women enter and leave. She flushed and grabbed her pack, left the restroom, walking closely behind two other women. Entering the concourse, she looked left and right, let out a breath of relief. No sign of the two men. She walked briskly to the taxi stand. *Get your shit together, girl. Your paranoia will kill you quicker than anything else.*

The night heat slapped her in the face as she headed to the

only available cab—a silver Aero Contaxi—and opened the back door. She threw her backpack in and climbed in.

"To the rail station, please," she told the driver, a squat Mexican man sucking on an unlit cigar.

"*Qué?*" he said between clenched teeth.

"Monterrey rail station. I need to catch a train."

The cabbie turned to look at her, a blank expression on his heavily lined face.

Feeling foolish, Elaine did her best to pantomime a train running over tracks, making locomotive sounds and blowing out a train whistle. After several attempts, recognition finally came to the driver.

"*Ah! Estación de carril! Sí.*"

Elaine didn't know if he had it or not, but he turned around and fired up the ignition as if he knew where to go.

Suddenly both back doors flew open. The two men who had been tailing her in the terminal jumped in on either side of her.

"Mind if we share a cab with you, Miss?" one of them said to her in perfect English.

Their abrupt appearance startled her. Brought all of her fears rushing back. "Um . . . this is, uh, this is *my* cab," she stammered.

"It's so expensive. Much better if we split the fare," the man on her left said calmly. "Better for you, better for us."

Elaine's mind reeled. *Could this be Derek's work? Did he send these guys to pick me up and get me across the border?*

She listened to the second man conversing in rapid-fire Spanish with the cabbie.

She hugged her backpack to her chest. "Let me out! NOW!" she screamed, her voice shrill in the tight confines of the cab.

The man to her left said, "The only place you're going is with us, my dearest one."

"I'll scream rape."

Both of them laughed.

The man to her left said, "You think there's anyone out here who would help you? Go ahead and scream. It'll be the last thing ever comes out of that pretty mouth of yours." He made a show of pulling back his jacket and displaying his weapon.

Elaine thought she would swallow her tongue as she glanced at the huge pistol tucked in a leather shoulder holster. Much of the long barrel was visible, and it gleamed in the sodium vapor lights of the taxi stand.

She dared to look up into his face, saw the serious intent of his expression. *No way this is Derek's doing. This is something else entirely.*

The cab pulled out into traffic and she began to pray.

The Killing Barn

BEFORE HEADING TO WINSLOW and Shangri-La, they went to Cottonwood. Parnell wanted to case out the site of their upcoming meet with Genevieve Thorssen. He and Jenn traveled in style, riding in Loretta Pesky's Rolls-Royce Phantom Coupe.

Cottonwood, 19 miles southwest of Sedona as the crow flies, was a sleepy ranching community nestled in Verde Valley, above the heat of the southern desert plains and south of the cool Arizona high country. The location was remote. Three-hundred acres of rolling hills and overgrown pastureland where sheep and cattle once grazed, prior to the bank foreclosure that doomed the ranch.

They traversed a deeply rutted dirt road for nearly a mile to get out to the feed barn where the meet was to take place. Madame Loretta complained with each dip and bump that her precious vehicle was not designed for off-road travel.

"You're the one who picked this godforsaken place." Parnell barked at her from the passenger seat.

The barn, ramshackle and falling down, had a slight lean to it. One corner of the roof had caved in. Wind whistled through holes in the walls where boards had rotted away, sheets of tin plugging the bigger gaps. A weathervane in the shape of a bantam rooster sat on top of the ridge beam and spun in the wind as though confused. A concrete grain silo towered over the barn like a disappointed parent.

Parnell heaved open the creaky barn doors. They stepped inside to the overpowering scent of fungus and cattle manure. A row of rusted milking stanchions lined one wall. Moldy hay bales were stacked along an adjoining wall.

He pulled Jenn aside and asked her, loud enough for Loretta to hear, "You think you could shoot Lars dead if we get him out here?"

The question didn't surprise her. She had been thinking about it the past few weeks. Emotionally she *could* pull the trigger on the albino beast who had murdered Russ. But if and when it came to actually doing it, she wasn't sure she was capable. Poppy believed in eye-for-an-eye justice. He'd killed more than a dozen people, but she questioned whether she could execute someone in cold blood. She was a Parnell, but she wasn't her father.

He broke the quiet. "I'll take your silence as a no."

"I *think* I could do it, yeah," she said. "It's just that—"

"Because if you can't, I certainly can. I just want you to have the satisfaction of putting him down. You doing it would be the ultimate justice. But it won't work if you're going to hesitate."

Satisfaction? Is that what it would be?

Loretta Pesky spoke up. "You two are heading down a bad stretch of road. I'd rather jump into a pit of rattlesnakes than be on the wrong side of Thorssen and Lars. This whole thing is a bad idea."

Parnell scowled at the woman. "Keep your editorial comments to yourself."

The fortuneteller shook her head in disgust, but kept quiet.

Jenn watched Poppy move through the barn, searching every nook and cranny for potential hiding places. The restaurant murder of her husband replayed in her mind—the giant approaching their table and calmly pointing his weapon; the gunshots, loud as cannon fire in the small dining room; the shrieks of horror coming from nearby diners; the sickening *splat-splat-splat* of bullets peppering Russ's head; blood splattering her and spraying across the white tablecloth; Russ dead, face-down in his plate of chicken parmesan. And worst of all, she recalled her moment of indecision as the restaurant erupted in chaos and her instinctive fight-or-flight response stalled. Her hesitant confusion almost got her killed. It all happened so fast. She would never be able to erase the vision of the albino's face in those excruciating eternal few seconds after the fatal shooting: the crooked grin on his bleach-white face, the glow in his weird pink eyes, the beaming happiness he projected after accomplishing his dark objective.

What kind of world is this where a man I have never seen walks casually into a restaurant and shoots my lover dead?

"Jenn, you're not looking so hot." Parnell said. "Are you okay?"

"I will be," she said, "after I kill the motherfucker."

Mexican Jumping Beans

THEY TRANSFERRED TO A WHITE Range Rover SUV on the outskirts of Monterrey. Elaine rode in the back seat, her wrists and ankles bound with plastic cable ties. Every movement caused her pain. The Mexican who smelled of peppers and onions sat next to her. The wheelman repeatedly checked her out in the rearview as he drove. His probing eyes—illuminated by the blue dashboard lights—were jumpy, like he was strung out on meth.

They were headed north, but to where and for what purpose she had no idea. Were these men drug cartel mercenaries abducting another American tourist for ransom? She had read stories about such goings-on in northern Mexico. But she didn't think that was the scenario. This was not a random pickup at the airport; she seemed to be a very specific target.

The man beside her held a gun in his right hand while he dug through her backpack with his left. He pulled out her cloth wallet and rummaged through it. He rattled off something in Spanish to the driver, which caused raucous laughter. The only thing she understood was *Karen Cooper*.

"What's so funny?" she dared ask.

The man waved her passport in front of her and said in clipped English, "This is not you. You are Elaine Leibrandt. Wanted by the gringo government. Worth *mucho dinero, mi muchacha*."

Elaine felt a chill traverse her spine as she heard her real name. "No, my name isn't Elaine," she said, trying to sound convincing. "I'm Karen Cooper from Costa Rica."

This brought more laughter from the two men.

"*De verdad.* If you are Karen Cooper, I am Tom Cruise, great Americano actor," said the man next to her with glee.

"And you *mala actriz, señorita,*" said the driver. "No award from academy of *imagen en movimientos* for you."

More merriment from the two men.

She felt the burn of humiliation. Her exhaustion fed her impatience, which fueled her anger. "I know damn well who I am," she said, her voice dripping with animosity. "I'm Karen Cooper, a Costa Rican artist doing business in Mexico. You have no right to—"

"*Callarse, perra!*" the driver shouted at her. "*Usted está* Elaine Leibrandt *de* Flagstaff Arizona *en los Estados Unidos.*"

A toxic pall filled the interior of the SUV. The man next to her continued to dig through her pack.

"What do you want with me?" she asked. "Where are you taking me?"

No response.

He dug out her cell phone and tried to operate it. Unsuccessful, he demanded she give him the password to open it.

"Look, I don't think—"

"Give me *el código* or I shoot," he said, roughly jamming the gun barrel into the soft place below her ribs.

She gasped as the deadly steel poked into her side. *No idle threat here.* She uttered the password with a shaky voice. He awkwardly navigated the menus with his left hand while keeping the gun planted in her side with his right. She prayed Derek had not yet sent meet instructions.

The gunman scrolled through the few text messages she had retained. Finding nothing of interest, he switched over to the log, finding the calls from Derek's burn phone. Derek's voice came through the tinny phone speaker as he played back his last voicemail:

"Hey, E, it's me. Wanted to let you know I made it. I'll be hooking up with you-know-who tomorrow. I just talked with her and she's fine. She made it to the camp. I'll be in touch again soon. I love you and miss you."

This brought about more Spanish chatter. The man beside her didn't look up from the phone, just kept scrolling as he conversed with the driver. He found the call she had made to her sister in Flagstaff from the San Jose airport, and he asked her who Gina was.

"A friend of mine," Elaine said, not wanting to implicate family.

"You talked for *dieciséis minutos*. Must have been *muy importante.*"

"Not really. Just catching up."

The driver said, "*Tu compañera, ella es en* Arizona, *correctomente*?"

She nodded. Nothing to gain by saying her "friend" wasn't in Arizona. They had the area code.

Her bound feet were going numb and she shifted on the seat, trying to get some feeling back. "Look," she said, "there's really no need to cuff my ankles. I can't exactly run away."

This brought about more discussion in rapid-fire Spanish between the two men. Ultimately, they left her feet tied together.

"*Dónde está* Derek Parnell?"

"Who?"

The gunman said, "Don't play *estúpido* with us, *mi mamá puta*. We know that's his voice *en su teléfono*. Derek Parnell. *También conocido como* King Midas. *Dónde está el macho*?"

"I don't know."

"Where are you meeting him?"

"Honestly, I really don't know."

"*Quien es* 'you-know-who' and what is *acampar*?"

"I don't know about any of this," she said. "He left me this one mysterious voicemail. That's it. I haven't heard anything else from him."

The man with the phone looked up. "So you admit *la voz en el teléfono es* Derek Parnell, *sí*?"

Elaine realized her mistake. They hadn't been sure it was her Derek on the voicemail, but they had expertly pushed her into a corner of admission.

"You were on your way to meet *el macho*, no?"

"I told you, I'm an artist. I came to Monterrey on business. I work with several galleries there."

The driver spoke up. "*Por qué lo hiciste di la taxista que le llevará a patio de ferrocarril?*"

Elaine told him she didn't understand the question.

The man with the gun had a better grasp of English, and translated for her. "If you are *artista* doing business in Monterrey, why you desire to go to rail yards?"

These men aren't stupid. They're calculating and cunning. Professionals. A wrong move and I'll be a corpse in the desert.

She uttered her best attempt. "I noticed you two following me in the airport and I was trying to lose you."

An awkward silence ensued as the two men studied her. Finally, the one with her phone said, "You need to work on your answers, *mi señorita*. Bullshit don't float where we're taking you."

That comment revealed quite a bit. They had no plans to kill her. If so, they would have already done it. They were taking her somewhere. They were hired thugs, doing a job for someone else who had an interest in her. Someone looking for Derek. More than likely they weren't Sinaloa or Gulf drug cartel personnel. And they were too crude and raw to be government agents. They had to be working for an independent operator.

"So where *are* you taking me?" she ventured.

The driver looked in the rearview at the man in the back seat, his jittery eyes questioning. "*Tejas*," he said. "*Un hombre ahí tiene mucho interés en ti.*"

The gunman glared at the driver with menace, like he had said more than he should.

"Texas?" she responded, going with it. "I got the Texas part, but not the rest of it. What'd he say?" she asked the gunman.

"He said, there's a man there who is very interested in you."

"Interested in me? Why?"

"Too many *cuestións, señorita* Leibrandt. Keep your mouth shut."

The gun dug deeper into her ribs. Her ankles burned from the cable ties. Her feet were numb. She felt miserable. But they had revealed a few things that gave her hope. They were transporting her to Texas. They had been instructed to deliver her alive and in one piece.

She sat back and remained quiet while the man with her phone tried unsuccessfully to reach Derek's burn phone with a return call.

The fear that consumed her was tempered by the knowledge that she had a little time. She began mentally reviewing possible scenarios in which she could make her escape.

And once I'm free, what then?

Home on the Range

PARNELL LOOKED OUT OVER THE RANGE his Shangri-La friends had constructed near the camp. His new crew took aim from behind crude wooden shooting stations, firing at a row of targets fifty yards away. The targets were large color portraits of hobo nation enemies: the president and select members of his administration, two Wall Street execs, a big pharma CEO, a Supreme Court justice. He smiled. His fellow breezers never lost their subversive sense of humor.

Parnell was pleased with the two men Weasel had recruited for his posse: Javion Wheeler, a muscular black man with a bushy Afro known as Flywheel, and Billy Dixon, a tall, wiry ex-rancher from Oklahoma whose hobo handle was Billy the Kid. They stood at their stations, shooting alongside Jenn and Weasel. The crackle and bang of gunfire echoed across the canyon. The air was tainted with the acrid smell of propellant.

At the first station, Jenn fired her nine millimeter Smith and Wesson M&P Shield he'd bought for her in Winslow. Most of her shots sailed high. Parnell worked with her, instructing her how to compensate for the recoil kick. She protested, wanting no part of this. Jenn hated guns. Referred to them as "tools of death and destruction." It had only been a month since she'd witnessed her husband being gunned down. But they would be facing some dangerous situations once they left camp, and he needed her to be ready.

He moved down the line, stopping behind the Oklahoman, Billy Dixon. Watched him fire off a few rounds. Parnell was impressed. The bull's-eye (the president's nose) was all but gone, shot to bits by Dixon's expert marksmanship. He'd bragged to Parnell that he had bagged his first coyote when he was just eight years old, thus earning him the nickname Billy the Kid.

Parnell clapped him on the shoulder between shots. "I see you weren't lying about your shooting ability," he shouted over cracks of gunfire. "Good work, Kid."

Parnell moved behind Javion Wheeler and watched him shoot. Flywheel was not a skilled marksman. Half his shots went astray, the inaccuracies due to Flywheel's impatience and the way he danced around as he shot, not planting his feet properly. Parnell instructed him on how to stand, how to relax his shooting hand and take his time. Wheeler's sloppy shooting didn't bother him, however. Flywheel's weapon of choice was a knife, a ten-inch Buck Hoodlum survivalist knife sharp enough to cut through a man's arm bone. Parnell had seen him wield the weapon expertly in a couple of tight situations in years past.

Behind him Loretta Pesky said, "How much longer do we have to stay out here? I'm burning up and going deaf from all the racket. You'll be hearing from my lawyer."

He turned. The fortuneteller sat in the shade, eyeing him with contempt. All the bitch did was bellyache. She had protested throughout the drive from Cottonwood to Winslow. She grumbled about having to wait while he made several purchases in Winslow (the Smith and Wesson for Jenn, a dozen rounds of ammunition, two more throwaway phones). She became belligerent when informed she would have to park her Rolls in a public lot and hike with him and Jenn to the hobo camp. Then during the hike she complained about the heat and her aching feet and legs.

Parnell yelled at her over the gunfire. "If you don't shut your yap I'm going to stuff you with straw and make you one of our targets. And it'll be me taking the killing shots."

That silenced her.

He moved on to Weasel. Greg Bethea was by far the most accurate shot in Shangri-La, as good with a pistol as he was a rifle or shotgun.

"Good work, partner," he said when Bethea stopped to reload. "I see advanced age hasn't taken the shine off your shooting skills."

Weasel laughed. "Look who's talking about age. Mister Cro-Magnon himself!"

Parnell gave his friend a mock laugh. "That's hilarious, coming from a Neanderthal. Or maybe you're older than that. Weren't you born near the end of the Cretaceous period?"

"Ha ha," Weasel harrumphed. "If I'm a dinosaur then you must be a Mesozoic reptile."

"A Meso *what?*"

Weasel slammed a fresh magazine into his Beretta. "You know, the Mesozoic era. The time before dinosaurs when reptiles ruled the Earth. For a smart guy you sure are illiterate, Derek."

Parnell laughed. "And you, my friend, will ruin your eyes if you keep reading as much as you do. Then you won't be able to shoot for shit."

The two men had long enjoyed this type of wiseass banter. Parnell met Greg Bethea ten years ago when Parnell first came west from New York, searching for Jenn and the killers who torched his house and murdered his wife. He knew Weasel Bethea to be one of the most intelligent breezers in camp. His dwelling—a crude structure of ponderosa pine walls, canvas flooring, and adobe roof—was packed floor-to-ceiling with paperback books.

Fifteen years ago Bethea pulled down a hefty salary as a fast-track Wall Street executive. He had been a high roller who wore custom-tailored suits and entertained wealthy clients. But then The Crash brought everything tumbling down. Bethea's financial services company went under. He couldn't find employment anywhere. Within three years he'd gone broke and was homeless. His high life among the privileged and rich had come to an end. He drifted west in search of his lost dignity, and found a home here at Shangri-La.

Parnell said to him, "Let's take a walk. Too noisy here."

Weasel holstered his Beretta. Parnell hollered to Jenn to watch Madame Crystal, then led Bethea down the storm drain culvert, up a slight ravine, then down the other side. The gunshots faded to muffled pops. A gentle breeze blew against their faces. They settled under the shade of a large desert willow.

Parnell said to him, "Good job on the two recruits you picked. They're both worthy of the task ahead. Thanks for that."

"It wasn't easy. When word got out that you were lookin' for a posse, I was overwhelmed. More'n twenty wanted a shot at it. Even two young ladies wanted to ride with us. You're a legend around here, Derek."

"Jesus," Parnell muttered in disgust. He'd hoped being away for three years might erase the hero worship lavished upon him. *Will I ever escape that stupid King Midas moniker?*

"A few of them weren't real happy when I told them they hadn't made the cut."

"Let me guess," Parnell said. "Ollie McKellar was leading that charge, right?"

"Yep. Our boy Ollie was irate. He's fifteen years younger than Billy and Flywheel. Thinks he's in better condition and would hold up better over the long haul."

"He thinks he's in better shape than Flywheel?"

"Yep. He's a cocky bastard. Big chip on his shoulder. He also thinks he can outshoot and outfight Billy and Fly."

Parnell shook his head. "Youth is wasted on the young."

"You got that right, padre. I've learned how to control him, but he would be a liability out on the rails."

"You ain't lyin' there." Parnell studied his longtime friend. "So, one thing I find curious, Greg."

"What's that?" Weasel said.

"When I asked you to recruit a couple of qualified hands for this posse of mine, you never asked me anything about the mission. Never asked me who we were going after."

"Well, you told me we were gonna bring down four criminals. That's all I needed to hear. I know about the two who murdered Jenn's guy. I figure the other two were involved with Jenn's kidnapping . . . and the ones who tried to ruin you. Don't need any names. Neither do Flywheel and The Kid. We're just honored to be riding with you, Derek. You're the man with the tombstone eyes."

"Will you cut the shit with the ass-kissin', Weasel," Parnell said, exasperated. "It's beneath you for Chrissakes."

"Sorry, partner, but it's true. You can't hide from your illustrious past."

"Maybe not. But I sure as shit don't wanna keep hearing about it."

"Understood. You want the truth of the matter?"

Parnell said, "Yeah, hit me with it."

"After all these years at Shangri-La, headin' up the security detail, I'm bored out of my gourd. I need some excitement in my life. Riding with you on this posse is exactly what I need."

"Glad to hear it, Weasel. But I gotta warn you. It's gonna get bloody and ugly."

Bethea smiled. "Even better. I've never been afraid to mix it up. You know that, Derek."

"Yeah, I *do* know that."

Weasel stroked his mustache whiskers and said, "I'm just happy you're back. We all wondered. We picked up bits and pieces from bounty hunters, but nobody seemed to really know what happened to you."

"We spent the last three years in Costa Rica. Talk about being bored out of your gourd. Fishing loses its appeal real quick."

"Costa Rica. Man, you *really* got the hell outta Dodge."

"Yeah, Lainey and I bought property on the beach down there. Figured we would need a safe house someday."

"I tried getting information out of Jenn. She told me you and Elaine were still alive, but wouldn't tell me where you were."

"So now you know." Parnell looked back at the shooting range. "Are you and your boys ready for this, Greg? It promises to be a rough ride."

"Yeah, we're pumped for this. Best thing to happen around here in years." Bethea's manner turned thoughtful. "I hate to ask this, Derek, because I know you don't have money these days—"

"You think I was asking you guys to put your lives on the line for no pay?"

"Well, no but—"

"I've got some cash stashed away in Utah. That's our second stop. I'll pay you guys there. In cash. It'll be generous. You can let Kid and Flywheel know."

"What's in Utah?"

"A deserted coal mine. You could say it's my last ATM in the States. And if all goes well, it'll be the burial ground for a couple of our targets." Parnell stood. "Sounds like target practice is over," he said. "Come on, let's head back."

As they retraced their route back to the shooting range, Weasel inquired about Elaine.

"She's well," Parnell said over his shoulder. "Or at least she was when I left her last week."

Truth was, he was worried about her, and had been conflicted about what to do. Elaine made it clear she was coming to join him. Much of the time, guilt gnawed at him for not responding to her. He missed her terribly, but now was not a good time to take chances. Cell phone communications between them could be intercepted by those interested in the reward for their capture. However, she was headstrong, and he had little doubt that she would foolishly leave their beach house in blind pursuit.

He had subconsciously made a decision when he'd purchased the burn phones in Winslow this morning.

As he and Bethea came into site of the range, he decided he would text Elaine a meet location—Hyacinth Mines in southern Utah. Three days from now.

Elaine knew where the mines were. She had been with him when he planted the money.

Shrink Wrapped Elaine

ELAINE AWOKE IN A STRANGE BED in a dark room under a blanket that smelled of dust and mildew. She was naked. Her head pounded with a hangover brutality.

She sat up, groaning with the effort. Her wrists and ankles were rubbed raw. Her body ached. Her nerves were on fire. Every movement caused her pain.

Where the hell am I? Dear God, what have I done?

She sifted through her fuzzy memory. Gradually details returned: the flight from San Jose to Mexico City, then on to Monterrey. The two Mexicans abducting her at the airport taxi stand. The long car ride through the dark desert. Crossing the border over the Rio Grande on a wide bridge. Dealing with U.S. Border Patrol and Customs. The feds gave their identification a mere cursory glance before waving them through. A mere formality? Did her abductors know someone important? Was the crossing at Laredo or Eagle Pass? She couldn't remember. Didn't matter. They had crossed into Texas. She was back in the U.S.

The wide strip of light leaking in from under the door brought her surroundings into shadowy focus. Small, windowless room. White dresser against one wall. Floor-to-ceiling bookshelves on the opposite wall. Framed print of a conquistador on horseback on a third wall. Night table with a lamp and clean ashtray. Ceiling fan with blades spinning lazily overhead. Indian throw rug at the foot of the bed.

The room spun. Dizziness made her woozy. She lay back on the pillows. They must have drugged her shortly after the crossing. Her mind was a blank slate after entering the States.

Am I still in Texas? Further north?

She took deep breaths, attempting to calm herself. The dizziness passed. She got up and wrapped the blanket around her, checked out her surroundings. Pain shot through her ankles and calves as she walked.

The house was quiet, a lifeless silence that convinced her she was alone. She switched on the lamp, bathing the small room in low-wattage light. The only color came from the spines of books lined up on the bookshelves. She perused the titles, some of which were in Spanish.

She searched through the drawers of the night table and dresser. Nothing there to give her a clue of her whereabouts. She checked the door, carefully wiggling the knob so as not to make noise. Locked from the outside. She got down on her knees and peered through the small opening under the door, could see just a few feet of floor in a dim hallway.

She checked under the bed. Nothing but dust balls there. And then she realized her backpack was missing, and her phone along with it. She was locked in and all her travel gear was gone. She tried not to panic.

She went back to the shelves, opening books, looking for clues about the identity of her captor. Her wrists were tattooed with blood-red marks from where they had cuffed her, and her hands hurt from the effort. She picked up a biography of Hernando de Soto and thumbed through it. A small sticker glued to the front endpaper read: **Property of Antonio Marquez.** *One of the Mexicans who abducted me?*

The far end of the shelves contained rows of textbooks. She moved to them, ran her finger along the spines. They all pertained to psychiatry. She perused the titles:

Stahl's Essential Psychopharmacology; Tarascon Pocket Pharmacopoeia; Handbook of Psychiatric Drug Therapy; Kaufman's Clinical Neurology for Psychiatrists. A well organized section next to it contained books about famous psychiatrists: Sigmund Freud, Carl Jung, Elisabeth Kubler-Ross, Alois Alzheimer. Some of the others were less familiar to her: Wilhelm Reich, Karl Jaspers, Alfred Adler.

She reached for one of the Freud texts but stopped short. A vehicle pulled up outside. The engine shut off. Two car doors squeaked open and slammed shut. Muffled voices. Laughter. Footsteps plodding on concrete.

She scrambled back to the bed and dove under the sheets, tried to slow her out-of-control breathing.

A house door squeaked open. The voices became louder, clearer. Two men, conversing in English, though she couldn't make out many words.

Elaine realized she had left the light on. Quickly she reached over and shut off the lamp, plunging the room into darkness. She pulled the sheets up to her chin and waited. Her heart thumped, a wild animal trying to escape her ribcage.

Breathe in, breathe out . . . Breathe in, breathe out . . . Got to keep your shit together here, girl!

Footsteps approached her door. One voice said: "Let's see how our pretty princess is doing." A mellow, well-educated voice. Not the Spanglish of her airport abductors.

She heard the metallic rattle of a key inserted into the lock. Tumbler turning. Lock clicking. Door opening. Hallway light spilling in, a wedge of light backlighting the two men in silhouette. One tall and thin, the other short and squat.

Squinting through her good right eye, Elaine watched the tall man move toward her, the biting lime scent of his cologne entering the room with him. He switched the lamp on. The second man remained at the door.

"Wake up, precious," he said, reaching down and jostling her shoulder.

She pretended to come awake, giving them a wide yawn for effect.

"Did you have a comfortable sleep?"

She looked at the man. Strikingly movie-star handsome. Chiseled cheekbones accentuated by a strong chin. Wide aristocratic nose, deep-set dark eyes like twin pools of oil. A scrubbed dusky complexion. He had a thick wave of glossy soot-black hair that swept over his head pompadour style, every strand gelled meticulously in place. He wore a custom-tailored tan suit and a red silk necktie. Everything about him was refined and impeccable. A man of distinction and import. Take away the suit and he could pass for an Aztec god.

"Are you back among the living, Elaine?" he inquired.

She stared at him, captivated by his blindingly white, perfect teeth and cover model smile. His dark eyes penetrated her in a way she found pleasurable. *Is this Antonio Marquez?*

The short man standing in the doorway said, "I think we got us a shy one, Tony."

Elaine shifted to check out the second man, who was younger than his accomplice and dumpy with an acne-pitted face. He was dressed casually in jeans, T-shirt, and black high-top sneakers.

She turned back to the man named Tony. He held a small black bag in his perfectly manicured hand.

"You drugged me," she said simply.

Tony smiled gently. "I assure you, I did not drug you, Elaine.

But I did give my crew permission to do so if you made things difficult. Apparently you were a very bad girl. My guys had to put you under for a while so they could get you here."

She didn't remember making things difficult or anything close to it. "Where is *here*?" she asked, her throat dry, her voice husky and cracking.

"You're back in the good old United States. You're a very popular lady in America these days, Elaine. You're a celebrity."

The man spoke flawless English. Much different than the two who picked her up at the airport and took her on the joyride.

"I don't have a clue what you're talking about," she said.

"Sure you do. You're worth a lot of money to the FBI. Wanted for the bombing of the Liberty Dogs compound in northern Colorado three years ago. Responsible for the deaths of forty-seven people. You and your boyfriend, Derek Parnell. But I'm not telling you anything you don't already know, am I?"

There was little to be gained by arguing her and Derek's innocence in that bombing, or even denying who she was. Better to try to get some answers. "Who are you?" she rasped.

"I'm a physician. You can call me Doctor Tony." He took a seat on the edge of the bed.

"What kind of doctor?"

"The kind that helps people."

"Doctor Tony is one of the best psychiatrists in Texas," the man stationed by the door said.

"I see," Elaine said. "So I'm somewhere in Texas, then."

Doctor Tony said, "San Antonio to be exact."

"And you're going to turn me in to the authorities for the reward money, right?"

His face flushed a deep bronze. His tone matched his dark complexion. "Don't insult me! I don't need the U.S. government's dirty money. I am a very wealthy man. A hundred large is petty cash to me."

"Then what do you want with me?"

"I want your lover boy—Derek Parnell. Where is he, Elaine?"

"Why do you want him?"

"I'm the one asking the questions here."

"I know." She decided to use the flattery approach. "I'm just wondering why a man with your obvious elegance and sophistication would be interested in Derek. Especially if it's not for the reward money. I think I deserve an answer to that after what you've put me through."

Doctor Tony studied her for a long moment before saying, "You're quite the plucky one, aren't you? I like that in a woman."

"So why the interest in Derek?"

She saw his eyes narrow and flash in anger. "Because he's a murderer. A cold-blooded killer. He snuffed someone very close to me."

This conversation had turned a murky corner. One of Derek's victims coming back to haunt him. "Who are you talking about?"

Doctor Tony hesitated, looked at his friend, then back at her. "My cousin, Tico. His name was Tico Samuels."

Elaine let out a braying laugh.

He grabbed her arm in a vise grip. "You find my cousin's brutal murder to be funny?"

"Ow, that hurts!" She tried to break free of him.

"I'll do more than just hurt you, bitch, if you make fun of my situation."

"Look, I didn't mean to laugh. But you have wrong information. Derek Parnell didn't kill Tico Samuels. The Colorado State Police did. I was there."

"She's lying, Tony," said the man at the door. "My bullshit detector's goin' off the charts."

Doctor Tony said, "It's common knowledge that Derek Parnell is a vigilante."

"That doesn't mean he killed your cousin. You've got it backwards. Tico Samuels murdered Derek's wife and burned his house to the ground. Then your cousin tried to murder both of us at Mesa Verde National Park."

The shrink smiled, a confident grin that showed off his straight, sparkling teeth. "So there you have the ideal motive. Where is Parnell, Elaine?"

This impeccably dressed man had his mind made up to kill Derek. But just maybe the doctor was the liar here. Perhaps this had nothing to do with Tico Samuels.

Her throat was sore and it hurt to talk. "Could I have some water, please?"

"Sure," the doctor said. "Diego, get our friend a glass of water."

"Not in a glass," she said. "Sealed bottled water if you have it."

He smiled again. "Sure. Not a problem. There's bottled water in the fridge, Diego."

Diego returned shortly with a frosty bottle of water. Elaine unscrewed the cap and gulped thirstily.

"We know you're going to meet him," Doctor Tony said, pulling her cell phone from his black bag. "A text came in this afternoon. We believe it's from your beloved."

He held her phone out so she could read the display:

Hi E. Meet us at the mines in 3 days (Thurs. PM).

"What are the mines, Elaine? Where is this place?"

Derek's timing couldn't have been worse but this was her fault. None of this would be happening had she not taken public transportation. She should have ridden the rails like any self-respecting hobo.

You're an idiot, Leibrandt!

"I'll ask again. Where are the mines, sweetcakes?"

She would prefer to die a horrible death before allowing harm to come to Derek. "I don't know."

"Oh, I think you know exactly where Parnell will be Thursday, Elaine. I'd like to join that party. You're my invitation." He glanced at his accomplice. "I believe the lady needs some coaxing to give us the truth, don't you, Diego?"

"Absolutely, Tony" Diego replied, moving to the side of the bed.

Elaine looked on in abject horror as the shrink pulled a syringe and a small vial of yellowish liquid from his bag. She recited a quick prayer in her head as she watched him load the hypodermic and squirt it once to test it. Diego pulled back the sheets and pinned her shoulders to the mattress, his eyes taking in her nakedness. She kicked and bucked but couldn't break free.

A pinching sting in her arm.

And then she tumbled through a tunnel of swirling, bouncing colors.

Breezers and Bloodweed

THE CAMP BUZZED WITH a festival-like ambiance. Parnell's posse would be leaving in the morning, and the Shangri-La breezers were throwing a bash to wish them good fortune and safe passage out on the rails. Biggest celebration Parnell had ever seen here.

A chill permeated the air this early-September night; the days were blisteringly hot and the nights frosty cool here in the high Sonoran desert this time of year. Two bonfires roared in a large clearing between the hobo dwellings and the river, illuminating the village in a flickering carnival midway brightness. Streamers adorned the tents and huts, blowing in the gentle breeze like brightly dyed strands of hair. Fred "Fingers" Johnston and his band played music on the makeshift stage where Reverend Ann delivered her sermons. Chef Alice cooked a bountiful banquet of fresh deer meat, grilled fish, and roasted vegetables. Blackberry wine and potato beer flowed freely. The pungent aroma of marijuana wafted through the night air, mixing with the smells of roasting meat and wood smoke.

Parnell, Jenn, Weasel Bethea, and Ann Finnegan sat near one of the fires scooping venison stew off of shiny hubcaps with plastic spoons and sipping homemade blackberry wine from Styrofoam cups. The camp enjoyed Chef Alice's venison steaks and deer stew thanks to the hunting prowess of Hopeful Harvey Henshaw, who bagged a big doe yesterday. The blackberry wine was compliments of Buttonhead Murphy, Shangri-La's party "pharmacist."

Parnell ate in silence, watching Chef Alice—a.k.a., Alley Cat—fillet rainbow trout caught this afternoon by Broadway Bling and Oshkosh Moss, the camp fishermen. Alice threw the fish on a pair of wrought-iron sewer grates the breezers had lifted from a downtown Winslow sidewalk one crazy night a few years back.

He took a gulp of wine, sopped up the remainder of his stew with a slice of stale bread. Parnell appreciated his fellow breezers giving him and his crew this splendid sendoff. He loved his Shangri-La friends, and tonight, steeped in weed, wine, and song, he felt that love profoundly.

The three-piece band finished a song and the public address speakers at the edge of the stage went silent. Parnell heard the portable gas generators chugging, the twin fires crackling. Laughter and splashing drifted up from the river. Dogs barked. And then Fingers Johnston's amplified voice echoed across the camp: "I've had a request for a tune all of you know, so we invite you to sing along with us, if the mood strikes."

Fingers started the intro on his battered acoustic guitar, and was joined quickly by his son, Zack on bass and some young guy Parnell didn't know on drums. Campers started singing along to a song that had been the American hobo anthem for as long as he could remember:

Ain't got no place to call my own,
Can't call nobody on the phone,
Ain't got no money for the rent,
Thanks to the U.S. government!

Ain't got two quarters to rub together,
My pocket's light as a goddamned feather,
So tired of this rainy weather
Time for a revolution,
for now and forever.

By the time they got to the chorus, most everyone had joined in. Jenn wasn't familiar with the lyrics, but did her best, picking up lyrics as she watched him sing along:

Uncle Sam did us wrong,
And we all went along,
A tax for this and a fee for that,
Till we're fuckin' busted flat, flat, flat
And now we know our Uncle's bent
So fuck the U.S. government!

Fingers ended the song with a guitar-strumming flourish, accentuated by the drummer's cymbal crash. The camp erupted in cheering applause and whistles. The celebration was in full swing.

Parnell called out to Chef Alice, displaying his wiped-clean hubcap. "Mighty delicious meal you've prepared for us tonight,

Alley Cat. Alice's Restaurant gets a four-star rating from me." Jenn nodded her agreement next to him.

"Only four stars, Derek?" Alice yelled back, brushing her hair back from her face as she flipped fish and stirred up a mound of onions, carrots, and garlic on the wide grill. A cloud of smoke escaped the pit oven and enveloped her. "Come here and try some of this trout," she said, coughing, her eyes watering. "Maybe this'll upgrade your rating to five stars."

He stood and went to her. She loaded his hubcap with two trout fillets and a mound of roasted vegetables. On his way back to his seat, he passed Loretta Pesky, who sat by herself, not eating or drinking, looking morose.

He showed her his heaping hubcap. "Not eating? You'd best snatch up some of this grub. You're going to need your strength, Loretta. We've got a big day ahead of us tomorrow."

She looked at Parnell's food and scrunched her face in disgust.

"Fine, have it your way, then," he said with a shrug, and went back to his place next to Jenn.

As if on cue, Fingers announced he was going to play a camp favorite in honor of Alice's superb culinary skills. The band promptly launched into "Alice's Restaurant" by Arlo Guthrie, which got the breezers singing along once again.

As he ate, Parnell was suddenly struck by an overwhelming sense of loneliness. The fact he was surrounded by good friends and scrumptious food and toe-tapping music only intensified his gnawing sense of aloneness. He missed Elaine. Lainey was his ballast, his steadying influence. They were a matched pair, two bookends on each end of the same shelf. He must have been crazy to leave her behind, rushing out without thinking what his hasty actions would do to both of them.

The happy times they'd spent together at her house in Flagstaff spooled through his mind. Flying kites and binge-watching movies while buzzed on peyote button. Drinking beer and smoking weed and laughing until their cheeks hurt. Playing with his model trains while they were eight miles high. Walking hand-in-hand through Lainey's botanical garden behind her house, breathing in the sweet fragrance of her desert marigolds and purple aster. The time they had brought back helium-filled balloons from the Coconino County Fair and spent the night inhaling the gas, talking and singing like Alvin and the Chipmunks, cracking each other up.

He missed her kisses, the feel of her creamy smooth skin rubbing against him when they made love. The scent of the perfume she favored—Obsession—the name said it all. Her excited whispers as she rode the edge of orgasm. Her intellect and creativity. Her face—scarred by the actions of a former violent boyfriend and the source of many of Elaine's insecurities—was beautiful to him. Each imperfection along her cheek and jawline the surgeons hadn't been able to correct only added to her unique beauty.

Had she received his text? Had she read his meet instructions? In spite of his reservations about the existence of God or a higher power, Parnell found himself praying. Prayed that she was okay. Prayed that she was safe and that they would be reunited at the Hyacinth mines on Thursday. He peered up into the starry skies. *Is anyone up there listening?*

Have I failed you for the last time, Lainey?

Jenn intruded on his wine-drenched introspection. "Are you okay, Poppy?"

"Yeah, I'm fine."

"You seem preoccupied tonight. Is it our meeting with the Swedes tomorrow?"

"No." He held up his cup. "I'm not used to drinking wine this strong."

Jenn dipped her head, looked into her own cup. "Yeah. Really tasty, though."

"Buttonhead says it's seventeen percent alcohol," Weasel Bethea said.

Ann spoke up. "Mister Murphy certainly knows how to pack a punch with his party favors."

Parnell looked down the line at Ann, saw her tip her cup and take a long nip of the blackberry brew. "I thought you abstained from alcohol, Annie."

"There're a lot of things you don't know about me, Derek."

Their conversation was interrupted by Buttonhead Murphy, who strolled up to them toting a long bamboo water bong. "Hey, guys," he said merrily, weaving in front of them, smoke spiraling up from the bowl. "You enjoying the party?"

"Speak of the devil," Weasel said.

Buttonhead tipped his trademark porkpie hat and gave them a goofy, stoner smile. "It would be terribly rude of me not to offer a roasty toast to you—our guests of honor—before you head off on your grand adventure. My latest harvest is derived from a hybrid cross of Panamanian Red and Purple Haze. I call it Buttonhead's Bloodweed. You get the mild cerebral high of the Red, coupled with the happy, chatty, psychedelic high of the Haze. It's my special strain that'll take you beyond the moon and stars. And you'll be talking and laughing your asses off the whole way. I've been saving it for a special occasion, and occasions don't get any more special than this, my friends. I'd be most honored if y'all would give it a try."

Parnell chuckled. He'd always gotten a kick out of the Shangri-La drug supplier. Buttonhead's wild, fright-wig bush of unruly red hair tucked under his frayed porkpie hat and wide, dilated eyes gave him a clownish look. He reminded Parnell of Harpo Marx.

"You know, Murph," Parnell said between chuckles, "you have a true salesman's gift. You would've been great as a carnival barker."

Buttonhead took a sweeping bow while still maintaining his grasp on the smoldering bong. "I accept that as a compliment, King Midas, but with one exception. Carny types sell deceit and trickery. There is nothing devious about my weed. Same goes for my peyote. I offer nothing but the highest-grade psychoactive experience."

Parnell said, "I can vouch for that." He pointed at the bong. "You've sold me, Murph. Let me at it."

"Absolutely." Buttonhead bent over and held the bong out to him. Parnell took a deep hit and held it in his lungs. Buttonhead paused briefly to check Parnell's reaction, then moved down the line, offering tokes to Jenn, Bethea, and Ann, each of whom took their turn drawing the Buttonhead Bloodweed smoke up through the long bamboo cylinder. Jenn and Ann both went into coughing fits, but Weasel managed to hold the smoke in. Through it all, Buttonhead kept up his patter: "Nice hit . . . that'll give you a good rush . . . you're getting spacey now . . . one more toke and you'll pass the Big Dipper . . . Have you reached Polaris yet?"

Parnell declined additional hits while the others continued to smoke. A relaxing calm overtook him. *Not too wasted. Nice mild buzz. Just right.* He sat quietly while the others became increasingly talkative, their voices escalating out of control until it sounded like a convention of speed freaks. Parnell couldn't hold back a boisterous laugh.

A clattering disturbance exploded on the far side of the village.

Loud voices rising over the music.

Gunshots.

A chorus of screams.

The band—well into the third verse of "Amazing Grace"—stopped playing. The camp plunged into a preternatural silence, as though someone had pulled the plug on the festivities. The partygoers looked around in confusion.

Fear replaced merriment.

Flywheel ran into view and shouted, "We got us some trouble brewin'. Ollie McKellar and his half-wit buddy are drunk as shit. They're shootin' up the camp. Knocked over some tents and winged Oshkosh's hand."

An electric jolt zapped Parnell as chaos erupted around him.

He jumped to his feet.

Goddamn, the one time I don't have my weapon.

Showdown at Shangri-La

OLLIE MCKELLAR STAGGERED UP TO THEM with a rough-looking guy Jenn knew as Palomino. Their guns were drawn, their faces set in drunken determination.

"What's going on, Ollie?" Weasel asked. "Looks like you've been hitting the 'shine a little hard tonight."

McKellar's face twisted into a scornful mask. "Shut yer face, Weasel! You got no right judgin' me." The barrel of his revolver shook along with his words.

Weasel kept his cool. "So what's your beef, Mick?"

"You know damn well what my beef is." He pointed the gun at Parnell. "You an' King Shit here passed me over fer your posse. I can shoot better than Flyboy over there, an' I ride iron horses better'n any of ya."

Flywheel stood in the shadows, eyeing McKellar with naked hatred. The blade of his deadly hunting knife gleamed in the firelight. Jenn had heard about the bad blood between the two men from Ann. Suddenly her giddy, drunken high had dissolved into fear and dread.

Parnell stared at the two inebriated gunslingers. "Put the guns away, kids," he said calmly. "Stop playing cowboys. Go sleep it off. We're trying to have some fun here, and you dimwits are muckin' it up."

"Go ahead and shoot him, Mick," Palomino urged his buddy. "That's what you said you was gonna do."

McKellar took a wobbly step forward, raised the weapon and trained the barrel directly on Parnell's forehead. His gun hand shook crazily.

"Go ahead, Mick," Palomino pressed. "Waste the motherfucker!" Pull the trigger."

Weasel spoke up. "Mick, c'mon. I know you don't have it in you to gun down an unarmed man."

"Don't I?"

"Don't do anything stupid here, Ollie." Parnell said.

A group of breezers gathered round to watch the exchange. Jenn made eye contact with Billy The Kid Dixon, who stood in the crowd with his gun raised, ready to take action if necessary.

Through his alcohol haze, McKellar realized he had an audience. He went into performance mode, spitting in the dust at Parnell's feet. "Mister King Shit speaks," he yelled dramatically. "Think you're a big-time celebrity in these parts, don't ya? Everybody kisses your ass and you think they love you. I got news for ya, Parnell. Nobody here loves you. They just want yer money. I'd hoped somebody'd finally filled you fulla lead. But now you show up with your slutty daughter and everybody's partyin' in your honor. What a crocka shit."

Parnell advanced on McKellar, rage boiling in his eyes. "What did you call my Jenny?"

Jenn threw out her arm to restrain him. "Poppy don't. He isn't worth it."

"*I'm* not worth it?" McKellar screeched at Jenn. "You ain't nothin' but a shanty whore with a big mouth."

Jenn felt the sting of his words. She released Poppy and balled her fists, made a move for McKellar. "You don't know anything 'bout me, twink-boy."

Ann jumped into the fray, stepping between McKellar and the two Parnells. That's enough," she said with conviction. "None of this is necessary. Give me the gun, Ollie. You've caused enough trouble."

McKellar let out a snide laugh and stepped back from her. "Well, look who it is," he said, his words slurring. Spittle dotted his chin. "Little miss self righteous. Little miss doctor do so little. You ain't no doctor. An' you ain't no mouthpiece fer God the way you claim. You live in yer castle all high an' mighty. But you know what? You're just a two-bit breezer loser like the rest of us."

"That's enough, Ollie," Ann said calmly. "Give me the gun. You, too, Palomino. Then I want both of you to leave."

"Fat chance, bitch!" Palomino said.

"Yeah," McKellar agreed. "We're here to take care of some long unfinished business. So get outta my face."

Flywheel moved closer, the blade out in front of him. Jenn glanced at Poppy, saw him clenching his fists at his sides.

Parnell said to him, "Since you've so eloquently described your opinions of us, it's my turn, McKellar. You're a cowardly little cocksucker. A scared, insecure little boy in a man's world—"

"Poppy, stop, or he's going to—"

"No he's not, Jenn," he said, eyes never leaving McKellar.

"He's a chickenshit and I've heard enough of his lip. You want the truth, Mick? I didn't want you on my crew. I don't trust you and I never have. If I was stupid enough to take you along with us, your hot-headedness would screw up the first jam we got into out on the rails. You'd get us all killed. I see by your actions here I made the right decision."

McKellar tried to get around Ann, but she held him back. "Why you bastard, I should—"

"You should what, McKellar? Shoot me? Go ahead. But you'll only get one shot and if it isn't a kill shot, I'll snuff you. I promise you, it won't be a pleasant way to die."

"You got a lotta balls, Parnell."

"Not a lot, no. Just a pair of them. But they're much bigger than yours."

Ann interceded. "Okay, enough of the anatomy lesson." A few anxious chuckles came from the crowd. "Let's stop the pissing contest and discuss this in a civilized manner, shall we?"

"Let go of me, bitch," McKellar blubbered, glaring at Parnell over Ann's head. "This ain't your business."

Parnell said, "I tell you what, Ollie old boy. You want to prove you're a man and not a sniveling, scared little twink?"

"Fuck you, Parnell!"

"I'm serious. I'm offering you the chance to prove your bravery."

"You callin' me out?"

"Yeah, I guess you could call it that."

"How so? A fistfight?"

"A fistfight? What're you, fourteen years old? That's minor league. Let's take things to the major league level."

McKellar thought it over, his eyes scanning the crowd. The hard, arrogant edge of his confidence seemed to be dwindling, giving way to fear. Suddenly, Palomino didn't look so sure of himself either.

"I'm listenin'. Whaddaya have in mind?"

"I propose a good old-fashioned duel. Just you and me, Mick. Your gun against mine. Last man standing after the smoke clears kinda thing."

A collective gasp whispered through the surrounding throng. McKellar swallowed hard and looked uncertainly at Palomino.

Ann said, "Dueling's not the way to settle anything, Derek. Remember how Alexander Hamilton ended up?"

"Yeah, I do. Hamilton was a fool. He fired into the trees thinking Burr would do the same. But Burr didn't fire high. He nailed Hamilton. I won't be that stupid."

Jenn couldn't believe this. Surely Buttonhead's Bloodweed and potent wine had transported her into some kind of *How the West Was Won* nightmarish alternate reality. Her head swam in incongruous thoughts. "Don't do it, Poppy," she pleaded. "*Please don't do it.*"

Parnell ignored her, keeping his focus on Ollie. "Whaddaya say, McKellar? Are we on?"

Ann, positioned between the two men, said, "Derek, I really don't think this is a good idea."

"Oh," Parnell huffed, "I think it's an *excellent* idea, Annie. I'm giving this cocky bastard a chance to back up his overblown ego. He runs his mouth all the time but I think he's all bluff and no balls."

McKellar looked around at the breezer faces fixed on him. His shaky demeanor revealed his fear. He looked at Palomino, who gave him a nearly indiscernible nod.

"Okay," he said weakly. "Let's do it."

Several of the more intoxicated in the crowd shouted out lusty hoots and hollers. It sickened Jenn. The mob wanted blood. She couldn't stand the thought of her father dying in a violent gun duel before a bloodthirsty crowd.

"Please don't do this, Poppy," she said. "For my sake, please don't go through with this."

He shifted his stare from McKellar to her. "Fetch my gun, Jenn."

"What? No. I won't do it. You've had a lot to drink and I—"

"Go get my gun *now*, Jennifer!" Parnell's eyes narrowed to scowling slits. His demanding, furious look scared her.

He turned to Weasel. She noticed something pass between them, some kind of nonverbal body language thing going on. Some kind of mutual understanding.

"It's okay, Jenn," Weasel said, his expression softening. "Go get Derek's gun for him."

A nervous buzz whispered through the crowd. All eyes were focused on her, glittering and flickering like the cut-out eyes of jack-o-lanterns. Her crazy father had finally gone off the deep end. A gun duel was outrageous even for Poppy.

She left the ring of firelight and went to retrieve Poppy's

Mauser. Worry consumed her. The odds were not in his favor. *Why is he pushing for a violent confrontation like this?* Jenn tried to think of a way out, but her mind and emotions were too blurred by weed and alcohol.

She heard a round of cheers go up when she returned toting Parnell's weapon. This thirst for violence shocked her. She knew the camp was rooting for Poppy, but it was little consolation. Someone was going to die out here tonight, and there was a good chance it would be Poppy.

Parnell was laying out the ground rules of the duel when she handed him his gun. "We stand back-to-back," he said loud enough for the crowd to hear, "and we walk in opposite directions as Weasel starts the countdown from five. When he finishes the count, he yells 'shoot' and we turn and fire our weapons. May the best man win."

"Wait a minute. Hold on," McKellar objected. "I ain't doin' it if Weasel's involved. You'll find some way to cheat, Parnell. I want Palomino to do the countdown."

Parnell nodded. "Okay, fair enough, Mick. Palomino will do the honors, then."

Palomino backpedaled into the shadows. "Uh, I really don't think I want any parta this shit."

"You already *are* part of this," Parnell said. "Put down your weapon and prepare to officiate."

Ann's voice was strained as she said, "Come on, Derek. This is completely insane. Let's call this whole thing off now."

"No way, Annie. I want to settle this once and for all. This has been bubbling up for years. Why don't you go see if you can help Oshkosh. Apparently this asshole wounded him."

"Poppy, listen to reason," Jenn intoned. "Ann is right."

"The duel is on," he said, ignoring her and checking his weapon. He stepped around Ann. "Come on, McKellar. Time to put up or shut up."

The throng erupted in an edgy cheer. As the two duelers took their positions, a hush settled over the spectators. The breezers standing behind McKellar and Parnell moved to the side, out of the line of fire.

The two men stood back-to-back in the clearing, Parnell taller by a couple of inches. As dictated by the rules Parnell had laid out, both men held their weapons down next to their thighs. McKellar took deep breaths, his face shiny with sweat. Parnell remained still and self-contained. *How can Poppy be so relaxed?*

Palomino's voice was unsteady as he began the countdown.

"Five..."

The duelers began walking in opposite directions.

"Four..."

Boots shuffling through the sunbaked dirt.

"Three..."

Jenn couldn't bear to watch. She covered her eyes with her arm and turned away. *What am I going to do if that bastard Ollie McKellar shoots Poppy dead?* Bile flooded her throat.

"Two..."

She heard a scrabbling sound followed by three shots in quick succession.

A loud gasp and a shout.

The sound of a body hitting the turf.

Screams and shrieks.

Cries of confusion. People milling around her.

She heard Palomino shout, "Holy shit!"

Against her will, Jenn forced her eyes open. She was stunned by what she saw: McKellar writhing on the ground, holding his right arm with his left hand, blood seeping through his fingers, his gun in the dirt five feet away.

"You cheated me, you fuckin' prick!" McKellar shouted at Parnell. "You shot me while my back was turned!" He groaned, a small puddle of blood pooling on the ground beneath his arm.

Parnell stood over him. "I have numbers dyslexia. I get all mixed up on countdowns like that."

"It's true," Weasel said. "Derek suffers from what is known as dyscalculia. It's a developmental disorder. Very difficult to discern numerical sequences."

Poppy and Greg Bethea exchanged smirks, and Jenn knew the duel had been a planned setup. Probably a sting they had pulled off together in the past.

"You ain't nothin' but a pair of low-rent, cheatin' grifter assholes," McKellar muttered through gritted teeth.

"You're lucky I didn't shoot to kill. Let this be a lesson to you, Ollie old boy. There're never any real rules in a gun duel. Also, never turn your back on a man with a firearm who wants to see you dead."

Palomino went for his gun on the ground and Parnell turned on him, trained the Mauser on his breastbone. "Stop right there, or

I *will* shoot to kill."

Palomino froze, his eyes wide ovals of fear. Parnell went to a knee to retrieve Palomino's weapon, a cheap Saturday night special .25 caliber pistol that had seen better days.

"You're a fuckin' coward, Parnell," McKellar ranted from where he lay. "Shot me in the back like a yella-bellied chicken."

"Quit fabricating things. I didn't shoot you in the back. I shot you in the arm. Big difference. You're lucky my aim is true. You should thank me for sparing your life."

McKellar moaned loudly. "Oh, man . . . this hurts like a goddamn motherfucker."

"Quit your whining, you little wimp." Parnell motioned to Ann. "You've got a new patient here, Annie. I hope you have pediatric training because this one's a big baby."

Parnell collected McKellar's gun. He then turned to face the crowd. "Sorry to spoil the party, folks. Me and my crew will be leaving shortly, so please, everyone go back to enjoying yourselves. Loretta," he shouted to Madame Crystal, whom he spied sitting well away from the action, "go collect your stuff and be ready for a night hike." To Weasel he said, "Get the posse together, Greg. I wanna roll outta here in an hour."

As Parnell walked up the hill with Jenn to gather their belongings, she heard threats coming from McKellar: "I'll get you for this, Parnell. I'm gonna fill you fulla holes, motherfucker, so you better be watchin' yer back."

Part 2:

THE POSSE RIDES

Barn Animals
Fun-time Juice and Open Pit Surface Mining
Swedish Sauna
Winging It In Winslow
Of Sin and Rectitude
Pornocopia
Canaries In a Coal Mine
The Belle of the Ball and the Southern Gentleman
Parnell's Amusement Park
Call From the Wild
Rolling Inferno
Superman and Captain Turnipseed

Barn Animals

THEY ARRIVED AT THE COTTONWOOD pastureland at three-thirty in the morning, worn and bedraggled. The two-hour drive in the Phantom Coupe was cramped, Loretta at the wheel and Parnell in the passenger seat. Jenn, Weasel, Flywheel, and Kid were jammed in the back. Interstates 40 and 17 were mostly deserted but Parnell made sure Loretta didn't exceed posted speed limits. They had an arsenal stashed in the trunk and he was a wanted felon. A bunch of grubby hobos armed like a small militia would not fare well if stopped by the Arizona Highway Patrol. Memories of the shootout with the Colorado State cops still haunted him and he surely didn't want a replay of that mess.

Talk during the drive centered around Parnell's fake duel with Ollie McKellar. The Kid and Flywheel relished it, laughing and whooping it up. Overbearing Ollie had finally been put in his place. Parnell told his rapt audience that he and Weasel had worked the gun duel ruse once before.

"We pulled the same trick seven years back," he said, keeping his Mauser trained on Loretta's right kidney. "Some wannabe cowboy drifted into camp talking a big game, telling us he was the second coming of Wild Bill Hickok. All macho bluster and bravado. Fulla lies and tall tales, which was the only way he resembled Wild Bill. This turd raped two of our women at gunpoint, Chef Alice being one of them. So Greg and I took action. We shamed him into a duel. That duel happened pretty much like it did tonight, except I shot to kill. Plugged him right between the shoulder blades. He died just like his hero, Wild Bill. Shot in the back. We buried him in the desert. A saguaro cactus marked his grave."

"Yeah," Weasel said. "The breezers rejoiced, especially the womenfolk. Justice had been served."

Jenn spoke up. "So you're telling me people in camp knew what was going on tonight? They knew McKellar didn't stand a chance?"

"Some of them did, yeah," Parnell said.

Flywheel said, "Yeah, I remember that day. I had a hunch you might be playin' the same scam tonight, but I wasn't sure. I was ready to jump in and slice an' dice that douchebag McKellar."

"I was ready, too," Kid said in his Oklahoma drawl. "I'm the newbie here. I didn't know what the hell was going on. But I wish you'd snuffed McKellar the way you did the Wild Bill dude."

Parnell shook his head. "Naw, Ollie didn't rape or murder anybody. He's a pain in the ass but he didn't deserve to die. He just needed to be taught a lesson."

"He shot Oshkosh Moss," Flywheel said. "Knocked down a few crash pads."

"Oshkosh'll be okay. Won't be able to use his hand for a while, but Annie's taking care of him."

Jenn's voice held an accusing tone. "Jesus, Poppy. You scared the shit outta me. You coulda died out there tonight."

Parnell emitted a soft laugh. "I wasn't gonna let that cocky little toad get a clean shot at me."

"One thing's for sure," Kid said. "Never play poker with Derek and Weasel."

Weasel laughed, saying, "FYI, playing poker is what got Wild Bill Hickok killed. He didn't pay up on a few losing hands so he got a bullet in his back."

Parnell didn't know that about Wild Bill Hickok. Greg Bethea was forever coming up with trivia gems like that. Unfortunately it brought back memories of his father, Louis, who had been shot in the back of the head, execution style, murdered over unpaid gambling debts when Parnell was thirteen. His mind flashed back to the rough looking men—loan sharks and collection agents—who showed up at their door making threats and shouting obscenities. His father's out-of-control gambling addiction had ruined their family, and his murder had thrown him and his mother into a depressing cycle of poverty and depression. The bank repossessed their house and he and his mother had to move in with his grandparents. His mother dealt with a never-ending parade of bill collectors and con men. The stress most certainly led to her early death. Parnell would always blame his loser father for that.

Arriving at the barn, they retrieved their weapons from the trunk and set up for the meet with the Swedes, which was scheduled for noon. Weasel, Kid, and Flywheel disappeared into the trees west of the barn where they bedded down to wait and catch a few winks. Parnell, Jenn, and Loretta moved their belongings into the barn. Parnell turned on the battery-powered LED lantern, a strong little unit that lit up much of the barn interior. He and Jenn looked for a good hiding place, a spot from where they could observe the exchange between Loretta and Genevieve Thorssen. They decided on a storage alcove behind the row of milking stanchions. Tight quarters that stunk of dusty hay, sour milk, and manure. But it was well hidden and knotholes in the boards offered them excellent vantage points.

Jenn fought to stay awake, but she finally conked out, nodding off on a blanket spread over hay bales. Adrenaline kept Parnell keyed up. Too much going on. He sat on a rusted milking stool, gun in hand, watching Loretta pace the hard-packed dirt floor.

He said to her, "You're wound up tighter'n a sealed condom."

She stopped her pacing. "Nice imagery, Killer."

He smiled. "That's rich, coming from you, Loretta. You've got blood all over your bank statements. Unless I have the wrong idea about fortune-telling pay scales, I'm betting a lot of folks died so you could buy that car out there and your castle in Sedona."

"My *castle?*"

"Yeah. Real estate on Inspirational Drive is pricey. You can't buy a place like that reading tea leaves."

"You're wrong, Parnell."

"About what? Tea leaves?"

"No. about me being a murderer. *You're* the killer. Not me."

He smiled at her. "I've never denied who I am. I've killed a few men in my time, yes. Every one of them deserved to die. But you? You keep deceiving yourself. Face it, you're a killer same as me, Loretta. The only difference is you murder by proxy. You're the go-between . . . the setup operative. You connect people who want to rid the world of someone with assassins willing to do the wet work. It's murder-for-hire and you're the architect."

She stared at him for a long moment, seeming to search for a retort but finding none. The lantern light reflected off the lenses of her glasses. Parnell waited, but she remained quiet. She returned to her shuffling, back and forth, from one side of the barn to the other, wringing her hands and rotating her head side to side as she walked. She started mumbling under her breath and Parnell wondered if she wasn't starting to lose it.

"What's that? What'd you say, Loretta?"

She stopped, turned to him. "I said I'm scared."

"Why? The hard part's over for you."

"Do you really think someone like Genevieve Thorssen is

going to let me live after she learns I've set her up?"

"Don't know. Guess that depends on her mood."

"She's ruthless. She'll have that monster Lars gun me down as soon as she realizes the cash bag is empty."

"Lars isn't going to be shooting anybody if we can help it."

"You seem pretty sure of yourself. What if something goes wrong."

"It very well *could* go wrong, but—"

"Because confronting Thorssen and Lars is a whole different thing from dealing with that Ollie character."

"Oh, I'm very much aware of that."

"So why haven't you killed me?"

"I told you that if you got me in front of Thorssen and Lars, I'd let you go. I figure this is your atonement, connecting me with the killer Swedes."

"And that's it? After my involvement you're really going to let me go?"

"Sure. After we take care of our business here. After that, you're free as a bird. So don't fuck it up by trying something stupid."

She shuffled closer to him, stood in front of him. "Thank you. Maybe you're not such a heartless man after all."

"That's debatable. I've done good things and I've done bad. You mean you can't reach into your all-knowing psychic mind and intuit all that, Madame Crystal?"

"I've tried. But your chakras are camouflaged. Your claircognizance factors are opaque and your spiritual being is all over the map."

"Enough of the psychic horseshit, Loretta. What are you getting at?"

"I'm saying you're a hard person to read."

"No news there."

"Why are you so against wealthy people?"

"Because I've seen what big money does to people. It's a corrupting influence, the dark side of capitalism. I've learned that most of the seriously disturbed assholes I run into have money to burn."

Loretta fingered the silver-and-turquoise bangles on her wrist, "*You're* rich. How do you come to grips with that?"

"I'm not rich any more." He looked away, reflecting on the way John Dobkin and Blanton Miles had tricked him out of his company and robbed him of his wealth before setting him up as the fall guy in the bombing of the Liberty Dogs compound.

"I'm sensing this is quite a dark memory for you," Loretta said, studying him, as though trying to peer behind his camouflaged chakras and clair-whatever opaqueness.

"I don't miss the money," he said. "Never felt comfortable having lots of it. I tried to give most of it away. Felt a huge relief when most of it was gone. But the pricks who tried to ruin me are gonna pay for what they did to me and others."

"Through your vigilante justice?"

"I prefer to call it *frontier* justice. An eye for an eye and limb for a limb. Let me ask you something, Loretta. Do you believe in the idea of karma?"

"Of course. Those of us with psychic awareness are attentive to the laws of karma . . . the cause and effect of all living things and situations. What goes around comes around, and all that. Karma is the foundation of metaphysics and the fundamental principle of psychic work. Why are you asking?"

"Because my kind of frontier justice is based on karma. I'm a firm believer, but sometimes karma doesn't move fast enough for me. I'm impatient that way. I can't wait months or years for it to come back around to crucify the deserving. So I speed things up."

"You're saying you're a karmic executioner?"

Parnell laughed. "Something like that, maybe, yeah. But there's another side to karma, and that's our personal karmic state. When I started giving most of my money away, I believe it balanced out my personal karma. I'm convinced it saved me in some situations where I should've been a dead man."

Loretta dipped her head in agreement. "Yes, I've always believed in the power of karma. Is it possible that we're more alike than either of us thought?"

Parnell made a sour face. "Not likely. But you could balance out your karma, too, and save yourself. By giving a lot of your blood money to deserving people. Folks like my breezer friends at the Shangri-La camp . . . good people at other hobo villages. Most of them lost everything in The Crash. Most of them are great people and aren't destitute by choice."

Loretta said, "I must say, you surprise me. You're a lot deeper than I thought."

"Think about what I've said. My hobo friends can use the help and since you are tuned in to the existence of karma, you can help your own state of being as well."

Loretta yawned widely.

"Am I boring you?"

"No . . . no," she said, blushing. "Just tired. It's been a long day."

"You should try to catch a few hours shuteye. You need to be at the top of your game when the Swedes get here."

She yawned again and covered her mouth with her arm. "You're right," she said, fatigue making the lines on her face stand out. He thought she looked ten years older than she did yesterday.

She removed her glasses and stretched out on the hay roll, wrapped her shawl around her tightly. Turned on her side and curled into a fetal position. Within two minutes she fell into a deep slumber.

Parnell watched Loretta Pesky sleeping and hoped she would be up to the task come high noon.

He sat in the otherworldly quiet of the barn in the middle of nowhere. It was eerie, this kind of stark silence. His thoughts turned to Elaine. He felt a physical ache bloom in his chest, seeing her face in his mind's eye, wondering where she was at that moment. Still in Costa Rica? On her way to the Hyacinth mines? Somewhere else? The not-knowing was killing him. Parnell never realized he could miss another human being the way he missed Lainey.

He stood, kicking his legs to get the circulation going again. Went to fetch his backpack. He pulled his remaining burner phone from the pack and sat down to send Elaine a text. He wrote:

R U OK? Please confirm our meet at the mines tomorrow. I'll keep this phone active until I hear from U. Miss U so much!

He pressed SEND, waited for the text to be transmitted. He stared at the tiny phone screen, seeing only half a bar of connectivity. He waited, watched, hoping the cheap phone had enough juice, praying there was a cell tower close enough to pick up the transmission. After an agonizingly long minute, he saw **MSG. DELIVERED.**

All he could do now was wait.

And then he heard the owl. Three long, spooky hoots coming from overhead, deep in the darkness of the rafters.

The calls sent a shudder through him.

He knew the Navajo legends about owls. They were considered helpers of witches and evil spirits. The Navajo nation thought of owls as messengers of bad news and harbingers of death. Based on his experiences, he knew the legends bore some truth.

He set his phone aside and picked up his gun, looked up into the dim ceiling of the barn, his eyes scanning the worm-eaten beams and struts above him. No sign of the owl.

Then he heard three more hoots, drawn out, like the nocturnal raptor was trying to emphasize something.

Parnell shivered.

Clearly an ominous sign.

Fun-time Juice and Open Pit Surface Mining

ELAINE TUMBLED HEAD-OVER-HEELS through a miasma of color and light, a free fall of such gravitational intensity it felt like being vacuumed into a vortex. But it was a beautiful vortex, this whirlpool of wonder, and she gave into its demands willingly. The colors—magnificently multi-hued—swept past her like bold brush strokes from an artist's palette. Diverse patterns twirled and lurched like whimsical chips inside a kaleidoscope. Extraordinary light intermingled with murky shadows, creating the illusion of trails behind the movement.

They had drugged her again. She was falling through another one of Doctor Marquez's hypodermic-injected dreams, and she went with it, welcoming the escape from the reality of her locked bedroom prison. These drug dreams took her back to her modeling days in Los Angeles, when she and fellow catalog models Heidi Walters and Valerie Kostov would drop acid on their off days. Usually their trips took place in Elaine's apartment, the three of them giggling for hours as they tried on weird outfits and spaced out to the psychedelic sounds of The Flaming Lips, My Morning Jacket, Ariel Pink's Haunted Graffiti, Electric Moon, and Hypnos 69. Sometimes Heidi and Valerie were in a retro mood and she would load up the CD platter with Beatles, Pink Floyd, Moody Blues, and Klaatu. They experimented with everything hallucinogenic in those days: Orange sunshine, blotter acid, microdots, windowpane acid, psilocybin mushrooms—any mind-expanding drugs they could get their hands on. They knew they were late for the counterculture '60s party, but they didn't care. Timothy Leary and Jerry Rubin and Allen Ginsburg were dead along with the "turn on, tune in, drop out" movement, but she, Heidi, and Valerie tried to revive it every chance they got.

The colors within Elaine's current trip started to fade. Spinning objects slowed. Trails shortened. She fought it, wanting to remain in this psychedelic dreamscape, but the free fall came to a halt. Her eyelids fluttered open. She had returned from her blissful high-def Technicolor dream, alone in bed in her locked-room jail.

She sat up and looked around. Nothing had changed. Still just her and the shelves overflowing with books. The ugly framed print of the Spanish conqueror on horseback.

How depressing!

She was still naked and had no idea how long she had been here. Hours? Days? Weeks? And without a window to peer out, she couldn't tell the time of day. She barely remembered how she got here. Her brain seemed to be wrapped in a thick gauze.

She felt a ravenous hunger and hoped the doctor would be back soon to feed her. And to inject her with another dose of the "fun-time juice." That's what he called it. She couldn't get enough of Doctor Marquez's medicine. At first she had been terrified of the psychiatrist's syringe. But when she experienced the beautiful somnolent trips the injections sent her on, her fears turned to cravings.

And then a chilling thought struck her. Maybe this doctor knew about her passion for psychedelic drugs. Maybe that's why he had been pumping her full of the fun-time juice. Was it possible that while she was gliding through these colorful trips he was taking a peek inside her mind? Examining her? Unlocking her deepest thoughts and secrets? After all, he was a psychiatrist. That's the kind of thing shrinks did. Poke around in people's heads. She recalled one of the textbooks on Doctor Marquez's shelves: *Handbook of Psychiatric Drug Therapy.*

She heard footsteps in the hall, saw the door open and Marquez enter the room with a burst of light.

"So how's my little girl doing today?" he said, flashing that dazzling movie-star smile, showing off his perfect white teeth.

Little girl? She hated the way he called her that. She remained quiet, noticing with some dismay that he wasn't holding a loaded syringe the way he normally did when he visited her. Instead he cradled her backpack under one arm.

He sidled over to the bed, laid the pack near her shoulder. "C'mon, get up," he commanded. "Take a shower. We're going on a little trip."

She wanted to tell him that she had just been on a wonderful trip and she wanted to return there. But this had interesting possibilities. He wanted her to take a shower. She would be escaping this dreadful windowless bedroom. "A trip where?" she asked, noticing he had her cell phone in hand and was looking at it thoughtfully.

"We're going to see your boyfriend," he said without looking up. "At the mines."

Elaine frowned. "I told you, I don't know—"

"Get your ass out of bed and get cleaned up! You stink and I'm not going anywhere with an unwashed urchin."

Unwashed urchin? Really? He had always been nice to her in his previous visits, had always treated her with respect. Now he addressed her in a mean-spirited way. *Something he discovered on my last fun-time-juice adventure?*

She wrapped the spread around her and put her feet on the floor. "What's so interesting on my phone?"

"Your boyfriend sent you another message. Take a look."

He held the phone out so she could view the screen. She read Derek's message, noticing that he didn't mention the geographical location of the mines (Utah), nor did he reference them by name (Hyacinth). She thought back to the first text Derek had sent. Same thing. No specific references to where the mines were located. Very smart on his part. Derek was always thinking.

"I want you to answer him," Doctor Marquez said. "Tell him you'll be there. But don't try anything funny. If you do, I'll take out your other eye."

Elaine shuddered. The thought of being completely blind horrified her. She would have to proceed with extreme caution around this man. *Don't let his matinee idol looks and quiet manner suck you in, girlfriend. He's a sociopath, through and through.*

She took her phone from him, a plan developing in her mind. She would convince the shrink that the mines were near Winslow, and not in Utah. She would take Marquez to the Shangri-La camp. She had friends there, Weasel Bethea and Ann Finnegan and a few others she had met when she and Derek spent time there three years ago. They would protect her. That is, if they were still around. Three years was an eternity in the hobo world.

She keyed in her text response, Marquez watching her with the focused eyes of a hawk scoping its prey. She would have to be careful. The doctor was very shrewd.

I'm fine. Will meet you at the Winslow mines tomorrow PM. I miss U 2!

"Let me see that before you send it," Marquez said, yanking the phone out of her hands. "Winslow? In Arizona?"

"Yes."

He eyed her suspiciously. "I didn't think there was much of a mining industry in Arizona."

Her mind raced. "Really? When was the last time you were there?"

"A few months ago."

"In Winslow?" She looked at him, held his disbelieving gaze.

"I've been through Winslow several times, Elaine. I don't remember any mining sites."

Suddenly her plan seemed lame, full of treacherous holes. She racked her brain, trying to recall the geography there. "There's a mining operation a couple miles east of Winslow," she said, improvising. "Near the Little Colorado River."

"East of Winslow?" He looked away from her, considering something. "I thought that was Indian country. A native American reservation. The Hopi tribe, if I'm not mistaken."

Shit, this man knows his stuff. "Well, you're right to a certain extent. The Hopi rez is further east of these mines. The mines are between Winslow proper and the reservation."

He scrutinized her intensely. "What type of mining?"

Damn, he's relentless. She thought back to her time living in Flagstaff and the information Derek had fed her about some of his hobo friends finding short-term mining jobs in the state. What were those jobs? Copper? Lead? Zinc? Silver? Probably any of those, but she quickly decided on an option that would be difficult to dispute. "Construction sand and gravel," she said with authority. "It's open pit surface mining."

He maintained his piercing examination of her. Finally he said, "What's the name of the mines?"

She knew she had to be careful here. Any name she came up with would not be verifiable through an Internet search. At a minimum, someone as sophisticated and educated as Doctor Marquez would surely run a Google search. This man was no fool.

"Oh, those mines were abandoned years ago," she uttered, searching for potential explanations. "There're no signs posted . . . no identification remaining. I've never known the name. It's just a good, private meeting place for me and Derek. As you are aware, we have to be careful."

He looked at her doubtfully. "I see, And just why did you have to specify Winslow? His text to you didn't mention any city."

Damn! I still haven't sold him on it. "Because Derek and I have met at several abandoned mines in Arizona through the years," she said, trying to keep her voice confident and controlled. "I just wanted to be sure we were on the same page."

He stared at her, combed his free hand through his thick black pompadour and sighed. "Okay, we'll go there, and if you are lying about this I guarantee I will kill you and go find Derek Parnell myself, without your help."

He transmitted the text message to Parnell and stood. "Go get your shower. The bathroom's down the hall. I put out soap and shampoo and a fresh towel for you. There's a toothbrush and paste there, too. And don't dawdle. I'd like to fly out before daybreak."

"We're flying?"

"Yes. Winslow's got to be somewhere around a thousand miles. Too far to drive."

Elaine worried about getting on a U.S. flight. "But it's dangerous for me to fly on a commercial jet. We run the risk of authorities identifying me. I could be arrested. That wouldn't be good for you either."

Marquez smiled. "Don't worry your pretty fugitive head over it, sweetheart. I have my own plane."

"You're a pilot?"

"I've done some flying, but I'm not licensed. The guy you met—my friend Diego?—he's a certified pilot. He's got thousands of hours flight experience flying in all kinds of conditions. He'll have us there in a couple of hours. Now go ahead and jump in that shower and wash that hobo stink off you. I brought you a change of clothes, too. You'll be like a new woman for the flight."

He smacked her lightly on her ass as she passed. She shot him a *don't-ever-do-that-again* look and he laughed, like it was all a game to him. Like she was his play toy.

She moved into the hallway, thinking maybe she could make a run for it, but Diego waited for her. He escorted her to the bathroom, then waited outside the door while she showered.

She took off her clothes and stepped into the shower stall, closed the glass door. The hot water pinged her skin like tiny massaging fingers. The slippery feel of soap and water against her body was luxurious. The steamy herbal scent of the shampoo sent pleasurable waves through her sinuses. She felt all the grime and frustration of her trip slide off her and circle the drain at her toes. She hadn't felt this clean since her last shower, before she left for the San Jose airport. How long ago was that? She had no idea. Time had become a murky concept to her.

She heard a knocking on the door, followed by "Hurry it up in there." Diego's voice.

She rinsed her hair and turned off the water, stepped out of the shower and grabbed the fluffy towel, began drying off. Elaine looked at her partially obscured image in the steamed-up mirror.

I have no idea what to do after we hit Winslow. How am I ever going to get Marquez and Diego to Shangri-La?

Swedish Sauna

NOON CAME AND WENT. 12:30 passed. Still no Thorssen and Lars. The heat in the barn was beginning to rise and Jenn was on edge. She felt herself dying a little more with each passing minute. This waiting amped up her bubbling anxieties.

She sat in the tight hiding space, shoulder-to-shoulder with Poppy, her legs cramping up, the rubberized grip of the gun slick in her hand. Sweat drenched her T-shirt. She had trouble breathing in the hot, dusty quarters, like sitting in a dry-heat sauna. It didn't help that she still felt hung over from last night's partying. Nausea gripped her. She had the shakes.

She studied the weapon in her hand, looking at the short stainless steel barrel, the white-dotted sights, the black polymer frame. Strange how a firearm this sleek and lightweight and resembling a toy gun could be so deadly. She had eight rounds in the Smith and Wesson and appreciated the raw power and potency of the small nine millimeter, yet even now, at zero hour, she had doubts as to whether she could aim it at another human being and shoot to kill. That uncertainty was eating her up as much as the waiting.

Poppy checked the time on his cell. 12:45. He yelled out to Loretta Pesky, told her to call Genevieve Thorssen to find out where she was. The gypsy woman connected with Thorssen and Jenn could hear Loretta's side of the conversation. The fortune-teller sounded nervous. Allegedly, Thorssen's limo had broken down and they were arranging for other transportation.

"That's bullshit!" Poppy roared. "It has to be a trick."

Loretta said, "I'm telling you, Parnell, I know Genevieve very well. She would *never* miss a payday like this one."

Poppy stepped out from the cramped storage area. Jenn gladly followed him out and took deep breaths, began stretching, working the kinks out of her legs.

"Yeah, maybe," he said. "She say how long they'd be?"

"They'll be here within forty-five minutes."

"Then there's no way their limo broke down."

Parnell got on his cell and called Weasel to update him. When he ended the call, he walked the interior perimeter of the barn, checking and rechecking each wall, looking at every opening and loose board, searching for points from where they could conceivably be ambushed.

Jenn observed Poppy. She hated seeing him like this. He had already performed this obsessive-compulsive exercise several times. He was a bundle of raw nerves, tense, angst ridden. Part of it, she was sure, stemmed from the text message he'd received near dawn from Elaine. Poppy told her that Elaine wanted to meet in Winslow tomorrow rather than the Hyacinth coal mines in Utah where they were headed next. That meant Elaine was in trouble, he'd said. Someone was interfering with her travel plans because if she had been on her own, she would have met them in Utah as he'd instructed. She watched him climb the rickety ladder and disappear up into the loft, continuing his search for ambush points.

She moved into a corner of the barn and sat, contemplating what had led to all this. She became misty-eyed as she thought about Russ. Russell Holt was one of the most honorable and decent men she'd ever known. He'd done the courageous thing by testifying against some very bad men, fearlessly going against the sub-humans who had been responsible for her seven years' incarceration in a human sex trafficking operation. He had testified against the men who framed Poppy and Elaine for mass murder. And Russ's reward for that bravery was a spray of bullets and a violent death at the hands of a vicious assassin by the name of Lars. Jenn could never erase the image of the massive albino Swede approaching their table in the Denver restaurant and opening fire, the goofy expression on his corpse-like face, the terrible pinkish-burgundy eyes that contained no sign of life whatsoever, the smirk on his tight mouth as he pulled the trigger.

It was all so unfair. Jenn knew she had never been destined to lead a normal life, whatever that was. But the way her life had gone to this point bordered on the absurd. She had been kidnapped and whisked away to the Rocky Mountains at age eleven. Her growing-up years were spent whoring herself out to nasty men deep in the bowels of a cave network. Her mother had been murdered in a house fire. Her father was a vigilante killer. The two people Jenn loved most—Lulu Solton and Russell Holt—had been savagely murdered. What did it all mean? Were these random events? Were they all connected on some perverse metaphysical path? Lulu used to talk to her of walking the metaphysical path to find your inner spirit. To discover your higher purpose through intuitive guidance. Lulu and a couple of the other girls were into meditation and mantras and tai chi, claiming those practices helped them find their inner peace. But none of that metaphysics stuff worked for her. She tried meditation and it just made her sleepy. She tried reciting mantras but it made her feel like a New Age airhead. She tried tai chi but it just felt comic-bookish. All of it was just abstract thinking to her. Nothing to do with reality.

So now at age twenty-two, she found herself still searching for her inner peace, still reaching out for her higher purpose. Would she find that higher purpose here today, in this decrepit barn on an abandoned ranch in Cottonwood, Arizona? Had the appalling violent happenings in her life led to this day? Poppy always spoke of karmic justice. *Is today the day I dish out some of that justice?*

Jenn heard the rungs of the ladder groan as Poppy came down from the loft. His phone buzzed and he answered. His eyes flashed as he muttered "yeah" and "got it" and "I'll text you when I want you to take out the driver" before disconnecting and saying to her and Loretta, "They're coming up the road. Weasel says it's a black limo. A chauffeur and two people in back. Let's move. You ready with your spiel, Loretta?"

She nodded and went to retrieve the empty cash bag.

Jenn thought her heart might leap from her chest. Weakness and nausea slammed her, but she managed to scramble back into the tiny storage alcove.

"You okay, sweetie?" Poppy whispered.

"I think so."

He tilted his head at her gun. "Safety off?"

Her hands shook as she felt for the thumb safety. "Yep."

"Are you ready for this?"

"We'll see," she said weakly.

He touched her gun hand. "You're gonna be fine. Try to slow your breathing. Relax."

"Easy for you to say."

"Whatever happens, remember I love you, Jenny."

She looked at him in the dim light, crouching next to her, clutching his Mauser, coiled like a snake ready to strike. With his weathered face and graying three-day beard, he appeared old and exhausted. But she felt safe with him by her side. He was the man with the tombstone eyes, a man feared by many. He was her father, the one who had risked his life to save her, the man who never gave up the search for her. Jenn realized she had never loved him more than she did at that precise second.

"I love you, too, Poppy," she murmured.

She heard the limo pull up outside, doors opening and closing, could smell the dust its arrival had kicked up. Heard approaching footsteps, the barn doors squeaking open, a female voice greeting Loretta and apologizing for their tardiness in a nasal, Scandinavian accent. Jenn bent over and peered through one of the knotholes, saw Genevieve Thorssen. Tiny woman with pale, freckled skin and strawberry blonde hair. Puffy face with enormous, protruding lips that looked like she'd had one too many collagen injections. Standing next to her, in stark contrast, was the giant Lars, scanning the interior of the barn with his bizarre laser-like eyes. The nightmare of the Denver restaurant shooting came rushing back as she watched him move toward Loretta and frisk her for weapons.

"Is this really necessary, Genevieve?" Loretta asked as the mammoth bodyguard checked under Loretta's shawl and patted her down her pants pockets.

"Just a precaution," Thorssen said in her clipped Nordic dialect. "One can't be too careful these days. You know that. Before we get down to details, Lars is going to check out the barn. Do your thing, Lars."

Jenn watched the monstrous hit man retrace the steps Poppy had taken, lumbering along, big-barreled gun out in front of him, waving it back and forth as he searched the corners and hidden places for trouble. It looked like the same weapon he'd used on Russ, the exaggerated barrel the silencer that had muffled the lethal shots in the restaurant. Suddenly her fear and anxiety switched to outrage and anger. This oafish, fluorescent-faced monster lurching through the barn was the source of her misery. He took Russ's life in exchange for a pile of cash. Hatred bubbled through her in repellent waves. She felt the Parnell killing gene click into place. She became dizzy with murderous lust, felt herself shaking as she nodded at Poppy and leaned forward. She was ready to go. Eager to kill.

Next to her, Poppy texted a message to Weasel outside: **Take out the driver. NOW!**

He pocketed the phone and picked up his weapon, nodded at Jenn, his eyes wonky with the same bloodlust Jenn was feeling. Together they crashed through the loose boards of their hiding place.

Poppy shouted in Genevieve Thorssen's direction, "Glad to

see greed is still alive and well in America, Thor."

Thorssen froze, momentarily confused.

Jenn moved in on Lars, who had turned at the loft ladder to see what the commotion was about. She opened fire, her first three shots hitting the albino in the cheek, neck, and chest. The giant let out a loud wheeze and grabbed for the ladder, trying to remain upright. Attempted to get a shot off, but she was on him, a red-hot rage sizzling through her as she pulled the trigger five more times, emptying the nine millimeter into him after he was down.

Thorssen looked on in horror, seeing her bodyguard lying dead in a pool of blood and a maniacal Jenn standing over him continuing to squeeze the trigger of an empty gun. She turned to Loretta and shouted, "You sold me out, you bitch!" and quickly pulled a small derringer from her purse. She took two shots at Loretta that went astray before turning on Parnell and firing.

Parnell rolled in the dirt, dodging the shots, then brought down Genevieve Thorssen with two well-placed head shots.

It was over in a matter of twenty seconds.

Jenn fell to her knees, sobbing. She trembled so hard she thought she might be having a stroke. She looked at the gun in her quivering hand and the dead man splayed out in front of her, his lifeless pink eyes staring up into the rafters, blood pooling around him on the dirt floor.

Did I really just do that?

"Oh my God! Oh my God!" Loretta's voice echoed off the barn walls.

From where she kneeled Jenn saw Genevieve Thorssen's body on the floor, two gaping wounds in her forehead weeping blood. She breathed in the cloyingly sweet metallic scent of freshly-spilled blood and nitroglycerine stench of discharged firearms. It was all too much for her. She flung her gun to the ground, dipped her head and vomited.

She was in the grip of dry heaves when she felt Poppy's arms pull her in. He held her close and rocked her tenderly, like he used to do when she was a child. Over Loretta's stunned babbling, he spoke into her left ear, consoling her. "It's all over now, Jenny. You did great. I'm so proud of you, sweetie. Justice has been served."

His loving touch and reassuring words helped. She clung to him with a tenacious grip.

Weasel entered the barn and shouted, "Everyone all right in

here?"

Poppy maintained his hold on her as he said, "Loretta's having some trouble, but we're okay."

The voices of Kid and Flywheel joined Weasel's as Poppy continued to whisper reassurances in her ear.

How can he be so calm after killing someone?

Winging It in Winslow

They got a late start flying out of San Antonio. One of the two runways at Boerne Stage Field was closed for repaving and air traffic was backed up. Their flight plan called for a 10 AM departure, but they didn't get away until noon.

The two-hour flight to Winslow in Doctor Marquez's Cessna single-engine plane had been memorable. The psychiatrist bought Elaine an outrageously expensive outfit from one of San Antonio's high-end boutiques, one of the few still doing business. She loved the clothes, especially the shoes, a thirteen-hundred-dollar pair of Manolo Blahnik pumps. But he also coerced her into painting her face with a heavy application of cosmetics, complete with a blazing red slash of lipstick. He thought the makeover made her look hot and desirable. She thought the overall effect transformed her into a clownish call girl.

Marquez had also shot her full of fun-time juice just before takeoff, which made the view from 5,000 feet quite interesting. She sat in the back of the four-seater, behind Marquez, who manned the co-pilot seat, and watched Diego pilot the small, sleek airplane. The cockpit dashboard fascinated her. She became transfixed on the movement of the gauges and the swirling colors on the pair of small monitors that looked to be GPS terrain shots.

The flight had been mostly pleasant, with the vibrating hum of the single engine lulling her into a comfortable trance and her side window providing her with magnificent views of rolling cottony clouds. Occasionally her eye drifted to the cockpit windshield where the whirring propeller held her spellbound. The spinning rotation of the blade mesmerized her, but after focusing on it for long minutes, she swore the propeller was slowing down. Twice she even thought it had stopped altogether and she freaked. And then, nearing Winslow, they hit a patch of turbulence and the small plane rolled and dipped in the crosswinds. She nearly lost it in spite of Marquez and Diego reassuring her everything was fine. The fun-time juice had lost its appeal.

When they landed at Winslow-Lindbergh Regional, Elaine had come down from her high (and her fears). When they hit the tarmac, she was clearheaded enough to think about her escape. As they taxied down the runway on their way to the fuel area, she thought about her last text message to Derek. He was headed to the Hyacinth mines in Utah to pick up his stash of money and she hoped he wouldn't change those plans on her account. Derek was smart that way. He could read between the lines. He was aware that she knew plenty of good people at Shangri-La who would take her in and protect her until he was able to join her.

Her problem was getting to the hobo camp. It wasn't a long hike. Having lived in Flagstaff for many years, she knew neighboring Winslow pretty well. The airport was a mile west of downtown; Shangri-La was two miles east of the city. She could get there, no problem. But how to get rid of the two men occupying the front seats of this plane remained her dilemma.

After refueling, Diego taxied the plane to the short-term tie-down area behind a whitewashed hangar while Marquez took Elaine to pick up a rental car. Then the three of them then checked into their rooms at the La Posada Hotel, where Marquez had made reservations. She didn't like the room arrangements. Diego got his own room while the doctor booked himself and her in a double-bed room. She worried about his intentions; Marquez had become more lecherous since they'd touched down. But then doubling up could work to her advantage. With the two of them sharing a room, she would probably have opportunities to make a run for it.

They spent a leisurely two hours over dinner at the Turquoise Room in the hotel, dining on elk and bison medallions, fried quail, churro lamb, and fresh vegetables. They drank Route 66 Cadillac margaritas. All very posh and elegant and expensive. Marquez had reserved a table out back where they could watch the trains chug past on the Santa Fe line. The thundering freighters brought back memories for Elaine. Three years ago she rode the rails with Derek and the late Razzy Jones. They had covered a lot of miles riding the iron horses, a trek that took them to the Colorado Rockies to rescue Jennifer, then hiking and riding through Colorado and Utah, evading authorities, before heading south to Costa Rica.

"Nice view out here," she said between train arrivals, just to be making conversation.

"Yeah," Marquez agreed, chewing his food. "I love watching the trains. Takes me back to yesteryear." He swallowed, then patted his mouth with his thick cloth napkin and sat back, took a slug of his margarita. "And I figure there's a good chance we might see your boyfriend hop off one of those railcars, Elaine."

Marquez sat studying Elaine over the salted rim of his glass. "So you think your boyfriend is really going to meet us tomorrow at this nameless sand and gravel mine near here?"

"Stop calling him my boyfriend."

"That's what he is, isn't he?"

"That sounds so . . . I don't know, so high school. Derek's in his early fifties and I'm . . . well . . . *Boyfriend* just doesn't fit."

Diego said, "How should we refer to him then?"

"Don't refer to him at all, I say."

Marquez shot her an angry look. "I'd like to refer to him as *dead*. I heard he used to be known as the man with tombstone eyes. I'd like to update that to the man who lies beneath a tombstone."

Diego burst out with a braying laugh. "That's a good one, Tony."

She sighed. This was exhausting. Even though she was eating a wonderful meal, she was tired of being held captive by this shrink and his pilot sidekick. She vowed to herself that somehow, some way, she would escape tonight.

Even if she died in the attempt.

"Tell us, Elaine. How did it feel to lose your eye?"

He winked at her and smiled, his implied threat obvious. She locked stares with him. She knew if she didn't produce Derek for them tomorrow, Marquez would take out her other eye. Probably worse.

She had to get away from these two tonight.

Only three miles to freedom.

A long and difficult three miles.

The task seemed impossible, but she had to stay positive and confident. Her life, and Derek's, depended on it.

Of Sin and Rectitude

PARNELL LED HIS CREW THROUGH barn cleanup detail. They retrieved shell casings, wiped up blood spills, removed shoeprints from the dirt, and dumped all trash that could pin them to the crimes committed here. They moved the bodies of Genevieve Thorssen, her chauffeur, and Lars into the rear compartment of Thorssen's limousine. Parnell wasn't able to find all the slugs from stray shots, but from a ballistics standpoint, the firearms involved in the shootings were either registered to aliases or not registered at all.

He felt comfortable with the job as he secured the barn doors.

Time to hightail it out of Cottonwood.

Parnell pulled Weasel aside and gave him special instructions for handling Loretta Pesky. He was to drive Loretta's Rolls. The two shots Thorssen fired at her had come close and the experience had left her stunned, so she let Weasel take the wheel without complaint.

He gave Kid and Flywheel the nasty job of making the three corpses disappear. Parnell instructed them to drive the limo to a remote mountain pass, well away from the main interstates, and run it off a cliff. "Make it look like an accident," he said. Weasel would follow them in Loretta's Rolls, pick them up after they finished the dirty deed, then make the short jaunt to Sedona to finish off Loretta at her home, making her death appear to be a suicide. From there, the three of them were to hop a northbound freighter into Utah to meet him and Jenn at the Hyacinth mines. Parnell drew a crude map showing them where to catch a boxcar or a piggyback, and scribbled detailed directions to the abandoned coal mines. He wished them luck and told them he would pay them handsomely for a job well done when they got to the mines.

The two vehicles moved out, kicking up trails of dust as they bumped down the potholed pasture road. Parnell and Jenn went behind them, brushing out tire tracks with leafy tree branches. When they were finished, they sat under the shady canopy of white mulberry trees, trying to regain their strength for the long haul north to Utah. They drank thirstily from their canteens and wiped their faces with cool, wet rags.

Jenn had been quiet since the shootings. She looked pale, sickly. In shock.

"Are you okay, darlin'?" he said, reaching out, running a finger down her cheek.

"I'll live, I guess."

Two pockmarks on her forehead gleamed an ugly wet scarlet. The shells of her weapon had ejected straight back into her face and clipped her above her right eyebrow. "Does it hurt?" he asked, touching the wounds gingerly.

"Ow!" she cried, pulling away from him. "Yes it hurts, goddammit!"

"Okay, okay," he said, backing off. Wow! No need to bite my head off, is there?"

Jenn looked at him from behind her dark sunglasses, but said nothing. She took another drink from her canteen, glanced back toward the barn.

"Look," he said, "I know you're struggling after what you did—what *we* did—this afternoon. I know it's affecting you, but you have to shake it off and move on. What you did was right. You brought down a mass murderer, a hired assassin . . . an evil thug who stole Russ from you. You made the world a better place and you should be proud."

"Yeah? Well, I don't feel proud," she said in a shaky voice. "I feel dirty and revolting."

"Look, Jenny, you shouldn't—"

"Dammit, Poppy! Don't tell me how I should or shouldn't feel, all right? I just fucking killed another human being in cold blood. Stood over him and emptied my gun into him like an insane madwoman. There's nothing admirable about that. It's nothing to be proud of."

"I know, but—"

"There're no 'buts' about it," she said, getting to her feet, walking away from him, out into the sunlight. She stopped after a few steps, turned back to him, the sun glinting off her shades. "I know it's easy for you to kill, Poppy. But I don't follow your warped code of ethics. I don't feel any sense of justice. I only feel, I don't know . . . dirty . . . full of shame . . . *sinful*."

Parnell got to his feet, went to her. She backed away, showing her fear of him. Her reaction tore him apart inside. He wanted to be here for her in her time of need, to console her, but she cowered in front of him, keeping her distance. He grabbed her by her arm and pulled her close, brushed a lock of hair off her face.

"Listen," he said, feeling her stiffen in his grasp, "I know exactly what's going through your head right now. I remember my first kill like it was yesterday. I couldn't sleep for two weeks after because I was so wrapped up in guilt. Believe me, Jenn, you did a very noble and courageous thing in that barn. You ridded the world of a vicious animal. It was karmic justice, plain and simple. You have no reason to feel dirty or sinful."

She remained rigid in his clench. "Easy for you to say. You're a professional killer."

The comment was a punch to his gut. Slowly, carefully, he reached out and slid her sunglasses up so they rested on top of her head. He wanted to see her eyes. "*That's* what you think I am?"

She blinked against the bright sunlight. With an annoyed tug, she reached up and pulled her sunglasses back into place. "What else should I think, Poppy? You've killed a lot of people. You've even said you lost count over the years."

"No, I haven't. I remember every one. Genevieve Thorssen is number sixteen."

"And you're proud of that?"

"No. Not proud. *Vindicated.* I *am* proud of you, however. For what you did today."

"That's really twisted."

"Maybe so. But it's reality, Jenn. Look, you didn't ask to be in this position. Fate put you in its crosshairs. You shot back. Nothing wrong with that, honey."

She considered that. A lone tear trickled down her cheek. He wiped it away with his thumb and kissed her forehead near her wounds.

"Thanks," she said wearily, looking up into his eyes, a small smile of gratitude on her lips.

He saw love there, mixed with confusion and doubt.

"You know, Poppy, you've never really talked much about your, um . . . well . . ."

"My kills?"

She nodded. "Who was your first, uh . . . victim?"

He and Elaine had covered this subject many times. But he'd never really addressed it with Jennifer. His daughter deserved to know no matter how painful the telling.

"Okay, well, my first wasn't any *victim*," he began. "He was a mobbed-up hit man who murdered my father in Philly when I was thirteen. Took me five years to catch up with the bastard, but I located him after I left boot camp. I took him down with nicotine poisoning. I was only eighteen—younger than you—and it messed up my head for a while. The military trained me to be a killer, but still . . ."

He went on to tell her about subsequent hits he'd made, including his killing of Elaine's attacker, Jessie Waltham, her sociopath ex-boyfriend who had taken her left eye with sulfuric acid. He told her he'd learned through the years that some people didn't deserve to continue drawing a breath.

She stepped back away from him. "I get it. But shouldn't God be the one making life and death decisions?"

Parnell looked at his daughter, took in her wounded face and her slight, willowy build. He saw her trembling fleshy upper lip, the mole on the bridge of her nose, the delicate cleft in her chin. She seemed so young and fragile and vulnerable in that moment. "Sounds to me like Annie Finnegan's been feeding you those bullshit biblical fairy tales, hasn't she?"

"No . . . I don't know . . . *maybe*. I'm on the fence about things Ann's been telling me. Some days I'm quite sure God exists. Other days—like today—I'm not so sure He's anywhere near."

"Well, you're smart. You'll figure it all out." He tugged gently at her sleeve. "C'mon, let's get out of the sun. I've got a call to make."

"To Elaine?"

"No. Annie."

He went to his backpack and pulled out his burner phone, sat with his back up against a tree. He knew it was dangerous to hang on to this disposable phone as long as he had. *One more call, then burn time.*

Jenn followed, sat beside him. "Why Ann?"

"Because I want her to be on the lookout for Lainey, and to protect her when she arrives."

"Aren't you worried about Elaine? I mean, you seemed pretty upset this morning when you got that text from her."

"Not worried," he lied. "Lainey can take care of herself. She's a survivor, just like us."

"So you're just going to leave her floating around god-knows-where by herself?"

"Listen, Lainey's tough. Resourceful. She's dealt with a lot in her life, just like you. I bet you didn't know she was a biker chick in her younger days?"

"Elaine?"

"Yeah. Lainey makes fun of it now, but when she was fifteen she shaved her head and rode a chopped Harley with a gang called the Hell Hogs. Rode with them for two years. Back before her modeling days."

Jenn was astonished. "The Elaine Leibrandt I know?"

Parnell nodded. "Yep. My sweet Lainey."

"When she was fifteen? Wasn't she in school?"

"She had a difficult childhood. Her father went AWOL when she was nine, which left her in the care of her abusive, alcoholic mother. An uncle molested her in her early teens. She got into drugs and shaved her head and rode with a motorcycle gang. Classic rebel with a cause story."

"Unfrickin' real!"

"Don't let her soft exterior fool you. She's way more street savvy than you'd think. She'll make it to Shangri-La. When she does, we'll figure out what to do from there."

Jenn mulled that over. "Okay. Say she does make it to the camp. Will she be safe there? That asshole Ollie McKellar has revenge on his mind. That Palomino dude, too."

"That's why I want Annie to look after her."

"Are we going back to Winslow?"

"No. I'll hire one of the breezers to bring her to us."

Jenn shook her head, not understanding.

He punched in Ann Finnegan's cell number, watching Jenn as he listened to the rings. Annie was one of the few in camp with a working cell phone.

"Hello?" she answered.

He was surprised Annie picked up.

"Hey, Annie, it's me . . . Derek."

"So I hear. You haven't been gone long. Are you in trouble?"

"No." He looked at Jenn. "We're not. But Elaine might be."

"Elaine? How so?"

"Last I heard she's on her way there. She might not be alone. I have reason to believe she's being held against her will."

"Really? Why do you think that?"

"A text message she sent me. I need a favor from you, Annie."

He heard her caustic laugh on the other end. "You want *my*

help after the way you insulted me? After all that Big Rock Candy Mountain nonsense?"

"Yeah, I do. Will you?"

There was a long delay, faint static buzzing on the line, then, "Of course I'll help you, Derek. It would go against my Christian values to—"

"I don't have time to listen to your pious routine, Annie. Here's what I need. Be on the lookout for Lainey. Make sure whoever's holding her, if anyone, is taken care of, if you know what I mean, And then—"

"You know, you're a very difficult person to like, Derek."

"So I've been told. Now here's the other thing I need. Find somebody to bring Elaine to me. I'll pay them well."

"I assume when you say somebody, you mean a Jack, not a Jill, right?"

"Yeah, maybe Oshkosh Moss or—"

"Oshkosh got shot in the hand last night by Ollie McKellar. Remember?"

"Oh yeah," he said, pinching the bridge of his nose. Christ he was tired. "How is that turd doing?"

"He's angry and hurting. You winged him pretty good."

"He's lucky I didn't kill him. If and when Elaine shows up, keep him away from her. And find somebody to bring her to me."

"Awfully demanding, aren't you? What if I say no?"

"Well, that would go against those Christian values of yours, wouldn't it, Annie?" He winked at Jenn.

"I swear, you're impossible, Derek Parnell. Okay, I'll do it."

"Who do you have in mind? Somebody I know? Maybe Harvey Henshaw?"

"No. Me."

"*You*? No fuckin' way!"

"Yes, Derek. I'll bring her to you. I'll make sure she gets there safely."

"Sure you will. And what're you gonna do when you run into trouble? Beat 'em up with your Bible?"

"Do you want my help or not?"

"That's why I'm calling you."

"Then let me handle it my way. I'll be in touch when Elaine shows up. Keep your phone handy and switched on."

"No, I need to dump this phone. I'll call you on another—"

Parnell heard the click of the disconnection. He couldn't

believe it. He'd been one-upped by Annie Finnegan.

"Women!" he said, shaking his head in disgust as he threw his phone into his pack.

He stood, flung his backpack over his shoulder. "C'mon," he said to Jenn, offering his hand to help her up. "The Verde River is just a few klicks from here."

As they walked away from the murder scene and hiked toward the river and the railhead beyond, he elbowed her playfully in her ribs. "We can wash away our sins and get some clean water for our canteens."

He looped an arm around her. She remained silent, but leaned into him and gave him the faintest hint of a smile.

Pornocopia

"How about you do a sexy striptease for us, sweetheart."

Doctor Marquez stretched out on his bed in their hotel room and eyed Elaine with a glazed look of lust. Diego gawked at her from where he sat in the easy chair.

She knew they would eventually get down to this. She stood before them, dressed in breezy cotton gaucho pants and a see-through, sleeveless silk blouse. Underneath she wore a lacy half-cup French bra and black silk panties. Black coral earrings dangled from her ears. A matching choker felt cool against her neck. Awesome Manolo Blahnik pumps with caged straps and heels boosted her five-foot-ten-inch frame to well over six feet. The expensive fashion ensemble was compliments of Antonio Marquez. He'd also bought her a full line of Estee Lauder cosmetics and instructed her to paint her face like a Bourbon Street hooker. She barely recognized herself in the bathroom mirror before leaving the shrink's house. The doctor had told her he wanted "his lady" to look classy for the trip. He'd even referred to her as *my statuesque pet*.

Tonight she would put an end to being the doctor's pet.

Tonight she would break free of him.

The psychiatrist and his pilot friend had been quite bold through the margarita-swilling dinner, making off-color jokes as they touched her legs under the table and slid their hands up her thighs. They had acted like a pair of frat boys on spring break, grabbing at her boobs and dirty-flirting. After dinner, when they'd retreated to their rooms, Diego showed up with a bottle of whiskey snatched from his room minibar, ready to party.

Now they watched her, excited, eager, wanting, their eyes swimming with desire. Like two teenage boys seeing their first peep show.

Disgusting.

Elaine had to keep her wits about her. She had to be the one in control. They planned to check out of the hotel tomorrow afternoon and she was supposed to take them to what she had described as abandoned sand and gravel mines. That would require a three-mile hike through high desert wilderness. She doubted they would go for that.

This was her chance. She had to make her move now.

Before these pigs raped her.

Time to take charge.

The radio blared AC/DC's "You Shook Me All Night Long." She swayed seductively to the music, feeling just tipsy enough to tantalize them, get them into vulnerable positions.

She would make them hers.

And then she would attack.

"All right," she said as she unbuttoned her blouse. "I'll give you gentlemen a little show."

The two men murmured their approval. Marquez slugged back his whiskey.

She worked her way down the front of her blouse, leaning over, exposing the tops of her breasts. Teasing Marquez and Diego. Giving them suggestive glances. Watching as their hands went to their crotches, rubbing themselves, vacant smiles plastered on their faces. They weren't just drunk. They were high as well. Both wore googly-eyed, spaced-out expressions. The shrink and his flyboy friend had shot themselves up with a dose of Marquez's fun-time juice and were soaring through multicolored clouds.

Perfect. Right where I want them.

She threw open her blouse, let it slip off her shoulders and fall to the floor.

"Wow!" Marquez exclaimed. "C'mon, let's see those tits, my pet. Get 'em out."

Elaine tossed her head flirtatiously, her thick, dark hair swirling around her face. She reached up behind her and unhitched the clasp of her bra, wiggled out of it, let her breasts bounce freely. Both men gasped at the sight. Marquez unzipped his pants and Diego rubbed himself vigorously, a determined grin on his face.

They were lost in their fun-time-juice fantasy.

"C'mon, fellas, no need to be shy," she cooed, rubbing her nipples and licking her lips. "Get out of those clothes. Let me take care of you."

"Holy shit, you are magnificent, my lovely!" Marquez called out, eyeing her dark swollen nipples.

The music changed to "Life In the Fast Lane" and she strutted across the floor, kicking off her pumps so she could maneuver better.

Diego bellowed, "Take off your pants, hot stuff! Let's see that juicy pussy of yours."

They were playing right into her hands.

She danced for them, teasing them, grinding her crotch against the bedpost, sighing breathily and wrenching her face into looks of orgasmic nirvana.

Diego was her target. He was the one with a weapon. She sneaked a glance at the chair where he sat, saw his gun tucked into the leather shoulder holster laying on the armrest. Within easy reach.

Can I do this?

She continued to hump the bedpost. Diego had his fully erect cock out, stroking himself, a wide sleazy grin creasing his face.

She went to him, played to his male ego. "Oh, Diego honey, you're so huge. You look so good right now I could just gobble you up."

She kept the doctor in her peripheral vision as she kneeled in front of Diego. "Oh, God, I can't wait to get that beautiful thing in my mouth! I want to taste you and swallow every drop, baby. You are sooh sexy."

She threw herself into it, calling up moves and lines of dialogue she had used in the two porn shoots she had done years ago in Los Angeles. She rubbed her breasts against Diego's engorged prick, leaned her face close in, let her hair brush against his throbbing cock. She turned her head, looked at Marquez, saw he had shed his pants and underwear, and was standing there with his dick in his hand.

His *limp* dick.

She reached out her left hand, encouraging him. "Come on over here and join us, doctor. I'll do you both. You don't want your friend to have all the fun, do you?"

Marquez mumbled, "No. Absolutely not." He dutifully moved next to her, swinging his penis near her face. She took hold of it and stroked him, tried a few tricks, but he remained flaccid. Didn't matter. She turned back to Diego, took his swollen purplish head in her mouth and sucked while continuing to fondle Marquez.

She had them where she wanted them. She eyed the holstered gun as she cupped the doctor's testicles. She went all the way down on Diego, his hardness filling up her mouth and rubbing the back of her throat. He moaned loudly, on the verge of coming. She started to gag and came up for air.

One last look at the weapon.

Three feet away.

Is the safety on?

Can I pull this off?

Both men were huffing, Diego riding the wave of sexual pleasure and about to slip over the edge, Marquez grunting, frustrated by his inability to raise his jolly roger. Their noises overwhelmed the music coming out of the tinny desktop radio speaker: "Dream On" by Aerosmith.

No matter how enthusiastic she got with her left hand, Doctor Marquez remained limp. His movements increased in intensity. He snorted and grumbled in irritation. He tugged her hair, jerking her head around, demanding she suck him. But she stayed with Diego (she had to stay with Diego to make this work) and her reluctance to please the psychiatrist orally only increased his frustration.

The doctor slapped at her breasts, hard exasperated smacks that hurt her. He kept trying to pull her head into his crotch, but she remained clamped onto Diego.

Diego thrust his hips in powerful strokes, savaging her mouth, rocking her head with each pounding plunge.

The moment of truth had arrived.

Can I do this? she asked herself for the hundredth time.

You have to, old girl. It's your only means of escape.

She moved her mouth as far down Diego's rigid shaft as her throat would allow and chomped.

Once . . .

Twice . . .

Three times. Three quick, wicked bites. Enough pressure to do serious damage but not enough to sever his organ.

Diego howled, a shout of intense pain, and spilled onto the floor. He lay on his side, curled up in the fetal position, hands pressed to his groin, wailing in agony.

In a swift, orchestrated motion, she scooted back on her knees and vise-gripped Doctor Marquez's balls. Twisted and yanked hard. He bellowed like a bear taking a shotgun blast and fell to the floor next to Diego.

Quickly she got to her feet and grabbed the gun off the desk, pulled it from its leather sheath, found the safety and clicked it off.

She stood over them, aimed the barrel at a spot between them. "Either of you perverts make a move for me, it'll be your last."

She backpedalled to the open closet where Marquez had stashed her backpack, keeping a wary eye on them. Hands shaking, she fumbled through her pack, found a black tank top and her denim jacket, slipped them on. She made sure her cell phone was there, then retrieved her hiking boots, sat on the edge of the bed and laced them up, listening as Diego directed a stream of tormented invective her way. She would have to wear the gaucho pants for now. Not a great fashion statement for hikers and probably too thin for the nighttime air, but she had to get out of here. The walls were thick in the La Posada Hotel, but her attack had raised a lot of ruckus. Surely a few of the guests would hear the commotion and contact the front desk.

Time for me to fly.

Elaine zipped up her pack and slung it over her shoulder, fastened the snaps in front. She caught a glimpse of herself in the mirror. Saw Diego's blood spattered across her cheeks and nose. *Can't go out in public like this.* She checked her gaucho pants, relieved to find no bloodstains on them. Keeping the gun on the wounded warriors, she moved into the bathroom and splashed water on her face with her free hand. Dried. The white towel came away a bright pink.

"Okay," she said, "I'm leaving this fun little get-together now. Thanks for getting me to Winslow, guys. That was really swell of you to provide me with free transportation." She looked around the room. "Nice accommodations, too. A shame I can't stay."

More cursing and threats from the floor.

Elaine leaned over Marquez. "You know, doctor. Maybe you should consult a real doctor about your erectile dysfunction problem."

Marquez was livid. He let fly with one of the most vulgar verbal attacks Elaine had ever heard, some of it in Spanish.

"I must say, doctor. Your bedside manner leaves a lot to be desired."

His face tightened into an angry mask. He tried to get up off the floor to come after her, but was too crippled. She leaned over and stuck the gun barrel under his chin. "Don't try it, my depraved little *pet.*" She pushed him back down on the floor and glowered at him.

Diego's blood had soaked the throw rug and was now seeping out over the hardwood floor. She listened to him groaning, his yelps of pain increasing in volume.

Will he bleed out before help arrives?

She couldn't stick around to find out. To Marquez she said, "Remember how all this went next time you think of kidnapping somebody."

From the floor he mumbled something unintelligible.

"Time for me to disappear," she said in a glib tone. "Toodle-loo."

She waited until she was out in the hallway and had the door closed behind her before she buried the gun in her backpack. She hurried down the long hall and through the lobby, out the front double doors and onto East Second Street.

The brisk night air cooled her heat. She walked quickly through downtown Winslow, but not so fast as to attract attention. Her pulse thrummed in her ears.

Twice she stopped to spit in the bushes. She couldn't seem to get the bad taste out of her mouth.

But she had done it. Elaine had used her charm and guile to escape her captors. She had used sex as a weapon. Derek had told her often that whenever trouble raised its ugly head, you should use whatever means you had to take matters into your own hands.

The ploy had worked.

She was excited, scared, relieved . . . *drained*.

Her only regret was that she'd had to leave the Manolo Blahniks behind.

A long three miles to Shangri-La.

As she made her way through downtown Winslow, headed to the trailhead leading to the hobo camp, she hoped no one would mistake her for a lady of the night.

That would be most awkward.

Canaries In a Coal Mine

GETTING TO THE HYACINTH MINES wasn't easy. Jenn and Parnell had hopped a Burlington Northern-Santa Fe boxcar on the other side of the Verde River at the Cottonwood rail line running parallel to Highway 89, and rode it west, circumnavigating the Grand Canyon. They then jumped off and hooked onto a Union Pacific freighter headed north into Utah. Parnell had traveled these routes many years. He knew freighter schedules and which runs would most likely have open boxcars or easily accessible intermodal flats. Jenn was glad she had Poppy with her. Left on her own, she likely would have ended up in southern California or Mexico.

She was exhausted after the hike to the railhead from the Cottonwood barn and the two sprint-and-grabs of moving trains. Poppy wasn't interested in conversation, wanting only to crawl into a corner and sleep. Jenn wanted to catch a few winks as well, but had trouble sleeping on the smelly, rumbling railcars. The horrors of this afternoon kept coming back to her. She had actually killed another human being—if the immense Swede assassin Lars could be dignified with that classification—and her mind refused to let go of it.

She watched her father snoozing. More than ever he was beginning to look his age. The past ten years had been rough on him. His hair, at one time black as a crow's wing, had skunk-like streaks of whitish-gray running through it. His stubble was salt-and-pepper. Deep lines creased his weather-beaten face, which sagged and showed the outline of jowls. His physique—once rock-hard and chiseled—had deteriorated during his three years of the soft life in Costa Rica. He was still an imposing figure, able to strike fear in others with just a glance from those gray tombstone eyes, but he had definitely softened. He now carried a slight paunch. And he had lost a step or two. When they ran alongside the trains today he'd had trouble keeping up. He winded easily and had a difficult time hooking on to the northbound. Poppy had been fleet and agile three years ago when they were running from the law. He'd been a track star, able to hop a moving train with the very best of the sprint-and-grab breezers. Today he reminded her of a once-great athlete still trying to compete in the big leagues well beyond his prime.

A troubled despair gripped her. Much of those ten years he had spent helping her. *Searching* for her. Never giving up the hunt for her despite long odds. He had come to her rescue, not just once, but twice.

As she took inventory of Poppy's decline, it struck Jenn that she was witnessing the swift passage of time. She couldn't hardly believe she was already twenty-two. But Poppy at fifty-two? Impossible! Seemed just like yesterday he was a doting young father in their nice suburban home in upstate New York, and she was his little Jen-Jen. He'd lovingly called her his 'pretty little flower girl' in reference to Thumbelina, the diminutive girl who lived in a flower in her favorite fairy tale of the same name. She remembered fondly nestling in his lap, captivated by his voice as he read her "Thumbelina" and her other favorite fairy tales. Every night after reading to her he would tuck her into bed and kiss her cheek before turning out the lights. Where had all those years gone? This aging man who slept in the corner of the rattling boxcar had dedicated his life so selflessly to her, and Jenn didn't think she would ever be able to repay him in kind. As she watched him, a profound love gripped her. She reached out and caressed his arm, tears welling in her eyes as he let out a tiny snore and turned over on his side.

They hopped off the Union Pacific freighter near the dead-end rail spur used by the Hyacinth Corporation back in the glory days of its mining operations. The mines lay in southern Utah, some one hundred miles due north of the Grand Canyon and forty miles west of the Grand Staircase-Escalante National Monument. It had taken them seven hours to get here. Midnight was approaching. It was dark and chilly. Poppy had described the terrain to her as a vast no-man's-land of sweeping desert, crimson canyons, red rock mesas, and spectacular multicolored rock formations carved out by millions of years of wind and rain. He told her that back in the good old days, before The Crash, when money flowed and Hollywood still made movies on location, many Westerns had been filmed out here, the best known being the Sinatra flick, *Sergeants 3*, and *The Outlaw Josey Wales* starring Clint Eastwood. Jenn noticed a misty melancholy in Poppy's eyes when he told her that Elaine—the self-appointed 'biggest movie fanatic on the planet'—

had been most impressed by that bit of trivia the last time he brought her here.

The path down the spur to the mines was dark and treacherous, so Poppy decided they would throw down and camp at the spur head. "Too dangerous to walk that section of track this time of night." He slept through to daybreak, but Jenn again had problems shutting down. The ground was hard and rocky. The desert night was chilly and she couldn't get warm in her threadbare bedroll. A fine dust filled the air, which gave her sneezing fits. She heard strange animal noises in the near distance. Coyotes? Wolves? Several times she heard something scratching in the sand. Snakes? Scorpions? Gilas? She picked up eerie, grunting bugle sounds that Poppy told her were the calls of bull elk. She tried to focus on the big beautiful sky overhead, even counting stars in an attempt to fool her mind into sleep. But the cold dusty air and her fear of unknown wildlife made it a long toss-and-turn night.

When daybreak arrived, they gobbled down trail mix and a few sticks of beef jerky before hiking down the spur to the mines. The track ran nearly a mile, winding through towering sandstone canyon walls and dropping down into a wide gorge where the mines were located. Jenn could see why Poppy hadn't wanted to hike it at night. Too many places for nocturnal predators to get at them. Too many crevices and holes to step into and break a leg or ankle.

Poppy described these abandoned coal mines as ghostly and Jenn thought his depiction was fitting. The landscape had a spooky, uninhabited vibe. It reminded her of photos she'd seen of NASA's lunar landings—a lonely, alien vista with evidence of humanity left behind. Footprints pock-marked the sand. Tracks had been gouged into the sandy surface by heavy mining equipment. A giant haul truck standing two stories high held a partial payload of sun-bleached coal fragments, its mammoth tires making it look like a lunar rover on steroids. A conveyance crane stood with its huge shovel buried in a mound of coal slag. A conveyor belt system snaked from half a dozen open mine entrances, feeding a centralized cradle bed. A small concrete building had lost one of its walls, chunks of cement scattered across the coal-dusted sand like gargantuan sugar cubes. A rusted aluminum sign hung crookedly over the tumbledown structure:

HYACINTH COAL, INC.
TODAY'S ENERGY FOR TOMORROW'S AMERICA

The scene in front of her seemed almost supernatural in its serene bleakness. "You had it right, Poppy," she said. "*Ghost mines*. It's like one day everyone just up and disappeared. Like the miners were abducted and whisked away by an alien spaceship or something."

"Yeah. They closed this one down and got out fast."

"Why? Because of the economy crashing?"

"No. Hyacinth was still pulling coal out of these hills a couple of years after The Crash," Parnell explained. "They left for other reasons. Underground coal mining got to be too expensive in these parts. Hyacinth shut down coal operations and got into uranium and silver mining. Much more lucrative."

"And they just left all this behind?" she said, waving her arm at the wood-framed shaft entrances and mining equipment.

He nodded. "They left even more shit underground. Purely a business decision. Relocating all this is expensive. Much cheaper to just leave it behind and write it off."

"What's that building over there?"

"That's the old headframe structure."

"Headframe?"

"Yeah. It's the place where mining engineers ran the below-ground water and ventilation systems. It was the nerve center of the operation."

Jenn smiled dourly. "Doesn't look like it has much nerve left now."

That made him laugh. She loved hearing him laugh. He didn't do it enough.

"C'mon," he said, "I want to show you a few things."

They made their way to the headframe housing, walking over glassy pieces of raw coal that dotted the sand.

He stepped over chunks of concrete and entered the open side of the structure, threw his backpack on a steel bench. "This here's known as the hoist room. We can stow our gear here while we go below."

"Below?" Jenn said, watching him dig through his backpack and retrieve his gun and a flashlight along with batteries he'd purchased in Winslow.

"Yeah," he said, kneeling on the far side of the room, working a combination lock on a set of large double doors hinged to the steel floor. He popped open the lock and grunted as he yanked the wrought iron handles, lifting the heavy doors.

She peered into the gloom of the gaping hole. "We're going down *there*?" she said, panic rising in her throat.

"Well, yeah. This is where my cash is buried." He looked at her. "What's wrong?"

Ever since Poppy had rescued her from the caves in northern Colorado, she'd been stricken with an incurable case of claustrophobia. She never wanted to see another underground enclosure as long as she lived. The thought of dropping down into that dark abyss terrified her.

Her expression reminded Parnell of that. "Oh, yeah. I'm sorry, honey. I wasn't think—"

"No. No, um . . . it's okay," she said quickly, mustering up her courage. "I'll go with you."

You're a Parnell, goddammit! Parnells aren't supposed to be afraid. Of anything. Ever. Do you want Poppy to see what a coward you are?

She had faced her husband's murderer yesterday and gunned him down. How bad could a dark mineshaft in the middle of the Utah desert be?

"You don't have to, Jenny—"

"I'm fine, really."

"Because you can stay up here while I—"

"Get your ass down in that hole, Poppy! Before I push you in. I'll be right behind you."

He smiled at her. "Yes, *ma'am*," he said, dropping into the opening.

She lowered herself to the floor and followed him down a crude wooden ladder bolted to the rock wall. The rungs squeaked as she descended. She prayed the steps weren't rotten as she peered below her feet, seeing Poppy's flashlight strobing the murky depths.

Down they went through the narrow shaft. The air became damp and smelled of fungus and sulfur. Floating shale dust made her eyes water. The temperature dropped. Cool air rose from below, flowing around her.

Thirty feet down, they came to a small opening, maybe twenty feet wide by five feet high. A tomblike enclosure. Jenn fought back her fear. They had to stoop to get around and she watched Poppy hunch over as he went to the far wall. He shined the flash on a steel breaker box recessed into the rock, a sealed cable running from it into the low ceiling. He opened the box with a squeak and flipped a switch. The tight space lit up like high noon.

A row of four light bulbs dangled from a socket bar overhead. "You have electricity down here?" she said, her voice deadened by the thick, dank air.

"Yep. Got power in all the tunnels," he said with pride. "At least the ones I'm using. I'll show you later how I made that happen."

She looked around. Stout wooden beams overhead supported the rocky ceiling. Thick tar-streaked timbers reinforced the walls every three feet. Water dripped somewhere close.

He pulled an earthen brick from the wall, exposing the face of a large combination safe. The heavy steel safe had been cemented into the wall between two support planks.

"*That's* where you've kept your money?" she said.

Parnell kneeled in front of the safe, twisting the combination knob. "Much more secure down here than trusting it with a bank these days."

"What if someone stole it? I mean, you told me you haven't been out here in almost four years. That's a lot of time for someone to find this place and steal your stash."

"Oh ye of little faith," he said between clicks of the rotating tumblers. "Elaine's the only one who knows about this place. She's the only one I ever told about the cash. In fact, she was with me here when I built this vault. But say somebody did find out about it and they wanted to rob me. It wouldn't be easy. Only two ways into this place: the way we came down, or up from below, more than six-hundred feet straight up through a narrow shaft."

One last twist on the combination knob and he popped open the safe, revealing a second, smaller safe inside. He went through the same motions again, spinning the knob on the interior safe, reciting the combination over the clicking tumblers as he twirled the knob—*left 82 ... right 16 ... left 49 ...* Jenn heard a click and a pop. The inside safe door sprung open. "Too many lock combinations to figure out," he said, reaching inside and pulling out a black plastic garbage bag. "Too much trouble. Easier getting into Fort Knox. So no, I've never been worried about anyone ripping me off. The biggest risk was me forgetting the combinations."

He slapped the plastic bag up on a flat-topped boulder. A haze of dust swirled around it causing him to cough.

"You hauled both of those safes down here?" she asked him. "You dug out the wall and poured the concrete casing?"

"Yes, ma'am. Eight, maybe nine years ago. I also built that ladder that got us down here. Wasn't easy, but I was a young stud back then."

She watched him pull decks of banded bills out of the bag and stack them on the stone shelf in front of him. She saw mostly Jacksons and Grants—twenties and fifties. He piled up the cash and the stacks quickly accumulated. There seemed to be no end to what was in the garbage bag.

"Jesus, Poppy. How much is there?"

"A little over two-hundred grand," he responded, not stopping, his hand a blur as he grabbed and stacked.

She whistled. "I knew you had some money, but I never dreamed you were this loaded."

He stopped and looked at her. "This is a pittance compared to what I once had." He pointed at the stacks of bills. "At one time my net worth was a million, closer to two mil, actually." He grabbed a few bundles and waved them around. "Aside from a bit I stashed away down in Costa Rica, this is the last of it."

She nodded. "I know you operated your own company at one time, and—"

"Yeah. Locomotion Enterprises. Big moneymaker."

"—you handed out a bunch of that money to your breezer friends. You were very generous. That's why they called you King Midas, right?"

He nodded.

"So, I'm confused about something, Poppy. Your relationship with John Dobkin? Didn't you tell me he made you rich?"

"Yeah, he did. But then . . . well . . . it's complicated, Jenny."

"You never talked about him much," she said. "Most of what I know about Dobkin came out in the trial."

"I didn't follow the trial, Jenny. American news was scarce in Costa Rica."

Jenn knew that was complete bullshit. Elaine told her that Poppy had indeed kept up with the trial, had followed every development in the Holt versus Dobkin Investigative Services proceedings. He'd had his nose in it from the beginning of jury selection to final judgment.

She wasn't going to challenge him on it. Instead she said, "So you're not upset? About losing all that money?"

"Not at all." He held up two stacks of bills. "I plan to give most of this away. Some will go to my posse. They do good work.

The rest goes to our breezer friends at Shangri-La and a few other hobo villages. I've got more cash stashed in Costa Rica for us, and Elaine has money from her artist days. We'll be fine."

"We?" Jenn said. "You're assuming I'm going back to Costa Rica with you?"

"Why not? It's not safe for you in the States. You can't go back to Vancouver. Our beach house in Manzanillo is a perfect safe haven for us."

She didn't think this was the time or place to let him know she wasn't interested in living with him and Elaine. She decided to change the subject. "You called Ann kind-hearted."

"Yeah. So?"

"I thought you despised her."

"No. I don't. She gets under my skin with all that religious nonsense of hers, but I certainly don't hate her."

"Could've fooled me. You really laid into her at Shangri-La. Then, yesterday, on the phone? You didn't want her joining us. Why not?"

"She would be a liability to us, that's why not."

"Because of her kindheartedness?"

"Bingo!" he said, pointing his finger at her.

She thought Poppy was being hypocritical and told him so.

"What the hell're you goin' on about, Jenny?"

"Isn't handing out large sums of money to people in need being kindhearted?"

"Yeah, I guess, but—"

"And yet you don't consider yourself to be a liability to our mission?"

His face reddened. "Christ, why the twenty questions today?"

"I'm just sayin', I don't think you give Ann Finnegan a fair shake. In fact, Poppy, I think you two are more alike than you care to admit."

"What?"

"It's true. You both have a generous side to you. You just show it in different ways."

She'd got him with that comment. First time she'd ever seen him speechless. "What's the matter?" she said, looking at him kneeling next to the flat-topped rock, his hands poised over a small fortune in U.S. currency. "Did I hit close to home?"

"Absolutely not," he said, stuffing two piles of cash into a canvas coin bag. He tossed the remaining stacks of money into the plastic bag, then threw the coin bag in the interior safe, slamming the door for maximum effect.

She had definitely touched a nerve. "Aren't you going to take all of it?" she asked.

"No. We'll be coming back."

"When?"

He scowled at her. "Why so many goddamned questions, Jenny?"

"I don't know," she said, wounded, afraid of him in that moment. "I'm just interested is all."

He picked up the flashlight and went to the circuit box, cut the power, throwing them into darkness. "Let's head topside," he said as he scooted around her. "There're a few other things I want to show you."

He started back up the ladder.

My father, the mercurial mystery, she thought as she climbed behind him.

The Belle of the Ball and the Southern Gentleman

WINSLOW WAS A SLEEPY DESERT TOWN running on life support. The city's population dropped after World War II with the rapid decline in rail travel. Construction of the I-40 bypass in 1979 diverted traffic away from the city square, and many businesses moved out to interstate sites to survive. The Crash twelve years ago hammered the final nail in the municipal coffin. The census marked it currently at 7,000+, and 800 of those residents were inmates at the state prison.

Elaine made her way through downtown, past boarded-up retail outlets and fast food joints. Country-and-western music rolled out of a grungy dive bar, the pedal steel guitar whining in the night. The brisk desert breeze whipped through her thin gaucho pants, chilling her. Thankfully her boots kept her feet warm. She buttoned up her denim jacket and trudged on.

At the corner of Second and North Kinsley she came to the bronze sculpture of the shaggy-haired guitarist known as "Easy." The intersection was a tribute to the Eagles' 1970s country-rock song "Take It Easy," which was set in Winslow. The statue glowed like a metallic deity beneath a streetlamp. A sign that read **Standin' On The Corner** stood behind Easy. The backdrop mural depicted a realistic storefront window reflection of a girl in a flatbed Ford and an eagle perched on the ledge of a windowsill. A group of tourists laughed drunkenly as they took turns posing with Easy, snapping selfies. Elaine loved the Eagles' music, but she could only shake her head. *A statue of a fictional guitar player? Everybody wants to be a star. Welcome to the Age of Narcissism!*

She walked five blocks on North Kinsley and cut over on East Maple Street, going another dozen blocks to pick up Oak Road, which took her under the I-40 bridge and to the trail leading into Homolovi State Park. She entered the park and passed the visitor center, the adobe building dark and forlorn, closed because of state budget cutbacks. She walked the open desert trail, past the replicas of 14th century multi-storied Hopi homes. The sandstone and mud dwellings stood like ancient sentinels underneath the shimmering moon.

The trail took her up a series of hills into high grasslands, then quickly narrowed into a dark corridor choked with scrub brush, ponderosa pine, and ironwood trees. She made her way through thickets of wild blackberry brambles. The thorny bushes scratched her arms. Burrs caught in her pants. Her feet ached and her ankles burned from the striations left by the Mexicans who had bound her in the taxi. Her backpack seemed to get heavier with each step. Her legs were rubbery. Her lungs burned.

She was miserable.

But she was free.

Free of the impotent psychiatrist and his perverted pilot friend. The damage she had inflicted on them brought a smile to her chilled face. They'd tangled with the wrong woman and paid the price.

She pushed on. A full moon shined down, painting the trees silver. She searched for the drainage culvert with the big steel aqueduct that led to the hobo camp. *How much farther can it be? I've got to be getting close.* Elaine had been down this hilly path with Derek a few times during daylight hours, but the distance seemed much greater at night.

She followed the overgrown trail, finally coming to where it opened out into a wide arroyo. The moonlight cast a hazy spotlight across the sandy, windblown terrain. She spotted the immense drainpipe across the divide.

She pumped a fist into the air. *I made it!*

She stripped a branch from a dead pine tree and entered the clearing. This area was a breeding ground for snakes and the last thing she needed tonight was to step in the path of a restless rattler. She swept the branch across the sand in front of her as she walked. Slowly and carefully she covered the three-hundred yards to the opening of the aqueduct.

She heard the gurgling rush of the Little Colorado River to her left. The air smelled sweeter here, less dusty and arid. Hobo signs were posted around the entrance of the big drainage tube, crude drawings scrawled on cardboard or tin with charcoal and chalk and brightly colored paint.

Derek had taught her how to read the cryptic sketches during their rail-riding adventures. She perused them in the silvery moonlight. Three forward slashes translated to "This place is not safe."

A tall cross meant "Food available for those willing to discuss religion in a positive manner." Two gun barrels facing each other for "This camp is heavily armed." A face in the upper right quadrant of a cross meant "Free medical assistance." *Mixed messages,* she thought. *What does it all mean? Is it safe to enter?*

Well, I've come this far . . .

She shrugged her shoulders and entered the drainpipe.

"Halt!" A male voice from above. "Do not proceed."

Footsteps banged across the pipe above her. Elaine backed out and looked up into a blinding white light. She flung the pine branch aside and brought her hand up to shield her eyes.

"State your business," the voice demanded.

A deep south intonation. Mississippi. Maybe Alabama. She moved to her right, trying to see around the bright light. The damned beam was powerful enough to burn sunspots into her retinas.

"I *said*, state your business, ma'am."

She squinted into the light. "I'm, uh . . . I'm just trying to get to Shangri-La."

"Well, you made it, ma'am. Please state your business. I won't ask again."

The angle of the light shifted, and she caught a glimpse of a man training a rifle on her. Caucasian, medium height, dark hair that flopped over his ears. A little younger than her. Late-twenties, early thirties. It certainly wasn't Weasel Bethea, the guard she thought might be watching over the camp.

The free medical assistance sign flashed in her mind and she saw her way in. "I'm hurt and I've come a long way tonight," she said. "I understand you have a doctor here. A Doctor Ann Finnegan?"

"You don't look hurt to me, ma'am. What's your injury?"

She wanted to tell him she was hurt by his insistence on calling her *ma'am*, the word Elaine reserved for women of her grandmother's generation.

"I'm losing my patience with you, ma'am. If you don't tell me who you are in—"

"My name's Elaine Leibrandt. I need to see Ann Finnegan."

"*You're* Elaine Leibrandt?"

"Yes. That's me. I'm Elaine," she said, stepping to her left while continuing to shield her eyes, getting a better look at his face in the moon's glimmer, trying to recall if she had met him before.

She'd been away for three years and faces could change. But no, she didn't recognize him. "I'm, uh . . . I'm confused. Do I know you?"

He leaped from the top of the conduit, landing sure-footed in front of her, agile as a cat, rifle cradled under one arm, the light firmly grasped in his opposite hand. It was a drop of ten feet or more and he'd executed the jump like an Olympian. The action startled her, but she held her ground.

"How do I know you're really Elaine Leibrandt?" he asked, standing uncomfortably close, looking her over.

"Well," she said, moving back a step, "I've been to Shangri-La before. I know a few people in the camp here. Other than Ann Finnegan, I mean."

"Yeah? Like who?"

"Um, I haven't been here in a few years, and I don't know if the people I knew are still here, but for starters I know Weasel. His real name is Greg Bethea."

"That's good. Who else?"

"Uh, well I also know the camp chef, Alice. Don't know her last name but she used to wear an *Alice's Restaurant* apron. You know, from that old song by Arlo Guthrie? I believe her breezer handle was Alley Cat."

"Very good. You're two-for-two. One more."

"Okay. How about Buttonhead Murphy?" she said, thinking about the jovial stoner with the bushy head of hair and porkpie hat.

"Excellent! One last question. Who is your husband?"

"Husband? I'm not married."

"Uh—that's not what I've been told."

She questioned whether she should even mention Derek, considering how many people were after him, then decided to take a chance. "You must be referring to Derek . . . Derek Parnell?"

He nodded. "I am. He's not your husband?"

"Oh, no. Derek's my . . . well, he's my *partner*. Is he here? Is he okay?"

The man smiled and leaned his rifle against the side of the aqueduct. His wary stance softened to a relaxed acceptance. "I know you two aren't a married couple. Just testin' you. Thought you might be one of those bounty hunters. We've been getting a lot of them lately."

"*Me* a bounty hunter?" she said, taking another step away from him. "That's a laugh."

"Well, it's not that you *look* like one of 'em. Ann told me you probably wouldn't be alone so I just figured that—"

"Ann? The Ann Finnegan I'm here to see?"

"Yeah. She told me to be on the lookout for you. Said you might be in trouble, that probably someone bad would be holding you captive."

This confused her. "How would she know that?"

"Your man Derek. He called her yesterday, gave her a heads-up."

Interesting. "Where was he calling from?"

"Don't know, ma'am."

"Hmm. So now that we've established who I am, how about telling me who you are."

"Oh, my apologies, ma'am. I've been quite rude, haven't I? Please forgive me. My name is Cale Turnipseed. Ann appointed me temporary camp security while Weasel is gone and Ollie McKellar recovers from his wound."

Now she was sure she had never met this man. A name like Turnipseed she would most certainly remember.

"Turnipseed?" she said. "Is that your breezer handle?"

"Oh, no, ma'am. Turnipseed's my real birth name. *T-seed* is my 'bo handle."

"Please stop calling me *ma'am*."

"Sorry, I didn't mean—"

"Cale Turnipseed? Your parents must love vegetables."

He laughed and looked away, toward the river. "I get that a lot. No, it's Cale with a 'C'. And my parents aren't big vegetable eaters. They hate kale with a 'K'. So do I. My folks were big fans of the old NASCAR driver, Cale Yarborough."

"That explains it," she said, having no clue about auto racing.

"I've never raced stock cars," he said, eyes twinkling, gentle grin on his face. "Rode a motorcycle for a while but never drove a race car."

This man's relaxed, happy-go-lucky demeanor warmed her, inviting further conversation. "So, Turnipseed," she said. "Such an unusual name. Are you anything like Johnny Appleseed? You know, the guy who spread apple trees everywhere he went? Do you leave a trail of turnips behind you?"

He laughed again, louder this time. "I get that a lot, too. No, I leave no turnip roots behind. I come from a long line of Swiss-German Turnipseeds who came over here in the 1700s and settled in the South. I happen to have some Cherokee blood in me as well. So I guess you could say I'm an Bavarian Native American Confederate who lives on a western hobo reservation."

She laughed. "How long have you been at Shangri-La?"

"Almost a year. Atlanta was my home. Born and raised there. Got a job working construction after high school. Unfortunately, The Crash happened the year I graduated and the economy flushed down the toilet. The firm I worked for had some big government contracts, so I was able to stay employed for a few years. But then it all fell apart about four years ago. Lost my job. Picked up some odd-job handyman gigs here and there. Drove a school bus part-time for two years. I loved those children, I really did. One of the saddest days of my life was the day the school system went belly-up bankrupt and I had to say goodbye to those kids . . ."

Elaine listened to him talk. *The man sure is a Chatty Charlie, an open book. Unusual in these paranoid times.*

". . . I scrapped and fought to survive. Got some help from my family, but all of them were hurting, too. Ended up having to sell my motorcycle to pay the rent. *That* about killed me, selling my baby. Big, beautiful vintage Harley Sportster, candy-apple red with high-flow heads and performance cams. Damn! The money from that sale helped for a while. But in the long run it wasn't enough. Like most everyone else I knew, I found myself homeless. I heard about the hobo camps out west and hitched out to California. Stayed in a coupla 'bo villages near San Diego, but it wasn't my scene. Drifted around a while before finding this place. The long-timers took me into their family—Weasel Bethea, Ann, Fingers, Oshkosh, Hopeful Harvey, Chef Alley Cat—they accepted me and made me feel at home. I love the camaraderie here, the sense of community. Do I wish I was back east driving those kids to school every day? Sometimes, yeah. But I love it out here . . . the mountains, the desert, the river and fresh air. It's beautiful. Every day is like a wilderness dream. I know that sounds crazy . . ."

"No, it doesn't," she said. She instantly liked this kind, earnest man who so easily shared the details of his life. She found his laid-back chattiness refreshing. "It doesn't sound the least bit crazy, Cale. My Derek feels the same way about Shangri-La."

He appeared relieved by her acceptance. "I know I talk way too much, but I can't help it. It's the Dixie in me, I reckon."

She smiled at him. "You sure it isn't the turnip seeds in you? I hear turnips make people verbose."

He searched her face for a sign that she might be putting him on. His brow wrinkled as he studied her. Elaine held a solemn pose as long as possible, then winked at him, which sent both of them into fits of laughter.

"You're a lot of fun, ma'am—sorry, I mean *Elaine*. I never expected Derek Parnell's, um . . . lady friend, to have a great sense of humor. And I absolutely never expected you would look the way you do."

She braced herself. "Whaddaya mean?"

"Well, please don't take this the wrong way, but after meeting your, um . . . *partner* Derek, I expected you to be harder looking. Maybe have some trashy tattoos and body piercings."

"Why would you say that?"

He glanced back toward the river. "Well, you know, Derek Parnell being who he is and all. I just had preconceptions about what you'd be like."

"Surely I must look a mess," she said.

"Oh no. Absolutely not. Just the opposite actually. You're *beautiful*," he gushed. "You look like you've come from a high society ball. You look like the belle of the ball . . . like Cinderella in search of her glass slipper."

She shook her head. "Jesus, Cale. I realize the light isn't very good out here, but you're either blind as a bat or a hopeless romantic. I assure you I haven't come from anywhere you'd call high society. I'm certainly no belle of the ball. Not even close."

"I'm not coming on to you, if that's what you're thinkin'."

"No, that's not what I'm thinking at all. I'm thinking about your opinion of my Derek. You've met him?"

"Oh yeah. He was here a coupla days ago. It was an honor to finally meet him. I'd heard so much about him. He's kind of a legend in these parts. His daughter Jenn got here a few days before he did. She seemed nice, but quiet."

"Are either of them still here?"

"No. They went to Cottonwood to take care of some business day before yesterday. Sounded like pretty nasty business, you ask me. Your Derek put together a posse. There was talk they were going to kill a few people."

"A posse?"

"Yeah. He and Weasel recruited two guys to go with them. Billy Dixon and Javion Wheeler. They interviewed a bunch of us before they settled on those two. I wanted to go. I thought it would be exciting to ride the rails with the guy they call King Midas."

"But they didn't pick you. Why?"

"Weasel doesn't think I'm tough enough. Besides, I really don't have enough experience hoppin' trains. It's okay though. I'm gonna get my chance now. Miss Ann said if you showed up, I would be accompanying you and her on a trip."

"A trip where?"

"Taking you to Derek."

"I thought you said you don't know where Derek is."

"I don't. Look, I think you should talk to Ann about this." He grabbed his rifle and moved to the pipe entrance. "C'mon. I'll take you to her. It's late but she'll be happy to know you arrived safe."

"Wait a minute, Cale," she said to his back.

"What?" He turned to her.

She pulled off her backpack and retrieved her phone. "I need to make a call before we head in to camp."

"Sure, no problem."

She leaned against the steel wall and scrolled through her phone log to find the number of Derek's current burner cell. She punched the Return Call icon and listened for the connection. After a long delay it went straight to voicemail. "Hey, love, it's me," she said, eyeing Cale as she left the message. "Hope you get this message. I finally made it to the, um . . . to the Winslow mines." She smiled at Cale, noticing his confused look, her look saying *Don't worry about it.* "Had to take a little detour getting here but all is well. Heard you were here a few days ago. I miss you like crazy, old man. Can't wait to see you. Just met a very nice, uh . . . miner here who will be escorting me to you." Another confused look from Cale. "If you get this, please call me back and let me know you're okay. I love you, babe. Be safe."

She disconnected, a hollow, disappointed feeling fluttering in her stomach. She wanted so badly to talk with Derek directly. She hoped he and Jenn were okay.

Cale spoke. "Pardon my curiosity, but what was that miner stuff all about? The Winslow mines?"

"Long story. Just think of it as a coded message."

"Oh, I see. Like in a spy novel or a James Bond movie, right?"

"Something like that, yeah."

"Because of all the bounty hunters searching for you two, eh?"

"Yeah. Them and a few others."

"Cool! Things sure have gotten exciting around here the past week."

"Whaddaya mean?"

"Well, we had people auditioning for Parnell's posse. All the stories goin' round about Derek's past . . . his legacy. The big sendoff party we threw for him and his posse. The gun duel . . . their quick getaway and—"

"Wait. A gun duel?"

"Oh yeah. Derek and Ollie McKellar. It was pretty intense."

Elaine remembered Ollie McKellar from her last visit to Shangri-La. He was a wise-ass punk with a quick-trigger anger and zero respect for Derek.

"What happened?" she asked.

"Well, the duel was a party-killer, that's for sure. Things were going along great, everybody drinkin' beer 'n wine, Chef Alice cookin' up some great grub, Fingers and his band playing the hits the way they—"

"Skip the party details, Cale. Tell me about the duel."

"Okay, okay. Ollie was drunker'n a sailor on leave and he and his buddy, Palomino, started roustin' the camp, knockin' over tents and shootin' off their guns. Raisin' hell. McKellar plugged Oshkosh in the hand, then he came after your Derek. Called him out, provoked him. Harassed Jennifer Parnell and Ann, too, callin' both of 'em filthy names. Derek suggested they settle things with a gun duel. They stood back-to-back. Palomino started the countdown and they walked away from each other, a step for each count. Derek turned and fired early. Hit McKellar in the arm."

"Derek didn't wait for the complete countdown?"

"No. He blamed it on some kind of numbers dyslexia. I can't remember the actual name for it."

Elaine smiled. Old Tombstone Eyes was at it again.

Parnell's Amusement Park

THEY WALKED ACROSS the mining grounds, Parnell explaining to Jenn what he knew about the place. He told her about the dilapidated headframe structure with its hoist room that sat above what once was the primary coal shaft. Tons of bituminous coal and anthracite had been hauled up and out through this main shaft during Hyacinth's glory days. In later years, the headframe had been reconstructed to house controls for operating the water, ventilation, and electrical systems that supplied the network of dig tunnels. They walked through the yard, Parnell giving Jenn the ten-cent tour of the heavy machinery that sat like mechanical dinosaurs in the desert sun. A hulking rock crusher that resembled a dumpster with jaws. A giant robotic gyratory crusher. The hydraulic mining excavator parked next to a heaping pile of slag, weighing in at close to 1,100 tons with a 60-yard face shovel and immense backhoe unit. Two conveyor belt systems peeked out from mine-shaft entrances and fed a main conveyor leading to a broken-down cradle bin. The belts had snapped and were disintegrating in the fierce desert sun. A yellow Caterpillar haul truck sat next to the cradle, its colossal tires mired in the sand.

The bean counters at Hyacinth hadn't seen it as fiscally prudent to rescue this equipment. Parnell got Jenn laughing when he mimicked a possible conversation between corporate stuffed suits sitting around a Hyacinth boardroom conference table: "Well, Jeeves, we can't take any more depreciation on this equipment, so let's just leave it where it is. We'll need a different configuration for mining uranium anyway and it'll be cheaper to leave this ancient technology behind." Parnell put his hand up to his ear. "What's this I'm hearing from the board? The environment, you say? Who gives a rat's ass! We own this godforsaken sandbox, and I doubt those lazy bastards in the EPA will get off their fat asses to come after us."

"How did you even find this place?" she asked. "It's so . . . I don't know . . . remote . . . *desolate*."

Her observation brought a smile. "There's beauty in desolation you know, Jenny."

She looked at him uncertainly. "How do you figure? This place is depressing."

He maintained his smile. "It grows on you. I'm gonna show you a few things that'll change your mind."

She shrugged, her body language saying *We'll see about that.*

He told Jenn he had discovered these mines shortly after coming west and beginning his search for her. He'd been killing time in a Phoenix Internet café when he stumbled on an article about the Hyacinth Corporation in southern Utah, how they were closing down their coal mining operations and moving to the northern part of the state to get in on the uranium rush. They would be leaving behind much of the infrastructure. Perfect! An isolated spot in the heart of the desert badlands. The closest town was Kanab, fifteen miles west, and it was half the size of Winslow. He could safely stash his cash here. He could disappear, go completely off the grid.

"So I take it you've spent a lot of time here," she said when he finished.

"Yeah. I've done a lot of work on this place," he said with pride. "Follow me. You won't believe what I'm about to show you."

He led her to one of three primary mine entrances. As they moved inside, out of the day's heat, he went to the circuit-breaker box mounted on a support post and flipped open the lid. He flicked two switches and was relieved to see the klieg lamps come on, lighting up the mineshaft entrance. He flipped another switch and heard the ventilation system kick in. A cool breeze swept over them.

He pointed to a sign he'd hand painted years before:

PARNELL'S AMUSEMENT PARK
Enter at your own risk!

"Is this one of your jokes?" Jenn asked.

"No joke. I'll show you later. I want to show you my living quarters first."

"Living quarters?"

"Yeah," he said, taking her to a rusty mining cart sitting on a stretch of rails leading into a dark tunnel.

"What's this?"

"An old mine trolley. They used these things to haul out coal before they were replaced by conveyor belt systems. Hyacinth used these things as people movers . . . *miner* movers. Go ahead, get in."

"What?"

He nodded at the strut bench in the cart. "Take a seat. This is how we get to my place."

Jenn looked skeptical. "I don't know about—"

"It's either ride the trolley or walk a quarter mile through some sketchy areas. I don't recommend walking."

Reluctantly she climbed into the cart and held fast to the roll bar in front of her. "You know how much I hate being underground, Poppy."

He climbed in next to her and patted her arm reassuringly. "This is safe. You'll be fine. I promise."

He reached down and opened the control panel he had engineered into the cart. Hopefully the tracks would still conduct electricity to propel them forward. He punched the green button in the panel and heard the buzzing hum. *Good, still working.* He pushed the throttle handle forward. The trolley car squeaked into motion. As they rolled into the mouth of the tunnel, more lights flashed on, lighting up the rails ahead. They moved slowly at first, but picked up speed after the first bend, then began a sharp descent.

"This is wild, Poppy," Jenn yelled, her short bob of dirty blonde hair blowing back in the onrushing breeze.

They rolled through the narrow tunnel, wheels screeching along the rails, earthen walls and wood beams flashing past, lights flickering in strobe-like flashes. They went into a curve and dipped downward, Jenn shrieking with glee.

Finally, the tracks leveled out and the cart slowed. They entered a cavernous area with a high rock ceiling. Parnell pushed the brake and they came to a stop. "We're home," he said, jumping out and extending a hand to assist Jenn.

"Amazing," she said, stepping out and patting her hair back in place. "You built this?"

"Hyacinth left the cart, rails, and transformer. I did the rest. Same technology as the model trains I used to mess around with. I repaired their transformer, then gave it juice through my power grid. Electricity runs to the rails and the trolley car wheels pull its power from the tracks."

"Where do you get the electricity?"

"Something I built up on the ridge. I'll show you later."

He led her to a small cave and flicked on more lights. Another hand-painted sign hung over the entrance:

Parnell's Paradise!

He inspected his old living quarters, Jenn following him. Nothing seemed to have been disturbed in his absence. A thick layer of shale dust covered the wood-plank flooring and every object in the rock-walled room. A sterno stove and small refrigerator on one wall. Shelves stocked with canned goods and cooking utensils on an adjacent wall. Mattress and box spring on a frame he'd constructed from the chassis of a mining car. A sink with running water and a stall with a working showerhead fed by an underground spring originally used by the Hyacinth miners.

"Jesus, Poppy," Jenn said, eyes wide, taking it all in. "All the comforts of home."

"Not quite," he said, slapping the mattress. A cloud of dust rose in the air. "I still haven't figured out how to get decent plumbing down here. I've got a latrine set up across the way, but it's a nasty business keeping the smell down."

She shot him a look of disgust. "Too much information, daddy dear."

"One thing's for sure. I could survive down here quite a while if and when those warmonger idiots in Washington get us into a nuclear war."

Jenn went to the shelves near the bed and spotted a group of framed photos of Elaine. Two of the poses were nudes, another pair showed her clothed with her eyepatch in place. She picked one of the nudes off the shelf and blew the dust off of it.

Parnell looked her way. "Those are my favorite shots of Lainey."

"The nudes?"

"All of 'em."

"She's a beautiful woman, Poppy. I always thought so."

"Yeah," Parnell said absently as he checked the sink, disappointed to see orange water running from the tap into the metal bowl.

Jenn picked up one of the photos of Elaine wearing her eyepatch. "She looks like a pirate. A gorgeous pirate babe."

"Yeah. The patch makes her look even sexier. But Lainey doesn't like wearing it. Says it draws too much attention. She thinks it magnifies her handicap."

"Handicap?" Jenn said, surprised. "I wish I was that handicapped."

"She's always been insecure about it. Her eye and the left side of her face where that psycho boyfriend of hers . . ." He felt himself choking up, so he said no more.

"You said Elaine's been here with you before?"

"Yeah," Parnell said with a disappointed grunt as he discovered the same rusty water problem in the shower stall. "Twice. I brought Lainey here right after I first built this place. Probably nine years ago now, when I made the first cash deposit in my vault room. Then she was with me the last time I came here, almost four years ago." He watched the showerhead continue to spray rust-colored water. *Shit! I'm going to have to flush the pipes with chemicals.*

Jenn put the eyepatch photo back. "How many times did you stay here without her?"

"I don't know. Quite a few, I guess."

"Dozens?"

He fiddled with the showerhead, trying to see if the connector was rusted out. "Yeah, dozens."

She gave him a critical glance. "You left Elaine alone in Flagstaff and stayed here? By yourself? Dozens of times?"

Oh, Christ! Here she goes again. Dread hit him in the chest with the weight of a punch. She was shifting into her judgmental mode—her head thrown back, eyes narrowing, her chin jutting out accusingly.

He stepped out of the shower stall and faced her. "Yeah, I did."

"And you think that was fair to her?"

"I did what I needed to do at the time."

"That's what *you* needed to do. What about Elaine?"

"Look, in case you forgot, I was out here looking for you. I never would've found you if I stayed holed up in Flagstaff with her."

"Elaine told me you never spent much time with her. Said you were more interested in gallivanting around the country. Told me you reminded her of Don Quixote, always running off on some gallant quest, attacking windmills and slaying dragons."

My ungrateful daughter just can't leave it alone. He did his best to keep his cool. "Do I have to keep reminding you that my gallant quest was all about finding you? And you do know Don Quixote is fiction, right?"

"That's not the point. You bring me out here to see this man cave you've built for yourself in the middle of nowhere and—"

"Man cave?" he snarled at her, feeling his blood pressure rise.

"Yeah, *man cave*. Your own *Parnell's Paradise* man cave. Elaine always seems to be an afterthought to you. You knew she was on her way to Shangri-La, making that dangerous trip by herself, and yet you don't really seem interested in her. What am I supposed to think, huh?"

"My relationship with Lainey is none of your concern."

"It's *all* of my concern! Do you love her?"

He took a step toward her and clenched his fists, then caught himself, blew out a heavy breath and turned away from her. "Of *course* I love her, Jenny. What the hell."

"You have a strange way of showing it. You haven't even checked your phone today to see if she made it to Winslow safely."

A bolt of shame struck him. He was so accustomed to being incommunicado he'd forgotten completely about his burner cell. With everything going on he'd forgotten about his conversation with Annie Finnegan. "You're right," he conceded. "I've been negligent. I'll call her when we get back to the headframe."

"Nothing like a sense of urgency for the woman you love," she said sarcastically.

"Man, that's cold, Jenny. Frigid in fact."

She gave him an icy look, which prompted him to say, "Look, I can't call her right this second. My phone's topside."

"How about Mom?"

"What're you talking about? Who?"

"Mom. You know, my mother? The woman you married? I believe her name was Barbara."

"What about her?" Parnell definitely didn't want to venture into a conversation with his daughter about his late wife.

"Did you love her? My mother?"

She had finally managed to crawl all the way under his skin. "Shit, Jennifer, what is this, the inquisition?"

"I'm just looking for answers to questions I've had for a long time. So did you love Barbara? Answer me. I need to know."

"So you're going *there*," he said, a statement of defeat, not a question.

"Yes I am," she said, chin protruding, defiance bringing color to her cheeks.

"Okay," he said, trying to think of the best way to approach this painful subject. "Yes, I did love your mother. At least in the beginning. But her family made things difficult. They came from a long line of money and I worked as a pest exterminator. They thought I was a lowlife, not worthy of Barbara. Behind my back they called me derogatory names, like 'Bug Man' and 'Cockroach.' Unfortunately Barb always sided with family, the Stevensons. She never had my back. It wasn't a good time in my life. You were too young to remember much of that, I'm sure."

Jenn shook her head. "You're so wrong. I remember the fights, the awful name calling. I remember hiding in my bedroom and hearing dishes breaking in the kitchen, both of you shouting at each other. I recall being scared and hiding under my bed."

"I'm sorry we put you through that, Jenny."

She scrutinized him. "Did you cry when she died?"

"Honestly?" he said, "I was sad that she died the way she did. Nobody should have to go out in a blaze set by murderers. But no, I didn't cry. We were too distant at the end. Barbara was very complicated and—"

"Just like you, Poppy."

Nothing like kicking a man when he's down. "Yeah, well—"

"I hated her," she said. "I want you to know that. She was a bitch, my mother."

He wasn't sure he heard her correctly. "*Excuse* me? What was that?"

"I said I hated Mom. In fact, I have a hard time even thinking of her as a mother. She was never there for me. I was the least important thing in her life."

"That's not necessarily true," he said, wanting to erase the hurt he saw on her face.

"Oh, but it is. You were the one who always took care of me. You were the parent who loved me, not her. She didn't give a shit about me. She only cared about her crazy, shallow yuppie friends. I never understood how you could stay with her, Poppy."

Nothing positive could come from Jenny thinking ill of her birth mother. His next words sounded foreign to him. "Barbara had her good points, and—"

"No she didn't. She was a selfish, narcissistic bitch!"

He couldn't really disagree with that, but still, he thought it a harsh assessment, and told her so.

"Really, Poppy? She treated you like you were her servant."

"That's true. She did treat me like shit. But I think you should have more respect for the woman who carried you for nine months and brought you into this world."

Jenn threw up her hands. "There's a lot more to motherhood than just giving birth. Hell, Elaine's been more of a mother to me than Barbara ever was, even though she's just twelve years older than me and I was only with her for ten months."

"So you like Lainey, then?"

"Are you kidding me? I *love* Elaine. Why do you think I've been goin' on about her? I think she's great."

"And yet you think I don't. Love her, I mean."

"I think you take her for granted. You're gonna lose her if you don't start giving her more attention, Poppy. Take it from a woman who knows a thing or two about love."

How can this 22-year-old girl-woman daughter of mine know anything about the complexities of love? He looked at her long and hard, saw the seriousness in her expression. She was so young, and yet so right.

"I'm worried about her, Poppy. You should be, too. I sure hope she made it to Shangri-La okay."

"Me, too," he said, starting back to the mine trolley. "C'mon, I want to show you the electrical grid I built."

The mining cart labored back up the track—much slower up the steep incline—retracing the route by which they'd descended.

He went first to the headframe and retrieved his burner phone, then dragged out a long extension ladder. He had Jenn follow him up the north ridge.

He trudged up a well-worn, narrow path, Jenn close behind. Up, up, up they went, high above the rim of Hyacinth operations. From up here, the heavy mining equipment far below looked like Tonka toys. The weight and awkwardness of the ladder slowed his progress as the broiling sun beat down. His lungs burned. Sweat dampened his shirt. His breaths came hard and he heard Jenny huffing and puffing at his back. Finally he came to the craggy shelf of rock that jutted out over the path, fifteen feet above. He stopped and positioned the ladder, secured it against the rocky ledge.

"You go first," he said to her. "I'll spot you, then follow you up."

She looked up, her chest heaving, unsure about it. "I don't know about this. Where are you taking me?"

"You'll see," he said impatiently. "Go on. You're gonna love this."

He held the ladder steady as she climbed, her steps tentative, cautious, then he followed. Up top, the sun became nearly unbearable. Parnell walked across the hard-baked plateau to the far side, the desert sun roasting his shoulders and top of his head. Jenn shuffled along behind him. He could see three states from up here: Nevada to the west, Colorado to the east, and Arizona due south. This high point would be easy to spot by plane or helicopter, and was easily accessible by hawks and eagles. But trying to get here on foot was a difficult proposition.

As they neared the downslope on the far side of the ridge, he saw that his prize creation was intact.

"So here it is," he said to her, pointing at four large glass panels recessed into the rock at his feet.

"What are we looking at here, Poppy?"

"High efficiency solar panels. The main power supply that sends electricity to the tunnels and mineshaft entrances."

"Really? *You* did this?"

"Yeah. I've spent a lot of time here. With and without Elaine."

"I'm sorry about that, okay? I was just trying to—"

"No harm, no foul, Jenny," he said, taking a knee and inspecting the panel frames.

Jenn scanned the large glass panels. "These things look like weird picture windows. They generate electricity?"

"Yep. It's solar power. Clean energy. The very thing the government avoids because the piggy-pigs in D.C. feed at the petroleum trough."

"Wow. I don't understand it, but *Wow!*"

"Let's get out of this frying pan and I'll do my best to explain it to you."

They went back down the ladder and sat in the shade of the rock outcropping. Parnell described the solar grid he constructed the first year he had come out here. He had known nothing about solar energy when he arrived, but Hyacinth had closed out their account with Rocky Mountain Power, so he had to learn how to build his own localized power grid. A lot of trial and error went into what she saw now, he told her. These four six-foot-by-ten-foot panels recessed into the rock were the energy gatherers that collected the sun's rays. Each panel was sectioned into arrays of solar PV (photovoltaic) cells. Underneath each panel were sophisticated photovoltaic modules, which converted the collected sunlight into electricity. A solar inverter converted the variable direct current (DC) from the captured light energy into a line frequency alternating current (AC) that could feed an off-grid electrical network. He tried to keep his explanation to basic layman's terminology, but Jenn's eyes glazed over as he talked.

"I see I'm either boring you or overwhelming you," he said.

"No . . . neither," she said. "I'm impressed actually. Were these already here or did you install them?"

"This is all my work. Did it with these two hands and this mush melon of mine," he said, tapping his forehead. "Had a helluva time getting these babies up here and hooked up. Same with the two safes in the vault room. But where there's a will . . ."

"Wow, Poppy. Don't you have to be a master electrician or something to wire up all this stuff?"

"Not really. Any moron who can read technical manuals could do this. Biggest problem was finding all the parts I needed. Had to go all the way to Vegas to get most of it."

"How'd you get these things out here?" she said, pointing at the panels. "Surely you didn't hop a railcar with them."

Parnell laughed. "Oh, no. No way possible to get these things on a train. I got one of Hyacinth's jeeps running."

He told her the coal company had left behind a couple of old jeeps with oversized off-road tires perfect for traversing rough desert terrain and potholed high-country roads. The batteries were dead, but he had pulled a working battery from an earthmover, then hotwired the jeep that was in the best condition. Parnell made multiple trips to Kanab and Mount Carmel, purchasing basic electrical components and how-to documentation, then drove to Vegas to find the solar panels and photovoltaic system equipment, such as solar trackers and charge controllers and solar-charging voltaic battery packs. The old Hyacinth electrical networks in the tunnels were still wired, and the big fans in the ventilation system were still in place and operable, so once he had his power grid working, all he had to do was connect it to those systems.

Jenn shook her head, amazed. "Incredible, Poppy. I knew you were smart, but I never figured you for a genius."

Parnell huffed. "I'm no genius, precious. Just resourceful. And so are you."

"You think so?"

"I *know* so."

She beamed at him, his compliment getting them past their antagonistic exchange. He wanted Jenn on his side. He *needed* his daughter to be on his side.

Parnell pulled the throwaway phone from his shirt pocket. "Time to make that call to Lainey. Then I've got one last thing to show you. I'm saving the best for last."

"What could that possibly be?"

"The amusement park ride to hell."

Call From the Wild

HER PHONE BUZZED. She glanced at caller ID and saw it was blocked. *Has to be Derek,* she thought.

She picked up. "Hello?"

"Hey, good lookin'. It's me."

Elaine's heart soared. She smiled and nodded at Ann Finnegan and Cale Turnipseed, who sat across from her in Ann's living room sipping wine. "It's him," she mouthed to them.

"Well, well, well," she said into the phone. "We were just talking about you."

"And here I thought my ears were burning because of the desert sun. Who are the royal *we* you're referring to?"

"Ann and Cale."

"Cale who?"

"Turnipseed."

"Oh, you mean T-Seed?"

She looked at Cale. "Yeah, I guess so . . . yes."

"I can't tell you how relieved I am that you made it to the camp. How was your trip?"

She dredged up thoughts of her long journey: the humiliation she'd endured at the hands of airport security, the kidnapping and her druggy captivity in San Antonio, her traumatic escape from the shrink and the pilot. Those events seemed like weeks ago, not days. "I ran into a few snags, but I made it in last night."

"You just got in last night? It shouldn't have taken—"

"Like I said, a few snags. I'm fine now. Ann and Cale are taking good care of me."

"I'm happy you made it okay, Lainey. I really am. I've been worried about you, hon. I miss you like never before."

She sensed genuine affection and a sincere longing in his words. An uplifting elation filled her. "God, I miss you so much, too. I can't wait to see you . . . to be with you. It's great to be able to talk to you. Where are you?"

"At the, um . . . at the mines. I'm here with Jenny."

"Give her my love. Anyone else there?"

"No, but my crew should be pulling in at any time."

"Yeah, I heard a little about that. Ann says you call them your posse."

"Yeah. Don't know what's keeping them. Shoulda been here this morning."

"I hear you were involved in a gun duel."

"Well, it wasn't really a duel. Just an opportunity to put down a loudmouthed asshole."

"So you cheated, then."

"I didn't *cheat*. I won. Mission accomplished. How is my juvenile delinquent friend Ollie anyway?"

"I haven't seen him, thankfully. But Ann tells me he's in bad shape. Apparently he's telling everyone he's going to learn to shoot with his left hand. Once he does, he's coming after you."

"Bring him on, I say."

Elaine said, "You know, love, you need to watch who you tangle with. I don't want to lose you over some silly machismo pissing contest."

He ignored her oft-repeated caution. "Just out of curiosity, what is T-Seed doing there?"

"He was working security when I arrived at the pipe last night. He's a nice young man." She saw Cale roll his eyes, then share a laugh with Ann. "Anyway, he's coming along with Ann and me. We're coming to see you, love."

There was an interminable delay and Elaine thought the connection might have dropped. Then finally Derek's voice: "Do you really think it's a good idea, E? You coming to the mines? It's a dangerous trip coming north. It's rough country. You'll need to hook two moving trains and I don't think Annie or T-Seed has ever done a sprint-and-grab before. Besides, we have some nasty business to take care of here over the next few weeks . . ."

Her heart sank as she listened to him go on listing all the reasons she shouldn't go to Utah to be with him. When he finally stopped talking, she said, "It really sounds like you don't want to see me, Der—"

She stopped in midsentence, hearing a muffled shuffling on the other end, as though he'd dropped the phone. Then she heard Jenn's voice: "Hi, Elaine—" more shuffling, irate cussing, then, "—give me that goddamned phone, Poppy! Elaine, are you still there?"

"Yes, I'm here."

"You and Ann and T-Seed come on. I can't wait to see you

guys. Poppy feels that way, too, but he's a little delirious right now . . ."

"Why's he delirious?"

"No idea, really, other than he gets all freaked out about cell phones sometimes."

Elaine grinned. "Tell me about it, girl."

"You know how to get here, right?"

"Yes."

"Well come on then. Come join Parnell's posse. Don't delay. The more the merrier."

Elaine heard a struggle ensue on the other end, a battle for control of the phone. Finally a perturbed Derek came back on the line. "Christ, E. You make things so difficult. Come if you must. But just so you know, when we disconnect, I'm trashing this phone. I want you to destroy yours, too. I don't want anyone tracking you here. That's the last thing we need right now."

Come if you must? Destroy my cell phone? Jenn is right. The man is delusional. "Do what you want with your phone, Derek, but I'm not destroying mine. We'll be leaving first thing in the morning," she said, looking at Ann, who bobbed her head and mouthed *Yes*.

"You're unbelievable, Lainey. You never listen to reason."

"Since when are *you* the voice of reason?"

"I'm just lookin' out for you, sweets."

How many times have I heard that sentiment from him?

"We've been on here long enough," he said. "I'm sure a dozen alphabet agencies know our whereabouts by now. I'm gonna end the call now. Be safe, Lainey. I love you, babe."

Her mood soared once again. "I love you, too," she said. But it was too late. He had already disconnected.

And so ended yet another strange exchange in their quirky relationship. She was in love with a temperamental, impulsive man.

In her heart of hearts, however, she wouldn't have it any other way.

Rolling Inferno

"AND NOW WE COME TO THE main attraction of Parnell's Amusement Park..."

Jenn stood inside the entrance of mineshaft #2, listening to Poppy describe his pride-and-joy thrill ride—his miniature roller coaster. Three wooden mining carts joined together by industrial railcar couplers sat on shiny steel rails. The wood looked ancient and worm-eaten. The wheels were heavy cast iron with *"Property of Hyacinth, Inc."* branded along the rims. Painted flames of fire flanked the sides of each car in blazing crimson-and-gold. The facing of the front car contained an aerodynamic design in a snappy fire motif that spelled out PARNELL'S ROLLING INFERNO.

"... and this little coaster will take you on a most fantastic hair-raising trip," Parnell went on in the booming voice of a circus impresario. "You'll travel through a mile of tunnels with so many twists and turns it'll make your head spin."

Jenn cut in on his pitch. "I've had enough hair-raising and head spinning the past few weeks."

"Oh come on. I'm offering you the ride of your life. Have some fun for once."

"Why'd you build this contraption?"

"For entertainment. Why else?"

She dragged a hand through her hair. "Whose entertainment? You told me no one other than Elaine has been here."

"That's true. Lainey's taken a few spins on the Inferno."

"But no one else?"

"Well, me. I've taken twenty rides or more."

"Really? Damn, Poppy. You're like a teenage dude."

"Why? Because I like roller coasters? I got news for you. Lots of adults are obsessed with coasters. They even have roller coaster clubs where members travel around the country riding them... at least the ones still in operation. They're serious about it. They rate them and discuss them."

Jenn smiled, amused with his childlike enthusiasm. "Maybe so. But this is different. You're all alone out here in the middle of the Utah desert. It's kinda creepy, Poppy, if I'm honest."

"Take a ride. You'll see. It's great fun."

She backed away. "I'm not gettin' in that thing."

"Don't be such a killjoy."

"I'm sure it's impressive, just like all the other stuff you've built out here. But I'm not takin' a ride. I know the truth about this thing."

"What truth?"

"I heard you designed this thing to be a killing machine. To execute John Dobkin and others who've crossed you."

"Who'd you hear that from? Lainey?"

"Yes."

"So you knew about the Rolling Inferno before I showed it to you?"

She nodded. "I'm not your little Thumbelina anymore. I would appreciate you treating me like an adult."

He put his boot up on the sideboard of the middle car, scanned her face for a long moment before saying, "You'll always be my little Thumbelina, Jenny, no matter how old you are. You'll understand that someday when you have children of your own."

She gave him a faint, appreciative smile. "Yeah, maybe."

"So since we're talking adult to adult here, Lainey told it to you straight. I built this coaster to knock off a few assholes."

Jenn looked over the three coupled cars. "A *few*? You've got twelve seats on this thing."

"Those seats are reserved for what I call my dirty dozen. At least they *were* reserved. That number has dwindled in recent years."

Parnell walked next to the cars, touching each one, looking down the tracks into the darkened tunnel, lost in thought. "When I first built the Inferno, I had this fantasy of bringing my dirty dozen to justice. I wanted to watch them all go down together, to hear them scream as they plummeted down the rails into hell. But I didn't foresee the difficulty in rounding up all twelve and getting 'em here for their final ride. I almost got the scumbag arsonists who murdered your mother. Had 'em in custody and was headed here. Unfortunately the Colorado State cops got 'em first. We maybe could've gotten Thorssen and Lars here too, but yesterday canceled them out. There were four others I had in mind over the years, but karma took care of them before I could get them. Two others I've lost track of. That leaves John Dobkin and Blanton Miles. I plan on putting both of them in the front car."

Jenn thought about this. "Let me see if I have this straight. You want me—your *daughter*—to climb inside your death machine and take a ride to hell?"

He reached out and touched her arm. "No. You misunderstand me. As is, this coaster is a thrill-ride adventure. Safe, exciting. As I said, I've been down these tracks many times. But when I get Dobkin and Miles, I'll adapt these cars for the final killing ride."

"I'm not following."

He patted the side of one of the cars lovingly. "You'll notice I used old, dry wood for these carts. For my purposes I couldn't use the coal company's steel carts. The shells had to be wood."

"Why?"

"I needed something that would burn fast and furious. It took a lot of work. I built the three cars from wood I found in the lower mines, oak planks used to bolster the walls down there. I pulled the chassis and wheels off three of the mining trolleys to give me my framework, and then secured my wooden cars to them. Bingo! The Rolling Inferno was born."

"So you're sayin' you cremate them as they ride?"

"Sort of. First thing I do is shut down the ventilation system in the tunnels. That'll build up pockets of methane gas and coal ash to dangerous levels. Then I drench the cars in gasoline and strap 'em in. I torch the cars and send 'em on their way. The first part of their ride is hot and terrifying. And then when they get into the lower tunnels and the flaming coaster hits the methane and coal dust . . . BOOM!" he slapped his hands together, startling her. "The earth trembles. The mineshafts rumble. It's Hiroshima and Nagasaki, baby! Welcome to hell, John Dobkin and Blanton Miles. Good riddance . . ."

Jenn watched him rant, his face flushed in an angry crimson. His voice was ragged and harsh, his brow set in diabolical seriousness. His eyes were aflame with a killer's bloodlust. He slapped the side of the front car to emphasize certain points, lost in his malignant, homicidal fantasy. She was terrified of him in that moment. Did he forget that she had narrowly escaped a similar explosion in the Colorado caves? Had he forgotten that her Lulu died in that same blast along with eighteen other innocent girls?

She let him finish his tirade, then said, "I have to ask you. Would sending Dobkin and Miles to fiery deaths on this coaster actually give you pleasure?"

"Like you wouldn't believe. It's all I've thought about the past three years."

"Really? That's *all* you thought about? You're tellin' me I'm not the reason you returned to the States?"

"That's what you think, Jennifer?" he said, going to her and reaching out to her. "It's not like that at all, sweetie."

She slapped his hand away. Jenn wanted to believe him, wanted it with all her being. She turned away from him, showing him her back. "I don't know anymore," she said. "I'm confused. About a lot of things."

"Of course you are," he said softly, moving behind her. He gently rubbed her shoulders. "You've been through so much, Jenny."

His strong hands felt good. His caresses to her shoulder blades and neck soothed her. She leaned back against him. "I'm doing my best to deal with things. It's just that I don't understand why you want to kill everyone who disagrees with you, Poppy. Why can't you just live and let live?"

He removed his hands and stepped back. "Shit, Jennifer. You need to toughen up. This is a desperate new world. A harsh world populated with dirtbags and clueless losers. Crooked people everywhere. Con artists who rig the system. Connected people escaping justice. The Dobkin trial should've taught you that."

She shook her head. She was having a difficult time understanding this man, a man who in his younger days had read her bedtime stories and tucked her in each night after giving her a tender goodnight kiss. A man who patiently helped her with her homework when she struggled with her studies, especially math and science. A man who'd comforted her in the middle of the night when she'd had scary nightmares. She pondered what had become of her father, the man who raised her practically single-handedly. The man standing before her with his lunatic expression and deadly roller coaster was a different man altogether.

She tried to reach him with a different approach. "Look, Poppy. I want you to know I'm extremely grateful to you for the way you've looked out for me. You searched for me even when things looked impossible. You've come to my rescue twice at great risk to yourself. Hell, if it wasn't for you I'd most likely be dead now. I get that. But I'm going to be completely straight with you. All of that creates a huge problem for me."

"How so?" he said, confused.

"I don't know of any way I can possibly repay you for what

you've done for me. I want to, but—"

"Christ, Jenny. Is that what's been eating at you?"

"Partially, yes."

"Well, get over it. We're family. I'm your father, goddammit, and you don't have to pay me back for anything. You give me your love—both the tough and gentle kind—and that's plenty for me."

"Really?"

"Yeah, *really*."

Maybe there is hope after all. She looked at him smiling at her, radiating his love for her through his serene grin. She returned his smile.

"You do seem to forget, however," he added, "that you saved my life, too. Have you forgotten?"

"What're you talking about?"

"On the trestle over the Yampa River in Colorado? When we were making our getaway from the caves and Burton Shanks went on the attack in the open boxcar?"

"I remember. What about it?"

"You yelled out a warning to me just as Shanks came at me. Razzy Jones took the thousand-foot-fall into the drink instead of me. Your warning saved my life. Don't you remember?"

She *had* forgotten that part of the horrific incident that claimed the lives of Lucious Jones and Liberty Dogs leader, Burton Shanks.

He made a move to her with arms outstretched and she willingly stepped into his embrace.

"I love you, Jenny, and no matter what happens, don't ever forget that," he said, rubbing her back.

"I love you, too, Poppy."

They held onto each other for a long moment before separating.

She said, "Lord knows I've seen enough murder and mayhem to last a lifetime. My experiences make it hard for me to understand why you seem to have a love affair with violence—" He started to object but she held up a finger. "Let me finish, please. You have your way and I have mine. I'll never be like you, Poppy, no matter how hard you try to make me that way. I couldn't possibly live the way you do."

His shoulders slumped and disappointment dulled his eyes.

Jenn felt an empathetic ache in her chest for him. How awful to go through life without hope. How dreadful to be so distrustful of everyone, to be so detached and . . . *alone* in the world.

She said, "I'm not condemning you, Poppy. I was merely pointing out our differences."

"I understand."

"Do you?"

"Yeah. I hear you loud and clear."

"Let me ask you something, Are you afraid of death?"

He frowned. "What kind of question is that?"

"An honest one. Answer it. Are you afraid of dying?"

He looked at her sharply, then said, "No, I'm not. It's the living part that gives me problems. How about you?"

"I'm fine with the living part."

"That's not what I meant."

She met his gaze. "Yes, absolutely," she said. "Most sane people are afraid of dying, Poppy."

A commotion outside in the yard interrupted their exchange. Men's muffled voices. Laughs and guffaws.

Jenn followed Poppy to the mineshaft entrance. The voices became clearer.

"Hey, Parnell. You around here somewhere? Yoo-hoo. Come out, come out wherever you are."

Weasel Bethea's voice.

Parnell smiled at her. "The posse has arrived."

Jenn followed him out. Greg Bethea, Billy Dixon, and Javion Wheeler stood in the mining yard, appearing scruffy and exhausted. All three wore sunglasses and tattered hats. She couldn't be sure from this distance and with the sun in her eyes, but it looked as though The Kid and Flywheel had splotches of blood on their shirts.

Parnell greeted them with: "I was beginning to think maybe you fools got lost or went to a strip club or something."

"Christ, Derek," Weasel said despairingly, "there are places in the Amazon rainforest easier to get to than here. The goddamned trains only run once in a blue moon."

"Bitch, bitch, bitch," Parnell said, walking out to meet them. "You guys look like shit."

"The same could be said for you, partner." Weasel Bethea clutched him in a loose hug. They clapped each other on the back then broke apart. "*You're* lookin' good, though, young lady," Weasel said to Jenn.

She waved him off. "You're an accomplished liar, Greg. But thanks."

Parnell said, "So how did things go?"

"Great," Weasel said. "Three bodies and the limo, gone from the face of the earth. It'd take expert archaeologists ten years to find any trace of any of 'em."

"What about Loretta Pesky?"

"The gypsy chick gave us some trouble, but we handled her."

"Yeah," Flywheel chimed in. "It wadn't easy. Bitch nearly clawed my eyes out. She was a helluva fighter."

Parnell shot Jenn a darting, anxious glance.

She could see now that it was definitely dried blood sprayed across their shirts. She felt sick to her stomach as the realization of what they'd done—apparently what Poppy had *instructed* them to do—sunk in.

"You *killed* her?" she exclaimed, the sick feeling intensifying. "You murdered Loretta Pesky? Jesus, God almighty!" She turned to Parnell. "You told me they were taking her back home to Sedona, that she didn't deserve to die because she helped us get the Swedes."

The three new arrivals were confused. They exchanged awkward glances, sneaked nervous looks at Parnell.

Parnell let out a heavy sigh. "I know what I said, Jenny. But we can't afford to leave loose ends. Loretta Pesky was a witness to the two murders in the barn. You and me? We were the killers, babe. You don't want to go to prison for the rest of your life, do you?"

She stared at him, speechless, her stomach churning.

"And don't forget she was bad news. She made piles of money setting up kills. She worked for Dobkin."

She looked away from him, to the men in his posse who shuffled nervously, eyes downcast, not meeting her scrutiny. She gave Parnell one last sharp look before turning and stomping away.

"Hey, Jenny, c'mon. Don't be that way," she heard Poppy say. "I'm only looking out for you. You don't want a price on your head like Lainey and me, do you?"

She walked toward the headframe structure, his voice trailing away behind her. She heard Parnell congratulating his posse for a job well done. "I've got pay for each of you. The best kind . . . tax-free cash."

She heard a round of thanks.

Then Parnell said, "You guys deserve to have a little fun. Time for a ride on my Rolling Inferno."

Superman and Captain Turnipseed

ELAINE, ANN FINNEGAN, AND Cale Turnipseed sat on the floor of an empty Union Pacific boxcar. They rode through the lush greenery of Kaibab National Forest north of the Grand Canyon near Jacob Lake. The rail line ran parallel to Arizona route 89 for long meandering miles, weaving in and out of thick woodlands and playing peekaboo with the sparse traffic. A truck hauling a load of timber motored alongside the train until it disappeared behind a curtain of trees.

Elaine sat near the open doors. Sunlight warmed her face as the scenery rushed past in a greenish blur. The rhythmic *clackety-clackety-clack* of wheels meeting track reverberated through the railcar. She glanced at Ann, who grimaced in pain, sprawled out next to Cale. Ann had taken a bad tumble while attempting the sprint-and-grab, slicing her knee open on a crosstie. Elaine had already pulled herself up and on when she saw Ann go down. It could have been disastrous, but quick-thinking Cale, running behind Ann, scooped her up without breaking stride and pushed her onboard before he hooked on. Lady Luck had been looking out for them. The train was going into a wide curve and had slowed to half speed. Lucky, too, that Ann was a petite woman. Cale had prevented a disaster and his quick reactions and athleticism impressed Elaine.

She envisioned him leaping down from the top of the aqueduct pipe when they'd met a couple of nights ago, the way he'd landed squarely and confidently on his two feet after the ten-foot drop. And now he'd performed this seemingly superhuman stunt to save Ann Finnegan. Elaine smiled as Cale's exploits brought to mind her favorite comic book hero: Superman. One of her guilty pleasures was watching the old 1950s television show starring George Reeves.

She dropped her voice into her best basso profundo announcer voice, reciting the monologue that opened that '50s show to Cale:

"Faster than a speeding bullet. More powerful than a locomotive. Able to leap tall buildings in a single bound. Look! Up in the sky! It's a bird. It's a plane. It's Superman!"

Cale and Ann looked at her as though she'd lost her mind, then erupted into laughing fits as they realized what she was doing.

Elaine decided to improvise two more lines: "But no, that caped man isn't Superman. It's the amazing, astonishing Captain Turnipseed!"

That brought on more hilarity. Cale got to his feet, mouth stretched in a wide grin, surprising her with a quip delivered in a rap-style rhyme, complete with tongue-clucking, mouth-popping percussion:

"And here on this train, Chick thinks she's Lois Lane. But the bitch ain't Lois Lane, yo, Just weird Lois E-Laine y'know!"

Elaine laughed so hard it brought tears to her eyes. She applauded him and said, "I didn't think a white boy Bavarian Native American Confederate hobo could rap so authentically."

He did a little hip-hop shuffle and bent over in a deep bow. "Street poetry from the 'hood ain't my only skill, yo!"

"You should hear him when he *really* gets rolling," Ann said from the shadows.

Cale nodded. "Yeah, I'm Kanye, Wiz Khalifa, Dr. Dre, and Fetty Wap all rolled into one. Maybe a little Diddy and Snoop Dogg, too."

Ann said, "I don't think Flywheel and his crew would agree with that."

"Flywheel?" Elaine said. "You mean Javion Wheeler? The man in Derek's posse?"

"Yes. Flywheel and his bunch don't care for Caucasian rap," Ann said. "They say it's unnatural and sacrilegious."

"Yo, they just a buncha jealous jive shucks who don't know ghetto pro when they eyeball it," Cale said, miming dropping his make-believe microphone and plopping down next to Ann.

Elaine hadn't laughed this much in ages. Soon, however, her thoughts returned to their reality.

"How's it going over there, guys?" she yelled above the rattle and clank.

Cale answered. "She's hurting but she just took a couple more painkillers. Luckily the bleeding stopped and nothin's broken. So far no infection."

"I'll make it," Ann said through gritted teeth.

Ann, being the camp doctor, had brought along a supply of Percocet and antibacterial ointment, which was fortunate. A bigger worry, however, was how they would get her off the train. She certainly couldn't jump from a moving train with her knee knotted up and sliced open. If they had to wait until this route was complete for the freighter to stop in a switching yard, no telling how far north of the Hyacinth mines they would end up. This train could run all the way to Provo or even Salt Lake City before stopping.

She reached into her backpack and pulled out her cell, tried to connect with Derek to give him a heads-up. No luck. Out of service. Apparently he'd made good on his promise to destroy his burner phone.

She cursed her poor luck. Very little had gone right since she left Costa Rica. *Why oh why did I ever attempt this impossible journey? I can't blame Derek for being ticked off at me. Shit, shit, shit!*

The train climbed to higher elevations. A chilly wind whipped at her. She grabbed a sweatshirt from her bag and put it on, knowing the heat would return once they hit the Utah desert. She had always liked the extreme shifts in climate and terrain in this part of the country. The changes in topology and temperature could be sudden and dramatic. She appreciated those variations much more now after having lived on the beach in Costa Rica for three years.

She inhaled the mountain air, her lungs filling with the sweet scent of spruce and pine. Clusters of bitterbrush and cliffrose interspersed with stands of golden yellow aspen reminded Elaine of her house in Flagstaff nestled in the foothills of the San Francisco Mountains. The sights and smells here brought on a longing for home she thought she had outgrown. Her thoughts swung to her sister Gina, wondering if she and Frank were really planning to leave her house and move back east.

They entered an open prairie where a herd of bison grazed. "Guys, take a look at this" she yelled to Cale and Ann. "There must be a hundred of them."

"Wow, cool," Cale said, getting to his feet and coming to get a closer look. "Man, they're huge."

Elaine checked out Cale from where she sat. He stood in the opening, his hand gripping the door handle, shock of dark hair flapping in the wind. She liked the way he marveled at the enormous horned beasts dotting the grasslands. With his prominent cheekbones, muscular athletic build, and endearing smile that was as quick as his wit, she thought he would make quite a catch for some young girl. *In fact, if it wasn't for Derek . . .*

"I'd hate to have one of those things come after me," he said, interrupting her erotic fantasy.

She smiled. "You especially wouldn't want that right now."

"What're you talkin' about?"

She put on her naughtiest face. "Because it's rutting season."

He tried to decipher her expression. "Rutting season? Yeah, right. Next you'll be telling me they shit golden road apples."

"Such language, Cale," Ann croaked.

Elaine said, "I swear to you, for once I'm not goofing on you. It's true. Late August through mid-September. That's horny time for American bison. You can look it up."

Cale laughed, free and easy, returning to his spot along the wall next to Ann. "I knew there was a reason I wanted to hang with you, Lois E-Laine."

Elaine went back to staring out the open doors, taking in the rustic beauty of the northern Arizona landscape. *Almost to the Utah border and still no plan for getting Ann off this train.* She began mapping debarkation possibilities in her head when she noticed a car on route 89, keeping pace with the train.

A raspberry-red Honda CR-V.

She thought it might be the same car she'd seen ten or twenty miles back, but couldn't be sure. Nonetheless, something about the vehicle set off her creepiness detector.

The train entered a canopy of trees, which cut off her view. Coming out the other side, she saw the Honda right there, keeping pace. Her alarm increased and she tried to quash it with reasoning. *Where else are they going to go, girlfriend? There are no exits on this stretch of interstate 89.*

The rail line swung wide, going around a high-crested bluff. She lost sight of the car again. But then, on the far side, road and tracks came back together, closer now, maybe fifty yards apart. Elaine saw sunlight flash off the tinted passenger-side window. The window came down. A man riding shotgun peered through binoculars.

He's scoping the train!

The road curved in closer to the train. Maybe thirty yards separated them now.

No other cars in sight.

The man wasn't holding binoculars, but rather a camera with a bulky telephoto lens. A black glass eye pointed directly at her.

Two men in a late-model Honda CR-V were following the train and snapping pictures of them. No mistaking it.

Why? Who are they?

Elaine held back a scream. She was freaked but didn't want to panic Cale and Ann.

Adrenaline zipped through her. Her heart pounded in her ears like a bass drum. She scooted back from the opening, behind the protective steel wall. Peeked around the wall, trying to pick up a plate number, careful not to expose herself. The driver stayed with the train, remaining directly parallel. No way for her to see the tag plate from this angle.

She looked back at her fellow travelers. Both appeared to be napping. She saw Cale's rifle propped against the wall next to him, sheathed in the shoulder carry bag. She thought about crawling across the floor to get it, but realized that would be foolish. She'd be exposed, an easy target. Then she remembered Diego's gun in her backpack. But just as quickly she rejected the idea. Getting into a shootout with a pistol trying to hit a car doing sixty miles an hour from a moving train seemed ludicrous.

She would just have to ride this out.

She blew out an exasperated breath and leaned back against the wall.

What else could possibly go wrong on this trip?

Too bad there wasn't a real Superman to save the day.

Part 3:

KINGDOM OF PUPPETS

PuppetMaster Central
Coasters and Crushers
Railside Reunion
Tunnel of Love
Satan's Wings
The Caveman's Desire
Elaine Sees a Ghost
Till Death Do Us Part
Operation Vagabond
In Memory of Luanne
Conquistador's Folly
Animal Chatter
Preparing For War
Remember the Alamo

PuppetMaster Central

HE PLUCKED THE FIRST SHEET off the printer and read with great interest.

> TIME: 16:22 PST
> FROM: Running Coyote
> TO: PuppetMaster
>
> These pics taken near Jacob Lake off Az. 89 today, early PM. Subject (Lady Cyclops) and two others (unidentified male and female) on UP train headed north. We picked them up west of Flagstaff where they transferred from BNSF to UP line. Unknown female hurt during transfer (photo included). Extent of injuries unknown. Subject lost after crossing Utah border. Request transfer of coverage to Utah agent(s).

The printer spit out the photos, crisp color shots of Lady Cyclops and her traveling party. He scanned them. Definitely her. No mistaking it. Several clear shots of her companions, a pair of shabby young hobos.

But why Utah? Is that where Lone Wolf and Little Tombstone disappeared to? He'd get eyes and ears in that area right away.

He smiled and leaned back in his leather recliner, watching activity flash across two banks of screens arrayed in front of him.

Things had heated up the past week. It was all finally coming together. He was jazzed, felt the old excitement returning. Three long years he'd waited for things to break, at times thinking Hyena would fire him, or worse, for his lack of progress. But Hyena was a patient and careful man, loyal to those in whom he placed his confidence.

Their primary target was Lone Wolf, who escaped their containment three years ago and gone dark. The man had gone so far underground, nobody knew if he was still alive until last week. There had been numerous rumors of his whereabouts, especially in the weeks leading up to the trial. But none of them panned out. Lone Wolf's ability to dodge their net frustrated PuppetMaster.

Two months ago, he'd devised a trap baited with something he knew would be irresistible to Lone Wolf: Lone Wolf's daughter (code name: Little Tombstone). The ploy worked, bringing Lone Wolf back into their fold and earning Hyena's effusive praise.

PuppetMaster's federal informants led him to where WITSEC had relocated Little Tombstone and her boyfriend (code name: Squeaky Wheel)—Vancouver, British Columbia. He knew it would be risky to go after them on foreign soil, so he had an operative scare them out of their safe house. He'd then manipulated Little Tombstone and Squeaky Wheel to Denver, arranging to have the young couple meet with one of his cut-outs. The cut-out agent had been at the Liberty Dogs compound in the Colorado Rockies at the same time as Squeaky Wheel, and had developed a brief friendship with him. So the meet was easily arranged. Platinum Goliath took it from there. The big Swede followed his instructions like a Boy Scout, performing the hit on Squeaky Wheel at Gilberti's Italian Restaurant without harming the girl. Squeaky Wheel went down hard and Little Tombstone ran for her life, straight to her father as hoped.

Their first sighting of Lone Wolf was with Little Tombstone in Sedona at Tipsy Gypsy's place of business. The northern Arizona agent, Crazy Horse, tailed the fortuneteller's Rolls-Royce from Sedona to Winslow, then tracked the three of them to the hobo village when they left the Rolls in a Winslow parking deck.

And then Lady Cyclops entered the scene. Another of PuppetMaster's operatives—Conquistador in San Antonio—had people casing the Mexican airports and border crossings. Two of his men picked her up at the Monterrey airport and brought her to San Antonio, where Conquistador interrogated her. He'd copped her cell phone and they'd run the number through their CCSS7 hacker network, which enabled them to pull copies of everything from Lady Cyclops's cell (phone logs, recordings of calls, transcripts of saved text messages, photos, contact data). PuppetMaster was pleased. The information gleaned from the phone was invaluable. But Conquistador had done something stupid. He'd tried to get frisky with Lady Cyclops in a Winslow hotel room and she had outfoxed them, escaping.

He accessed a file downloaded from Lady Cyclops's phone. All indications were that she was on her way to meet Lone Wolf.

The chance of netting Lone Wolf, Little Tombstone, and Lady Cyclops in a single sweep loomed large. The perfect trifecta. They would finally eliminate all of Hyena's loose ends from the trial.

PuppetMaster turned his attention to the nearest monitor. More information coming in from Cottonwood. They'd tracked Lone Wolf and Little Tombstone to an abandoned barn on a foreclosed ranch by way of the GPS device Crazy Horse had attached to Tipsy Gypsy's Rolls in the Winslow parking deck. Crazy Horse's inspection of the barn revealed slugs buried deep in two walls, a pair of shell casings, and spots of dried blood in the dirt. No bodies found. Evidence that at least two vehicles had been there recently.

An incoming e-mail flashed on another screen:

TIME: 17:46 PST
FROM: Golden Bear
TO: PuppetMaster
SUBJECT: RE: Thor and Goliath Watch

Unable to establish contact with Lady Thor or Platinum Goliath past 48 hours. Limo service informs us Thor limo not returned to garage same timeframe. Attempts to reach Chauffeur-1 negative as well. Awaiting further instructions.

PuppetMaster rose from his chair and paced through his cluttered office. He feared the worst. Thor, Goliath, and their driver, all missing for two days. And the scene at the Cottonwood barn? *Did Lone Wolf capture his prey there and take them somewhere? Did he kill them? Is Tipsy Gypsy involved?*

Lady Thor had been doing more work off the books lately, going rogue, looking for a bigger cut of the action. PuppetMaster hadn't worked with her recently. Per Hyena's demands, he'd hired Platinum Goliath for the Squeaky Wheel hit without going through Thor as was usual protocol. He'd used Tipsy Gypsy as the go-between on that job. Had Thor and Goliath finally jumped in over their heads? Had they been reckless? Too greedy?

He sat at his console and pulled the keyboard close. Time to send out some communiqués.

They were zeroing in on Lone Wolf.

Just a matter of time before they flushed him out.

Coasters and Crushers

A CHILL FROSTED THE NIGHT AIR. Parnell, Jenn, Weasel Bethea, Billy Dixon, and Javion Wheeler sat in the mining yard, roasting their skewers of meat, onions, and carrots over an open fire. A cooler full of beer sat close by. Overhead the big sky dazzled, splashed with a million stars and a fat orange moon.

"Hyacinth, huh?" Weasel said. "You're telling me this coal mining outfit named their company after a *flower*? Little wonder they went out of business."

Parnell bit off a chunk of meat. "It wasn't named after a flower," he said, chewing. "It's a family name. And they didn't go under. They're doing quite nicely. Two uranium mines up near Moab and a silver mine in Colorado."

The Kid took a slug of beer and wiped his mouth. "Uranium and silver, eh? Corporate pigs can't get fat on coal anymore?"

"Oh, they can, yeah, with above-ground strip mining," Parnell said. "But most underground operations like this one are losin' money. Too much overhead. At least for coal. Coal's a common commodity. Uranium and silver are more scarce. Uranium's dangerous to handle. Less competition."

Flywheel said, "Uranium. Lemme guess. Guvmint's payin' top dollar for warhead materials."

"You got it, Fly," Parnell said. "Millions of folks're starvin' and homeless, but Uncle Sam keeps printing money to pay for atomic rocks. Gotta keep those nuclear subs afloat. Gotta keep those silos stocked with missiles."

Silence ensued. The fire crackled and popped. Sparks spiraled upward, floating into the night sky. A cool desert breeze whispered across the site.

Parnell stared into the fire as he enjoyed his meal. The talk of uranium got him thinking about John Dobkin and Blanton Miles and the way they had set him up as the fall guy for the takedown of Burton Shanks and the Liberty Dogs in Colorado. They'd devised a fake suitcase nuke for him to deliver to Shanks, a nuke the Liberty Dogs were allegedly going to use in an act of domestic terrorism. In exchange, Parnell was to get his daughter back.

His thoughts carried him back to the days leading up to that exchange. He'd studied up on enriched, weapons-grade uranium, neutron generators, plutonium, and other technical concepts of mobile nuclear weaponry so he would be able to pass himself off as knowledgeable. *Was that really only three years ago?* It all seemed so audacious and impossible to him now. Somehow he'd pulled it off, thanks to Lucious Razzy Jones, who'd accompanied him on the crazy mission, posing as a veteran arms dealer. In the end, however, the fake suitcase nuke was a live bomb that Dobkin's people detonated remotely, destroying the Liberty Dogs' Colorado munitions bunker and killing 47 people.

He looked across the fire at Jenn, who sat by herself, blanket draped over her shoulders, her face a joyless mask as she picked at her kebob with indifference. She continued to stew over his latest transgression, unable to forgive him for lying about their handling of Loretta Pesky. Truth was, he'd planned all along to have Madame Crystal knocked off. It was the *only* thing to do. He knew damn well they couldn't leave a witness to three murders behind.

Why can't I be honest with Jenny? Why is it so hard for me to relate to her?

Yesterday he'd attempted to win her back, but the result was disastrous. He'd paid the three men in his posse and they had gone to Kanab in the jeep to spend some of their hard-earned cash. Shortly after they left, Parnell handed her a pack of banded hundred-dollar bills.

"What's this?" she'd said, staring at the cash in her hands as if it were poisonous contraband.

"What's it look like? It's your pay. You're part of this posse."

"You're paying me for *murdering* someone?" she said, offended. "You're no better than Loretta Pesky! Take it back. I don't want it. It's dirty."

She waved the bills in his face and he couldn't hide his annoyance. "What the hell is wrong with you? I do something nice for you and you rip into me. What is it? You can't handle it when someone shows you a little kindness?"

She threw the cash at his feet. The bundle broke apart. Bills blew across the sand. "You think you can buy my love with money?" she shouted. "Mom tried that. It doesn't work with me."

"Damn, Jennifer," he said, bending down to gather up the cash. "First you equate me with a gypsy con artist, then with your mother. I deserve better than that."

"Do you?"

"Yeah, I believe I do," he said, straightening, glad they were alone, that the others weren't around to see this miserable exchange. He stuffed the money in her pants pocket. "That's for you, whether you want it or not."

He was walking away when he heard her say, "And just what am I supposed to do with it?"

"Buy something nice for yourself," he said without breaking stride.

"How? Where? This place isn't exactly Bloomingdales or Saks."

He came to an abrupt halt and turned, faced her. "Well then, maybe you can buy yourself a little gratitude."

"That's not something you can buy," she said, her voice a flutter of runaway emotions.

He stared her down. "Well, *there's* something we can both agree on," he said before trudging away.

Last night Jenny refused to sleep down in his mineshaft room, electing instead to spend the night in the headframe structure where she battled the cold and insomnia. "I've spent a third of my life living in caves and I won't spend another night sleeping in one," she had complained. He let her have her way, but ordered Weasel to stay above ground with her. He didn't sleep much himself for worrying about her.

Yesterday's friction carried over into today on their two trips to Kanab to pick up food and supplies. Jenny didn't want to go, but he insisted she accompany him with hopes they could work things out. The rides were silent, awkward affairs, the only real conversation being about Elaine. Jenny wanted to know, since they were out in the jeep, why they weren't looking for Elaine and Ann? They should have been here yesterday, she said. Wasn't he worried about them? Didn't he care about Elaine?

Jenny's continual reproaches exhausted him. He'd purchased another throwaway phone in Kanab in an attempt to reach Elaine. Unfortunately, no pickup or voicemail. Just dead air. Had she destroyed her phone? Was she out of cell tower range? Something more sinister at work? He also tried Ann's number with the same result. He promised Jenny that if Elaine didn't show by tomorrow afternoon, he'd lead a search party out to find them.

Flywheel's voice brought him back to the present. "This place is the bomb, Derek. Even better than Shangri-La."

"Yeah," Kid agreed. "Your coaster's got big balls."

"Thanks, Kid," he said proudly.

Jenny rolled her eyes.

Weasel said, "I agree. I've done some coaster cruising in my days and I gotta tell you, Derek, your Rollin' Inferno blows away the best of 'em . . . the Bizarro or the Nitro or Apollo's Chariot . . . the Inferno tops 'em all. How 'bout we take another spin on it after dinner?"

"No way. You guys've had too much beef and booze. I don't want you pukin' in my coaster. Besides, we have business to discuss."

Parnell told them the same thing he told Jenn yesterday. He built the Rolling Inferno initially to serve as an execution machine for his wife's murderers, then to fry John Dobkin and Blanton Miles when he captured them.

Weasel said, "It's a shame you have to destroy your great thrill ride for two creeps like them. Seems like a waste of brilliant mechanical engineering."

Parnell made an A-OK sign with his thumb and forefinger. "Easy enough to build another coaster, Greg. An even better one."

Kid said, "You're sayin' there'll be a big bang down in the tunnels?"

"Yep. Fire meets methane and coal dust . . . an explosive combination. It's a three-step process: Strap 'em in, light 'em up, and turn 'em loose. I want Dobkin and Miles in the front car. They deserve the best seats in the house."

"Cool, man," Flywheel said eagerly. "Let's go get 'em right now!"

"Hold on, Fly. It's not that easy."

He briefed them on John Dobkin and the reasons they had to be cautious in their attempts to apprehend him. Parnell's research revealed that Dobkin had moved his operations out of the Las Vegas Bellagio penthouse and into a palatial mansion in the suburb of Henderson, near Sloan Canyon. Dobkin had designed the house and had it built to his specs, which emphasized privacy and security in addition to luxury. A twenty-foot-high electrified fence surrounded the twenty-acre property. A gatehouse with a thirty-foot gate spanned the front entrance and was manned by a high-priced security team who patrolled the grounds 24/7. The security team was top-drawer with most of the officers being ex-Vegas police or Nevada State cops. It wouldn't be easy getting at

Dobkin. They were going to have to exercise patience and creativity to abduct him.

"Grab another beer, guys," he continued. "There's more about Dobkin. The man is seriously connected. Before he came out west he spent a dozen years working in the Office of Naval Intelligence in Bethesda. His bosses were rear admiral directors, high-ranking military types with close ties to Beltway politics, and all the graft and corruption that goes with it. His duties got him top security clearance where he was able to make contacts within the NSA and CIA. Dobkin started compiling dossiers on anyone and everyone he thought might make a difference, and he has used those contacts very much to his advantage."

"What about the other dude?" Flywheel said. "Blanton Miles?"

"He won't be so easy to find. Even when he supposedly worked for me, I never knew where he was. All of our communications were by phone. Miles is one of Dobkin's top lieutenants and he's definitely the sharpest knife in the drawer. He's mobile and elusive. They used to call him the ghost agent. He's like smoke in the night. You can smell him and you can feel his presence. You know he's there, but you can't see him. Since we know where Dobkin is, we start with him. We get Dobkin and he'll lead us to Blanton Miles."

Flywheel got up and went to the cooler, grabbed beers for himself and Kid. "So how're we gonna get to Dobkin, with all that security around him?" he asked, returning to his spot near the fire and handing a beer to Dixon.

"Good question," Parnell said. "I want you and Kid to find an answer." He looked at Weasel. "Greg, I want you to take the jeep first thing tomorrow morning and drive Fly and Kid to Vegas. Take them to some out-of-the-way car rental place and rent a nondescript vehicle for a week under an assumed name. Pay cash, of course. Make it a comfortable car because you'll basically be living out of it. I don't want you guys getting hotel rooms. Got it?"

"Yeah," Flywheel said. Dixon nodded.

"And absolutely no casinos or titty bars. Any drinkin' and druggin' you want to do, get it out of your systems tonight. I want you guys to spend the next four days casing out the Dobkin place. I want eagle eyes on the property round the clock. I want to know when and how Dobkin comes and goes. I want to know where he goes when he leaves. I want an hourly journal of all activities on the grounds there, including security patrolling schedules. I want you to come back with recommendations on how we can capture Dobkin and get him back here with the least amount of hassle. Understood?"

"Sounds good, boss," Kid said.

"Ditto for me," Flywheel agreed.

"You're going to need some surveillance gear—top of the line cameras with powerful zooms, a non-glare day cam, a night-vision camera, high-end listening devices . . . say a bionic ear with an amplification booster and a parabolic microphone. You'll need headphones to monitor audio and a DVR unit to capture all incoming video and audio. You'll probably also need a few good GPS units to track vehicle movement. Again, just as a reminder but it bears repeating. Do not, I repeat, *do not* purchase a laptop or phone or any kind of device that provides Wi-Fi service. If you do, you might as well paint bulls-eyes on your backs. These people we're dealing with are technologically savvy. And don't buy all the equipment in one place. Spread out your purchases. There are several good surveillance equipment stores in and around Vegas. Lots of observation and people-watching goes on there. They call it Sin City for good reason."

Flywheel said, "No disrespect, Derek, but we don't know shit about all this technology stuff."

"Yeah," Kid chimed in. "I wouldn't know where to begin."

"I've got it all written down . . . addresses of retail shops, model names and numbers of surveillance devices. The models I recommend come with easy-to-follow documentation. I'll give you the cash you need. I want you guys focused, with an eye on the prize at all times. You'll be rewarded nicely upon your return."

Weasel seemed concerned, saying, "These guys make good points, Derek. I'm not sure sending two techie novices on this assignment is the best way to do it. You're well versed with all this surveillance equipment, how to use it, where to buy it. Why not go yourself?"

"Because Dobkin and several of his associates could identify me on sight. They know Jenny, too. My cover would be blown in a heartbeat. Plus, in case you've forgotten, I'm on the FBI Most Wanted List. Lots of folks are after me."

"Fair enough," Weasel said before tipping his head back and chugging a mouthful of beer.

Parnell said, "After you drop them at the car rental, you head back. We need the jeep here."

"How far is it to Vegas?"

"A little more than two-hundred miles. Much of it's interstate highway, an easy drive. But it'll be a long day."

"What about the other jeep?" Weasel said. "Can we get it running?"

"No. I've tried. The transmission is shot."

Kid said, "Does any of this other shit work? Man, it's always been a dream of mine to drive a dump truck as big as that one," he said, pointing at the titanic haul truck that gleamed in the firelight.

Flywheel laughed. "Dude, you dream really small."

"Ain't nothin' small about that truck, Fly."

Flywheel took a swig of his beer. "I'm just sayin' your dreams are kinda microscopic, Billy. Dreamin's fer big things."

"So what would you call a big dream?"

Flywheel ran a hand through his bushy 'fro, thinking, then pointed at the pair of rock-crusher machines. "I dream we get that Dobkin motherfucker back here and crunch him up into tiny pieces in that bone-crusher thing fulla teeth."

Parnell couldn't help but smile. "Now you're talking!"

Railside Reunion

AT THE BREAK OF DAWN, Bethea, Dixon, and Wheeler left for Las Vegas. An eerie quiet had settled over the mining yard. Jenn slept in the headframe structure and Parnell was up on the ridge, cleaning sand and bird crap off the solar panels before the day's heat became too intense. He'd been working for thirty minutes when he heard Jenn's shouts from below.

"Poppy! Poppy! Come quick!"

He raced to the edge of the promontory and looked down, out across the yard, saw Jenn running toward something hidden from his view. He threw his towel and spray bottle aside and grabbed his gun, quickly descended the ladder. His legs were shaky as he headed down the meandering path.

He ran into the middle of the yard, past the smoldering pile of charred wood from last night's fire. The smoky smell tickled his nose with a barbecue scent. He trotted in the direction of Jenn's voice, moving through the mining site entrance and coming to the rail spur.

Elaine stood there, appearing dazed and weary. A rush of emotion caught in his throat as an overpowering sense of elation filled him. She wore her black eyepatch, frayed jeans ripped in the knees, filthy tank top. Her hair was a rat's nest. But to his eyes she was more ravishing than ever. A vision from a sexy dream. Annie Finnegan, obviously favoring one leg and grimacing in pain, leaned against her, with T-Seed propping Annie up on the other side.

Jenn ran to Elaine and hugged her, shooting rapid-fire questions at her in a breathless voice. Lainey smiled tiredly and wrapped her free arm around Jenn while struggling to maintain her grasp on Annie.

Parnell peered down the tracks to where the rails disappeared behind a bluff. He spotted what looked to be a green, late-model Toyota Camry. His first thought was: *Please tell me they didn't steal a car. Or even worse, rent one.* The easiest way to track someone was over the road.

He kicked into a full sprint, seeing as he got closer that

Annie's knee was a dark purplish blob that looked like a grapefruit gone bad.

Elaine kissed Jenn's cheek and broke away from her, came to Parnell with her arms wide open. The vision of Lainey rushing to him with her long, rangy strides and welcoming smile inflated him. Her eager smile was the sweetest thing he'd ever seen. The only woman he'd ever truly loved was safe. They were together again. Nine days apart had felt like nine *years*.

They came together in a crashing, body-bashing collision of unbridled passion. They hugged and kissed and squeezed and grabbed and fondled with such ardor they tumbled into the hot sand. They giggled like carefree teenagers. They cried sloppy tears of joy. They kissed and clutched and clasped and squeezed as they rolled through the sand as one, holding on, laughing as they spun and slid. Over and over they went, unable to get enough of each other. Lainey's kisses tasted sweet. Her touch electrified him.

When they rolled to a stop Jenn said, "Wouldn't it be ironic if after all this, they killed each other right here and now?"

Everyone laughed.

Down on the ground, still wrapped around each other, Parnell felt the tickle of Lainey's whisper in his ear. "Don't ever leave me like that again, old man."

He grinned into her shoulder and pulled her closer. "No worries, milady," he murmured. "You're stuck with me forever."

"I'd better be."

"I've missed the hell out of you, E. I love you, babe."

"I must be crazy, but I love you, too, Derek."

Jenn said, "Maybe you two should get a room."

That got Annie and T-Seed laughing again.

Parnell looked up from where he lay beneath Elaine in the hot sand. *My daughter the comedienne. It's good to see her beaming face again.*

He and Elaine got to their feet, brushed themselves off. He looked at Annie and Cale Turnipseed and said, "Welcome to the eternally dysfunctional Parnell family."

Tunnel of Love

THE MEMORIES CAME RUSHING BACK to Elaine. The dark, dank mine entrance smelling of shale dust, creosote, and old wood; the short drop down the squeaky tracks in the mining cart; the solid, preternatural quiet of Derek's rock-walled living space where miners once gouged out tons of coal.

They lounged side by side on Derek's mattress. She filled him in on Ann's injury and the circuitous route they'd had to take to get here. Their freighter had traveled north to Gunnison—two-hundred miles out of their way—before stopping, allowing them to get Ann safely off. Ann's knee had swollen to frightening proportions and she couldn't walk far without immense pain.

"Lucky for us, she brought a good supply of Percocet," Elaine said. "In the Gunnison switching yards, we pumped her full of drugs. Only way we could get her on a bus. Trailways brought us south to Kanab where we rented the Camry."

"I knew Annie would be a problem. I just knew it."

"Relax." She rubbed his arm. "Ann's been very good to Jennifer. She's treated me well, too."

"What about T-Seed? How'd he get involved in all this?"

"Ann wanted him along for protection."

"Protection? What's he gonna do, talk your attackers to death?"

She grinned. "Cale is certainly chatty. But Ann might be dead right now if it wasn't for him. He's good people, Derek." She recounted Cale's trackside superhero exploits and Parnell listened attentively. "You know, Cale's hurt you didn't pick him for your posse," she said.

"That's why I passed on him. Too sensitive."

"But he idolizes you."

"Yet another reason why I passed."

She sighed. "You know, Derek, this world could use a little more sensitivity."

He pulled her closer and began caressing her breast, tweaking her nipple through the thin fabric of her shirt. "How does this sensitivity feel, E?"

"Wonderful. Oh, God . . . absolutely . . . *delicious*."

He nuzzled her neck, his breath warm against her skin. His fingers fluttered down her stomach as he slipped his hand between her legs and rubbed her mound through her tight jeans.

Oh, my . . .

She closed her eyes, relishing the feel of his fingers working her down below, his hand teasing, tantalizing.

He tugged at her zipper, his breaths coming harder and faster in her ear.

His erection poked her thigh, straining to escape his pants. She reached down and touched it through the rough cotton material, felt him respond. She ran a finger up the shaft and circled the swollen head, teasing him. Squeezed gently. Heard him moan.

He unbuttoned her jeans, snaked two fingers under the elastic band of her panties and worked his way to her sweet spot. Found her clit and teased it, moving his hand in a circular motion.

Oh, sweet Jesus . . . I'm . . . so . . . wet!

And then thoughts of her personal hygiene intruded. Against her will she reached down and grabbed his wrist. "I've got three days' hobo stink on me," she said, the words difficult to get out.

"So do I. So what?" he panted, shaking off her hand and continuing with his seduction. "Just go with it, E. A little ripeness heightens the experience."

His assurance relaxed her. Heat rose to her face, inflamed her mind. She whispered crude, raunchy sentiments in his ear, knowing how much her vulgarity turned him on.

He tugged off her jeans and panties and went down on her. She gasped loudly as his head bobbed between her legs, his whiskery cheeks rubbing her thighs, his lips and tongue working their wet magic.

"Stop, babe," she croaked.

"What?" he said, raising his head, confused, eyes glazed, mouth and chin glistening. "What's wrong?"

"Absolutely nothing," she uttered, her body trembling. She got to her knees with great difficulty. "Get those clothes off," she commanded. "I want you inside me. Now! I want you to fill me up!"

Her hands shaky, she helped him strip off his shirt and pants, removed his underwear. She lay down, stroking him, guiding him, letting out a delirious moan as he entered her.

Oh, my fucking word, it's been so long!

He pumped and bucked. She moaned loudly and called out his name with each deep thrust, their rocking and plunging sliding the grimy mattress halfway off the mining cart chassis that served as the box spring.

Each stabbing push of his hips made the ticklish pleasure nearly unbearable.

So beautiful! I'm about to . . . oh, I'm . . . so . . . CLOSE . . .

She wanted to hold back, to wait for him, but the dam was about to burst.

He rode her hard, his face and shoulders shiny with sweat.

He bucked one last time and shuddered. "I'm gonna come!"

He erupted inside her, his body convulsing spasmodically, his fingers digging into her shoulders.

His climax sent her over the edge. She gasped as orgasmic waves rushed through her. Her body trembled in jittery tremors.

He rolled off of her with a satisfied sigh.

They lay side by side, drenched and drained, trying to catch their runaway breaths.

When her breathing slowed, she spoke in a hoarse whisper. "That was so awesome, Derek. I love you, babe."

He answered with a rip-snorting snore.

Satan's Wings

POPPY AND ELAINE HAD DISAPPEARED belowground and Ann Finnegan slept through Percocet dreams in the headframe structure. Jenn was alone with Cale Turnipseed, or T-Seed as everyone called him.

She and Cale strolled through the yard, walking between the silent mining machines. Cale chattered nervously and Jenn tried to absorb his rambling thoughts.

"Are you afraid of me?" he said, stopping next to the big haul truck, the massive tires dwarfing him.

Jenn let out a huffy chuckle. "Why would I be afraid of you?"

"I don't know. Just seems like you are. You keep your distance and every time I say somethin' you look . . . *afraid*. Like I'm about to attack you."

He really thinks I fear him? That's hilarious.

Her sarcastic impulse kicked in. "What'd you have in mind? Maybe us takin' a romantic stroll, holding hands, stoppin' to share a kiss every once in a while? Maybe hookin' up in the shade?"

His face reddened. He didn't know what to do with his hands. "Oh, I'm, uh . . . I'm really sorry. I didn't mean to—"

"Hey, it's okay." She realized her words had stung him. Unbelievable. A sincere, thoughtful man. A rare quality in male breezers these days. Most of them were macho fools. "I'm the one who should apologize," she said. "I'm not used to men treating me with kindness. Thank you, Cale."

He blushed again.

She spoke to relieve his awkwardness. "Elaine told me all about the heroic stunt you pulled off out on the rails. The one that saved Ann. Said she christened you Captain Turnipseed."

"Oh, my God. She told you that?"

"Yeah."

"Well, it was just my instincts takin' over. Nothin' heroic about it. Your dad's the true hero."

"I don't know about that. Poppy's just a regular screwed-up human bein' like the rest of us."

"He looks out for the little guy . . . for all of us down-and-outers. We need more like him."

"That's debatable."

"I thought you two were close."

"I'm discovering that we barely know each other."

Cale looked at her hesitantly, appearing to struggle with something.

"What is it?" she asked.

"Well, I don't know if I should go there—"

"Come on, out with it."

"Okay. Well, I know you and your dad spent many years apart. I heard all about your time in captivity with those creeps in Colorado. That lunatic fringe bunch."

"Where'd you hear that?"

"You sure you wanna know?"

"Yeah, I do."

He sighed. "Okay, here goes," he said hesitantly. "After you showed up at Shangri-La, the stories about you spread like wildfire. Once information gets on the hobo hotline, it's community knowledge. I don't believe much of it myself. A lot of it seems so outrageous. Grotesque."

She gave him a probing stare.

"Oh, I don't mean to imply anything negative by it," he said, flustered. "I mean, well . . . I know some folks thought . . . Oh, hell, I don't know what I'm tryin' to say, Jenn."

She threw her head back and laughed. "You're really cute when you struggle to be honest."

He turned away, embarrassed.

"It's not any big deal, Cale. I know what I am and what I'm not. I don't have any shame about the things I did in those caves. No guilt whatsoever. I did the things I did to survive. Period."

"Hey, I'm sorry, all right? I didn't mean suggest anything or to judge you—"

"It's all right. I don't give a damn what people think. I learned at the trial that the truth rarely matters."

"Yeah, I heard about that, too. The jury acquitted that asshole your father is after. Him an' all his cronies. Then they . . ." He hesitated, looking unsure.

"Go on, you can say it, Cale. Then they murdered my partner, Russ."

"I thought he was your husband."

"No, we weren't married. We talked about it. I loved Russell so much, but . . ." Her eyes misted up.

"Hey, I didn't mean to dredge up bad memories for you, Jenn. I'm sorry."

"Quit apologizing," she said, wiping her eyes. "You haven't done anything wrong."

"Okay, right, yeah. I just want to say that even though we don't know each other, any kin of Derek Parnell is a friend of mine. Anytime you need to talk, about anything, you can come to me. I know I'm a chatterbox, but I'm a really good listener, too. You can trust me, Jenn."

She smiled at him. "I appreciate that, Cale. I really do."

She heard a droning noise in the distance and turned her head in that direction. "You hear that?" she said.

"Yeah, what is it?"

"Don't know."

The noise increased in volume. A motor of some type. They looked at each other, silently questioning, waiting. The buzzing engine sound got louder. Jenn thought: *A car? Dune buggy? Drone?*

Thirty seconds later a small airplane flew into view, its wings reflecting the sunlight. Single propeller engine. Blue and white with red striping. Three-wheel landing gear. Windshield tinted a deep charcoal. It came in low, flying just above the top of the ridge that enclosed the mining yard. So close Jenn could make out the registration number on the fuselage. The plane passed over, buffeted by crosswinds, engine buzzing, propeller cutting the air, then swooped upward and disappeared beyond the far peak where Poppy's solar panels were located.

"That was weird," Cale muttered.

"Yeah, *weird*," Jenn said, wondering why a private plane would come in so low over the basin. This place was so far out in the middle of nowhere it might as well be a crater on Mars.

They're searching for something.

She heard the plane sputter, then increase in volume.

It's coming back!

Jenn grabbed Cale by the arm. "C'mon, we need to get out of sight."

"Why? What's goin' on?" he said, confused.

She pulled him forcefully behind the big balloon tires of the hydraulic mining excavator, in the shade underneath the multi-ton machine. Peeked out.

The plane had turned and flew back towards them, coming in across the far ridge. The engine changed pitch and the aircraft slowed. The closest wing dipped, the pilot changing course. The plane soared along the rim.

The aircraft circled the perimeter three times, then flew off.

Silence returned to the mining yard.

"What was that all about, Jenn?"

"Don't know for sure, but it's obvious they're very interested in this place."

She needed to let Poppy know.

The Caveman's Desire

ELAINE AWAKENED ON THE SHABBY MATTRESS, naked and sticky, an arm draped across Parnell, who slept contentedly. She brushed her fingernails down his thigh and nibbled his earlobe. They were together again, sharing an intimacy she thought had been forever lost. Their lovemaking had been scorching, affectionate, sweet. Pleasingly coarse. Magical.

He stirred, yawned. Opened his eyes, gave her a heavy-lidded glance.

"Hello there, super stud." She smiled at him, planted a kiss on his cheek.

"I must still be dreaming," he said, licking his lips, eyes scanning the length of her body.

"That was quite the wild ride, wasn't it, babe?"

"Oh, did we just take a spin on the Rolling Inferno?"

She slapped his chest playfully. "Derek!"

He snickered. "Yeah, it was fantastic. Thought maybe they'd hear us up in the headframe."

"They probably did. Damn, the things you do to me." She reached around him. "My hand is telling me you're ready for round two."

"Jesus, woman. You're insatiable."

"Just makin' up for lost time, old man."

He brought his face close to hers, rubbed his nose against hers. "I love you, Lainey. I hope you know that."

She stopped playing with him and pulled away. He turned to face her, leaning on an elbow.

"Of *course* I know that," she said. "You just proved it in so many ways." Elaine searched his face. "Why would you say that?"

"Well, because Jenny doesn't think I do. She's been riding me constantly. Thinks I abandoned you."

"Well . . . you kinda did. But if it makes you feel any better, I forgive you."

That one stung him.

"Look, I'm really sorry about the way things have gone, E. I never should have come north without you. Never should have left you behind."

"You left to get your daughter out of a life-or-death jam. I get that, Derek. I really do. I was in one of my bitchy moods the day you took off."

"No," he said, "I'm not gonna let you take any of the blame. I handled it poorly. It's my bad, Lainey."

He got up from the mattress and went to the shelves, pulled a joint out of a coffee can. "I've been doin' a lot of thinking." He looked at her, the doob clenched between his teeth. Fired up the joint and sucked the smoke deep into his lungs. Chest thrust out, cheeks puffed, face red, he retraced his steps back to her, his semi-erect manhood bobbing as he walked. He held the hit for a long minute, then exhaled. The room filled with the burnt herbal smell of strong weed.

He coughed twice and cleared his throat, handed her the doobie. "After I take care of this business with Dobkin and Miles, I wanna settle down. With you. No more hobo hotfoot. No more ridin' the rails and playing vigilante. No more King Midas or man with the tombstone eyes bullshit. No more rigged gun duels. Just you'n me, Lainey."

She took a toke, her eyes never leaving him. The smoke was mild and very sweet. Citrusy. Powerful.

"No offense, honey," she croaked, the smoke escaping her mouth with her words, "but I've heard this pitch from you before. You said Costa Rica was the place we'd live out our days as man and wife."

"That was then. This is now."

"And what makes now different from then?" She took another pull on the reefer, handed it back to him.

"I've finally come to my senses. I realize I can't live without you, E. Let's get married. I mean it, sweets. I love you and I don't want to be apart ever again."

She coughed out a cloud of smoke. "*What?* Holy shit!" she exclaimed. "Well, this is certainly out of left field. Jennifer has really done a number on your head, hasn't she?"

"Jenny has nothin' to do with this. It comes from right here," he said, thumping his chest. "And here." He tapped his head. "I'm serious. Let's make it legal, babe. Nothin' has ever felt so right to me."

She tried to pull her rampaging thoughts together. This was so out of character for Derek, a man who believed that marriage was "only for conformist dolts." He'd told her numerous times that his late wife Barbara had ruined any chance of him getting married again.

She considered the joint pinched between her fingers. "Great weed. Is it Costa Rican?"

"No. I got it from Buttonhead. His newest crop. He calls it Bloodweed. Says it's a hybrid of Panamanian Red and Purple Haze. Murph claims it'll take you beyond the Big Dipper and on to Polaris. He just might be right."

Elaine laughed. "Buttonhead's a character, that's for sure."

"Don't get off the topic, babe. How 'bout it? Let's get hitched."

"Are you asking me or telling me?"

"I'm *proposing*," he said, drawing out the word dramatically. He took a knee next to the mattress. "Will you marry me, Elaine Leibrandt?"

She couldn't count the number of times she'd fantasized about hearing these words from him. How often she'd dreamed of a big wedding—her in a beautiful Vera Wang gown and him in a formal tux. The many times she'd envisioned Derek slipping the ring on her finger under a flowered arch of roses and hydrangeas and exchanging vows of everlasting love in front of a gathering of friends and family. But at this moment she was blazed on Bloodweed and he was kneeling on the floor in front of her, naked, hands clasped together, peering at her with a pleading, desperate puppy-dog expression. It wasn't the least bit romantic. Nothing to get starry-eyed and dreamy over.

It was comical. Hilarious.

She passed him the joint. As much as she wanted to maintain control, she couldn't. The thought of them being legally married was suddenly a strange concept. Elaine tried to hold back but it was impossible. A quiet chuckle exploded into full-blown gleeful laughter, her shrieks filling up the small cave.

He got to his feet, watched her roll across the mattress hooting and cackling. A stunned look of hurt crossed his face. Miserably, he brought the joint to his mouth and toked.

"Oh, come on, Derek," she managed between laughs. "You've gotta admit, it's pretty goddamned funny. Us a married couple?"

Their eyes met. Smoke swirled around them. Her actions were humiliating him. Here he was, putting himself out there, taking a vulnerable leap with his proposal of marriage, and she was carrying on like a brainless, giddy schoolgirl. *We never should have gotten high before starting this conversation.*

And then a light came into his bloodshot eyes, as though he suddenly understood her amusement. He plopped on the mattress next to her and held up the joint. "I should have forewarned you about this stuff," he said brightly. "One of the side effects is laughing your ass off."

"Your ass or mine?"

"Both."

Her face hurt from grinning so much. "Well, you're partially right."

"Whaddaya mean?"

"The laughing part is true . . . however," she placed one hand on her butt cheek and reached across him with her other hand to grab his backside, "our asses are still attached."

That started another round of laughing, which soon led to a second round of lovemaking.

Elaine Sees a Ghost

JENN BENT OVER ANN, who lay in the makeshift bed they'd set up in the headframe.

"How're you feelin'?" she said, glancing at Ann's elevated leg.

"Much better, thanks to you, young lady. I'm beginning to think you might have a future as a critical care nurse."

Jenn smiled. "Ha! Me, a nurse? Has all that Percocet you've taken affected your brain?"

"I know a budding health care professional when I see one."

Jenn squeezed the plastic trash bag they had filled with ice and strapped to Ann's damaged knee. Squishy. "Looks like you need a refill." She unbuckled the leather belt and removed the bag, took a look. "Still discolored, but the swelling has gone down some," She checked the small cooler next to the bed. "I'll go see if I can find more ice."

"Where's Cale?"

"Don't know. Haven't seen him in a couple of hours."

"I need to thank him for what he did for me."

Jenn tucked the ice pack under her arm. "I'll see if I can find him."

"Thank you. Cale's a wonderful man."

"Yes, he is that."

Jenn turned to leave and Ann caught her by the wrist. "Don't go. Please. Won't you stay and talk with me for a while?"

"Don't worry. I'll be back soon."

"You're very sweet, Jenn. And really pretty, too."

Jenn looked down at her, seeing a needful longing in Ann's medicated eyes that made her uncomfortable.

Ann said, "People like you and Cale give me hope for this troubled world."

Jenn smiled uneasily. *God help this world!*

She left the headframe and went to mineshaft #3 where the men had moved a large tub of ice after the party wound down last night. As she walked across the yard, she thought about the plane they'd seen earlier. She needed to let Poppy know about it, and she was frustrated by her inability to get the news to him. Great danger was possibly lurking and he and Elaine were underground, screwing their brains out. She wished they would come up for air soon.

She reviewed her options. She could attempt the treacherous hike down the tunnel to Poppy's living space. *No way I'm going to do that.* She could stand at the mouth of the tunnel and yell her lungs out, but that wouldn't accomplish anything either. Three-hundred feet straight down, under a mass of solid rock. Poppy would never pick up her shouts.

It's maddening. I'll just have to wait on them.

She entered the mineshaft and went to the big aluminum tub that sat next to the green Camry Elaine had rented. A pool of slushy ice remained. She used a plastic cup to scoop ice into the bag.

"Ah, there you are."

Cale's voice. He stood in the mine entrance, his body a black cutout against the sunlit backdrop.

"Hey, Cale. Where'd you go?"

"Did some explorin' out near the rail spur. Ran into a coupla big rattlesnakes, but nothin' else. This place is deader'n Death Valley."

"You didn't see anymore of that plane did you?"

"Naw. That was freaky, huh? Whaddaya think that was all about?"

"I wouldn't have thought much about it if they'd just flown over. But they circled three times. Means they were lookin' for somethin'. Probably Poppy and Elaine. I need to let them know."

"They aren't finished with their, um . . . carnal relations yet?"

Jenn snorted. "*Carnal relations*? You're too funny, Cale. No, they haven't finished *fucking* yet if that's what you mean. You gotta stop bein' such an altar boy, Captain Turnipseed."

She tied off the end of the ice bag and walked past him. "C'mon, I need to get this ice to Ann before it melts. She was askin' about you by the way."

"How's she doing?"

"Her knee is better, but . . . I don't know. She seems really lonely. I kinda feel sorry for her."

"Yeah, I know what you mean," Cale said, following close behind.

They walked out into daylight and were halfway across the yard when she heard Poppy's voice.

"Hey, wait up, you two."

She turned to the shouts. Parnell and Elaine walked toward them, holding hands. Lainey wore her black eye patch and matching head scarf. Jenn waved and doubled back to meet them, Cale pulling up beside her.

"Well, if it isn't Fred and Wilma Flintstone!" Jenn said. "You guys sure look a lot more relaxed than the last time I saw you." *Actually, Poppy looks utterly exhausted.* "Must be all that quality sleep you got down in Bedrock Manor, wink-wink, nudge-nudge," she said, elbowing Cale in the ribs.

Cale started to snicker, but stopped when Parnell said, "Not funny, Jennifer."

"Oh, come on, Derek," Elaine said, laughing. "Don't be a grumpy old fart."

They both look wasted, Jenn thought. She said, "I'd love to stay and chat but I need to get this ice to Ann. I'm glad you've come out of hibernation. There's somethin' you should know."

"What's that?"

"We saw an airplane earlier. It came in low and flew around the perimeter three times."

"What kind of plane?"

Cale said, "Small, private aircraft. Single engine Cessna . . . propeller on the nose cone, tricycle landing gear."

"What color was it?" Elaine asked.

"Blue and white with red trim," Jenn answered.

Elaine let out a sharp breath. Brought her hand to her mouth.

Parnell turned to her. "What is it, E? You look like you've seen a ghost."

Elaine tugged on her scarf, readjusted her eyepatch. "Did you get a look at the pilot?"

"No," Jenn said. "The windshield was tinted. But I did get the registration number."

Parnell focused on Elaine, who had become noticeably panicky. "You know something about this, Lainey?"

"No." She looked away. "I don't know . . . *maybe.*"

All eyes were on Elaine.

Till Death Do Us Part

"Lainey?" Parnell said. "Do you know somethin' about this?"

The revelation of the plane stunned her speechless. *Is it possible Doctor Marquez and Diego tracked me here? Is it really them?* Cale's description of the plane matched what she remembered of the shrink's aircraft. But those details could apply to hundreds of planes. Thousands . . .

"Elaine?" Parnell demanded.

Jenn and Cale watched her, perplexed.

Elaine met Parnell's inquiring stare. "I, um . . . I'm really not sure," she said meekly.

She had hoped to avoid discussion of her problematic trip. But now her actions had possibly brought them trouble. She needed to come clean with him.

"We need to have a talk, babe," she said.

Parnell's curiosity turned to concern. "What's goin' on, E?"

She peered at Jenn and Cale.

Jenn took the hint. "C'mon, Cale, let's get this ice to Ann."

Elaine watched them walk through the yard and disappear into the headframe. "Those two seem to be getting along well," she said.

"That's not the topic here, Lainey. Tell me what you know about that plane."

She snatched the scarf from her head and wiped her neck. "It's like a microwave out here. Can we go someplace cool to talk?"

"Sure," he said. He took her by the hand and led her inside the mineshaft entrance where the Rolling Inferno sat. He helped her up into the front car and climbed in after her.

"Okay, let's have it," he said.

She took a deep breath. *Where to begin? How much do I tell him?*

She started with Doctor Marquez's identity. "Do you remember Tico Samuels?"

Parnell nodded. "Of course. The firebug murderer. How could I forget? Couldn't be his plane. He's dead."

"Just bear with me, okay? When I got to Monterrey I ran into this Mexican—Antonio Marquez—who claimed to be Tico's cousin. Marquez told me he wanted to get his revenge on you for killing Samuels. You familiar with anyone named Marquez?"

Parnell thought, then shook his head. "No. But I never knew anything about Samuels' family."

"I told Marquez you didn't kill Samuels, that the Colorado State pigs did. But it didn't seem to matter to him. He still wants your hide, Derek."

"So what do you mean when you say you 'ran into' this Mexican?" he said, putting air quotes around the *ran into*. "On the train? Is he a rail-rider?"

"No. Marquez is a doctor. A psychiatrist. He kidnapped me. Him and a buddy of his named Diego. They knew me by name and knew of my association with you. They drugged me and took me to San Antonio. To Marquez's house. They cuffed my wrists and ankles. Look," she said, holding out her arms, "you can still see the marks."

"Jesus, Lainey. I'm sorry."

"They put me under with drugs and stole my phone. They saw our texts and listened to my voicemails. Marquez interrogated me as to the location of the mines where we planned to meet. Since you hadn't indicated Utah, I tricked him into going to Winslow."

"To Shangri-La?"

"Yeah. I figured I'd have some protection there. I convinced him that's where the mines were, where I was gonna meet you. But we didn't quite make it there."

"What's this have to do with the plane?"

"Marquez owns a plane. Diego is his personal pilot. The three of us flew from San Antonio to Winslow. Marquez's airplane matches the description of the plane Jenn and Cale saw."

"I see," Parnell said, mulling it over. She could tell from his reaction that he appreciated her resourcefulness. "How'd you break free of 'em?"

He didn't seem upset with her story thus far. Best to just put it out there and be done with it. "I used the only weapon I had."

"What's that?"

"Sex."

Her frank admission hung out there, the words stark and naked, an embarrassing confession. She didn't want to look at Derek. *Couldn't* look at him. The silent interlude dragged on.

What is he thinking? Will he press me for more details?

She broke the silence. "Before you get all bent outta shape, just let me say that—"

"You did great, E. I'm proud of you." He caressed her shoulder blade then worked his hand down her back. "Jenny was so worried about you. I kept telling her you knew how to take care of yourself in tight situations and I was right."

Sweet relief. She'd expected something else entirely from him.

He leaned in and kissed her on the mouth. "Don't get me wrong. I was plenty worried about you myself." He kissed her again, this time more hungrily. "I love you, Elaine. I won't ever leave you like that again."

She beamed at him.

"Do they still have your phone?"

"No. I took it from them when I made my escape. Remember, you called me when I was at Shangri-La?"

"Oh yeah. You don't still have it, do you?"

"No. I destroyed it before we left to come here. Just like you told me to do."

"Excellent. What about Annie's phone?"

"She lost hers trackside when she took the tumble."

"Okay, so there's no way they could have traced you here by triangulating the cell signal on either phone."

"No, I don't see how." *Should I tell him about the men in the car chasing the train?*

"What's this doctor look like?"

She described Marquez, relating more of the psychiatrist's swarthy Aztecan features than his movie star good looks.

"So you think he's really related to Tico Samuels?" she asked.

"Doubtful. It sounds too rehearsed. Besides, Samuels was such a loser I don't think anyone in his family would give a shit about him."

"You think Marquez and Diego are bounty hunters, then?"

"I don't think so. You've got a hundred large on your head, same as me. If they were looking to cash in on the reward they would have collected on you before trying to find me."

"I don't know, Derek. They needed my help to find you. They might have been planning to turn us in together. Only thing I'm sure of is that Antonio Marquez is desperate to find you. And he made it very clear what his intentions are."

"He's probably one of my long lost enemies with a score to settle," he said, grinning at her. "The list is quite long."

Unbelievable. He's smiling. "None of this scares you?"

"Hell, no. Life is good. I'm here with you. And Jenny. What more could a man want?"

"I appreciate that, babe, but this shrink wants to *kill* you. That doesn't bother you?"

"Look, anybody who shows up here looking for trouble will take a ride in this baby." He slapped the coaster car wall in front of them. "I'll strap 'em in and light her up, let her rip."

Elaine had long thought his roller coaster preposterous, more than a little over the top. Still, she admired his brilliance with all things technical. He had transformed this deserted coal mine into a livable space, bringing electricity with his solar power grid, running water with his underground spring taps, ventilation with his restored tunnel fans. Elaine thought that in better times, Derek could have done well as an innovative engineer.

He broke into her thoughts. "What say we head back out and check on Annie." He moved to get out of the coaster car.

"Wait," she said. She placed her hand on his arm. "One more thing before we join the others."

"There's more?"

"Yes. Earlier? Down in your room? When we were discussing marriage? I just—"

"There's no need to go there, sweets."

"I think we do, Derek. It's important."

He sat down with a heavy sigh. The coaster car shifted with his weight. "Okay shoot."

"Well, earlier I made a mockery of marriage. I laughed about the thought of us being a married couple and I saw how it hurt you."

"Hurt me? But I laughed along with you, Lainey."

"*After* the fact, sure. But when I started laughing and saying mean things, I could see it wounded you, and I'm sorry for that."

"Hey, no harm, no foul, sweetie."

"It was the smoke . . . the Bloodweed. That shit'll make you crack up over anything and everything."

"Understood, E. I didn't take that conversation seriously."

"We never should have had that discussion stoned. Now that we're straight, there're some things I want to say."

"Okay."

"I have loved you since that first day you visited me in the burn center . . ." She opened up to him, professing her love for him, telling him things she'd held close to her chest for years. As she talked, her mind took her back to those horrid days following the acid-throwing attack. Those lonely, frightening days laying in that Los Angeles hospital bed wrapped up like a mummy. The skin-graft surgeries. The excruciating pain. The endless parade of hospital staff and surgical specialists trooping through her hospital room at all hours. Laying there, hour after hour, knowing her left eye and catalog-model beauty had been stolen from her by an unstable, jealous boyfriend.

". . . when you walked in that room something happened to me, babe," she continued. "Something good. Something *wonderful*. I loved the sound of your voice, the things you talked about, the way you laughed when I said something goofy. The way you *listened*. But I detected a sadness in you, too. I realized you were broken, just like me. You opened up to me, a complete stranger. You told me about your murdered wife and your missing daughter. The more we talked that day, the more I realized our meeting was kismet. You're a big fan of karma, Derek. There's no better illustration of karma in action than the day we met. A meeting of two broken souls. That day was the beginning of my healing and I know it was for you, too." She looked away, the warm blush of embarrassment rising in her cheeks.

"That's beautiful, Lainey," he said, misting up. "You've been thinking about this for a while, haven't you?"

She nodded. "I love you with all my heart, babe, and I want to marry you in the worst way. I would be proud and honored to be your wife. I want very much to be Mrs. Derek Parnell. We can make a wonderful life together. You said earlier you were proposing to me. Was that just the weed talking?"

"No. That was me *asking*," he said, tears in his eyes.

"Then let's do it, Derek. It doesn't have to be a big fancy wedding. We could have a small ceremony here. Or Shangri-La. Or even Las Vegas for that matter."

He frowned. "We can't get married in the States, Lainey. We're wanted felons."

"Okay, then we'll do it once we get back to Costa Rica."

"I'm all for it. I really . . ."

His words trailed off and he tilted his head, listening.

She looked at him. "What's wrong?"

He held up his hand, quieting her.

Soon she heard what he was hearing: the sputtering drone of an airplane engine outside.

"Well, well, well, could that be our esteemed doctor?" he said, jumping out of the coaster car and extending a hand to her. "Let's go see who's come calling."

They went to the cave entrance, peeked out. Elaine sucked in her breath.

Parnell peered up at the airplane as it banked over the far ridge and flew over the mining yard. "Is that the shrink?"

She nodded. *Without a doubt—Antonio Marquez's airplane.*

"He sure is a persistent bastard. You must have really pissed them off, E."

She bobbed her head dumbly as she watched the plane make several passes. *Oh, if he only knew.*

Operation Vagabond

AN EXHAUSTED WEASEL BETHEA returned from Vegas just after dusk. He sat with Parnell at the pallet table in Parnell's underground abode and briefed him on the day's activities.

"Kid and Flywheel are in place. They got a rental car and I helped 'em purchase the necessary surveillance gear. Gotta say, Dobkin's mansion is a real fortress. Enough security there to rival the Pentagon."

Parnell smirked. "Someone like him can't have enough protection. You think Billy and Javion can handle it?"

"Oh yeah. They pick at each other a lot, but that's good. They keep each other on their toes. They'll get us what we need."

"Tell me somethin', Greg. Does the name Antonio Marquez ring any bells for you?"

"No. Don't think so. Should it?"

Parnell scratched his head. "I don't know. Something about that name is familiar to me, but it's hazy."

"Why do you ask?"

Parnell filled him in on Elaine's run-in with the psychiatrist and his pilot friend—her abduction, the shrink detaining her in San Antonio, their flight to Winslow, today's flyover with Elaine identifying the plane.

"That could be problematic," Weasel said. "Which reminds me." He reached into his backpack and pulled out a newspaper, spread it out on the tabletop. "I hate to be the messenger of more potential problems, but there's an article on the second page you should see."

Parnell pulled the newspaper close. "The Las Vegas Sun is still publishing a daily?"

"Yep. The only rag between Denver and LA still goin' to press with print versions."

Parnell flapped the paper open to the second page. Weasel pointed a grimy finger at the story below the fold:

WAR ON VAGRANCY TOP PRIORITY
By Winston Furtaldo, Associated Press

WASHINGTON DC — There was jubilation on Capitol Hill this week. A dozen Army National Guard units rolled out to begin the cleanup of the ever-present homeless blight that has become an ugly eyesore for our once beautiful nation. The effort, known as Operation Vagabond, will focus its initial thrust in the Southwest, where the homeless situation is most prevalent. It is estimated that 40 million people are squatting illegally in the United States, most living in abject poverty and squalor.

Joseph P. Barnabas, National Guard Bureau Chief and member of the Joint Chiefs of Staff, has this to say about Operation Vagabond: "The administration has directed me to put my most qualified personnel on this important initiative. As such, I have appointed Lieutenant General Michael J. Gollinger to head this mission. I have every confidence that General Gollinger's troops will quash this scourge that has been worsening since the Great Crash. These indigent refugees from society are squatting on government lands, taking up residence in foreclosed private structures, and trashing our national parks. These freeloading tramps pollute our lands and waterways and do not pay taxes. Their presence has a negative impact on our once-thriving tourist trade and they are hampering our efforts to stimulate our sluggish economy. We now have taken on the look of a destitute third-world country and it's time to do something about it. Our economic recovery begins with this cleanup effort."

Parnell couldn't read any further. "Are you shittin' me?" He pushed the newspaper away from him in disgust. "Indigent refugees from society? Freeloading tramps? Hampering their efforts to stimulate the sluggish economy? I guess it never occurred to these rich jackoffs that a jobs program just might turn the economy around. I mean, most of the folks we know want to work, there just isn't any work to be had. Shit, Greg. They're declaring war on the hobo nation."

"Sure seems that way."

"Are they gonna just deport everyone who's unemployed?

That'd be almost half the country."

"I'm not real sure deportation is what they have in mind, Derek."

Parnell felt a black rage coming on. "Typical political bullshit! First they bankrupt the country and then they point their cannons at the victims. And they have the balls to call themselves civil servants. A government for the people by the people? My fuckin' ass!"

"Settle down, Derek. Let's think this through, okay?"

"I should've seen this comin', Greg. Everything's a war to those turds in Washington. How much time you think we have?"

Weasel slid a hand down his long neck. "Can't say for sure. I dug around while I was in Vegas, trying to learn more. This article was all I found."

"You think we have time to build an army? To fight the bastards?" As soon as the words left his mouth, Parnell realized how insane he sounded. *Going to war against the juggernaut U.S. government? The same fool's errand the subversive Liberty Dogs planned to carry out three years ago. Get a grip, Parnell.*

Weasel looked at him with a mixture of admiration and concern. "You mean a hobo army?"

"Never mind," he said, waving him off. "Just one of my feverish fantasies talking."

"Because, I hope you know, Derek, that they would crush us in a heartbeat—"

"Yeah, yeah, yeah, I know that," he said irritably. "But we *can* lessen the damage."

Weasel questioned him with a curious look.

"I need to get down to Shangri-La soon," Parnell said, worry etching his voice. "They're one of the bigger camps and they're on Hopi reservation land. Got to get our friends relocated."

"Uh . . . reality check, Derek. How're you gonna do that? There're a hundred—maybe *two* hundred—breezers in Winslow. And even if you could move them all, where're you gonna relocate them to? It's admirable, my friend, it really is, but you're dreaming. You can't save everybody."

Parnell thought on that for a moment. "We could get a couple dozen of 'em out here. I could find legitimate housing for another dozen or so. Maybe save the families with children."

Weasel smiled knowingly. "Again, very commendable, partner. But the reality is, we just don't have the resources to get that done. Besides, think about it. How do you choose who to move and who to leave behind?"

Parnell realized his friend spoke the truth. He felt the world closing in on him.

"Don't look so defeated," Weasel said.

"I've got to find a way to help our friends, Greg."

"I'm with you. We can work on some kinda plan. But first, after what you told me about that airplane, I say our first priority is to start a round-the-clock security detail. Somebody is interested in us and they know where we are."

Weasel yawned, got up from the table and put his hand on Parnell's shoulder. "Been a long day. How 'bout givin' me a lift back topside. I'll get T-Seed on the first watch tonight. Come daybreak, I'll take over. We can work out a security schedule tomorrow."

As the mine cart squeaked its way up the track, taking them to ground level, Parnell struggled with what he saw as his responsibility to his friends at Shangri-La. Government troops would round up and deport a small number of breezers on immigration charges. They would be the "lucky" ones.

The remainder?

I absolutely have to do something!

In Memory of Luanne

A BRISK NIGHT BREEZE WHISTLED through gaps in the walls of the headframe. Jenn lay nestled in the warm cocoon of her bedroll attempting to find sleep. A coyote howled in the distance, its wail a long and forlorn reminder of her loneliness.

Ann Finnegan stirred under a pile of heavy blankets, breathing the deep, easy breaths of narcotic-induced slumber. She mumbled something unintelligible and rolled over on her side, facing Jenn. The swelling in her knee had lessened the past three days, and she could get around for short periods during the heat of the day. But when night fell and the chill descended, her pain returned. The drugs helped her sleep.

Jenn watched her sleeping. *Maybe I should dig into her Percocet stash.*

Her thoughts turned to Cale Turnipseed as they had so often lately. Such a nice guy. An interesting man. Good looking in a clean-cut way. Always seemed to be in a good mood, no matter the situation. Crazy how she'd immediately gravitated to him when he smiled at her that first time in the Winslow camp. She smiled, thinking about how the man they called T-Seed could converse intelligently on almost any topic. The others seemed to be annoyed by his verbosity, but she loved listening to him talk.

She wished he was here now. Jenn had seen little of him since he started guard detail. Weasel Bethea had organized a 24/7 watch rotation and Cale had taken the graveyard shift while Poppy and Weasel shared daytime duties. Billy and Javion were due back from Vegas tomorrow, so hopefully their return would give her more time with Cale.

She yawned widely, stretched. For some reason memories of Luanne Solton flooded her head. Jenn recalled the warmth of Lulu's body snuggled up against her on those cold winter nights deep in the Colorado caves. The emotional and physical intimacy they had shared was like a supercharged umbilical. She and Lulu had become inseparable down in those prison cells of dusty rock walls and hard granite floors where depraved men raped their bodies and minds and souls for seven long years. Lulu knew just how to hold her, how to touch her, what to say to her to take the bitterness out of her contaminated heart. Jenn drifted off to sleep thinking about her late girlfriend . . .

. . . Lulu's warm breath tickles her exposed breast, her tongue circling Jenn's hardening nipple in tantalizingly moist loops. Jenn breathes in Lulu's hair and perfume—a sweet scent of shampoo and floral-tinged vanilla that excites her. Lulu takes Jenn's breast into her mouth and Jenn lets out a small gasp of pleasure. She strokes Lulu's long hair as Lulu slurps at her left breast. Jenn feels Lulu's fingers dance down her belly and snake through her pubic hair, teasing her with a skillful and assured touch, then probing, finding the spot of no return.

Jenn can't catch her breath. *Oh, my freakin' God! She rocks my world!*

Lulu whispers, "You are so gorgeous, Jay-Jay," using her pet name for Jenn. "You're like a fucking fountain down there, girl," she says, her hand exploring. She brings her face close. Jenn can get lost in those big chocolate eyes. Lulu kisses her, slowly runs her tongue across Jenn's upper lip the way Jenn loves. "I want to taste you, Jay-Jay," Lulu pleads, her voice husky, sexy.

Jenn smiles at her in the dim light. "You're gonna make me come, Lu. Let me do you first." She kisses Lulu, relishing the softness of her full lips, her silky skin, the heat of her compact body. "No need to rush, love," Jenn says, her voice shaky, her body quivering. "There're no guards around tonight. Let's take our time. Let's enjoy every minute of this. I love you so much, Lu. I want to please you."

Lulu caresses her cheek. "You *do* please me, Jay-Jay. In every possible way."

Jenn closes her eyes and brushes her lips against Lulu's mouth. Teases her with her tongue. Gently nibbles on her lower lip. Lulu moans, her breath hot and musky sweet against Jenn's face . . .

Jenn came awake, the spicy dream evaporating. Ann was in her bedroll, face-to-face with her, kissing her, fondling her. The shock brought Jenn out of her sleepy stupor. She jumped out of her bedroll into the cold night air, backpedaled several feet. "Whoa! What the hell!" she shrieked.

"I—I didn't mean to . . . uh," Ann stammered. "I just thought that . . ."

"You thought *what* exactly?" Jenn said, the words escaping

her mouth on tiny clouds of frosty air. "That I'm a lesbian? Is that what you thought?"

"No, um . . . not really, no. It's just that . . . well, you confided in me and, uh . . . you told me about the relationship you had with that girl in the caves and I just—"

"Ann, I told you, that was a close friendship that developed because of the dire circumstances we found ourselves in. It wasn't an invitation to jump my bones."

"Oh, dear God, please forgive me," Ann said. "I'm so embarrassed, Jennifer. I'm really sorry."

Telling her about Lulu was a mistake. Why did I ever open my big mouth?

Jenn shivered. The small battery-powered heater in the corner wasn't enough to ward off the frigid night air. She reached down, grabbed one of the blankets and pulled it around her. The moonlight pouring in through the missing section of the headframe roof lit up Ann's face. She peered out from the bedroll with a wounded expression. "No need to apologize," Jenn told her. "Look, I loved Luanne and she loved me. But it never would've have happened if we met somewhere else."

Jenn watched her climb out of the bedroll and crawl back under the pile of blankets, favoring her knee as she moved. She peeked out over the edge of the blankets looking ashamed, rejected. *She really wants to be with me in that way,* Jenn thought with amazement. Ann had shown a few signs of interest the past week, but Jenn thought it was nothing more than an innocent girl crush. It never occurred to her she would actually make a move. After all, Ann was a pastor, a woman of the cloth.

Jenn liked her. She was a good hearted person. It would be cruel to leave her floundering in her vulnerability. "Actually, I'm kinda flattered, Ann."

"You are?"

"Yes. You're an attractive woman—"

"You think so? You don't think I'm a frumpy religious crone?"

A crone? She's only a few years older than me. "Hardly," she said with a laugh. "You've got a unique beauty about you. You're super intelligent. You treat everybody with kindness. You're well respected in camp."

"Your father doesn't like me much."

"Poppy doesn't care for a lot of people. You shouldn't take

that personally."

"I worry about Derek," Ann said, clearly relieved at the opportunity to change the subject. "He's obsessed with revenge." She shifted into her preacher voice. " 'Never take your own revenge, beloved, but leave room for the wrath of God, for it is written, vengeance is mine, I will repay, says the Lord.' Romans chapter twelve, verse nineteen."

"You've got a biblical passage for everything, it seems."

Ann smiled. "Those passages were drilled into me from an early age. Scripture is my subconscious. It's helped me through some rough times." She made eye contact. "Surely you must think I'm strange."

"No. Not at all. I'm all for anything that eases people's minds, anything that gives them strength."

"You're a sweet girl, Jenn."

"No, I'm really not." *I'm a murderer, just like Poppy.* She wanted to get back to the start of this conversation. "So you're gay, then, Ann?"

A long pause, then, "You're very direct. Just like your father. You handle it much better than he does, however."

"Well? Are you? Curious minds want to know."

Ann exhaled a long, exasperated sigh. "Yes. I've known it since grade school. I used to play nurse with my childhood girlfriends. Every time your dad calls me Nurse Annie I'm reminded of those scenarios," she said with a dry laugh. "Those were heady times . . . my awakening, my early days of exploration and discovery . . . finding out who I was. Discovering the joys of the female body. And later, cherishing the companionship and love of another woman . . ." Her voice faded away in a dreamy whisper.

An honest, forthright confession. Jenn appreciated her courage. "Wow. Thank you for trusting me, Ann. That admission couldn't have been easy for you."

"Oh, it's never been easy, Jennifer. My sexual preference has always been at odds with my faith and religious upbringing. I was constantly bullied in school, called horrible things. When I was fifteen, my mother caught me and Katy Greer naked and, um . . . pleasuring each other in the basement. My father—the most straight-laced, buttoned-up religious man you'd ever want to meet—was furious. In his myopic vision, anything even hinting at homosexual behavior was an abominable sin. He enrolled me in one of those dreadful conversion therapy programs, thinking it would 'cure' me. Surprise! It didn't. In fact, just the opposite happened. I fell in lust with another girl my age who was going through the program."

Ann remained quietly pensive for a moment, then said, "Oh, listen to me going on and on about myself. Like a narcissistic fool I am, telling you about how hard things were for me when you were the one who really had it rough. I can't begin to imagine what you had to go through, Jennifer. Please forgive my vanity."

Jenn moved closer to the heater, seeking warmth. "I'm interested, Ann. This is nice. I feel honored that you're opening up to me like this."

"Really?"

"Yeah. Tell me more."

"Okay. Well, I guess all of this—the clinic and the bullying—eventually brought me closer to God. It set me on my path of spiritual awareness."

"How so?"

"I prayed after each of those ugly encounters. I asked the Lord to enlighten the misguided, to make them mindful of the fact that we are all His children and that loving someone, regardless of their sex, race, or creed, is a beautiful thing. Sharing your love and pleasing other people should be honorable, not sinful. That's what I try to promote now. That message is needed more than ever in these difficult times. The word of Christ should open people's minds, not close them."

"That's really nice. Has it worked?"

"Sometimes. It's been successful at Shangri-La. My efforts there have turned around quite a few nonbelievers. It's an amazing thing to witness. God's love is very powerful."

"So you don't have to answer if you think I'm bein' too nosy, but are you involved with anyone in camp now?"

Ann looked at her with a sharp eye. "You're not being nosy. Yes, there was someone. Past tense. An older woman. It ended more than a year ago."

"Is she still there?"

"Yes. It's awkward sometimes, but we've remained friends."

"Was your relationship public knowledge?"

"Everybody knew about it, yes. Most folks embraced it. There aren't many secrets in the village."

The cold night air penetrated the thin blanket. Jenn pulled the wrap around her tighter. Her teeth chattered. "So you really thought we could have something? You and me?"

Ann nodded timidly. "I did. And I still do. I have a strong feeling you're attracted to me."

"As a lover?"

"Yes."

"What gives you that idea?"

"The way you look at me. Like you're undressing me with your eyes."

"Wow. Really?"

"Oh, yes. You do. It turns me on quite a bit, even if I don't show it. True confession time, Jennifer. You're the only reason I'm here. I wanted to see you again. I *had* to see you again."

"You're makin' that up."

"No, I'm not. After you and your father left, I couldn't stop thinking about you. I had dreams about you . . . about us together. Like the one you apparently just had about Lulu."

This conversation was beginning to make Jenn uncomfortable. "And you think I have a natural desire to, uh . . . to be with you?"

"I can't speak for you. I just know how you make *me* feel."

Jenn had long been conflicted about her sexual leanings. She'd certainly dedicated a lot of thought to the subject. Her childhood had been stolen from her, corrupted by forces of evil. Had that unfortunate twist of fate pushed her toward lesbianism? *Was it circumstance or nature that made me love Luanne?*

Ann said, "You're confused, Jennifer. I get that. I know all about that feeling. You're also freezing. I can see you shaking from here." She brought her hand out from beneath the blankets and motioned to her. "Come here, darling. Climb in with me and get warm."

Darling? "Oh, I don't know if that's a good idea," she said with a shiver.

"Come on. I won't bite. Just a friendly cuddle to get warm."

"How friendly?"

"I won't do anything against your will. I promise."

"I don't know."

"Come on. I'd hate to see a lady I care so much about freeze to death. The Heavenly Father might not forgive me for that."

Jenn laughed. "You're a piece of work, Ann Finnegan."

She went to the bedding where Ann lay. Three slow, tentative steps and Jenn was there. She looked down and locked eyes with Ann, a message of invitation and acceptance passing between them. And then, as if directed by an unseen hand, she dropped to her knees and dove under the pile of blankets into Ann's warm embrace.

Ann gave her a chaste kiss on the cheek as Jenn snuggled in close to her. "Isn't that much better?"

"Yeah, this is nice," Jenn said, getting comfortable in the crook of Ann's arm. "I don't want to hurt your knee."

"Don't worry, you're not. Holding you like this erases the pain. You're better medicine than the Percocet tabs."

"There's one compliment I've never heard before."

Ann laughed. "Stick with me and you'll hear lots of things you've never heard before."

"God, Ann, your body is like a blast furnace."

"It's my way of letting you know you're welcome in my bed anytime."

"Now don't start jumpin' to conclusions. If it wasn't so cold I wouldn't be here with you like this."

"You're so cute when you're telling a lie, Jennifer." Ann rubbed noses with her, Eskimo style.

The close intimacy and Ann's bold admissions put Jenn in a confessional mood. "You know, the years I was in the Liberty Dogs compound I grew to hate the male of the species. It was appalling the things those pigs did to us. What they made us do. I mean totally disgusting. After Lulu and I hooked up, we learned how to play their game, how to work situations to our advantage. We figured if we did everything they wanted and more, we wouldn't be sold to a high bidder and we could stay together. It was the old 'devil you know is better than the one you don't' kind of thing. Many of the girls came and went, never to be heard from again. But Luanne and I remained, together for almost seven years. We were dubbed the Cave Queens by those perverts. We were their favorites. The things Lu and I did were adventurous, to put it mildly. But it worked. We were there for each other, had each other's backs. We fell in love. We survived. Well, I survived, thanks to Poppy. But Lulu . . . ?"

"You really cared for her, didn't you?"

"More than I can put into words."

"So much loss in your life," Ann said, wiping a tear from Jenn's cheek and pulling her closer. "I'm sorry."

"It's okay," Jenn said, weepy. She sniffed back her tears and continued. "So I turn eighteen and I'm thinking I'm a full-blown lesbian. What else could I think? I'm completely and irreversibly in love with Luanne and have been for years. And then, out of the blue, Russell Holt enters my world. We started seein' each other on the sly. He blew me away with his kindness and compassion. He told me he was workin' undercover for an operation designed to bring down the Liberty Dogs. He knew about plans to bring my father into the mix. He told me Poppy would soon be coming to my rescue. Russ ultimately restored my faith in men. He was a beautiful man in all respects. He wanted to save all the girls, but couldn't. I loved him deeply. I miss him as much as I miss Luanne. So I don't really know what that makes me. Lesbian? Hetero? Bi?"

"How about a loving human being?"

Jenn smiled at her. "You know how to make a girl feel really good about herself."

"I'd like to do that all the time."

Jenn didn't know how to respond to that. All she could think of was, "I come with a warning, Ann."

"What's that?"

"I'm bad luck. Everyone I get involved with ends up dead."

"Well, then, I'll just have to take my chances, won't I?"

Ann leaned in and kissed her with a hunger that surprised Jenn. Jenn took the plunge, letting go, giving into the pleasures of being with this attractive, complex, intelligent woman.

They were lost in each other when the door creaked open.

A powerful flashlight beam spotlighted them.

"Oops! Holy shit!" Cale Turnipseed uttered in surprise. He quickly snapped the flashlight off. "I, uh . . . I was on my rounds and . . . well, I see you ladies are busy. So sorry to barge in like this . . ."

His voice drifted away as he backed out of the headframe and closed the door behind him.

Conquistador's Folly

PUPPETMASTER SAT AT THE CONSOLE, composing his update to Hyena. His e-mail reflected the pride he felt over the progress they'd made the past four days.

> TIME: 23:18 PST
> FROM: PuppetMaster
> TO: Hyena
>
> Good news. Recent activities indicate we are closing in on Lone Wolf. One of my operatives located Lady Cyclops on a Union Pacific train in southern Utah Monday traveling with two companions (one male, one female; photos attached). Pics gave us potential identities of both. We believe the male to be Cale Allen Turnipseed, formerly of Atlanta, Georgia, current residency unknown. Criminal background check indicates Turnipseed is wanted on a federal warrant for tax evasion. The female is believed to be Ann Josephine Finnegan, former nurse on staff at El Pueblo Medical Associates in Albuquerque and missing for 37 months. Ms. Finnegan, who has no criminal record, injured her leg in transit and is believed to be immobilized.
>
> Having narrowed the search area to the southern quadrant of Utah, I put eyes in the sky (Conquistador) in that area. Yesterday, during flyover routines, Conquistador reported seeing a young couple at an abandoned coal mine in southern Utah, near Kanab (37.74 degrees North, 108.52 degrees West). Visuals of the pair reveal a close resemblance to Little Tombstone and Mr. Turnipseed. Because of this sighting, and due to the fact that Lone Wolf was last seen with Little Tombstone, we believe Lone Wolf to be in the vicinity. Requesting permission to enter the mining site to get an up-close look at the situation. Time to roust Lone Wolf and Lady Cyclops.

He sent the communication and sat back, pleased with himself. Derek Parnell and Elaine Leibrandt would soon be his. And it was possible they would snag Parnell's daughter as well. Three years of hard work and diligence was about to pay off handsomely.

The iridium satellite phone buzzed on the corner of his desk, startling him. The flashing red light on the display told him it was

Hyena. Probably calling to congratulate him. He reached for the phone.

"Hey, boss," he said pleasantly.

There was a two-second delay filled with clicking noises as the ciphony voice encryption system kicked in. "Funny you should call me that," Hyena said in his sandpapery voice. "I just read your update. I'm thinkin' maybe you're under the impression *you're* the fuckin' boss now."

"What?" PuppetMaster said, not sure he heard him correctly. "What're you talking about?"

"I believe you stated: 'Time to roust Lone Wolf and Lady Cyclops.' Since when are you callin' the shots?"

"No. I, um . . . I was requesting perm—"

"I know exactly what you're doin'. You're undermining my authority and I won't have it."

"I wasn't trying to—"

"And not only that, your reporting is sporadic and threadbare. I only hear from you once or twice a week, and this update you just sent me sucks."

"Sucks?"

"You heard me. It's for shit. There's no meat to it. It doesn't tell me much more than I knew last week . . ."

PuppetMaster could do nothing but listen to him fume.

". . . and that agent Conquistador you've got workin' for you? He's a lobotomized loser. Your sorry excuse of a report gives me vague information about his flyover routines and visuals. No specifics. How many times did the pinhead fly over the site?"

"Six."

"Christ! And would I be correct in assuming you didn't include that in your so-called report because you knew how I'd react?"

"No, I—"

"And I'm also assuming by visuals you mean naked eye identifications and not real photographic proof."

"Well, yes, but—"

"Get your head out of your ass, Puppet Man! Even a greenhorn CIA spook newly graduated from the Camp Peary Farm knows you don't hang around a surveillance locale once you've been made. Conquistador should have flown in, taken aerial photographs, then gotten the fuck out. But does he do that? Shit, no. He flies over like he's a fuckin' float in the Macy's Thanksgiving parade. Did he wave to everybody on the ground and smile real big?"

"No, of course not, but—"

"It's extremely sloppy work! And you never got my approval to have your guy fly over in the first place. You just went ahead and did it before you even sent me the coordinates of this coal mine. Conquistador is incompetent. You're even worse. You failed to follow proper protocols."

"Honest, sir, I only did what I thought was best. We're finally about to nab them and—"

"Do *not* insult my intelligence!" Hyena roared. "I'm goin' to spell this out for you so you'll understand it. You work for me, not yourself. Everything goes through me and has to be approved by me. You take orders from me and only me. When you receive orders from me you carry them out to the letter. Got it?"

"Yessir."

"So I'm orderin' you to eliminate Conquistador. You've got one week to make it happen. He's no longer an asset to us. It's dangerous to keep him in play."

"What? But he's the one who found Lady Cyclops. He's the one who got her back into the States and tracked her, we think, to Lone Wolf. Without Conquistador we'd still be in the dark."

"Yeah, he's also the moron who lost her. Get rid of him. And start sending me daily reports that tell me something. It'll be your jugular next if you don't get your shit together."

"But sir, Conquistador has all kinds of inside information about our operation. He's a loose cannon. He could do a lot of harm."

"Even more reason to eliminate him. You've got your orders. Make sure neither of us ever sees him or hears from him again. Do I make myself clear?"

"Crystal clear, sir."

"One more thing. I don't want you or anyone in your employ near that mining site. If I catch wind of that happening, you can kiss your ass goodbye."

The line went dead.

PuppetMaster sat, stewing in anger for several long seconds before placing the satphone back in its cradle. He knew what this was all about. The big man was giving him his pink slip. He'd outlived his usefulness. Hyena was cutting him loose.

This called for the expensive whiskey. He went to the liquor cabinet, grabbed a fresh bottle of Glenfiddich and a glass, cracked the seal and poured. He carried the bottle and glass to his chair at the console desk and sat. Took a long slug of the whiskey. Stared at the bank of monitors in front of him and thought.

Twelve years he had worked for Hyena and never had there been an exchange between them like the one they'd just had. PuppetMaster had seen Hyena's brutish behavior before. He'd witnessed the sudden disappearance of other top operatives in the organization, never to be heard from again following similar tirades from the big man. Hyena wasn't to be taken lightly. He was a dangerous, manipulative, extraordinarily powerful man who could destroy people with a couple of phone calls. He could have people killed with a single text message. He had critical segments of the U.S. government in his back pocket. He had eyes and ears everywhere. He had the capacity to bend others to his will. Hyena was not someone you crossed and lived to tell about it.

He's ordered me to kill Antonio Marquez.

That sick call to arms bounced around in his brain.

He drained his glass and poured another tall one, thinking about who he could commission to carry out the gruesome task. Too bad Lars was missing. He'd be perfect for this hit. A few other names came to mind, but ultimately, PuppetMaster knew this was one he'd have to handle himself. If it was bungled in any way, Hyena would hold him responsible, and would come after him with a vengeance.

His head hurt, the pain intense, like a cold steel chisel prying his brain from his skull. He'd never killed anyone before. At least not with his own hands. His skill was in manipulating others to do the dirty deeds. For years he'd sat in this cluttered control room and pushed buttons, talked with operatives, written communiqués, listened in on wire taps, watched videos, examined surveillance data, ran background checks, ordered stakeouts and hits. For a dozen years he had been the quarterback calling the plays. And now the head coach demanded that he make an illegal dirty hit on one of his own players.

He felt sick.

Another long, burning gulp of whiskey. His eyes watered and he retched, but he held it down.

How best to pull this off? Booby trap Marquez's plane? That wouldn't work. He knew very little about the mechanical side of airplanes. And that would require breaking into the shrink's hangar and having the know-how to rig the plane to bring it down in flight without inviting pre-flight suspicion. Too many things could go wrong. Maybe summon the psychiatrist here to congratulate him on a job well done and then lace his drink with poison? No, that would mean a body on his own property he'd have to dispose of. Perhaps just go to San Antonio and shoot the man? *Right, you've shot a gun maybe three times in your life, all at paper targets at the shooting range.*

The cleanest way would be to have Marquez picked up on a series of charges—kidnapping, aiding and abetting a wanted felon, false imprisonment, among others. But that would require a lot of time and red tape, not to mention getting the feds involved. And Marquez, although out of harm's way, would still be alive and able to talk. That certainly wouldn't satisfy Hyena.

Such a fucking mess!

And then he was hit with a startling insight. *Maybe I'm thinking about the wrong target. Possibly it's time for the quarterback to take down the head coach.*

Or maybe he could get Marquez to do the hit.

His attention was drawn to an incoming e-mail flashing on a console screen.

>   **TIME:** 23:47 PST
> **FROM:** Golden Bear
> **TO:**   PuppetMaster
> **SUBJECT:** RE: Thor and Goliath Watch
>
> Three mangled and burned bodies have been found at the bottom of Whitman Gorge in Northern Arizona. The scorched frame of Thor's limo was located a half mile away. Bodies are believed to be Lady Thor, Platinum Goliath, and Chauffeur-1. Arizona Criminal Investigations Division has been called in to assist with the identification of victims and to determine cause of deaths. Will keep you posted as events unfold.

Can this day possibly get any worse?

PuppetMaster reached for the Glenfiddich and drank straight from the bottle.

Animal Chatter

THE MADNESS STARTED WHEN Billy Dixon and Javion Wheeler returned from Vegas. Elaine sat in, listening as they debriefed Derek and Weasel on their stakeout of John Dobkin's mansion.

"The man is a major league pimp," Flywheel told them. "All that's missing is the purple crushed velvet suit with fluffy wide lapels and a leopard-print hat."

"Yeah," Kid said, "Dobkin's runnin' girls outta two casinos. High-roller clientele."

Parnell nodded. "I told you the man's a back alley sleazeball."

"Too bad we can't nail him on prostitution charges," Weasel said.

Parnell said, "Actually we could, Greg. Prostitution's illegal in Vegas and Reno and a few other major cities. It's legal in *rural* Nevada, but only through licensed brothels. It's certainly against the law to run whorehouses out of Vegas casinos."

"So let's report him, get him picked up for that," Kid said.

"Wouldn't work. Dobkin's got the local law in his back pocket. And even if a prostitution rap would stick, I want Dobkin back here where I can fuck with him personally. How accessible is he, Billy?"

"Very accessible. He visits both clubs every night. We think to collect on previous day business."

Flywheel said, "He spends alotta time at the second casino. Every night. Coupla hours. Consistent. Prob'ly dippin' into the goods. Gettin' his dick wet."

Smiles around the table.

Weasel said, "How does he get around?"

"Three chauffeured limousines," Kid said.

"Just the driver? Any muscle?" Parnell asked Dixon.

"The drivers are armed. And he's got protection with him on his rounds. Always one dude ridin' shotgun and carryin'."

"Where are the limos parked when not in use?"

"In a shed at the rear of the property."

"Any way of getting into the shed without detection?"

Kid and Flywheel looked at each other. "Not if you wanna live to see another day," Flywheel said.

"Yeah," Kid agreed. "It's a goddamned police state. The guards inside the fence are shoulderin' AK-47s. But as I said, Dobkin's vulnerable when he leaves his castle. You can set your watch by his schedule. He makes his rounds the same time each night. Hits the first casino at eleven-thirty. Always quick. Thirty minutes tops. Then on to the second where he spends two or three hours. Like Fly says, probably gettin' his horns clipped. Best time to nab him is after his second pickup. He's all relaxed after gettin' laid and collectin' his money. His protection has their guard down then, too, waitin' on him all that time. And the muscle doesn't always wait. Two nights the bodyguard left the driver alone while he went inside for an hour or more. Probably gettin' a little poon-tang of his own."

Flywheel said, "Dobkin's an easy mark, Derek. We coulda already grabbed his nasty ass and had him back here for you to strap into your hell coaster."

"Trust me, we'll get him soon. What kind of intel did you pick up?"

Kid said. "Not sure how meaningful it is, but we intercepted some phone conversations using that listening device you had us buy. That thing's amazing. Could probably pick up a whisper on the moon. Of course, we were only able to hear his side of the conversations, so the information is scattered at best. We also were able to hack into his Wi-Fi network and read some e-mails. Took some doin' to crack his login, but we finally got in on the third day. The e-mails were all heavily encrypted but that app with the decrypt translation routines worked wonders."

"Find anything interesting?"

Flywheel said, "Don't know what it means, but we picked up a lot of chatter about animals."

"Animals?"

"Yeah, strangest thing—coyotes, bears, hyenas, wolves—those animals came up often. There was also some shit about puppets. And somethin' about a conquistador, both in the e-mails and phone calls. Couldn't make much sense of it to be honest, but Dobkin was plenty steamed about somethin' every time he mentioned a conquistador."

"You have all this recorded?"

"Yep, right here on this laptop. That and a bunch of video

surveillance. Just like you asked."

"Outstanding. You guys do good work."

Kid said, "There's something else you might need to know, Derek. There was a lot of talk about an airplane and longitude/latitude coordinates."

Parnell raised an eyebrow at Elaine, an accusing glance. He pointed at the laptop and said, "It's on here?"

"Yep."

"Open her up. Let's have a look."

The geographical coordinates marked the exact location of the Hyacinth mines. Weasel used the laptop to run a check on the registration number of the flyover plane that Jenn had picked up. The plane was a 2007 Cessna 172 Skyhawk owned by Antonio Rodrigo Marquez of San Antonio, Texas. A home address was listed for Marquez. Elaine recognized it, felt her stomach turn over. Same street where he'd kept her drugged and imprisoned.

At the conclusion of the debriefing, Parnell showed them the newspaper article about the government crackdown on the homeless.

"A war is coming, people," he informed them, "either with the feds or with Dobkin's syndicate . . . probably both. We need to be ready."

"So what're we waitin' for?" Flywheel said. "Let's go get that motherfucker."

"Soon, Javion," Parnell said. "No one wants him more than I do. But a shit storm's comin'. I'd like to save as many of our brothers and sisters as we can."

Kid and Flywheel weren't happy. Elaine could see it in their body language. They were cowboys, gunslingers with itchy trigger fingers. They had just spent the better part of a week living in a rental car, casing their target. They had been recruited for a posse and were eager for some real action.

Wheeler and Dixon left. Weasel stayed behind. He clapped Parnell on the shoulder. "They're young and eager, Derek. Ready to mix it up."

"You mean what we did at Cottonwood wasn't enough to satisfy their bloodlust for a while?"

"They wanna see justice done."

"So do I. And the young guns will get their opportunity soon."

Weasel left. Parnell and Elaine were alone. He said to her, "Incredibly small world, isn't it, E? The plane that flew over checking us out and this Marquez asshole who owns it, is connected with Dobkin in some way. Marquez is also the one who picked you up in Mexico and says he wants me dead because he thinks I killed Tico Samuels, who is allegedly his cousin. Very karmic shit."

Elaine thought about the man photographing them from the road when they rode the Union Pacific freighter. *Is the mystery shutterbug also connected with this? How wise is it to keep that from Derek? Is it too late to tell him about it?*

"I have to ask you, Derek. Are you angry with me about the plane? Do you think I caused all of this?"

"What? No. None of this is your fault, babe. Why would you even say that?"

"I don't know. I just don't believe Antonio Marquez would be in the picture if it wasn't for me."

"He's after *me*," Parnell said with assurance. "My gut's tellin' me that he was probably activated the second I crossed the border."

Elaine wasn't sure he really believed that, but she loved him for saying it. "Then why didn't he pick you up instead of me?"

"Because he couldn't find me. Besides, I'm not as good lookin' as you."

He smiled at her, but she knew that look. He had figured it out. He knew she hadn't ridden the rails from Costa Rica. Derek knew she had flown to Monterrey on a commercial airline and that she had been abducted at the airport. Although nothing was said, she felt like she had let him down, betrayed him in the worst way.

"I'm so sorry, babe," she said to him.

"You have no reason to be sorry for anything, Lainey."

"Oh, but I do. I have a lot to be sorry about."

And that's when she told him about the two men in the raspberry red Honda following the train and snapping zoom-lens photos of her, Cale, and Ann.

His pasted-on smile disappeared.

Preparing For War

BIG TROUBLE BREWING.
Elaine's disclosure about the overly curious photographer only threw more kindling on the fire that was beginning to burn out of control. Parnell wondered who the guy was. Who was he working for? Dobkin? One of the federal alphabet agencies? Was he an independent bounty hunter?

The news about the government crackdown on squatters also distressed him. It impacted his plans to go after Dobkin. The feds wouldn't hesitate to use force in dealing with the so-called hobo problem, and he felt the need to take action. Parnell envisioned another Ruby Ridge shootout or the federal siege of David Koresh and the Branch Davidian compound in Waco by the FBI, ATF, and Texas National Guard. Would the feds storm into Shangri-La and the Hyacinth mines as they had done in those incidents? Would they pull a stunt similar to the MOVE blitzkrieg in Philadelphia, where a police helicopter dropped bombs on a row house, killing eleven black liberation members and starting fires that destroyed 65 homes?

The federal government loved to play hardball.

This country that had so unjustly disowned him took no prisoners.

Parnell wouldn't go quietly. He'd had enough. He was tired of running. Tired of hiding. He'd be ready for them. He'd be lying in wait for Dobkin, too, should he elect to make a move. Elaine had lobbied heavily the past few days for them to just pick up and leave, go back to their safe house in Costa Rica. "Let's take Jenn with us and get out while we still can," she'd pleaded with him.

He refused. He had a duty to his fellow breezers, he'd told her. Dobkin and Miles had to be eliminated. Time to see justice done.

"And just why is saving your hobo friends your job?" she'd railed. "Why are they your responsibility? You're talking like a crazy man, Derek. Listen to yourself. It's insane. You can't take on the U.S. government, hon. You used to laugh at the Liberty Dogs for wanting to do the same thing. I remember you saying the military would make them a tiny grease spot on the map. What makes you think it'll be any different for us?"

"Look, E, I hear what you're saying all right? But I'm not gonna run anymore. It's time to stand up to the bullies."

"I'm just asking you to listen to reason, babe. Let's get out of this screwed-up country and go back to our beach house. Let's get married the way we talked about and enjoy the rest of our lives together, lay on the beach and listen to the waves lap the shore."

"If you're scared, why don't you take Jenn and go back to Flagstaff. You'll feel a lot safer in your house with your sister Gina. Frank's there, too."

"No," she'd said adamantly. "That'd be way worse for me. The feds would find me there. And I'm not spending another day without you, Derek. I've had enough of being alone."

He'd sighed, considered the situation. "Okay, how about this? How about we leave after I get Dobkin and Miles?"

"But that could take weeks. Months, maybe. You don't have a clue where Blanton Miles is."

"My gut says he's close."

She'd given him a crooked smile. "Your gut does an awful lot of thinking for you."

"Hasn't let me down yet."

She stared at him, a penetrating gaze. "You really make things difficult. I must be a loon, but I'm with you till the bitter end, you crazy bastard."

He laughed and kissed her. "What makes you think the end will be bitter?"

She answered with a measured look that gave him pause.

He'd worked feverishly over the next four days, creating more living spaces down in mineshaft #3. His breezer friends would need decent places to stay after their transfer from Shangri-La. Elaine and Jenn helped him install plumbing and run electrical wiring. Weasel made daily runs to Kanab to pick up needed parts, air mattresses, blankets, and food. T-Seed, Flywheel, and Kid traded off security shifts. T-Seed also assisted Parnell with the construction of a crude shack up on the north ridge so those keeping watch over the solar panels would have shade from the intense sun during the day and protection from the cold winds that gusted over the peak at night.

Human watches were effective to a point, but one—or even two—guards couldn't possibly cover the entire Hyacinth periphery sufficiently. The mines covered acres. The area had hundreds of nooks and crannies. They needed electronic detection to alert them of perimeter breaches. On his trips to Kanab, Weasel purchased motion detection sensors that enabled them to build an invisible electronic fence around the mining yard circumference. They got the infrared beam apparatus and zoom cameras installed the first day, and hardwired the monitoring station in Parnell's underground quarters that night. After many test runs the following morning, he felt confident they had all ground intrusion exposures covered.

They remained extremely vulnerable from the air, however. Fortunately, there had been no more flyovers since the day the psychiatrist, Marquez, had paid them a visit in his single propeller plane. Parnell didn't really know how much of a threat Marquez posed, but they had to be vigilant concerning attacks from the air. John Dobkin owned a small fleet of helicopters and could inflict substantial damage on their power grid with them. Of course, the feds also had tremendous firepower from the air. It would be like shooting fish in a barrel for the National Guard. A single chopper with a sharpshooter could hover over the north ridge and take out their entire electrical system with a few well-placed shots.

Next on his list was building up their defense. Parnell knew a black market arms dealer who operated out in the desert near Mount Carmel, an old Nam vet by the name of Buster who owned a large warehouse stocked with illegal military ordnance. Buster sold quality dependable arms and ammo—no cheap knockoffs—and his prices were reasonable. He was also known to be discreet.

Since this was to be a large purchase and Parnell wanted someone watching his back, he took Kid with him. Billy Dixon had done two tours in Afghanistan and was very familiar with military weaponry.

Buster greeted them as they entered the spacious depository. He was tall and wiry with a gray ponytail trailing down his back like a squirrel's tail. He moved with a nervous energy and talked around a lump of tobacco in his cheek. A frayed, faded-red MAKE AMERICA GREAT AGAIN baseball cap adorned his head.

Buster showed them around his warehouse and pointed out his best sellers. Parnell hurried him along, wanting to make his purchases and get out quickly. He didn't want to be here if and when the feds swooped in on this place. He bought a hand-held M203 40-millimeter grenade launcher mounted under-barrel on an M16 rifle with half a dozen high explosive grenade cartridges. He also picked up a pair of Bushmaster assault carbines with ten 30-round magazines, four Glock automatic pistols, and a Tec-9 semi-automatic with four clips of ammo. Total price tag came close to ten grand. Buster was so happy with the sale he threw in two police-issue tasers Parnell was eyeing for the Dobkin abduction.

The arms dealer locked up the warehouse for an hour and drove them out into the desert to a firing range he'd constructed to give them a live tutorial on how to use the grenade launcher. He showed them how to attach the launcher to the rifle and the quickest and safest way to load the bright green-and-gold cartridges into the single-shot weapon.

"This baby's a lightweight marvel," Buster said in his croaky voice before spitting a wad of chaw into a tin can. "Only about twelve pounds. But it has the explosiveness to blow a ginormous hole in the Great Wall of China, you can be sure of that. It'll annihilate anything unfortunate enough to be within a hunnerd feet of point of impact." Buster took aim on a target painted on the facing of a large boulder a hundred yards off, the gob of tobacco puffing out his cheek. "You got yer dual sighting—a leaf assembly in front and a quadrant scope on the rear. Makes for pinpoint accuracy. This here's the trigger, in front of the magazine. The mag serves as your hand grip . . . like this." He moved his arm out of the way so they could see his hand position. "Soft pull, and . . ." He squeezed the trigger. The grenade left the rifle with a muffled *plink*, the projectile whistling toward the target. Parnell and Kid watched in awe as the boulder blew apart in a cloud of dust and rock fragments. Nothing left but a smoking hole.

Buster lowered the weapon and admired his shot. "You'll notice the lack of recoil," he said. "Also, good thing it's extremely accurate because that awesome little bang just cost four-hundred bills. These cartridges are super expensive so make your shots count, gents. And by all means, be careful how you handle 'em."

Parnell asked, "Will this thing bring down a small airplane?"

"Whoa! Hold on there, King Midas." Buster laid the modified M16 in the back of his pickup. "I don't know what you have in mind, bro, and I don't wanna know. It's difficult to hit a movin' target. And remember, this launcher is only accurate up to about two-hundred yards. That's over land. You shoot up into the sky and miss, that grenade might come right back down and blow your ass to smithereens."

"He's right about that," Kid said.

Parnell said, "You got any kind of anti-aircraft weaponry,

Buster?"

"Well ain't you the evil terrorist," he said with a snide grin. "Sure thing. I got somethin' that'll bring down a plane. But it'll cost ya."

"How much?"

"Eight grand."

"What do I get for eight large?"

"A Russian SA-7 MANPAD."

Dixon told Parnell, "A MANPAD is a shoulder-launched surface-to-air missile system. They're deadly."

"You're goddamned right they are," Buster said. "The rockets contain a guidance system that locks in on flyin' machines. Ya let it rip an' it finds the target for ya. Blows it right outta the sky. Ya hardly even hafta aim. It's a sweet deal."

Parnell figured Buster was trying to gouge him. "How many missiles do I get with it?"

"Two."

"Just two?"

Buster cringed. "Methinks King Midas is wantin' to bring down an entire air force."

Parnell laughed. "And methinks Buster the Guster is ripping me off. I'll give you five grand."

"Make it six and I'll throw in a third missile."

"I'll take the third missile, but my offer is still five."

"Shit, partner. A man's gotta make a livin'."

"Looks to me like you're not struggling any, Buster."

"Well, I think you owe me four-hundred for the grenade we just shot."

Parnell shook his head. "Sorry. Cost of doin' business, my friend. Five grand. Not a penny more. Take it or leave it."

"Shit, man. I already gave you two free tasers. All right, goddammit, I'll take it. Let's see the money."

"I'll settle up after I inspect the merchandise."

Buster smiled a gap-toothed grin and spat a wad of tobacco in the sand. "Your mama didn't raise no fools. Let's get back to the shop," he said, climbing behind the wheel of his pickup. "Just remember, this sale is off the books. No paperwork. You get caught with this shit, it's on you. We ain't never met and we don't know each other. Understood?"

"No need to recite the fine print to us," Kid said, opening the passenger-side door and scooting into the middle of the front seat.

Buster dipped into his bag of Red Man chew. Pulled out a plug and shoved it under his cheek. He gave Kid a sidelong glance and said, "There's *always* a need to recite the fine print in this business, son. Don't you ever forget that."

Parnell tried to hide his smile as he climbed in the pickup and closed the door behind him. On the ride back to the warehouse, he thought about the purchases he'd just made. Fifteen thousand in cold hard cash to defend themselves against the U.S. government and John Dobkin's syndicate.

Such a waste.

Suddenly he felt clammy. He could hear his own voice rumbling in his head, a phone conversation he'd had more than three years ago with Blanton Miles concerning the Liberty Dogs' plans to go up against the U.S. military:

"They still planning on driving their armored vehicles up Pennsylvania Avenue, guns blazing? Morons! They'll end up a tiny grease spot on the map. The feds will annihilate them. Don't these whack jobs know what they're up against?"

He thought about the cache of lethal arms they'd be hauling back to the Hyacinth mines.

He trembled. Felt shaky and weak.

Do I really want to go to war with the world's mightiest military? The smart thing would be to go to Vegas to pick up Dobkin immediately. Dobkin could lead them to Miles. Parnell could get the pair back to the mines and strap them into the Rolling Inferno, send them straight to hell. Get out before the U.S. Army juggernaut moved in on them. Escape the States and live out the rest of his days in peace with Lainey.

But there were his breezer friends to think about. So many good people who needed protection. He couldn't abandon them.

A small tremor rolled through him. Cold fingers of angst crept up his spine. Bubbling, burning bile filled his throat. He felt faint, needed to lie down but couldn't. Parnell stuck his head out the truck window and vomited, the wind carrying it away.

Kid touched his shoulder. "You okay?"

"Yeah, just dandy," Parnell said, wiping his mouth.

Buster looked across Kid at Parnell. "Methinks King Midas got a bit too much of the grenade gas. I've seen CS gas make men twice your size keel over and spew their guts out. I got a good deal goin' on gas masks if you're interested."

Kid shook his head. "We shot off a grenade cartridge, not tear gas. There ain't any CS gas in grenades."

"Young punks these days," Buster said with disgust. "Think they know everything. Gimme a break, dude. A man's gotta make a livin'."

Remember the Alamo

THE HYACINTH SITE HAD TRANSFORMED into a small community. The mines buzzed with new arrivals—a dozen Shangri-La breezers taxied in from Winslow by Javion Wheeler and Greg Bethea in the rental cars. Jenn knew most of them from her brief stay at the large hobo camp: Chef Alice, Fred "Fingers" Johnston and his son Zack, Buttonhead Murphy, Harvey Henshaw, Broadway Bling, Oshkosh Moss. Jenn did not know five of them: two young women close to her age, two men in their fifties, and a teenage boy who never went anywhere without his skateboard.

A revitalizing spirit came with the new guests. Fingers Johnston strummed his guitar and sang accompanied by son Zack on bass. Their music filtered through the mining yard while folks partied and laughed and danced late into the night. The sweet smell of Buttonhead's grass perfumed the air. Booze purchased in Kanab flowed freely. Chef Alice prepared tasty meals of store-bought meats and vegetables and they ate like royalty.

This Hyacinth renaissance did wonders for Jenn's well-being. But occasionally her spirits would flag. Something would remind her of their current predicament. She would glimpse the hardware that controlled the infrared security fences. Or see the guards walking patrol carrying serious assault weapons. Yesterday she caught a look at the scary-looking rocket launchers Poppy and Kid brought back from Mount Carmel. In one of her weaker moments, she had wept.

How have we come to this?

Staying busy helped to calm her nerves. Jenn worked long hours with Poppy building out the new living spaces. Poppy was patient with her, teaching her the finer points of plumbing, electrical wiring, and basic carpentry. Their first big project was fixing the water corrosion problem. Water pumped in from the underground aquifer had been running a rusty orange since the day she and Poppy arrived. This week they saw sand, calcium, and algae clouding up the flow. The water had become unsafe to drink and nasty to shower under. To fix it, they'd pumped chemicals into the spring and replaced the old Hyacinth galvanized steel pipes with

PVC tubing. Twenty-four hours later they had clean running water. On top of the new plumbing system they'd built three new shower heads with fiberglass stalls and two sinks. They'd even fashioned a crude community loo out of discarded aluminum cisterns, creating a urinal trough and two toilets that flushed. Not stopping there, Poppy had also reworked a large tipple tank the miners once used for washing raw coal, creating a rudimentary septic system. Jenn wouldn't miss the old smelly privy. No more squatting down on rough outhouse boards and holding her nose.

    She cherished this time with her father. In her eyes, he was an engineering wizard. She marveled at what he'd accomplished here, converting an abandoned coal mine in the middle of the Utah desert into semi-comfortable living accommodations. In his more playful moments, he referred to it as his Hotel Sahara.

    And there's that weird roller coaster of his, too.

    She laughed. *My father, the amusement park impresario.*

    She loved him. Now more than ever. She was ashamed of the way she'd treated him. He deserved better.

    This morning he and his posse left for Vegas to go after John Dobkin. She was a bundle of nerves. She wanted to go with them, as did Elaine. But Poppy had been resolute. Told them this was no job for women. Elaine got all bent out of shape, accusing him of being sexist. But Jenn knew what he meant. He was just protecting them. Poppy didn't want to risk losing the only two people he loved in a risky endeavor. Still, Jenn would have preferred to face the fire with him. This waiting without knowing was punishing her.

    The departure of the posse left Cale Turnipseed heading the Hyacinth security detail. Poppy had left him in charge and appointed Broadway Bling, Oshkosh Moss, and Shawn Fikespaw as guards. Jenn wanted to see Cale. *Needed* to see him. She felt compelled to explain that embarrassing situation he had walked in on several nights ago in the headframe, with her and Ann cuddling under the blankets. Cale was up on the north ridge standing watch this afternoon. It was the perfect opportunity to talk to him.

    She went to the coolers in mineshaft #3, picked out two bottles of iced tea. Shoved them in her backpack and headed up to the ridge.

    Jenn thought about Cale as she walked through the yard. Something about him consumed her. Completely. He invaded her thoughts often. Every time she saw him she experienced a wonderful hormonal rush. When she was with him she became warm and tingly. Felt like she was flying nestled inside a fluffy cloud. The mere sight of him made her feel like she was defying gravity.

There's definitely something happening here, Jenn.

Something sweet. Something powerful. Something blindly and mysteriously significant.

She'd only known him for a couple of weeks, but there was an acute familiarity about him.

Strange.

Some kind of bizarre déjà vu thing going on?

They'd shared only a handful of conversations, but she remembered every word. She liked the way he talked, his drawn-out Georgia cadence giving his speech a lovely lilting rhythm. And he *listened*, a rare quality in most men. His broad shoulders and athletic build? *Oh, my God!* Lately she found herself fantasizing about running her hands over his lean body and making love to him.

But he thinks you're gay, Jenn.

Time to clear up that misconception.

She climbed the ladder up to the ridge.

He gave her a wide smile as she approached the wood-frame guard shack.

"Well my day just became ten times more awesome," he said, dark sunglasses shielding his eyes.

She returned his smile. "Thought you might be thirsty sittin' up here all by your lonesome." She handed him one of the bottles.

"Oh, thanks. You're so sweet, Jenn," he said, popping the cap and taking a swig. "Ahhh . . . good stuff. Glad you came up. This watch is pretty boring."

"I guess it's good for all of us you're bored," she said. "Is it against Hyacinth security policy to have company while you're on watch?"

"Not when it's the boss's beautiful daughter," he said, pointing at the bench seat next to him.

Did he really just call me beautiful? She sat and opened her iced tea, took a sip. "You and Poppy did a great job on this shack."

Cale waved his hand. "Ah, nothin' to it, really. Just slapped some wood together and anchored the frame to the rock. Only took a few hours."

She looked out over the grid of solar panels to the sprawling desert canyon below. "It's a gorgeous view here. How high up are we?"

"I reckon it's close to a thousand feet down to the desert."

"Sure is beautiful. All the crimson mesas and hills. It's like we landed on another planet."

He scanned the desert landscape. "Yeah. It does have that cool alien vibe to it."

"Ann Finnegan says God exists in every cell of nature," she said, thinking this might be a good lead-in to explaining her actions with Ann. "Do you believe that?"

"I guess, yeah."

"So what we see from up here is a true work of art, right? A celestial masterpiece?"

Cale nodded. "That's an interesting description."

"Ann's made me see things in a new light. Oh, she annoyed the hell out of me at first. But now I realize the woman's got a good grip on things. Better than most of us, I'd say."

He studied her from behind his shades. "You two seem to have gotten pretty close."

She wished she could see his eyes. "Not the way you probably think, Cale. I came up here to tell you about that thing with Ann and me the other night? When you walked in on us?"

"Aw, no . . ." he stammered, looking like he'd rather jump off the ridge than discuss this. "You don't need to explain any—"

"But I *do*. I feel like what you saw gave you the wrong impression of me."

"Really, Jenn. It doesn't matter what I think about—"

"It matters to *me*. I know you're good friends with Ann. You know she's a lesbian. I can get a little wild now and then, but I don't swing that way. I'm not gay and I want you to know that about me. I *need* you to know that about me."

He stared at her, unable to find any words.

"Say something, Cale."

He looked down into his lap, absently ran his hand over the stock of his rifle. Remained silent.

Her nervousness made her ramble on. "I'll tell it to you like it is. I had a relationship with a girl in the Colorado caves. Her name was Luanne . . . Lulu. We were best friends and lovers. But that was a very different time and headspace. Those were my man-hating days, for obvious reasons. Lu and me, we just clicked from the beginning. We looked out for each other. Had each other's backs. I loved her, but that was then. This is now. I am *NOT* attracted to other women."

"Jenn, you really don't have to—"

"Yes, I do, Cale. My whole world came crashing down when you saw me with Ann. You must think I'm a real tart."

"Stop beating yourself up. I don't think any of those things about you. And I don't care what you were doin' with Ann. I only care that you're with me here."

He smiled and it comforted her. She felt an overpowering urge to kiss him. Wondered whether she should risk it. Decided against it. Determined she'd gone this far and should finish coming clean with him.

"There's more you need to know about me."

He removed his sunglasses and eyed her with mock suspicion. "Are you trying to make me *not* like you, Jenn?"

"No. Oh no. Not at all. I just—"

"You have skeletons in your closet bad enough to turn me against you?"

"I murdered a man last week. In Cottonwood."

"Wait. *What*? You mean the hit man who killed your Russ? *You* pulled the trigger?"

"Yeah, I did," she said, dropping her head and looking down into her lap. "I shot him. Five or six times. Like a homicidal psycho. I've been having a hard time dealing with it."

"But Derek told us *he* gunned him down."

"Really?"

"That's what he said."

Poppy is covering for me? Interesting.

"No, unfortunately, I was the shooter, Cale. I'm a killer. Like father, like daughter as they say. I'm tryin' to purge it from my memory, but you just can't forget somethin' like that. Only thing keepin' me halfway sane is what Poppy keeps telling me. The scumbag deserved to die."

Cale reached across and rubbed her shoulder. "Wow, Jenn. I'm so sorry. I can't imagine going through that."

"Me either, really. Never thought I had it in me."

They sat next to each other, gazing out over the arid landscape, quiet, absorbed in their individual thoughts. The talk of killing had reawakened Jenn's fears. She trembled as she imagined what might be ahead for them here at the mines.

She stole a look at Cale. Looked past him to see the binoculars and walkie-talkie on the shelf near him. "Do you think we're gonna be attacked?"

He came out of his reverie. "Sadly that's the talk goin' round. I can't escape the feelin' that we're here in the Alamo and General Santa Anna is organizing his troops for the big push."

"The Alamo?" She spied the deadly-looking semi-automatic rifle in his lap, the case of rounds at his feet, the rocket launcher standing next to his right elbow with the long missile locked in and ready to fire. "I don't think Santa Anna had the firepower to compete with you. The Mexican infantry only had flintlocks and muskets and short range cannons. You've got . . . well, you've got an arsenal."

"Yeah, so do those we might be tangling with. Too bad it isn't still 1830, huh?"

"You mean the Alamo? The Alamo siege was 1836," she said, hoping she didn't sound too smug. "Late February through early March to be exact. Thirteen days total."

"How'd you know that?"

"Most Americans know about the Alamo, Cale."

"Not those specific details." He tilted his head, scrutinizing her. "You know, I think you've been holdin' out on me, Jenn."

"Really? Enlighten me."

"I think you're more intelligent than you care to let on. You've said things that blow me away, and I've wondered how a girl who, um . . . who had no education past the fifth grade—"

"Sixth!"

"Excuse me," he said with an impish grin. "How someone with a *sixth* grade education can be so smart. I mean, you were held captive for what? Six years?"

"Seven. I was eleven when I was kidnapped and Poppy rescued me right after my eighteenth birthday. Seven years. My *lost* years."

"So how'd you get to be so smart? Surely those pedophile bastards didn't let you out for school every day."

"No, but—"

"And I'm quite sure those idiots weren't teachin' you math and science and English. So what I'm left with is you're just a natural genius."

"Stop it," she said with a blush and playful slap on his arm. "I'm self-taught. Did a lot of reading when I was inside. Read hundreds of books. Not much else to do during the, um . . . down time."

"Those twisted bastards supplied you with a bookmobile?"

She laughed. "No, silly. I learned how to play the game to get books. A lot of us girls figured out how to get things we wanted from those . . . *pigs*. Not braggin', but I had two of the men wrapped around my little finger. They brought me books. Mostly non-fiction. History, biographies. Fodor's travel guides. Memoirs. Condensed encyclopedias. I told them what I wanted and they got it for me. I devoured those books. At least when I wasn't . . ." she bowed her head, her mind flooded with memories of the revolting things she had to do to get favors. ". . . well, you know. Those books were my picture window on the world I couldn't see. They were my education. And Greg Bethea just brought his library over from Shangri-La. I can't wait to dig into his stacks."

"Yeah, Greg's always been a big reader," he said. "You wouldn't think a guy with the 'bo handle of Weasel would be all that literate. But he's really smart. Like you."

"You're sweet to say that, Cale. But I have to confess. I got lucky on the Alamo. You hit on one of my favorite topics. I've always been fascinated by the Texas Revolution. I can tell you all about the Battle of San Jacinto, where we got our revenge on Santa Anna for the atrocities at the Alamo."

She looked at him, but he remained focused on the desert vista below. She said, "Poppy gave me my love of the printed word. He spent a lot of time with me when I was a little girl. He doted on me. He used to read to me before I learned how."

He turned to face her. "It must've been incredible growing up with Derek Parnell as your dad."

"It had its moments," she said. "I'll tell you, though. When Poppy showed up at the Liberty Dogs' compound and freed me from that hell, I hardly recognized him. He was a different man. Completely changed. Not at all the quiet, loving dad I once knew. He had a hard edge to him. He was violent and cold blooded. Suspicious of everyone and every*thing*. I was shocked. He scared me, Cale. Still does sometimes."

"We have something in common, then. He intimidates the hell outta me, too."

"He does?"

"Yeah. I think that's the main reason he didn't want me in his posse. Derek wants guys who won't back down from him. He recruited hardboiled types who are like him. Weasel tells it to him like it is without fear. Greg's a hard case. Your father and him go way back. Kid and Flywheel are cut from the same sheet of steel. Hard and unbreakable. No disrespect to your dad, but I don't really wanna be like those guys."

She couldn't hide her surprise. "I'm glad you feel that way."

He regarded her for a long beat. "I misread you, Jenn."

"In what way?"

"I thought you were attracted to bad boy types."

"My Russell wasn't that way," she said, the thought of her late lover bringing her close to tears.

"Was he an altar boy?"

"Huh? What're you talking about, Cale?"

"You called me a altar boy, remember? Put a negative spin on it, like there's something unmanly about bein' polite."

She hid her face behind her hand. "Jeesh, yeah. Unfortunately I do," she said, feeling her cheeks burn. "I'm sorry about that. I've said a lot of snarky things to people lately. Poppy included. I haven't really been myself, with all that's happened."

"Understood completely. But do you think I'm a lightweight goody-goody two-shoes? A nerdy kind of guy?"

"No, I—"

"Because that seems to be the general opinion of me."

"Oh, Cale, no. I don't for a second think you're a lightweight or a nerd or anything close to those things. You're Captain Turnipseed. Remember? You rescue damsels in distress."

"Yeah, sure I do," he said with a chuckle. He reached across and placed his hand on top of hers. His touch sent her floating. "I know it's probably too soon. You just lost Russ and I want to honor that. But I can't hold back anymore. I have to tell you . . . I like you, Jennifer Parnell. A lot. It might surprise you to know that I've been thinkin' about you the past few days."

She thought she might pass out from pure joy. "Good thoughts?"

"*Wonderful* thoughts."

She beamed at him. He caressed her knuckles. Her throat went dry. She tipped her bottle and took two long swallows of iced tea. Jenn wanted to blurt out right then and there that she thought she might be falling in love with him, but thought it too crazy to verbalize.

He seemed to be struggling to find the right words. Finally he said, "I have to tell you that my, um . . . my thoughts about you haven't been . . . well, they haven't been entirely pure. I think I know you well enough to tell you I have kind of a dirty mind and—"

"Jesus, Cale!" She burst out laughing. "Of *course* you do! You're a healthy hetero male. I'd be worried about you if you *didn't* have dirty thoughts. I'm flattered."

"Really?"

"Absolutely," she said, setting her tea aside and wrapping her hands around his, squeezing gently. "I've tried not to be obvious about it, but I've grown awfully fond of you, too. You think my thoughts have been pure?"

"I don't—I don't know, Jenn."

"Pure thoughts are for altar boys, Cale."

He laughed. "Well, that's certainly not me," he said before leaning over and kissing her. His approach was tentative at first, moist pecks along her upper lip and cheeks, his slow, sensual movements making her crazy, giddy.

Jenn wanted him. *Craved* him. He propped his gun against the bench and took her in his arms, began kissing her with a hungry open-mouthed passion. She felt his hand move to her right breast, his deft fingers massaging her nipple through her blouse. She was soaring, hovering over a desert dreamscape where fantasy dovetailed with reality. She wanted him to take her right here in this open-walled lookout shack high atop the north ridge. Her hand ventured up his muscled thigh. She brushed her fingers across the bulge in his pants, felt him respond. Heard him sigh and whisper her name between kisses.

And then they heard the drone of an airplane engine.

Their hands stopped moving. They sat rigid, their mouths pressed together, listening.

The engine noise increased in volume.

Cale pulled away from her and grabbed the binoculars. Scanned the horizon.

"Damn, this can't be good," he said, holding the field glasses steady. "I think it's the same plane that buzzed us last week."

Jenn could see the outline of a small aircraft in the far distance, coming in low, making a fast approach.

"Here, have a look," he said, handing her the binoculars.

She trained the glasses on the plane, adjusted the focus. Single propeller Cessna. Blue and white with red trim. The plane banked in a slight turn enabling her to read the registration. Anxiety gripped her.

"Yep, it's definitely them," she said.

They watched as the pilot brought the plane down close to the desert floor.

Cale shouted, "The crazy bastard's tryin' to find somewhere to land. He'll rip the shit outta that landing gear."

Jenn said, "They're gonna crash."

But she was wrong. She held the binoculars steady. Watched in stunned disbelief as the aircraft bounced twice, kicking up small explosions of sand, then set down on a long strip of hardpan and coasted to a stop.

Cale snatched the walkie-talkie to notify Oshkosh. "I think General Santa Anna just arrived."

Part 4:

FLASHPOINT

The Psychiatrist's Prescription
Las Vegas Shuffle
Jailbirds Will Sing
The Snake and the Mongoose
Love for the Java Angel
Limousine Testimony
Doctor Strangelove's Plan
Karmic Mood Swings
The Omniscient Scriptwriter
Prairie Dogs and Bible Lessons
Miles From Nowhere
Evacuation Strategy
Fire In the Hole
Dirty Birds
Parnell's Westbound Whistle Stop
The Last Train to Winslow

The Psychiatrist's Prescription

ELAINE EMERGED FROM MINESHAFT #1 and entered the yard. The bright sun warmed her face. She shook her head, her freshly shampooed hair brushing her shoulders. She adjusted her eyepatch to a more comfortable position and inhaled deeply, the fresh air invigorating her.

She'd spent the morning belowground in gloomy despair. Derek had left at dawn and she'd been mired in a melancholic funk as deep and dark as their subterranean living space. He'd motored off to Las Vegas with his posse. Said he'd never leave her behind again, and yet he had. She'd raised a big stink yesterday when he'd informed her of his plans. The scene, played out in front of several of the newest Hyacinth residents, embarrassed her, but she finally got him to agree to burner phones. A way to keep in touch. A victory of sorts.

Still she worried. He was on a dangerous mission.

Will I ever see him again?

Oh, quit being such a drama queen, woman!

She touched the phone in her jeans pocket for reassurance. Her lifeline to him. Wondered if he had made it to Vegas yet. Wanted to call him but knew she shouldn't.

She squinted across the yard, which was strangely empty this early afternoon hour.

Where is everybody?

And then she heard shouts. From outside. Near the rail spur. Angry male voices.

BLAM, BLAM, BLAM! A trio of gunshots resounded, loud as sonic booms.

She ducked instinctively. Looked around.

Warning yells. *That sounds like Cale.*

More shots fired, the sound of each concussion piercing holes in her nerves.

Screams came from the rail spur.

She raced inside the mine entrance and grabbed her rifle, the one Derek had instructed her to keep close at hand. On rubbery legs she ran toward the altercation, buzzing voices becoming more distinct as she ambled through the yard. The rifle was heavy in her shaky arms. She prayed she wouldn't have to use it.

She rounded the bend and stopped. Two bodies on the ground, fifty feet apart, both pocked with bloody bullet holes. A small clutch of people—Broadway Bling, Buttonhead Murphy, Chef Alice, two of the young women—gawked from the fringes, keeping their distance. Ann Finnegan leaned over a body, shaking her head as if acknowledging defeat. Elaine ventured closer, saw the body Ann tended to was Oshkosh Moss, the older black man who had been walking point security.

"Mister Moss is gone, may God bless his soul," Ann announced, backing away, mouthing a silent prayer.

Cale Turnipseed and Jenn stood in rigid shooting stances, training their weapons on two men who stood near the other dead body. The two men held their hands high in surrender. A pair of revolvers lay in the sand at their feet.

Elaine gripped the rifle so tight her hands hurt. She advanced cautiously. The faces of the visitors became clear: Antonio Marquez and Diego. *Oh shit no! Please tell me this isn't real!* Her legs trembled. Dizziness overcame her. Their faces transported her back to that Winslow hotel room when they tried to have their way with her. Their being here in this time and space was so odd it threw her off kilter. Like one of those scenarios in a nightmarish dream that, while vivid and convincing, made no logical sense.

She focused on Cale, keeping Marquez and Diego out of her line of sight. "What, um . . . what happened here?"

Broadway Bling answered for the group of bystanders. "We all saw the plane land the other side of the ridge. Saw these men get out and approach the railhead, lookin' for a way in. We got here just in time to see the shootout. Just in time to see Mossy go down."

Tears glistened on Broadway's face. Chef Alice and Buttonhead Murphy were stunned. The two young women sobbed, obviously in shock.

Cale spoke without turning away from his prisoners. "Crazy bastards brought their plane down in the desert, other side of the ridge. Jenn and I saw them come in. It was insane. By the time we got down here to assist Mossy they opened fire on the old man and killed him. I put down the shooter. Jenn clipped the short dude in the hand."

Marquez spoke. "We fired in self defense. I'm sorry anyone had to die, but your security guy went crazy. You have to believe me when I say we come in peace. We harbor no ill will toward you folks."

"Bullshit!" Broadway answered. "Your guy shot first. Mossy didn't stand a chance. In fact, if T-Seed and Jenn hadn't shown up, we'd prob'ly all be dead."

Marquez kept his voice level. "I believe you're being a bit melodramatic, sir."

Cale glanced back over his shoulder at Elaine. "These assholes say they know you. You know these guys?"

"Unfortunately I do."

Marquez said, "Lovely to see you again, Elaine."

Diego gave her a scornful look with those predatory eyes of his.

Elaine resisted the urge to pull the trigger, put them both down.

Cale nodded in Elaine's direction. "You have business with this woman?"

Marquez shook his head. "Not directly. Actually, we came looking for Derek Parnell. We have a proposition for him."

"What kind of proposition?"

"We can deliver someone he's wanted for a long time. A man named Blanton Miles. That name ring a bell with anybody here?"

Elaine maintained a poker face as the familiar name floated in the air.

"Can't say we have," Cale said.

The doctor said, "Well, I hear Parnell's got a heavy score to settle with Mister Miles. I can help him accomplish it."

Jenn said, "He already told you. We don't know any Blanton Miles."

Marquez chuckled. "Oh I believe you do, sweetheart. You might not know him personally. Probably never seen him in the flesh. He's like a ghost. A digital entity. He's there in the phone lines, the cell towers. He's embedded in computer systems and databases. Doesn't like to show himself. Completely a behind-the-scenes type. But I happen to know Blanton Miles is a real, flesh-and-blood human being. I've worked for him for many years. His code name is PuppetMaster. He worked for your father during those years he was looking for you, Jennifer. Actually your father worked for *him*. Parnell just didn't happen to realize it at the time."

"Why does Miles need a code name?" Cale asked.

"Because he works for a syndicate headed by a man I'm quite sure you know, Jennifer . . . John Dobkin. Code name Hyena. You and your late boyfriend—Russell Holt—testified against him at the trial, if I'm not mistaken? Please accept my condolences. I'm very sorry for your loss."

The code names PuppetMaster and Hyena were familiar to Elaine. She had sat through a couple of long briefings with Derek and his posse. The intel brought back from Vegas was liberally sprinkled with references to puppets and hyenas, along with coyotes and wolves.

Jenn said, "So you're saying you can deliver Blanton Miles to my father?"

"Yes, I can. *We* can."

"Why would you turn on your boss?" Cale wanted to know.

"My own survival. I've reached the end of my usefulness to the organization. I've discovered there's a contract out on me and Miles plans to execute it. We have a meeting planned for day after tomorrow."

"Where?" Jenn asked.

"Las Vegas."

"Why Vegas?"

"Because that's where Dobkin is."

Cale looked confused. "I'm not following."

"Dobkin and Miles have had a huge falling out. Miles wants me to take out Dobkin and hopes that I'll go down in the process. If not, I'm sure Miles has a backup plan for me to make sure my life ends. He's very diabolical. Ask Parnell. I'm sure he'll agree with my assessment."

Jenn said, "So why do you need my father?"

"Because contrary to what you see here, I'm not a killer. I'm a licensed psychiatrist, not a hit man . . ."

No, you're not, Elaine thought bitterly. *You're a wealthy kidnapping rapist scumbag.*

". . . I need Parnell for protection," Marquez continued. "I know he'll jump at the chance to do the necessary dirty work. This is his golden opportunity. Without me, he'll never find Blanton Miles. And without him, I'm for sure a dead man. It's a win-win for everybody."

Broadway Bling shouted out, "Screw that! They're murderin' lowlifes. I say we just shoot 'em both now and let the vultures feast on their sorry carcasses."

Elaine was inclined to agree. She would like nothing more than to finish off these two sexual deviants and leave their corpses for desert scavengers to consume. But she knew an advantageous opening when she saw one. Marquez's story held up insofar as what she knew. Sure, his was a twisted tale of erratic allegiances and violent encounters. But Elaine imagined this to be the way sinister, big-money organizations with dark objectives ran. She was familiar enough with John Dobkin's history to know that things could be playing out just as Marquez suggested. The possibility existed that he had something very valuable to trade.

"Take them inside, Cale," she instructed. "We have a lot to discuss."

Cale and Jenn escorted the two men into the yard. Marquez walked with his head held high, his pomaded hair glistening in the sunshine like polished coal. Ann limped beside Diego, tending to the pilot's wounded hand as they walked. The rest of the gathered followed.

Elaine pulled her phone from her pocket and called Derek. This was news that couldn't wait.

Las Vegas Shuffle

Murky neon light filtered through the limousine's heavily-tinted windows. Three of them sat in the back with Weasel up front behind the wheel, the privacy partition open. The clock above the full-length bar showed 1:37 AM. Exactly one hour since they'd carjacked John Dobkin's sleek black stretch Lincoln in the rear parking lot of the Bellagio. An hour and fifteen since Dobkin had gone inside for his nightly pickup.

The operation had gone off without a hitch. They'd surprised the driver and bodyguard, zapped them into submission with the tasers. Bound them, duct-taped their mouths. Locked them in the rental car. Minimal resistance. Taken all of five minutes. No gunshot blasts. No shouts for help. No witnesses.

A carjacking of quiet efficiency.

Parnell felt the fatigue in his muscles and bones. It had been a long day. The 220-mile drive to Vegas. Another 25 miles down I-515 to Dobkin's mansion near Henderson. He worried the entire trip, with their rental loaded with illegal assault weapons and surveillance equipment.

And then there was Elaine's call this afternoon. Trouble at the mines. The shrink with the plane had returned, had flown in with two of his flunkies. A shootout. Two dead, one of them Oshkosh Moss, his longtime Shangri-La friend. Moss's death hit Parnell hard. He felt responsible for it somehow. An angry venom coursed through him. He was itching to get back to the mines and make somebody pay for it.

A messy situation. Parnell didn't like messy. *What's with this head doctor, Marquez?* Out of the blue, the shrink claimed to know Blanton Miles, claimed he could lead Parnell to him. Wanted to team up with Parnell to put Miles down. Did he really know Miles? If so, how? And why the quick shift of marks? The whole thing was sketchy and reeked of a setup.

He'd kept Elaine's call to himself. No sense upsetting the others when nabbing Dobkin was the current order of business.

So tired. Drained. So much crowding his mind. Surging adrenaline was all that kept him going. He eyed the bar beneath the mounted flat screen TV. Wanted a drink so bad it hurt, but knew they had to stay sharp and focused for what was to come.

He scanned the parking lot for the umpteenth time. Ran his fingers along the barrel of the Mauser in his lap. Bounced his knee up and down. Looked through the limo window at the double glass doors where Dobkin would be coming out.

Where the hell is he? What's taking him so long?

"You seem awful jittery, boss," he heard Flywheel say from his corner of the plush leather couch.

"I wanna grab the son of a bitch and get back to the mines. Don't like bein' away from Lainey and Jenn."

Weasel turned his head, spoke through the open privacy panel window. "Don't forget. We still have our friends at Shangri-La to think about. My last trip over there wasn't pretty, Derek. A lot of them don't understand why they were left behind. They're angry, confused. I told you that would happen if you tried to save a select few of 'em."

"Yeah, I know you said I can't save them all," Parnell said wearily, wishing Bethea would have kept that painful subject to himself for now. "I'll go over to Winslow after we get back. Hand out some money and do my best to explain what's going on." He thought about what had happened to Oshkosh Moss before saying, "Thing is, though, Greg, I'm not sure folks're any safer at the mines than they are in the camp."

Kid, peering through the window on Parnell's side, sat up straight. "It's showtime, guys. Here he comes."

Parnell felt an electric charge surge through him. His pulse thumped in his ears. John Dobkin came through the automatic doors, his sawed-off, stocky frame illuminated by the casino lights and wavy glare of the sodium vapor lamps. Expensive suit. Gray fedora, pulled down low and tight. Leather-bound attaché case in his grasp. Thick cigar in his mouth, a cloud of smoke trailing him as he walked.

He strutted toward the limo.

Weasel keyed the ignition. The Lincoln roared to life.

Parnell gripped his Mauser.

Flywheel slid his blade out of its sheath.

Kid's Glock shone in the dim light.

Showtime indeed. This was what Parnell had waited three-plus years to accomplish. He was finally going to grab John Dobkin. Take him to Utah. Give him a ride on the Rolling Inferno. Make him pay for his long list of criminal activities.

Dobkin walked between parked cars, getting closer. When he got within thirty feet, Parnell gave the command. "Okay, let's go!"

Doors opened and they stepped out into the chilly night.

Strobing neon flashed across the parking lot in colorful lightning strike bursts.

Music and traffic noise reverberated from the Strip.

The Bellagio fountains swished in a continual hiss.

Shoe leather scuffed across the pavement.

Flywheel circled around behind Dobkin; Parnell came at him from the side, grabbed his shoulder. Flywheel pressed the knife against Dobkin's side, said in a loud whisper, "Make a sound I'll slice you to ribbons."

Dobkin's jaw dropped. His cigar hit the ground in a spray of sparks.

Parnell pushed him forward. "Get in," he commanded, looking around to ensure there were no witnesses.

Dobkin willingly got in the back without uttering a word. Parnell climbed in after him. Kid used both hands to help keep Dobkin contained. Flywheel hustled around the other side and jumped in, pulled the door shut behind him.

Parnell sat rigid.

Something is very wrong here.

The man they had wasn't John Dobkin. The realization rocked him.

He told Weasel to turn on the interior light. The back of the limo lit up.

Parnell flipped the bill of the man's fedora up with the barrel of his gun.

"You're not Dobkin," he said.

The man gave him a greasy smile. "You're quite a detective."

Parnell wanted to pistol whip the wiseass into submission. "Who the hell are you?"

"Name's Fuzzy. Mister Dobkin's body double."

Parnell stared at him. "Body double? You gotta be shittin' me!"

Fuzzy chuckled. "You didn't really think a man of Mister Dobkin's distinction would be openly accessible, did you? He's too valuable to be out doing his collections and pickups."

Parnell was furious. He looked between Kid and Flywheel, his glare silently asking the question: *Did you think you had the real*

John Dobkin in your sights?

"I swear to you, Derek," Kid said, desperation in his voice, "we *were* trackin' the man himself."

"You mean last week?" Fuzzy said. "Nope, that was me."

"Christ," Parnell said, exasperated, disgusted that they'd come this far only to be thwarted. But he really couldn't lay too much blame on Dixon and Wheeler. He'd been fooled, too, by the body double ploy. Should have seen it coming. Should have *expected* it. There was no denying the resemblance. Fuzzy could easily have been John Dobkin's twin brother.

"You've got pretty big balls, Fuzzy," Parnell said. "You do realize we could kill you right now."

"This ain't my first dance," he said arrogantly. "Just know that if anything happens to me, you'll never get a meeting with Mister Dobkin."

"*Meeting?* We're not here to schedule a meet-n-greet with the asshole," Parnell said, frisking the man, finding a cell phone and a pistol.

"I'm just the messenger," Fuzzy said as Parnell patted him down. "I'm just the man's proxy collection agent."

"Yeah, right." Parnell grabbed the attaché case by the handle and opened it. He stared at three rows of bright green packets. Cash, neatly banded and stacked. The slight moldy ink smell of used bills filled the limo.

"Wow! Pimping is a lot more lucrative than I ever dreamed. Count it," Parnell said, passing the attaché to Kid.

"That's not all from our girls," Fuzzy said.

Weasel stuck his face in the partition window. "*Your* girls?" he said with marked revulsion.

Parnell said, "I hate to inform you of this, Fuzzbrain, but slavery ended in this country a long time ago."

"Our girls willingly provide a legal service."

Parnell scrolled through Fuzzy's cellphone contact list. "There are *so* many things wrong with that statement," he said, a scowl creasing his forehead.

Kid finished counting the money. "Close to forty grand," he announced.

Flywheel whistled. "For one night? What the hell do your broads do for that kinda scratch?"

"Only about a third of that's from our escort services."

"What's the rest from?" Weasel wanted to know.

"It's our take from the—" Fuzzy stopped. Looked doubtful. "I think you'd better discuss this with Mister Dobkin. I'm not at liberty to talk about our operations."

"Shut down the lights," Parnell said to Weasel.

The back of the limo went dark. Back to muddy neon colors streaming through the charcoal tint.

Parnell closed the top of the attaché, latched it and set it back on the floor. Thought about the firearms and the two phones they'd seized from the driver and muscle. Both phones were new burners. Pretty much clean, no info. Used just for communications. Fuzzy's phone was different. There were hundreds of contacts. Almost as many text messages. Dozens of calls displayed in the log. A valuable acquisition.

He cycled through some of the texts. "So, *messenger* man," he said while reading, "what's your procedure on collection nights?"

"I—I don't know what you mean." Fuzzy sat between Parnell and Flywheel, showing a look of confusion that Parnell recognized as a bad piece of acting.

He gave him a grim smile, flipped the fedora off his head. "Don't play dumb with me, Fuzzy. I know you're not as stupid as you look."

"Seriously, we don't have any strict procedure in place."

Parnell remained calm. "You and I both know that's bullshit, Fuzzy. Your call log states otherwise," he said, swiping through the phone records with his forefinger. "It's showing a call to the same local number at about this time every night going back at least two weeks. What's that all about?"

Fuzzy remained quiet. He'd lost his confident swagger.

"Is this Dobkin's private line?" Parnell asked. He recited the number.

Fuzzy shrugged his shoulders, refusing to divulge anything.

Parnell brought the phone close to his face. "We can do this easy or we can do it hard. Your choice. The easy way is you provide truthful answers to my questions and we all smile at each other. The hard way is you clam up, or, worse, you lie to me. If you wanna take the hard road, I'll have my blade man stick you good. He's got a knife that can cut through steel. It'll slice your kidney and liver like a razor through butter."

Fuzzy took one look at Flywheel and knew he was doomed. "Okay, okay," he said. "Yes, I call Mister Dobkin every night after the Bellagio pickup."

"To tell him what?"

"The cash pickup amounts."

"What else?"

"That's it," Fuzzy said weakly.

"Really?" Parnell said. He waited . . . five seconds . . . ten. He could sense the wheels turning in Fuzzy's warped mind. Felt him twitching next to him.

"You sure that's all you wanna tell me?"

Fuzzy nodded, the motion almost imperceptible.

"Cut him, Fly."

Flywheel pulled the blade across the top of Fuzzy's hand, just below the wrist. Parnell leaned in and clamped his hand over Fuzzy's mouth to stifle the scream. Kid jumped in to help. The man had the strength and determination of a wounded bull. They struggled to keep him down and quiet.

"Take it like a man," Parnell yelped through clenched teeth as he struggled to contain him. "It's just a little paper cut. The next one goes through your vital organs."

He bucked and snorted and kicked, blood dripping down his wrist, staining the front of Kid's shirt.

Parnell said, "You don't stop wiggling you're gonna bleed all over the upholstery. That would make your boss mighty angry. He might even fire you. Now I'm sure you don't want that, do you, Fuzzy?"

He shook his head, no. Kept his eyes trained on Flywheel and the wicked survivalist knife he held near his abdomen. Became very still.

Parnell said, "That's a good boy. Now I'm gonna let go of your mouth and if I hear a peep outta you my blade man will start slicing and dicing. Got it?"

He nodded, fear swimming in his eyes.

Parnell pulled his hand away. Kid backed off. Fuzzy held his bleeding hand with his good hand. Sat back on the couch seat, breathing heavily, whining over the pain, but not uttering a word.

Parnell grabbed a cloth towel from the bar. "Here, wrap your hand up tight. Unless you're a hemophiliac, the wound will clot up pretty quick."

Fuzzy grimaced as he wound the towel around his damaged hand.

Parnell went back to examining the data on Fuzzy's phone. "You know, in your line of work you really should learn to erase your history on these little gizmos. Big mistake. I'm sure your boss won't be thrilled when he discovers the security breach you've left here. Lots of incriminating evidence. You take one of those fly-by-night online secret agent courses, Fuzzy?"

Muffled chuckles from the others. Fuzzy remained impassive.

"You like workin' for Dobkin?"

He nodded.

"How long have you worked for him?"

"Seven years."

"Seven whole years and you're still making rookie mistakes? I'm surprised the big man has kept you around. Maybe it's just your good looks and bubbly personality, eh, Fuzzy?"

No response.

Parnell set the phone down on the couch. "Tell you what I'm gonna do for you, my friend. I'm gonna give you the chance to redeem yourself."

"I don't need redemption," he ventured. "I work for a legitimate businessman. I provide a legal service for him."

Parnell laughed. "Sure you do. Keep telling yourself that if it makes you feel better. Now here's what we're gonna do, Fuzzy. You're gonna describe the layout of Dobkin's compound. Then you're gonna tell me how you deliver the night's receipts to him. After that you're gonna call him and tell him you're on your way. If I detect any tricks or suspect you're feeding me bullshit information, you're a dead man. Got it?"

Fuzzy looked from Parnell to Kid to Flywheel, back at Parnell again. "Mister Dobkin might not be home tonight."

Parnell sighed deeply. "You really are a stubborn bastard, aren't you?" He looked across the couch at Flywheel. "Cut him again, Fly."

Wheeler's blade sliced across Fuzzy's lower arm, opening a new bloody gash. Fuzzy howled in pain. "*SHIT!* What the hell was that for?"

"That's for your poor attitude," Parnell said. "I'm looking for team players." He handed him another bar towel. "Here, you know the routine. Now start talking. Give us a clear picture of the layout of Dobkin's villa."

Fuzzy began talking nonstop. Parnell plotted accordingly. Night crew security at the mansion was beefed up. Three heavily armed guards manning the front gate. AR-15s and sidearms. Long, twisty drive around the main house to the back of the property and the limo garage. Two more armed guards there. Monies and receipts taken to an underground vault beneath the main house.

"Do you deliver the cash to Dobkin personally?"

"No. My responsibility ends at the garage. The armed guards take it from there. I rarely see Mister Dobkin."

"Are there other collection runners besides you?"

"He's got networks in other states, but it's just me in Vegas."

"What about perimeter security? Any guards making rounds at this late hour?"

"Yeah, two guys on the fences. Takes them about forty-five minutes to make a full sweep of the grounds."

Parnell pondered all of this. *Seven guards on duty versus four of us in two vehicles, a pair of taser guns, a grenade launcher, plenty of firepower. The element of surprise on our side. This could work if choreographed properly.*

Parnell knew from past experience that Dobkin was a notorious night owl. "So where does Dobkin usually hang out this time of night?"

"When he's home, he stays mostly in his office or his game room. They're off of his bedroom on the third floor at the back of the house. When he's not entertaining his lady friends he likes to shoot pool and smoke his cigars, keep watch over his investments."

"Any guards up there?"

"No. He's got bulletproof glass in the windows and dozens of cameras but no human security."

"How will we know if he's there?"

"If the lights are on, he's there. When he's away, he keeps that area of the house dark."

"Was he there when you left tonight, Fuzzy?"

"Yeah, he was. Doesn't mean he will be now. The man gets around."

Parnell picked up Fuzzy's cell and handed it to him. "Call him. Put it on speakerphone. Let's get this show on the road."

Jailbirds Will Sing

николай **NEAR MIDNIGHT. ELAINE COULDN'T SLEEP.** She'd spent the past hour tossing and turning on the dusty mattress, wondering how things were going in Vegas. Fretting whether Derek was okay. Imagining all kinds of horrific scenarios unfolding in Sin City.

She finally decided to go topside and get some fresh air. She put on her denim jacket, wool jeans, and hiking boots, and rode the mining cart up to ground level. She crossed the dark yard, her flashlight beam leading the way. Frosty out tonight.

She decided to check on Marquez and Diego, and went to mineshaft #2 where they were being held. The cave entrance was lit up via the electrical grid, and the bright lights hurt her good eye at first. She walked around Derek's crazy roller coaster to the small alcove that served as the makeshift jail.

She heard Jenn and Cale's muffled voices as she entered. They sat with rifles across their laps watching the two prisoners, who were strapped to heavy wood beams. A battery-powered lantern cast dappled light against the alcove walls.

"You two doing okay here?" she said, waving her light across their faces.

"Yeah, we're fine," Jenn said.

Jenn didn't sound fine to Elaine.

"What're you doin' here?" Cale said.

"Can't sleep."

"Perfectly understandable," Jenn said.

"Rough day today, wasn't it?" Elaine said to them while aiming the flash at Marquez and Diego, taking a long look at the two men she had come to despise. She then took a seat across from Jenn, putting her back to the prisoners.

This afternoon they had buried Oshkosh Moss near the rail spur where he died. Reverend Ann gave a tearfully profound eulogy. Dinner in the yard tonight had been a somber affair. They had suffered their first casualty and even Chef Alice's best Brunswick stew and vegetable mélange couldn't revive their spirits. Nor could Buttonhead's Bloodweed or gallons of beer erase the devastating feeling of loss that hung over the Hyacinth community.

"Cale and me, we've been talking," Jenn said to Elaine, her voice a near whisper to keep the conversation removed from the detainees. "This has gone too far. We think some of us should hold an intervention with Poppy. I love him dearly but he's setting us up for Armageddon."

Elaine nodded. "I know what you're saying. I plan to have a talk with Derek when he gets back."

"Well," Jenn said, "no disrespect, Elaine, but that hasn't worked in the past. I say a bunch of us confront him, try to talk some sense into him."

"That won't work with Derek. He's a bullheaded man. The more we throw at him the harder he'll push back. Believe me."

Jenn said, "We've got to do *something*. I don't think I can survive losing someone else I love."

"I know that, dear," Elaine said, patting her hand. "We'll get through this." She looked at Cale. "How are you holding up?"

He shrugged his shoulders. "I killed a man today," he said in a dazed monotone.

Marquez spoke from the shadows. "The law will have something to say about it, that's for sure."

Elaine turned around to look at him. "I'd say the law isn't exactly on your side, considering the shit you've pulled."

"Maybe not. But then, I haven't murdered anybody."

Elaine countered. "Well, I don't know that for sure. But what I *do* know is you have a long list of felonies. And that's just with me. Abduction. Kidnapping. Illegal transport across international borders. Attempted rape. False imprisonment. Assault. Shall I continue?"

"*Assault?*" Diego nearly screamed. "You're the one who should be brought up on assault charges, bitch!"

Elaine spied the blood-soaked compress on his left hand. *Is his cock bandaged as well?* She laughed a tired chuckle. "Still a little sore are we, Diego?"

Diego tugged aggressively against the ropes that bound him, yelling profanity-laced insults at her before Marquez settled him down.

Jenn rubbed Cale's arm consolingly. "I'm trying to help him deal with the shooting. It's not an easy thing."

"I know," Elaine said. She reached out and kneaded Cale's shoulder. "All you need to keep in mind is that you saved a lot of lives out there today. You did what an armed guard is supposed to do. You protected the village."

"Yeah, maybe," he said dully. "Thanks, Elaine."

All remained quiet for a long beat. Then Marquez said, "I came here to give Derek Parnell something he wants very badly, and this is how you treat us?" He shook his tethered arms, the rope scratching against the support post.

"Could be worse," Cale said. "I could have stripped you naked, tied you up in the yard, or latched you to the shack up on the ridge. Let you freeze your nuts off. I *should* have done that, actually. You're both animals. I heard all about what you did to Elaine."

"I want to talk to Parnell," Marquez demanded, ignoring Cale. "Valuable time is slipping away."

"He's not here," Elaine said, standing, going to him, stopping ten feet in front of him, pointing the powerful light in his face.

Marquez brought his hand up to shield his eyes. "Where is he?"

"Just a phone call away."

"He's going to lose out on getting Blanton Miles."

"So you keep saying. Are you even really a doctor?"

He looked taken aback. "Of *course* I am. I'm ABPN certified to practice psychiatry in the state of Texas. Look me up."

"Was Tico Samuels your cousin?"

"No. Samuels was a contract killer in Dobkin's organization. I knew about him and what he'd done to Parnell, but I never met him."

"So why'd you lie to me when you first picked me up? Why did you claim you were out to avenge his murder?"

"I knew that was the only way you'd lead me to Parnell."

Elaine ran a hand through her hair. "That doesn't make sense. You had to know I wouldn't lead you to Derek after you talked about killing him. If your real end game was having Derek help you take out Dobkin and Miles, why didn't you present it that way to me?"

"Would you have believed me? Would you have taken us straight to your man?"

"No."

"There you go," he said smugly. "We figured the quickest way to get Parnell involved was to say we wanted him dead. Trust me, Elaine, I know a lot about the way people think and reason. I've spent my life studying it. The mind is easy to read when you know the signposts, the telltale markers. I learned a great deal about you when you were drugged. I knew all your talk about sand and gravel mines in Winslow was bullshit. I knew Parnell wouldn't be anywhere near there. It was an amateur attempt at misdirection. Very transparent, I must say. But it doesn't take a trained psychiatrist to understand your deep love for Parnell. I knew you'd eventually lead us to him. And you did."

Elaine felt something deflate deep within her, her internal spark losing fire. An unpardonable sense of violation overwhelmed her. *He actually probed my mind when I was on those fun-time juice trips. Jesus God! What else did he probe?*

She said, "But I ditched you two that night at La Posada. I got clean away."

"Oh, Elaine," Marquez sighed. "You have the naiveté of a ten-year-old. Blanton Miles has a sophisticated network of eyes and ears all over these parts . . ."

The cameraman in the Honda on interstate 89 tracking us on the train.

". . . we picked you up again forty-eight hours after you so rudely departed—"

"Yeah, bitch," Diego cut in. "Next time I get my hands on you I'm gonna—"

"Shut up, D-man," Marquez barked. "I'm talking here." He turned back to Elaine. "We did our flyovers to determine who was here. Mighty fascinating collection of tramps you have gathered here. Like a hobo hall of fame, it is." He snickered at his joke. "Anyway, the last few passes we scouted for a suitable landing strip. I just wish it had gone better. No one needed to die out there today. Both of those men would still be alive if your guards had listened to reason."

Cale jumped up and joined Elaine. "You're a goddamned liar!" he bellowed, pointing his rifle at the two prisoners. "Your guy shot first. There wasn't any reasoning to be had."

Elaine reached out and eased the barrel down with her hand. Gave him a reproachful look.

"Look," Marquez said, his tone pleading, "there is no way we would risk our lives and my two-hundred-thousand-dollar aircraft if this wasn't a very serious deal. As I said this afternoon, this is a winning proposition for all of us. You've *got* to let me discuss this with Parnell. Time is of the essence. If you keep us locked up here, Miles will know something is up. Something not in his favor. Let me talk to Parnell."

Elaine stared at Marquez. "I'll take it under advisement," she said, then turned on her heel and walked away.

As she was leaving the alcove and entering the main shaft, she heard the psychiatrist say, "I'm sure you don't want Lone Wolf to become Dead Wolf."

The Snake and the Mongoose

PARNELL WAS JAZZED. Plugged in. All of his senses buzzing.

These were the moments he lived for. These do or die situations. Made him feel alive. Vibrant. Liberatingly reckless.

He sat in the back of the limo, on the couch behind the privacy panel. Aimed his Mauser at the driver through the open partition window. Kid sat next to him, the barrel of his Glock against the fiberglass panel, ready to plug either Dobkin employee if the situation called for it. Flywheel sat on the opposite couch, keeping Fuzzy quiet with the threat of his survivalist knife. Weasel Bethea drove the rental, tailing the limo on the half-hour drive from Vegas to Henderson.

Parnell spoke to the two men in front. "First sign of anything funny and we shoot to kill."

He knew the warning was probably unnecessary. When he'd freed them from the rental car trunk, they were dazed and confused. Jittery from being tasered. They'd seen what Flywheel had done to Fuzzy. Their will to live far outweighed their loyalty to their boss. Parnell didn't think they'd give him problems. Still, he knew he had to keep guys like this in line. Let them know they have skin in this gambit.

They pulled off I-15 heading toward Sloan Canyon. The rental car headlights bounced behind them. Just their two vehicles on this dark and lonely stretch of desert highway.

Parnell mentally reviewed their plan—plan B—the emergency backup scheme he'd hoped they wouldn't have to go to. Dobkin had outfoxed them at the Bellagio, so now they were faced with this risky endeavor. He knew the potential risks but he wasn't about to back out now.

Getting inside the fence shouldn't be a problem. The rear section of the Lincoln sported tinted windows so dark they were nearly opaque. The regular driver and bodyguard were up front as per usual. Everything would appear normal. Should get them past the guards at the front entrance.

Once inside, they would drive to the rear of the property and pull into the limo garage, overtake the guards, then bind and secure their captives. He, Kid, and Flywheel would then proceed to the main house to seize Dobkin. Weasel would park the rental out front, on the country road, and wait for instructions, with the grenade launcher locked and loaded. Three throwaway phones would keep everyone in contact.

So many moving parts. So much could go wrong. But Parnell wouldn't allow himself any second-guessing. He had to remain positive. He was ready to pull this off. He knew this team could handle it.

They turned off the country road and onto the long driveway leading to Dobkin's estate. Weasel dropped behind in the rental, parked. Killed the headlights. They continued on, driving up to the front entrance, industrial spotlights lighting the area. Solid redbrick guardhouse. Wire mesh gate standing thirty feet tall. Twenty-foot electrified privacy fence surrounding the sprawling 20-acre property.

Parnell took a deep breath. Reminded the driver to act natural. The driver nodded and slid the partition window shut.

The limo pulled to a stop in front of the gate. A guard with a graying military brush cut and steely countenance came out of the gatehouse and approached the vehicle. He wore a shoulder holster with the grip of his .38 fully exposed.

"Everything go well, Arthur?" he asked the driver with a bored smile.

"Yeah. No problems. Big payout tonight."

The guard bobbed his head. "Good. Chief will be happy. Maybe he'll give us all a big raise."

The muscle in the passenger seat said, "Right. Look for *that* to happen."

The three Dobkin employees shared a noisy laugh before the guard stepped back and punched a button on a small console near the gatehouse. The gates parted with a lurch and a clang, squeaking as they slowly slid open along a track.

The limo rolled past the gatehouse window. Parnell saw three guards studying video monitors. Camera views of different parts of the property. He smiled. *Their command center. Dobkin's Achilles heel. This is where they're most vulnerable.*

The gates closed behind them.

They were inside.

The limo followed the winding drive, coming into view of the main house, which looked like a small hotel. Four stories of floor-to-ceiling mirrored glass. Well manicured hedges along the front. Tall, spindly date palms lining the sides, their leafy illuminated canopies rippling in the gentle breeze. Sloped copper roof. The fourth floor showed the only light—Dobkin's penthouse and offices.

They rounded a sweeping curve and passed a cactus garden with a gurgling creek meandering through it. Water sluiced down the red rocks of a brightly lit waterfall. Another turn and they drove through a thicket of Texas mountain laurel. Parnell glanced through the rear window. They were out of sight of the main house. Much too far to hoof it on foot to get Dobkin. Too time-consuming. They'd need to drive the limo back to the mansion.

They approached the garage, a low-slung warehouse with three oversized doors. Spotlights mounted on high stanchions lit up a wide stretch of asphalt. A metallic, dark blue stretch limousine glimmered under the artificial light. Two cameras, halfway up the stanchions, recorded their approach, their glowing red lights like the eyes of nocturnal predators.

The middle garage door rolled up. A guard brandishing an automatic rifle stepped out into the glare of headlights. Arthur the driver slowed, lowered his window and called out to him. The guard swung his weapon toward the garage bay, signaling them inside.

The limo rolled into the shadowy interior. The driver shut off the ignition and the door rolled down behind them. Bright lights came on, illuminating the garage bay. Parnell saw only the lone guard.

Maybe karma is smiling on us, he thought as he gave the nod to Kid and Flywheel.

Events unfolded in a blur.

Rear car doors swung open.

Shouts.

Grunts and groans of struggle.

The surprised garage guard mumbled "What the hell?" as Parnell came at him and shot him with the taser. The guard dropped to the floor, convulsing and twitching like an epileptic suffering a grand mal seizure. Flywheel pulled Fuzzy out of the limo and held him at knifepoint. The Kid kept the driver and his muscle covered with his Glock.

Parnell looked down at the tasered guard, who writhed on the concrete floor, groaning, eyes rolling crazily. The two electrode darts and the connected conductor wires gave him the appearance of an electrocuted puppet. Parnell took his AR-15, turned and pointed it in the direction of their captives.

To Kid and Flywheel he said, "Wrap 'em up. Make it quick."

Dixon and Wheeler went to work, binding the wrists and ankles of their hostages with zip ties, then duct-taping their mouths.

Parnell got on his cell, called Weasel. "We're in the garage. You in position?"

"Sure am."

"We're goin' after him. Stay tuned."

Parnell disconnected and slipped plastic cuffs on the garage guard. "Any of your friends out here?" he demanded.

"No. No one else."

"If you're lying to me I'll use your own rifle on you."

The guard shook his head vehemently, fearfully. "No—not lyin'. Just me here."

Parnell unspooled strips of duct tape and plastered them across the guard's mouth, then detached the electrode darts from him and reloaded the taser. Grabbed him and stood him upright, helped him take a few steps. "Open the door," he barked, "Now!"

The guard moved to the wall in an awkward, stumbling duck walk and pulled a switch. The garage door squeaked up. Parnell peeked out, looking for other guards who might have been alerted.

No one. No sign of activity. Just the pair of videocams with their red lights glowing.

Dobkin definitely knows we're here by now.

He ordered Kid and Flywheel to latch the four captives to workbenches that were bolted into the floor. "Spread them out so they can't help each other."

Dixon and Wheeler worked quickly while Parnell anxiously stood watch. Less than three minutes to get their detainees secured to the benches. Then they were in the limo, Parnell behind the wheel, retracing their route back through the thicket of mountain laurel trees and the floodlit cactus garden.

Parnell pulled the limo up behind the main house in the paved turnaround. Parked. Told Flywheel to get in the driver's seat and Kid to come with him. If Fly hadn't heard from them in twenty minutes, he was to take off and rendezvous with Weasel.

Parnell and Kid entered the house, stealthily, weapons drawn, on high alert. They waited in the dark for an alarm to sound, but none did. They made their way along the outside wall, slowly, carefully, noiselessly. Fuzzy had told them there would be no guards here this time of night, but Parnell didn't believe him.

He heard a bubbling sound, like an aquarium air filter. Picked up the scent of wet vegetation. As his vision grew accustomed to the dark, he made out an elevator on the far side of the expansive room, floor indicator lights above the doors. A wide spiral staircase wound its way to the upper floors. Parnell jerked his head in the direction of the staircase and Kid followed.

They were almost to the base of the stairs when the lights flashed on. They crouched against the wall. Parnell scanned the room, sweeping the barrel of the AR-15 from wall to wall. Waited for the attack.

None came.

He realized they had set off a motion sensor.

They were in a spacious atrium with a vaulted ceiling that encompassed the first three floors. Glimmering crystal chandeliers. Onyx floors. An island of tropical flora with bubbling koi ponds on either side. Indian marble elevator doors. Italian tile staircase with polished mahogany railing. A grand ballroom befitting a wealthy pig like John Dobkin.

This sensor-tripping intrusion had surely alerted him.

They had to move fast.

Parnell signaled Dixon to follow him up the stairs. They half-jogged up the winding staircase, stopping at every turn to ensure the going was safe.

Second floor. A dim, nondescript area overlooking the ballroom. Several closed doors. No sign of activity.

Up to the third floor. Quiet and dark.

Fourth floor. Lights in brass wall sconces illuminated the long hallway leading to Dobkin's suite of rooms.

They padded down the hall, weapons raised. A tight knot formed in Parnell's gut. *Can't be this easy. Surely the man has protection up here.*

That thought had barely registered when shots thundered from behind them, deafening in these close quarters.

They spun around in unison.

Parnell dove for the floor, shots whizzing over his head.

A bald security guard came at them with a vengeance, firing

rounds from a semi-automatic pistol. Kid remained upright, returning fire, crying out as he took a slug in the shoulder. Kid returned fire, nailing the guard with two killing strikes—one in the cheek, the other in the chest. The guard went down with a loud *thump*.

A second guard stepped out of one of the rooms, ducking low, firing a .38 revolver. Kid took four direct hits. A fifth shot tore a chunk out of the wall near Parnell's head. Kid let out a shriek and a loud wheeze, then tumbled forward, doing a face plant near the body of the guard he'd killed.

Parnell sprayed a volley of shots from his prone position, striking the guard in the face and chest. The guard slammed against the wall, a look of surprise on his blood-pocked face, then crumpled to the ground.

Silence ensued.

The ringing in his ears was intense.

A murky haze clouded the hall. Parnell breathed in the cloying metallic scent of freshly-spilled blood and discharged firearms. He waited several long minutes, stooped in an edgy crouch, his head swiveling, scanning the hallway, fully expecting another attack.

None came.

He crawled to Dixon, felt Kid's neck for a pulse. There would be no saving Billy the Kid Dixon. He was gone.

A fierce anger filled Parnell as he retrieved Kid's Glock and slid it in his waistband. An anger so ferocious and molten it made him dizzy. Brought out the savage in him.

He heard footsteps. Slow, shuffling footfalls coming from Dobkin's penthouse suite.

Parnell checked his rifle clip, ensuring he still had ammo in the magazine. Stood. Moved toward the double doors at the end of the hall. Stopped halfway. Listened.

The footsteps shuffled closer, then stopped on the other side of the doors.

He smelled cigar smoke. Dobkin loved his Cubans.

The double doors swung open.

John Dobkin stood facing him, dressed in a blue satin bathrobe, puffing on a thick cigar. He was exactly the way Parnell remembered him. Mid-sixties. Imposing. Short—no more than five-six—but with a powerful build that made him appear taller. Deeply lined face tanned to a dark copper. Shifty, intelligent gray eyes peering out from under a thick brow. Wiry silver hair. Crocodile thong sandals that showed off professionally pedicured feet.

The look screamed aging playboy. A Hugh Hefner wannabe.

He pulled the cigar from his mouth. "It's about time you showed up." He looked beyond Parnell, assessing the sprawled bodies and destruction in his hallway. "I was beginning to think you'd lost your moxie in your old age."

Parnell moved closer, aimed his rifle at his breastbone. "Raise your hands up high, where I can see 'em."

Dobkin smiled at him, took another draw on his cigar. Exhaled the smoke casually. "There's no need for drama, Parnell. I'm not armed. I absolutely detest violence."

Parnell emitted a snide laugh. "Yeah, right. More than a hundred death certificates say otherwise."

"I said *I* detest violence. That doesn't apply to those who work for me." Dobkin pointed at the corpses littering the hallway. "Look where violence gets you." He shook his head. "Goddamned fools."

It took all of Parnell's self-restraint to keep from pulling the trigger. "Anybody else in there with you?" he said, trying to get a peek into the suite behind Dobkin.

"Just two of my favorite ladies. Your timing really sucks, you know that?"

"No other security?"

"Relax. The shooting is over." Dobkin shook his head. "You know, Parnell, all of this could have been so much simpler. Cleaner."

"Yeah? How so?"

"I've been waiting a long time for you to contact me. More than three years. I was hoping you'd do it the classy way. The professional way. With a phone call or friendly visit."

"Why would I want to contact you? Classy or otherwise?"

"To discuss our differences. To work out a resolution like two civilized gentlemen."

"*Gentlemen?* That's rich, Dobkin. There's nothing to discuss." Parnell took two more steps forward, jabbed the rifle at him. Kept enough distance between them to prevent Dobkin using his cigar as a weapon. "Let's go, asshole. Time to take a ride."

Dobkin stared at him, sucking on his cigar. Clouds of smoke swirled around his face. "Such disrespect. You need to know that I can get those federal charges against you and your lady friend dropped."

Parnell's indignation had his finger tightening on the trigger. "You're fulla shit. Let's go!"

"Christ, Parnell. Don't you know you'll never make it out of here alive?"

"Wrong. I'm leaving and you're coming with me, even If I have to shoot both your kneecaps and drag you out of here."

"My guys at the entrance will never let you out."

"I got in, and we'll get out." Parnell kept the rifle trained on him as he reached into his pocket with his left hand, pulled out his cell phone.

Dobkin looked on with interest. "What're you doing?"

"Calling the bomb squad." He connected with Weasel. "Hey, we're ready to roll. I need you to hit the front entrance. Launch one grenade at the gatehouse. Any survivors, launch a second. Got it?"

"Roger that," Weasel replied.

Parnell disconnected and slipped the cell in his pocket.

"Grenades?" Dobkin said doubtfully. "As in *hand* grenades?"

"Something like that, yeah. Let's go. Get a move on."

"I don't believe you. You're bluffing, Parnell."

"Start walking or I shoot."

"I'm not going anywhere with you."

"Do you value your kneecaps?"

"You won't shoot me."

The man's arrogance was off the charts. He stood there, nonchalantly smoking that smelly cigar, challenging him with an audacious stare. His smug expression radiated contempt, daring him to take action.

Parnell didn't want to risk any more loud shots, and he certainly didn't want to have to drag Dobkin out to the waiting limo. Lightning quick, he swung the butt end of the rifle around and clipped him flush across the forehead. Dobkin dropped with a stunned groan, his cigar throwing off sparks as it hit the floor next to him.

Parnell stomped on the lit cigar, scorching the hardwood.

A look of astonished resignation crossed Dobkin's face as he lay in the threshold of his penthouse suite doors. Parnell had him. The man had been counting on his crackerjack security force to protect him. Now he was alone, facing the fire. Just a pathetic bully-coward, spread-eagled in his monogrammed bathrobe, gingerly pressing a hand against his swollen, purpling forehead.

Parnell seethed with anger. He kicked him in the thigh. "Get up."

"Can I at least change clothes?"

"No." Parnell scanned the hallway, worried further delay might bring more security. "The bus is leaving. Let's go."

"Shit, Parnell," he said, woozily getting to his feet. "You make things so difficult."

"Many people would agree with you. Now move your ass."

As they made their way down the shot-up hallway, stepping over the fallen bodies, Dobkin said, "You'll pay for this."

"I already have," he said, looking down at Billy Dixon's bullet-riddled body. "*Dearly*. And now it's your turn to make a payment. Keep walking."

"Let's take the elevator down," Dobkin suggested.

"No." Parnell didn't want to be trapped in the elevator. Could turn out to be his coffin. "Head for the stairs."

The going was slow back down the winding staircase, Parnell prodding him forward with the barrel of the AR-15. Light leaked out from under several doors on the third floor; some of the mansion staff coming awake after all the commotion upstairs. Parnell got up close behind Dobkin and whispered, "Keep your mouth shut or I shoot. Anybody comes out into the hall, they're dead." But all doors remained closed.

Down to the second floor. Dark. No activity.

They walked through the ballroom atrium and out to the parking area.

"It's fucking cold out here," Dobkin complained.

"You should have dressed for the occasion."

Flywheel stood outside the Lincoln and, seeing them coming, opened the rear door. "I heard shots fired. I was startin' to get worried," he said. "Where's Kid?"

"He didn't make it," Parnell said, shoving Dobkin into the limo and climbing in after him. "Let's go, Javion. Roll. Stop when I tell you."

Wheeler dashed around the car, plopped into the driver's seat. "What's goin' on?" he said, shifting the limo into DRIVE.

"You'll see," Parnell said through the partition window.

Flywheel took them down the long driveway, stopping when Parnell gave him the order. They waited about forty yards from the front gate.

Ninety seconds later a flash of blinding light enveloped the gatehouse.

A muffled boom reverberated across the property, rocking the limo with the impact of an earthquake tremor.

Flying debris rained down on them, showering the Lincoln with brick shards and Plexiglas.

Smoke wafted up the drive, toward them. The gatehouse had been reduced to one wall and sections of the foundation. Half the front gate had folded over.

A second grenade cartridge hit the standing gate.

The ground shook.

A section of the steel mesh gate struck the side of the limo with a screeching thud, cracking the tinted glass window.

More debris pelted the Lincoln.

"Holy shit!" Flywheel shouted.

Nothing but a smoking, gaping hole where the gatehouse had been. Both sides of the gate had blown out. Twenty yards of electric fence had crumpled, reduced to a smoking, buzzing rubble.

Dobkin turned to Parnell, a look of horror etched on his dark, bruised face. "You're a fucking lunatic, Parnell."

He responded with a menacing smile. "Wow. Nothing like the snake calling the mongoose a predator."

Parnell spoke to Flywheel through the partition window, eyes never leaving Dobkin. "Onward, Javion. Let's go pick up Greg."

Love for the Java Angel

JENN WAS TRAPPED IN A disturbing nightmare and couldn't escape. She tried to scream but her vocal cords wouldn't respond. Tried to run, but her legs wouldn't budge.

An enormous hyena feasted on Poppy, snarling and drooling with predatory lust as it ripped long shreds of flesh from his motionless body. A second hyena dipped its snout into Poppy's bloody abdomen and yanked out a steaming organ.

She awoke, gasping. Drenched in sweat.

Terrified.

Disoriented.

She pulled in deep breaths. Tried to still her rampaging heart. Thought pleasant thoughts while attempting to put the nightmare into perspective.

Is Poppy okay? He'd told her often that dreams were omens, a foretelling of things to come. He was away on a dangerous mission. Could the nightmare be telling her something about his fate there? But as her head cleared, she realized this vicious dream was preposterous. Just a reaction to all the stress she'd been under.

She wiped the sleep from her eyes. Remembered where she was—stretched out in the back seat of the rented Toyota Camry parked inside mineshaft #3. Jenn had taken to sleeping here since her embarrassing tryst with Ann Finnegan in the headframe. She liked Ann and had nothing but respect for the woman, but she couldn't look her in the eye after what they'd done. She didn't know what to say to her and had gone out of her way to avoid her.

The digital clock on the dash showed 4:42 AM. She yawned drowsily, the fatigue of the past few days dragging her down.

Thoughts of Cale Turnipseed pushed away the remnants of the nightmare. She had left him just a few hours before, but it felt like days. She had been able to catch a little shuteye, but he hadn't been so lucky. With Poppy and the posse away, Oshkosh Moss dead, and two prisoners to watch, the security detail was spread thin. Not enough available guards. Cale had been pressed into double-shift duty, now standing watch out by the railhead where Oshkosh had been killed. He had to be exhausted. She'd take him some coffee, keep him company. His day had been a much more real nightmare than what she'd just awakened from. He'd killed a man. Pointed a gun at another human being and shot him dead. Jenn knew all too well what that experience was like. If you had any level of empathy for the sanctity of human life—and she knew Cale did—it tore out your insides and raped your conscience.

She threw on her jacket, slipped into her boots. Jumped in the front seat and flipped down the lighted sun visor mirror. Applied light makeup, brushed out her hair. Painted her mouth with a quick swipe of peach-colored lipstick.

She exited the car and switched on the mineshaft lights, squinting in the overpowering glare. Went to the long wooden worktable Chef Alice had set up as a food prep area. Brewed a carafe of coffee in the battery-powered AeroPress machine. Poured the rich black coffee into her thermos. Added hazelnut creamer, the way she knew Cale liked it.

She grabbed a flashlight and went out into the yard. The nippy night breeze stung her cheeks and slapped her awake. As she rounded the bend that led to the tracks, she saw a flashlight beam coming from the opposite direction.

"Hey, is that you, Jennifer?" she heard Elaine calling out as they approached each other.

"Elaine? What're you doing out here?"

"Great news. I just heard from Derek. They picked up Dobkin and are on their way back."

"Awesome! So Poppy's okay?"

"Yeah, he is."

"Whew. I'm so relieved. I know you have to be, too."

"I am. But there were complications."

"Complications?"

"They lost Billy Dixon."

"*What?*"

"Yeah. He was killed in a shootout inside the mansion."

"Oh, shit no!" Jenn hung her head. She liked the rangy, slow-talking Okie. Couldn't picture him dead. "But Poppy told me the operation would be slam-dunk easy."

Elaine laughed. "What Derek calls slam-dunk easy is batshit crazy to the rest of the world."

"Billy was a great guy."

"I know. It sucks. Derek was really torn up about it."

"Are the others all right?"

"Yeah. Just exhausted. They should be here in a couple of hours." Elaine shined her flashlight on Jenn's thermos. "Going to see Cale?"

"Yeah. Bringing him some coffee."

"He'll like that. I just came from there. I was on my way to get him some joe myself."

"How's he doing?"

"Okay, I guess. Not his usual carefree self—especially after hearing about Billy—but he's holding it together. He'll appreciate the caffeine boost. He's been working on his rap routine trying to stay awake."

Jenn grinned. Cale had busted out one of his rhyme schemes for her a few days ago, and she thought he was quite good. At least for a white guy.

Elaine said, "He was talking about you a lot."

"Really?"

"Yeah. It's obvious he's got a thing for you, Jenn. And I've seen how you act around him . . ."

"Look, I don't think we should—"

"Hold on," Elaine said with a sharp chuckle. "You thought I was going to warn you away from him, didn't you?"

"No, not really," she said, but that's exactly where she thought Elaine was headed.

"You and Cale are wonderful together. Go for it, girl. Don't let that one get away. He's quite a catch. I'm happy for you. I'm glad something beautiful is going to come out of this dreadful mess we're in."

"Really? You mean that?"

"With all my heart, sweetie."

"Thank you, Elaine. That means a lot to me."

"Oh, it doesn't matter what I think. The important thing is how you and Cale connect. What you two think of each other." Elaine fiddled with her eyepatch. Shuffled her feet. "Hey, listen, Jenn. There's something I've been meaning to talk to you about. With all that's been going on I haven't had a chance. This is kind of a weird place to talk, but—"

"Go ahead. Now's as good a time as any," Jenn urged, feeling a creepy-crawly warning sensation in her stomach. *Is she about to lay more bad news on me?*

"Okay." "Derek told me what you said about me."

Jenn tried to remember her conversations with Poppy. "Something I said about you? Was it derogatory?"

"Oh no. Not at all. Derek said you raved about me, that you said some wonderful things. He said you told him you thought I was more of a mother for you than your birth mother, even though you and I were together less than a year. He said you worried about me incessantly while I was in transit, that you shamed him for appearing not to care about me as much as he should. He told me you think I'm sexy and beautiful and that you love me. Is that true, or is it just Derek flapping his jaws?"

Jenn was glad the darkness prevented Elaine from seeing her embarrassment. "Poppy should learn to keep his mouth shut," she said. "But, yeah. It's all true, Elaine. Every word of it."

Elaine shrieked like a giddy schoolgirl. "Oh wow! I can't begin to tell you how happy that makes me. Come here and give me a big hug."

Jenn stepped into Elaine's welcoming arms. A hug had never felt so comforting, so reassuring.

Elaine rubbed her hands across Jenn's back. "I love you, too, Jennifer," she said into her ear. "So much. Just as if you were my own biological daughter."

They held their embrace, trembling, overcome with emotion. Jenn hugged Elaine to her tightly, doing her best to hold back a deluge of tears. Happy tears. A magnificent euphoria struck her. This strong, courageous woman loved her like her biological mother never had. Elaine Leibrandt loved her the way Barbara Logan Parnell never could.

Elaine patted her twice on the back. Kissed her on the cheek and stepped back. Wiped a tear from her good eye and looked at Jenn, a smile brightening her face. "One thing, however."

"What's that?"

"Just keep in mind that I'm *much* too young to be your actual mother."

They shared a laugh as Jenn dried her eyes.

"Go," Elaine said, rubbing Jenn's arms, "Cale is waiting. His coffee's getting cold."

"Thanks, Elaine."

"For what?"

"For being the best, *youngest*, substitute mom a girl could ever hope for."

Elaine snickered. "You're something else, girl. Save your sucking up for Cale. Go on now," she urged, "go see your man. He needs you."

Jenn stood and watched Elaine's back as she walked away. She took a moment to cherish what had just happened. She smiled. *That is one amazing woman.* She watched as Elaine disappeared into the darkness, then turned and walked down the tracks to where Cale was stationed.

"Don't shoot," she said, shining the flashlight on her face as she approached. "It's just me. I brought you coffee."

"Ah, it's a sexy java angel bringing me nectar from heaven," he said, taking the thermos from her and giving her a quick kiss on the cheek. He unscrewed the lid and poured the steaming coffee into the cup. "You're so sweet to think of me." He took a sip. "You get some sleep?"

"A little," she said, planting a kiss on his mouth, tasting the sugary hazelnut on his lips.

"Wow! A *kissing* java angel! I must be dreaming."

She pulled her head back, studied him. "Are you okay, Cale?"

"Yeah. Why wouldn't I be?"

"You've been through a lot."

"We all have. Elaine and I were discussing that very thing. She was just here."

"I know. I ran into her."

"She tell you about Billy Dixon?"

"Yeah. It's tragic. Poppy told me they had a foolproof plan going in. But something went wrong. They did get Dobkin, though."

Cale took a few more careful sips, steam billowing from the cup. "At what cost?" he said, wiping his mouth. "Billy was a decent dude. He was my friend. He arrived at Shangri-La the same week I did. I can't believe he's gone. It makes no sense."

She caressed his arm. "Things are tough right now. I know that."

He looked out into the darkness that cloaked the desert. "Please don't take this the wrong way, Jenn, but I used to think your father was the bomb. That he was this superhero kind of cool dude who could conquer the world. I heard all those stories about him, those King Midas stories. Him helping all us down-and-outers. But lately I'm not so sure. I'm thinking he's a mess. That he's unstable. A danger to us all."

"You know I'm with you on that, Cale. This crusade he's on scares me. Poppy's dragged all of us into this personal war of his.

That's why I suggested the intervention earlier. But hell, he won't even listen to Elaine."

"There's definitely a war coming, Jenn. Some things are worth fightin' for, but for me, this isn't one of them. I didn't sign up for this shit."

She rubbed the top of his hand, thinking Poppy would probably still be in Costa Rica if it wasn't for Russ's murder. Jenn just couldn't get past the burdensome thought that all of this was her fault.

Cale seemed to be lost in another world. "You know, it's just a matter of time before the feds show up here," he said faintly. "When they do, I'm gonna have to disappear."

"What're you talking about?"

The seriousness in his expression scared her. "There's something I should have told you before now."

Jesus. Another true confession? What a night!

She questioned him with raised eyebrows.

"I'm on the run from the law. I'm a wanted felon."

"*What?*"

"Yeah. Tax evasion. I owe the U.S. government four years of back taxes."

"Are you serious?"

"As a heart attack."

Jenn tried to process this. "Elaine told me about your biker days, but I didn't know you were a real outlaw, Cale."

"Aren't most of us these days?" he said with a wink and a touch to her wrist. "You and Elaine have opened up and let me in your lives. You've both been honest with me, revealed things of a very personal nature. But I've kept things from you all and that's been bothering me. Remember I told you about my days as a school bus driver?"

"Yeah?"

"Well, I wasn't laid off like I told you all. I went on the run after federal marshals served me with a lien against my personal property and the government started garnishing my wages. They were gonna repo my motorcycle, which was the only possession I had that was worth anything. I got the hell out of Atlanta and rode west. Kept on the move. Spent some time on a Sioux reservation in North Dakota. They're some of the finest folks I've ever known. I would've loved to stay there longer, but the law caught up with me and I had to move on. Wandered through a few hobo camps until I hit Winslow and found Shangri-La. Ended up sellin' the bike to a guy from Phoenix."

Jenn could only stare at him open-mouthed.

"The Internal Revenue Service gave me an ultimatum—pay a fine of two-hundred grand or do the time. Four years in the Atlanta pen. I couldn't afford to pay and I certainly wasn't gonna let 'em lock me up. This all went down almost four years ago. I've been on the lam ever since."

"Holy shit, Cale. Didn't you have anywhere to go? Anyone who could help you out?"

"No. My father died years ago. My mother was, and still is, homeless. She's doin' the hobo thing, same as me and you and millions of others. I don't have any brothers or sisters. I've got an uncle in Mississippi, but he can barely keep his head above water with a wife and five kids."

Jenn couldn't believe this. "You must've made a lot of money if the government came after you."

"Not really. I was a contractor handyman and driving a school bus for Chrissakes. What I owe is far less than the fine they levied against me. Uncle Sam says I owe interest and late fees on my unpaid taxes. Two hundred grand, they say. They're nothin' but thieves. Fuckin' bureaucrat pirates. The whole thing is a sham, Jenn."

"Why didn't you pay your taxes? Couldn't you afford to?"

"Oh, I did pay for a few years. Through the nose. My contracting business boomed when I was doin' it full time, and I paid my taxes diligently. But it always bothered me. I'm against taxation. Always have been. It's nothin' but grand larceny, you ask me. What gives the government the right to steal a quarter or more of our income? I mean, I never saw a government employee on site with me, workin' beside me, handing me tools or helping me haul shit. What entitles them to my hard-earned money? I finally started realizing the income they pilfer from us regular folk goes to support the organized crime syndicate run by the super wealthy.

"So when I started driving the school bus, I decided I wouldn't contribute to crooked politicians' financial portfolios anymore. No more buying political favors or propping up third-world dictators with *my* money. Oh, the school system withheld my taxes, sure. But I stopped reporting my handyman income. It was a matter of principle. It took the IRS a few years to catch up with me, but when they did, they came down hard."

Jenn thought for a minute, then ventured forth. "The tax thing has never made sense to me," she said. "The politicians drained the unemployment fund for their own gain. Same with Medicare and Social Security. They've bled the country dry with their self-serving greed, and yet still feel entitled to pick the pockets of those lucky enough to have jobs. And nobody says anything. Nobody stands up to them."

Cale smiled. "Couldn't have said it better myself. I'll have you know that I'm not alone. I know a half-dozen others at Shangri-La with tax evasion warrants out on them. We haven't been hassled yet. But the time is coming."

"If you run, I'm coming with you."

"Why would you do that? You don't really know me."

"I know you well enough, Cale."

He looked at her doubtfully. "What about your father?"

"What about him?"

"Well, I just thought that whatever is gonna happen here happens, you'd go off with him and Elaine and I'd never see you again."

"Cale. I'm twenty-two years old . . . a grown woman out on my own. What makes you think—"

He cut her off with a deep, aggressive kiss, his tongue probing the back of her mouth.

When they parted, she looked into his eyes and said, "That was awesome. Do it again, please."

And he did.

She said, "I wish you weren't on guard duty."

"Why?"

She frowned and pushed out her lower lip in a mock pout. "Are you really that clueless, Cale?"

He shrugged his shoulders.

"Well, let me put it bluntly. I wanna fuck you senseless."

He pretended to look shocked. "You really are a java angel! A *wet dream* java angel. Harvey Henshaw will be relieving me in a couple of hours. Can you wait that long?"

"Only if you keep kissing me."

Limousine Testimony

They drove through the dark Nevada night, taking back roads, Flywheel keeping the limo to well within posted speed limits. The tires thrummed over the desert asphalt. The wind whistled around the Lincoln. The engine purred.

Parnell sat in back, facing Weasel and John Dobkin, pointing his Mauser at Dobkin. The Vegas mobster's wrists and ankles were tightly cinched. He sat motionless, quiet, gazing out the spider-webbed window at the nightscape rushing past. The knot on his forehead had swollen to the size of a small egg and had bruised to an ugly purple. Dressed in his silk robe and nursing the nasty head injury, he resembled a heavyweight boxer who had just lost a prizefight.

Parnell broke the silence. "That was some great shooting back there, Greg," he said to Weasel. "Just two grenades to take down the front entrance?"

"I got lucky. That launcher has a ballbuster kick to it."

"You catch any return heat?"

"No. I moved fast. Caught 'em completely by surprise."

"You get everything outta the rental?"

"Yep. I wiped everything down, too."

"Good work, my friend."

"Thanks."

Dobkin came out of his trance. He leveled his hooded eyes on Parnell. "You'll never get away with this, Parnell."

"Looks like I already have."

"You're a moron. As soon as word gets out you killed five of my guys, destroyed my property, and abducted me, there'll be a storm of hellfire comin' down on you. We know where you live, you know. My people know exactly where you're taking me. They're gonna crush you."

"I look forward to their visit," Parnell said cheekily. "But if they want to save your ass they'd better make it fast because you don't have much time left on this earth."

Dobkin tittered. "Always bringing the drama. You're such a punk. I'm disappointed. I expected better from you."

"*You* expected better from *me*?" Parnell felt his emotions getting away from him and he tried to dial them back. "Let's talk about expectations versus reality, shall we? You think everyone on your staff loves you, don't you?"

"My staff doesn't give me any problems. They're very loyal."

"Loyal? You're out of touch, Johnny boy. I had an enlightening chat with Fuzzy—your doppelganger—in the Bellagio parking lot. He had some unkind things to say about you. Your driver Arthur and his muscle also shared a good laugh with the front gate guard at your expense."

"I don't believe that."

"No? It's obvious to me that many of your people just plain don't like you. And who could blame them. You treat them like a pile of dog shit you just stepped in."

"You don't know a goddamn thing about my relationship with my employees. I compensate them quite nicely. They couldn't go anywhere else and make the kind of money I pay them."

Parnell exchanged a smile with Weasel. He'd landed a verbal punch. Touched a nerve.

"Do you believe this guy, Greg?" he said to Weasel. "A man like this who's overseen a huge organization all these years and he doesn't know jack squat about managing people?"

Weasel bobbed his head. "Yeah, I picked up on that."

Parnell returned his attention to Dobkin. "Guys like you think everything is about money. It's not. People need to know they're appreciated, that their work is valued. They need to hear positive words from the boss once in a while. You just heard me congratulate my friend Greg here on his good work with the grenade launcher. I'm willing to bet you rarely do that with your folks. If you had, maybe someone would have tried to save your useless ass when we were goin' down that staircase. But nobody came to your rescue, did they? Nobody bothered. Why is that, I wonder?"

Dobkin glared at him. "I care *plenty* about my employees. Each and every one of them."

"Do you? You mentioned that we killed five of your security staff. That accounts for the two in your hallway and three in the gatehouse. You never asked about Fuzzy and his bodyguard. Or Arthur the driver, or the limo garage guard. Maybe we killed all of them as well. But apparently you don't think they're important enough to ask about. Shows me how much you care, Dobkin. Not one whit."

"I know you didn't kill them, Parnell. That's why I didn't inquire about them."

"Oh, that's right. I forgot. You've got videocams everywhere. Big Brother Dobkin. Those cameras didn't do you much good tonight, did they?"

Dobkin brought his shackled hands up to his wounded forehead, winced as he felt the damage. "Go ahead," he said. "Have some fun. Soon it will be my turn for fun. Soon you'll be begging for your life. My organization has implicit instructions on what to do should I suddenly disappear."

"Don't be too sure about that. After your employees learn of our attack and the casualties you suffered, I'm sure you'll have a lot of worried personnel lookin' for employment elsewhere. The rats will desert your sinking ship in huge numbers. It doesn't matter how much you pay them, Dobkin. All the money on Wall Street doesn't do a corpse any good."

Dobkin rolled his eyes and went back to staring out the cracked window at the passing night.

They rolled on toward the Utah state line, the rear of the limo quiet. After twenty minutes, Parnell caught himself beginning to nod off.

"You got any coffee in this overpriced yuppie mobile?" he asked Dobkin.

"How the hell would I know? This is Arthur's limousine."

Parnell grumbled and scooted over to the bar, checked the cabinet underneath, saw bottles of every conceivable type of hard liquor lined up like colorful glass bowling pins. But no coffee.

"Shit, no coffee?" he said. "What kinda transportation service are you runnin' here?"

Dobkin only glared at him with disgust.

"Well, this'll do, I guess," Parnell said, snatching a bottle of very expensive Macallan single malt scotch and three glasses. He set the glasses on the padded bar and poured generous amounts of the whiskey into each. Handed one to Weasel and shouted to Fly through the privacy panel window, "Sorry, Javion, yours will have to wait since you're driving. We don't need you gettin' a DUI if we get pulled over."

Flywheel, his bushy 'fro blowing in the wind like an overgrown tumbleweed, looked up in the rearview and told him, "If some pig stops us, a DUI will be the least of our worries."

"Good point," Parnell said, and handed him a whiskey through the partition window. He went back to the bar cabinet and grabbed another glass, poured another and handed it to Dobkin, who accepted the drink between his bound hands.

"A toast to our success tonight," he announced. "We got our man. Drink up, fellas."

He tossed back his scotch, felt the smooth burn in his throat. Flywheel and Weasel did the same.

Dobkin observed the proceedings with contempt. "I'm not drinking to *that*."

"Suit yourself," Parnell said, quickly grabbing Dobkin's drink and slugging it back.

"I propose a second toast," Weasel offered. "To Billy."

"Excellent idea, Greg." Parnell collected the glasses, poured again, smaller portions this time. Handed them out. In a somber, commemorative tone, he said, "To Billy the Kid Dixon, the Okie with brass balls. A man who bravely and courageously served with the Parnell Posse to bring criminals to justice. Tonight he took the westbound train and we will miss him."

The three men tossed back their whiskey.

"The Parnell Posse?" Dobkin said from his end of the couch. "You're a loony tune, Parnell,"

"Maybe so. But unlike you, I care about my people. I bet you don't even know the names of your security guys who died tonight."

Dobkin appeared flustered. "I know *everything* about the men I pay to protect me. Those men were like family to me. You think I'd hire just any ol' sleazebag off the street to watch my back?"

"Well, I'd say your *family* didn't perform too well tonight. Five of 'em gone, just like that," he said with a snap of his fingers. "Another four compromised in the limo garage. Pretty useless, all of 'em. Wouldn't you agree?"

John Dobkin just stared out the window.

"And here we are with you, the big Vegas high roller, the notorious criminal overlord, tied up like a roped steer and headed toward the slaughter pens."

Dobkin turned and directed his steely gray eyes at him. His bruised and battered face communicated pure loathing. "You're history, Parnell."

"We'll see about that."

Keeping his eyes on Parnell, Dobkin said, "You know, one thing I don't understand."

"What's that?"

"If you have such a hard-on to see me dead, why didn't you just shoot me in my penthouse and be done with it?"

"What fun would that have been? I have something very special planned for you, Dobkin. Don't I, guys?"

Flywheel and Weasel chuckled in agreement. The Rolling Inferno awaited.

Parnell moved in front of Dobkin, said, "After what you did to my daughter, you deserve only the most horrific sendoff, you son of a bitch."

"I have no idea what you're talking about."

He wanted to strangle the smug asshole with his bare hands. "For seven long years you knew my Jennifer was with those animals up in the Colorado mountains. Yet you didn't utter a word. You knew who torched my house and killed my wife, but kept it to yourself. You orchestrated all of it while you had me running around chasing my tail."

Dobkin sat there, looking amused. "I believe all that you speak of was in Blanton Miles' purview. Not mine."

"Really? You're gonna throw Miles under the bus? Nice."

"I'm not throwing anyone under the bus, Parnell. As I recall, Miles reported to you. It was his responsibility to keep you informed."

"Blanton Miles never reported to me and you goddamn well know it. He was always your puppet. You pulled the strings and he danced."

Dobkin laughed. "You have quite an imagination."

Parnell wanted to lash out at him, tattoo the other side of his forehead with a matching bruise. "I'm not imagining that. Miles was your consigliere when you stole my company . . . when you cleaned me out. You know it and I know it. But then, you've always been an accomplished liar, haven't you? I followed your trial with great interest. You committed perjury no less than a dozen times by my count. You swayed that stupid-ass jury with the most outrageous lines of bullshit I've ever heard."

Dobkin smiled easily and said, "Speaking of stupid, your daughter and her boyfriend were incredibly dumb to come after me with their ill-advised lawsuit. No one has a prayer of beating me in a court of law. Too bad your daughter's sweetheart—Russell Holt, wasn't it?—had to pay for their mistake with his life."

Parnell felt something twist in his gut. "Uh-huh, and you

murdered him."

"I did no such thing."

"Oh yes you did. I have proof. Not only for Holt's murder, but a few others as well."

"I told you, Parnell, I abhor violence. There's no way I could take another person's life. I don't have it in me the way you apparently do." He squinted up at Parnell and pursed his lips, scrutinizing him. "But just out of curiosity, can I ask what kind of proof you have?"

Parnell nodded. "Bank statements showing large payments from one of your offshore accounts wired to the account of one of your longtime operatives—Loretta Pesky. Surely you remember her. Doing business as Madame Crystal in Sedona. She was the go-between. I followed the money trail, which led to two people I know are on your payroll—Genevieve Thorssen and her fellow Swede, her assassin partner Lars. Don't sit there and tell me you don't know them. They brought us to see you three years ago at the Bellagio."

"Sure I know them, Parnell. All three of them. Or I should say, I *knew* them. Terrible thing you did to them at that abandoned barn in Cottonwood. So vicious and cutthroat. No chance for proper burials."

Jesus, this guy is all-seeing, all-knowing How could he possibly know about activities at the Arizona ranch?

"Not that it matters, but tell me more about this proof you have."

Parnell continued. "Well, I have Loretta Pesky's bank statements going back a few years. There are several big wire transfers from you to Pesky, each followed shortly thereafter by outgoing payments to Thorssen. The dates line up perfectly with known hits Lars made, the last being on Russell Holt in a Denver restaurant. They're obviously blood money transactions, Dobkin. Murders for hire. People who got in your way."

John Dobkin studied Parnell, a look of approval softening his suntanned features. "You're smart, Parnell. I'll give you that. You're resourceful and crafty. That's why I recruited you for my war against that fringe militia bunch in Colorado."

"Yeah," Parnell said, "you tried to kill me and my daughter up in those mountain caves after I did your dirty work for you. You tried to take out Elaine, too."

"And I failed. One of my few failures in recent years. In hindsight I see it was a monumental mistake that has cost me dearly."

"I'm curious about something, Dobkin. Your surveillance network seems to be pretty sophisticated. Why didn't you come after me? Did you know where I was?"

"Of *course* I knew where you went. I know all about your beach bungalow in southern Costa Rica, your stilt house on the Caribbean. Lovely place. I've known about it since the day you purchased it. I knew you and Elaine Leibrandt were there. I figured since you were being quiet and minding your own business, there was no need to mess with you. Too many other things needed my attention."

"Did Blanton Miles know where I was?"

Dobkin's laugh was a mirthless sound. "No, he didn't. The three years you've been gone I let him go on a wild goose chase pursuing you. I encouraged him to find you. Offered him big bonuses and incentives. He pumped a lot of time and energy into it, but he never located you. It kept him out of my hair and was quite entertaining to watch."

"But isn't he one of your top lieutenants?"

"He *was*. Past tense. Back when you were in the fold and we were pulling your strings. He's done a lot of good work for me, but he's outlived his usefulness. It's time to cut him loose."

"And by 'cut him loose' do you mean you plan to kill him?"

"Interpret it however you want, Parnell."

Does Dobkin not realize his time is short? That he's in no position to call the shots? He appears to be sedated by his enormous arrogance. Seems to be boosted up by his abundant narcissism.

Parnell said to him, "I still don't understand why you didn't come after me."

"Oh come on, really? Do you think you're all that important, Parnell? After you helped me wipe out the Liberty Dogs compound, I had no need for you anymore. Of course I would've preferred eliminating you and your pretty accomplice. But Costa Rica was a universe away, and truthfully, I didn't want you anywhere near the trial."

"Why not?"

"Think about it. You were the only one who could prove I was lying. Well, you and Miles. But I made sure Miles wasn't called to testify." He gave Parnell a studious look. "Your Jennifer and her traitor boyfriend made a fatal mistake dragging me into court the way they did. Russell Holt was a festering boil on my ass. He did his damnedest to bring me down."

"So you had Lars kill him."

"Yes. Good riddance, I say."

"You're scum, Dobkin."

"Hey, you should be thanking me."

"*Thanking* you? What the hell for?"

"I gave instructions that under no circumstances was your daughter to be harmed. My orders were to nail only Holt and let your Jennifer go."

"Mighty kindhearted of you," Parnell said with a sarcastic edge. "Why would you leave Jenn alone?"

"Because I knew she would lure you back to the States."

"You're pathetic, Dobkin."

"It worked. That's all I care about."

Parnell clenched his fists. Liquid fire pulsed through his veins.

Dobkin said, "But that's all yesterday's news. Let's get back to current events . . . this so-called evidence you have on me? The money trail? Just what good do you see it doing for you, Parnell? You gonna take it to the authorities? Have you forgotten you have a large bounty on your head?"

"No, I haven't forgotten. You laid that curse on me, the curse that keeps on giving. And as you stated, you're unbeatable in a court of law. I just wanted you to know that I have the goods on you. So, I'm taking you to Utah, where I oversee my own system of justice. Where the guilty pay the ultimate price."

Weasel said to Dobkin, "It'll be so much fun. You're gonna get to go on Derek's special amusement park ride. You like roller coasters, John?"

Dobkin gave Parnell a look of confusion. "What the hell is he babbling about?"

Parnell smiled. "You'll find out soon enough."

Doctor Strangelove's Plan

ELAINE WATCHED A WORN AND BEDRAGGLED Derek step out of the sleek black limousine. He looked like he'd aged ten years. She tried her best to get him down to their living quarters for some much needed sleep, but he wouldn't hear of it. His entire focus was on their new prisoner, John Dobkin.

She followed Derek and Greg Bethea as they ushered Dobkin to where Antonio Marquez and Diego were being held in mineshaft #2. The Vegas mobster was quite a sight, dressed in a rumpled silk robe, purpling wound sprouting from his forehead like a bloated mushroom, restraints limiting his movement as he shuffled along in a daze.

They entered the small, rocky alcove. Parnell eyed the two men chained to wall timbers. "You're the two idiots who landed that airplane in the desert?"

Silence.

Marquez and Diego looked past Parnell, staring at Dobkin in disbelief.

"Not gonna own up to it, huh?" Parnell said. "Surely car travel would have been easier. You guys suffering from brain damage or somethin'?"

Marquez cleared his throat. "It's a long way from San Antonio," he said, eyes still on Dobkin. "A thousand miles to be exact. We're on a tight schedule. We wouldn't have made it if we drove."

Parnell fixed his bleary eyes on Marquez. "You the Texas head doctor?"

"Um, *psychiatrist*, yes."

"So you chanced crashing your airplane to get here."

"Diego here is a world class pilot. I have complete confidence in his aviation skills. He's landed in much more hostile environments than this."

Parnell glanced at Diego. "Why is your hand bandaged up?"

"Your daughter shot me."

"I'm sure you deserved it." Parnell looked in Elaine's direction. "Jenn was on guard duty?"

"No, not really. She was with Cale up on the ridge when these two flew in. She went with him to help Oshkosh when these guys tried to storm the entrance."

He turned back to Marquez. "So, the million-dollar question. What's so urgent you had to risk landing in the desert?"

"We're chasing someone I know you'll be interested in, Derek. May I call you Derek?"

"Only if you want me to shoot you in the head. Tell me what's goin' on. Twenty words or less."

Marquez shuffled uneasily. "We've got your old nemesis—Blanton Miles—in our crosshairs."

Weasel addressed Marquez. "Whaddaya mean you have him in your crosshairs?"

"Well, we work for him. We're supposed to meet him in Vegas tomorrow."

"Why?"

"He didn't provide me with an agenda. But reading between the lines, I think Miles wants me to murder this man." He jutted his chin at Dobkin.

Parnell said to Dobkin, "You're quite a popular guy these days. You know these two?"

Dobkin shook his head. "Never seen them before."

"He's lying!" Diego erupted. "We've worked for him for years. We take our orders from Miles, but he calls the shots."

"Yeah, he knows exactly who we are," Marquez said, scowling at Dobkin. "He wants us dead for buzzing your mining compound. Says we compromised his operations, that we're a danger to the security of his organization. But he won't get involved himself. He's getting Miles to do it. He's a master at covering his tracks. Always works it so there's never any blowback. Leaves nothing that would link him to his crimes. The Holt trial was a classic example of how this man operates."

"Yeah," Parnell muttered, "I'm familiar with how this prick works."

Marquez continued. "Blanton Miles is just like him. I've worked for Miles a long time. I've learned his thought processes. I discovered that Mister High Roller here came down hard on Miles after we reported our flyovers. Blamed him for our actions. Threatened his life if he didn't eliminate us. It really pissed Miles off, being ordered to do something like that. Miles figures his best bet is to turn the tables and take down Mister Moneybags. But he's incapable of doing it himself. He wants *us* to get our hands bloody and leave *our* fingerprints all over it. I would stake my entire psychiatric practice and my airplane on it. Admit it," he said to Dobkin, "you ordered Miles to kill us."

John Dobkin glowered at the psychiatrist, anger and hatred pooling in his cement-gray eyes. "You're damn straight I did. You're a loose cannon. An incompetent fool. You need to go. Both of you."

Parnell said to Dobkin, "So you *do* know these two. How lovely." He pressed the Mauser up against Dobkin's spine and said to Marquez, "You don't have to worry about this douchebag anymore. He's all mine now."

Dobkin continued to glare at Marquez, wincing as the gun barrel stuck him in the back.

Marquez said, "I'm glad you're going to do him. I'm not a killer. Neither is Diego."

"No, you're certainly not killers," Parnell agreed, visibly tensing up. "But you *are* misogynist, rapist kidnappers."

"*What?*"

Parnell snorted disgustedly. "Don't give me the surprise act, Doctor Strangelove." He jerked his head in Elaine's direction. "This beautiful lady told me all about what you barnyard animals did to her. The way you drugged her and took advantage of her. It's repulsive, what you did."

Marquez threw out his shackled hands in a supplicating gesture. "Look, we didn't mean anything by it. Just some fun and games between consenting adults. In fact, I treated her like a queen. Bought her expensive clothes and a nice dinner. Put her up in a luxurious hotel room. I wouldn't call that taking advantage of her."

"*Consenting adults?*" Parnell spat on the dirt floor. "You're depraved, El Shrinko. Fun and games you say? I've got a few of my own in mind for you two later. But let's get back to Blanton Miles. You're supposed to hook up with him in Vegas tomorrow?"

"Yes," Marquez said, looking at Elaine, obviously taken aback at Parnell's suggestion of retribution. She held his stare and thought: *Are you really all that surprised I told Derek about what you did to me? You're shocked that my man would just let something like that slide?*

"When and where?"

"One o'clock. At the North Las Vegas Airport."

"The small airport? Not McCarran International?"

"Correct."

"Why there? Why not a casino or a club on the strip?"

"Miles doesn't like crowds. He's got an obsession with privacy. Rolls under the radar as much as possible."

Parnell nodded. "Yeah, I know all about that weird kink of his. Still, why a small, out of the way airport?"

"That's where he's comfortable. We've met there before. I figure if we fly out of here in the morning, we can be there by—"

"Wait a minute, hold on there, Strangelove," Parnell said, throwing up a hand. "I'm not goin' anywhere in that plane of yours. It's a deathtrap and this whole thing smells like a setup. A trap with teeth."

"It's *not*, I'm telling you," Marquez practically whined. "Why would I set you up when Miles is the guy we're both after?"

"Oh, I don't know," Parnell mused, "maybe because you convinced my Lainey you were after *me*? That you were Tico Samuels' cousin and wanted to avenge his death?"

"No—no! I already explained that to her," he said, tipping his head at Elaine. "I used misdirection to fool her into leading us to you. Just Psych 101 stuff, really. Embarrassingly elementary, I'm afraid. But it worked."

Elaine watched Parnell turn this over in his mind, staring off into space the way he did when contemplating the logic of a situation. Finally he said, "Why would Miles need to meet with you in person? If he wants *you* to snuff Dobkin, why wouldn't he keep his distance?"

"Because he's not about to arrange a hit over the phone or through electronic media, even with all the encryption software we have in place. It'd leave a trail back to him. He's way too savvy for that. More importantly, he wants to keep an eye on us, see us actually carry out the dirty deed, to be sure firsthand that Dobkin is eliminated."

"And then Miles would be in a good position to remove both of you," Parnell deduced.

"You got it. But he wouldn't do it himself. He'd contract it out. Miles has a couple of hard-case executioners on retainer."

Parnell thought for a minute, then said, "Look. I *do* want Miles. But the only way I'm going to Vegas with you is driving our rental car with my friend Greg along for the ride." He clapped Weasel on the shoulder. "You haven't exactly earned my trust,

Strangelove."

"I wish you wouldn't call me that."

"And I wish you hadn't raped my woman."

"I didn't rape anybody."

"I'd say otherwise," Elaine said, flushing with an anger she thought she'd gotten past. She stared him down until he looked away.

Dobkin said to Marquez, "I don't suppose you've heard yet what these jerkoffs did to my home, have you?"

"No, what?"

"Nearly wiped out my entire security team before they abducted me. I'm sure it's all over the news media by now."

Weasel spoke, pride brightening his tone. "He's right. We did a little landscaping using explosives. It's the newest craze in home gardening techniques. I believe they call it grenade-scaping."

Nervous laughter filled the cave.

"Is that true?" Marquez asked, a look of worry crimping his dark, Aztecan features.

"Yeah, we bombed the shit out of Dobkin's front entrance," Parnell said. "Left quite a mess. That leads to another issue. How do you think Miles will react when he sees the destruction there? When he learns that a handful of guards were killed and the head honcho is gone? When he sees the place lookin' like a war zone? You think he'll still show at the airport?"

"Maybe not. *Probably* not," Marquez said. "But that gives me an idea."

"I'm listening."

"Miles undoubtedly knows by now that John Dobkin's place has been attacked and that he's missing. Right?"

Parnell put his free hand to his ear. "Is there an echo in here? That's what I just said."

"So, how about I call Miles and give him a half truth?"

"Half truth?"

"Yeah. He knows about these mines, where they're located. He suspects this is your base of operation, even though he hasn't got verification on that yet. I'll confirm it for him. Tell him we've seen you here. With John Dobkin. I'll tell him we can't leave for fear of losing you and him. I think he'd make the trip here."

"What are the chances?"

"Excellent, I'd say."

"Bullshit!" Dobkin snarled. "Miles won't come here. He

doesn't want to deal with me."

"He *won't* be dealing with you," Parnell said. "That knock on your head must've caused short-term memory loss. Have you forgotten I have a gun stuck in your back? That you're shackled and on your way to hell? You're in no position to influence anything."

"We'll see about that," Dobkin grumbled.

Diego chimed in. "Miles will definitely come. He'll trip all over himself to get here." He tilted his head at Parnell. "Miles has been obsessed with finding this man for three-plus years. He'll hustle his ass off to get here."

Elaine could see Derek starting to accept Marquez's plan. At least she hoped she was reading him correctly. She didn't think she could survive him traipsing off to Vegas on another high-risk venture without her.

"What do you think, E?" Parnell said to her. "You think this could work?"

She was surprised by his asking her opinion and tried not to sound too eager. "Yes, I do. Everything you've told me about Blanton Miles says his knowing you're here is a big incentive for him. Having Dobkin and these two here as well . . . I don't see how he'll be able to resist. You ask me, the plan holds water."

Parnell nodded, mulling it over. Looked at Weasel. "What do you think, Greg?"

"I'm with Elaine. I say let's try it. Worst that could happen is Miles turns tail and runs. Drops off the grid. But we'd still have our number one public enemy here," he said, pointing at Dobkin.

"Miles won't run," Marquez said. "His monumental ego won't permit it. He'll come if I call him."

"It's all a moot point, Parnell," Dobkin said. "My people will be here soon to crush you."

"So you keep saying. And as I keep telling you, we look forward to their visit." Parnell turned to Marquez. "Where is Miles based these days?"

"He works out of an underground bunker near Los Angeles. Far under the radar."

"LA? How far is that from here? Five hundred miles?"

"Something like that, yeah," Weasel said.

"That means he probably wouldn't be able to make it by tomorrow," Parnell said.

"He could definitely be here tomorrow afternoon," Diego said.

"He'll come by chopper. That's how he's traveled in the past."

"And he won't come alone," Marquez said. "He'll have a couple of bodyguards with him. The man is excessively paranoid."

Parnell bobbed his head in understanding. "Good to know. All right. Let's try this. Go ahead and call Miles, try to get him here."

"I'll need my phone."

"Where is it?"

"One of your guards took it. The guy who killed my man on our way in."

Elaine said, "Cale has it, Derek."

"T-Seed shot somebody?"

"He sure did," Elaine said. "After Oshkosh went down. He and Jenn brought these two in."

"Well I'll be damned," Parnell said. "Didn't think T-Seed had it in him. Where is he now?"

"Probably sleeping. He pulled a double watch last night."

"Okay," Parnell said, giving Dobkin a light shove. "Let's get our prisoner down into lockup and then get Doctor Strangelove's phone."

Dobkin turned and looked at Parnell. "I'm not staying here?"

Parnell gave him a wicked grin. "Oh no. This is a minimum security lockup. You're a prize prisoner. We're taking you down to *maximum* security." He turned to Marquez. "And you, Doc, if you attempt anything funny when I bring you your phone, I'll decorate this cave with your gray matter. Got it?"

"No worries. I'll convince Miles he needs to come here. You can even listen in on the call."

"Oh, you bet your ass I'll be listening. To every word."

Parnell led Dobkin down a winding, rock-walled corridor, Weasel trailing, prodding Dobkin along with his rifle. Elaine brought up the rear. They carefully made their way through the dim, narrow passageway, descending three levels to an area she had never seen, coming upon a dark, depressing ten-by-ten fissure in the rock with a wrought-iron gate bolted across the opening.

"Where are we?" she asked, her voice deadened by the rocky tomb.

Parnell told her Hyacinth once used the area to store explosive materials, primarily black powder, dynamite, ammonium nitrate, and blasting caps. The space was empty now, save for an old cot and a steel slop bucket.

He pushed Dobkin into the rock cell and slammed the heavy

gate shut with a clank, then secured the two jumbo padlocks.

"Even your most loyal peeps will never find you down here, Dobkin."

"You're not gonna give me a change of clothes?"

"No. You won't be here long. Just until I get Miles."

"What about food and water?"

Parnell smiled at him sardonically. "Water drips down the walls when it rains. And the cave rats down here are nice and plump. Good eatin' if you can catch one."

"You're a sadistic bastard, you know that?"

"I treat folks the way they treat me."

"I never treated you like this, Parnell."

"No you didn't. You treated me worse. You've had me in a cage without bars for ten long years. My Jennifer, too."

"C'mon, this is inhumane. Have some compassion. I haven't eaten in close to twenty-four hours."

"Then why don't you call room service."

They left him there in his dim and dusty cell, Dobkin rattling the wrought-iron door and shouting threatening obscenities at them as they made their way aboveground.

They re-entered the spacious entryway of mineshaft #2, walking alongside the Rolling Inferno, past the alcove where Marquez and Diego were being held. They entered the yard, the sun blinding after their time underground. Elaine and Parnell headed to Cale's living space while Weasel left them so he could catch some shuteye.

Cale's dwelling was in mineshaft #1, at the opposite end of where Elaine stayed with Derek. She worried at what they might find, knowing Jenn was probably shacked up with Cale. *Why are you always so concerned about what Derek thinks?*

They entered mineshaft #1, walked to the far end. Cale's area was small and secluded. Open. No privacy door. Parnell charged into the gloom of Cale's small cavern, Elaine following close behind. Cale and Jenn were asleep, sprawled atop a large air mattress, completely naked. The sight of his nude daughter spooning a bare-assed Cale didn't seem to faze Derek at all. He strutted up to the air mattress and jostled Cale's elbow.

"Hey, T-Seed," he said. "Sorry to barge in on you but I need the shrink's phone."

Jenn came awake. "Poppy?" she said, groggy, confused.

Cale opened his eyes and scrambled to pull a blanket over

them. "What the—?"

"Where's Doctor Marquez's cell phone? That's all I need. Tell me where it is and I'll let you two get back to sleep."

Elaine picked up the unmistakable smell of sweat-drenched sex. *Good for them,* she thought, wondering why Derek was so uncharacteristically taking this scene in stride.

Cale pointed to his pants that were draped over a boulder. She watched Derek go to them and dig the phone out of the front pocket.

"Sweet dreams, kids," he said, turning and walking out.

Elaine caught up to him and said, "Really? No comment about what we just saw?"

"C'mon, E. You think I've never seen my daughter naked before?"

She grinned ear-to-ear as she followed him out into the yard.

Karmic Mood Swings

SEVEN HOURS OF UNINTERRUPTED SLEEP did wonders for Parnell. He had collapsed into a dreamless slumber and slept the afternoon away after retreating to his subterranean abode. Upon waking, Elaine coaxed him into the shower where they made wet, sloppy, exquisite love. He felt recharged. Revitalized. Ready to take on the world that had rocketed off the rails.

He sat now in the mining yard hunched over his second plate of beef stew, his favorite Chef Alice dish. Weasel sat next to him, mopping gravy from his hubcap with a hunk of wheat bread. Annie Finnegan's nightly prayer session had just wrapped up and the Hyacinth breezers were in a festive mood. A light marijuana haze hung over the clearing, intermingling with the mouthwatering scent of smoked meats and roasted onions. Music and discordant voices rolled across the clearing as the gathering sang folk songs and protest anthems to the accompanying guitar work of the Johnstons (Fingers Johnston and his son Zack on guitars, with Ricky 'Radboy' Stindahl busting a mean tambourine).

Parnell spotted Elaine and Jenn near the bonfire, heads thrown back, singing boisterously, laughing as they belted out familiar lyrics. He smiled, grateful they were enjoying each other's company. Seeing the two women in his life together like this filled him with a joy that had been missing in recent years.

He leaned back and peered up into the wide sky, taking it all in. The half moon brightened the infinite clusters of stars, bringing the tiniest pinpoints of light into crisp focus. He never tired of this breathtaking nightscape. The southern Utah sky was true celestial theater, reminding him of the Hayden Planetarium his mother had taken him to when he was a boy. He would forever remember her for her obsessive interest in astronomy. He'd never felt closer to her than he did that night, when she'd leaned close and whispered to him, pointing out various constellations and planetary systems and describing in great detail what she knew about them. He knew she could ill afford the cost of the trip into New York City and the planetarium's high price of admission, but she'd done it for him nonetheless. She had found a way to bring him happiness for one unforgettable evening.

"You okay, partner?" he heard Weasel say.

"Yeah. Got a lot on my mind is all."

"I hear that, bro. Sucks about Blanton Miles, huh?"

"It's only an extra day or two," he said. "We'll get him, Greg."

"Hope so."

Earlier today, Doctor Marquez had contacted Miles on his cell phone and they'd all listened in on the call. Miles had seemed genuinely excited that the psychiatrist and Diego tracked Dobkin here. Miles admitted to knowing about the destruction and killings at Dobkin's mansion, and wondered to where Dobkin had disappeared. He seemed hot on the idea of coming to the Hyacinth mines, but claimed he couldn't make it for a few more days. Could Marquez keep Dobkin contained until he could get here? Marquez had done a good job at sounding put out over the delay. Asked Miles if he could possibly make it sooner, because no telling how long the situation would hold. After much back-and-forth, Miles agreed to come within 48 hours. They agreed to meet at Marquez's airplane on the western side of the Hyacinth ridge. Miles said he would text the psychiatrist when he was in transit.

Hearing Blanton Miles' voice in the speakerphone had ignited a fit of rage in Parnell. The bile rose in his throat and an angry fire burned in his gut as he'd listened, wanting so much to reach through the tiny speaker and strangle the man who had so expertly hoodwinked him for seven long years.

Parnell had told Weasel that they'd get Blanton Miles, but he now questioned their chances. He knew how Miles rolled and the man's delay tactics bothered him. Why had he requested extra time—a whopping four days at first? Hadn't he originally planned to be in Las Vegas tomorrow? Was he onto them? Now that the airport meet was off and he knew all the principals were gathered here, was he plotting something? Miles had all his marks lined up like ducks in a carnival shooting gallery. Doctor Marquez had told them they had Blanton Miles in their crosshairs, but Parnell wondered just exactly who was in those gun sights. Parnell didn't like it at all. The change in plans troubled him greatly.

Weasel's voice cut into his thoughts. "You know, I was able to get connectivity on the laptop earlier. I discovered something distressing."

Parnell didn't need *distressing* right now. "What's that?" he said, irritated.

"That government cleanup movement I told you about? Operation Vagabond? It's on the move. The National Guard just steamrolled two hobo camps in southern Colorado—one in Alamosa, the other in Cortez. The report said Northern New Mexico and Arizona are next. That means Santa Fe and Winslow, Derek. We need to get back to Shangri-La soon."

Parnell felt like he'd been run through with a sword. "When you say steamrolled, what does that mean exactly?"

Greg Bethea ran a hand down his long neck. "Means the villages were flattened. Destroyed. Our breezer friends tear-gassed. Those without proof of citizenship—and that's a great many of them—were deported. Those who put up resistance were shot."

"Jesus! How many dead?"

"Dozens."

Parnell did his best to hide his fuming anger. "Shit, Greg, it's certainly not a government for the people, is it?"

Weasel shook his head. "Hasn't been for a long, long time, my friend."

Parnell felt the night closing in on him. He stood, told Weasel he needed to walk off his dinner.

"Want some company?"

"Nah. Thanks. Got a lot on my mind. Just need some alone time."

"Understood. Give some thought to us heading to Shangri-La, will you?"

"Sure thing, Greg."

Parnell took his hubcap dinner plate back to Chef Alice. Complimented her on her cooking, then went to his underground quarters and threw on a heavier jacket. Grabbed his pistol, a flashlight, and a wad of money. Checked that his Mauser was loaded, then rode his mining cart back up to ground level. Walked through the yard toward the site entrance where he knew T-Seed was standing night watch. He had a few things to discuss with him.

The music and singing faded to a muted hum behind him as he neared the deep cut in the rocks that served as the Hyacinth entrance.

"Hey, Mister Parnell," T-Seed called to him from near the rail spur. "What brings you out his way?"

"What's with this *mister* shit, T-Seed? Makes me feel like an old man."

"Sorry, sir. It's just out of respect, sir."

"I'm not a *sir* either. Far as I know, the Queen of England hasn't knighted me for anything. You can call me Derek."

Cale let out an uneasy chuckle. "Sorry. I'm a bundle of nerves around you."

"Why is that?"

"I dunno. I guess because of who you are. Your reputation and all. And, no disrespect intended, but I get the feeling you're here to scare me away from your daughter."

Parnell lifted the flashlight, shined it on his face. "*That's* what you think?"

"Yeah. I mean, after you, um . . . after you found us together this morning the way you did . . . the way we *were* . . . I, um, I just thought that—"

"Jesus, T-Seed. Get a grip, son. I came here to congratulate you on your taste in women, among other things."

"Really?"

Parnell nearly laughed at the incredulous look on Turnipseed's face. "You've made my Jennifer happier than I've seen her in many a moon. She was in a bad place before you came along. I'm grateful."

"Are you serious?"

"Don't I look serious? I will give you a word of warning, however. You'd better continue to treat her right. She needs a lot of TLC right now. She and my Lainey are all I've got in this sorry world. If I catch word that you've mistreated Jenny in any way, you'll have me to deal with. Got it?"

"Oh, sir—I mean *Derek*. There's no way I would ever think of doing her harm. Jenn is one of the most fascinating and beautiful girls I've ever known. She captivates me. I knew she was special the first time I laid eyes on her. Wasn't sure I'd ever see her again after she left Shangri-La with you. But thank the Lord, it all worked out."

"Yeah. Jenny is *very* special. I'm glad you see that, Cale."

"You called me Cale."

"That's your name isn't it?"

"Well, yeah. But you've always called me T-Seed."

"If you're callin' me Derek, I should call you Cale. No?"

"I guess. I'm honored."

"Don't be. It's no big deal."

An awkward silence ensued as they scanned the moonlit desert.

"Anything happening out there tonight?" Parnell asked him.

"No. Nothin' but a few coyotes callin' each other. Lookin' for love, I guess. In other words, a pretty boring night."

Parnell reached into his pocket, pulled out the cash, peeled off a few hundreds and extended the bills to him.

Cale looked at the cash fluttering in the cool night breeze under the flashlight beam. "What's this?"

"Take it," Parnell demanded. "It's your posse pay."

"But I'm not in your posse."

"Consider yourself officially recruited."

"But—"

"I greatly underestimated you, Cale. I apologize for that. My mistake. When I was putting my crew together, I thought you were too soft. Not fit for the rough-and-tumble I knew was ahead of us. I didn't think you could handle the bloodletting that had to be done. I also mistakenly thought you wouldn't be able to jump moving railcars. But Lainey told me about your acrobatics on the Union Pacific . . . the way you saved Annie. And yesterday? Shit, Cale. Jenny said you took down that guy from over two-hundred yards out. That's incredible marksmanship. Especially under duress. Your first kill?"

"Yeah. It's hard for me to accept that I killed another human being."

"You did the right thing, Cale. The guy you nailed was a really bad dude. If not for your quick actions yesterday, many of our friends might be dead right now."

"Maybe, yeah. But it makes me feel kinda sick when I think about it too much. I really don't know how you do it, Derek."

"Every mark I've killed deserved to die. Every time I snuff someone, I feel like I'm doing the world a favor. And I know for a fact that yesterday *you* did the world a favor. Karma will be kind to you."

"Karma?"

"Yeah, y'know. Lady Luck. Father Fate . . . whatever you wanna call it. More importantly, where the hell did you learn to shoot like that?"

Cale said, "I spent a couple of months on a Sioux reservation in North Dakota. Couple of guys there could shoot the eyes out of a mosquito at that distance. They made good money at sharpshooter competitions. They taught me how to shoot a rifle, taught me how not to miss, no matter the circumstances."

Parnell was impressed. "You're every bit as good a shot as Billy Dixon was."

"That's high praise. I was truly sorry to hear about Kid."

"Yeah, I was right there in that hallway with him when he took the westbound. It was devastating. Abducting that turd Dobkin has cost us a lot." He thrust the cash at Cale. "Take this goddamn money! My arm's getting tired."

With great reluctance, Cale stepped forward and plucked the cash from his hand. "Thanks, Derek. You're a good man."

"Quite a few folks would disagree with you." Parnell watched Cale stuff the money in his hip pocket before saying, "I have a feeling this area is about to become a hot zone. You ready for that, Cale?"

"Well, I've given that some thought lately. Jenn and I both have. This place reminds us of the Alamo before the siege."

"The Alamo?" Parnell grinned, getting a kick out of the analogy. "Does that scare you?"

"Some, yeah. Jenn's more worried than I am."

"Well, I've always said a little excitement never hurt anyone. We'll be fine." He clapped Cale on the shoulder. "Listen, I'm gonna take a stroll into the desert, maybe go check out the shrink's plane."

"That's a long hike. You want me to go with you?"

"No, I need you to stay put. When I come back I'll spell you for an hour or so, let you go get some grub. Alice's stew tonight is out of this world."

"I appreciate it, Derek. Be safe."

He left Cale and walked away from the mines. The night engulfed him. The music and singing faded away behind him and a preternatural quiet blanketed the desert. A brisk breeze kicked up, biting at his face. His breaths matched his strides and he fell into a comfortable hiking rhythm. The half moon glimmered, painting the sand and rocks a dreamlike silvery patina. The western ridge jutted out over the desert basin, a monolithic bronze monument. He headed for the ridge, flashlight out in front, the strong beam illuminating his way.

So good to stretch his legs. He considered his options as he walked. He'd intimated to Cale he thought big trouble was on the way. The mines would become a 'hot zone' is what he'd told him. Probably not a good thing to do. Cale would relay it to Jennifer, which would only feed her already high sense of anxiety. Lainey would surely hear about it, too. He'd made a mistake, being so forthright with Cale. He needed to be the one with the cool head and calm demeanor. He needed to provide the leadership this bunch needed right now. But then again, Cale and Jenn had apparently already discussed the idea of the second coming of the Alamo, so he really hadn't sprung anything new on Cale. And it was pointless to ignore the hard truth. A war was coming to Hyacinth. He felt it in his bones. Could sense it the way he could foretell the coming of a thunderstorm. Karma was calling soldiers to the war. And with Dobkin out of the picture, Blanton Miles would be the architect of that war.

So, what to do? Should he head back to the mines and strap Dobkin, Marquez, and Diego in the Rolling Inferno, send them to their fiery deaths, then get the hell out of Utah? He'd already shut off the ventilation system in mineshaft #2 in preparation of sending his roller coaster on its final ride. Or should he wait and see what developed with Blanton Miles? After hearing that prick on the psychiatrist's phone this morning, he wanted to include him on the hell coaster in the worst way. But he hadn't lost sight of the fact he had a lot of other people to think about.

And to throw a wrench into an already dangerous situation, Weasel had brought up that Operation Vagabond mess the feds were running. Greg was pushing him to get to Winslow to help the Shangri-La breezers. Lots of urgency there. But really, how much good could he and Weasel and maybe Flywheel and Cale do at Shangri-La? Right now he needed to be at the mines, protecting his family and friends. They stood a better chance here at Hyacinth, cloistered within their rock walls and deep tunnels and armed with lethal weaponry. But when he thought about his hobo friends at Shangri-La and their vulnerability against attack by U.S. National Guard units, his guilt kicked in.

He trudged on, the ridge looming larger as he neared it. His breathing became more labored. His calves hurt from hiking through deep sand. The cold breeze penetrated his jacket, making him shiver. *Not as young as you once were, old boy.*

Marquez's plane came into view, looking like a Matchbox toy from this distance. Moonlight reflected off the cockpit windshield in shimmering sparkles.

A scuffling sound came from behind him and he spun around. Scanned the desert floor with his flash, sweeping the light across fifty yards of terrain. Nothing but rocks and cactus and his footprints in the sand.

He switched the flashlight to his left hand, pulled the Mauser from his waistband with his right. Gripped the gun tensely. Stood still. Held his breath.

His heart thudded in his throat.

Something big rustled behind the sandstone boulders that lined the base of the ridge. He jerked the flashlight there, trained his pistol above the beam. Nothing but ghostly shadows projected against the wall of the ridge.

He listened. Heard footsteps shuffling through the sand.

Thought he heard a human voice.

Whispers.

A snicker.

His pulse was crazy, erratic. Frantically, he searched for some cover. Realized with dismay he was out in the open.

A familiar voice called out to him. "So we finally meet again, Parnell. Looks like I'm the one in control this time."

Parnell couldn't believe his ears. "McKellar?" he said. "Ollie McKellar?"

"Oh, don't act so goddamned surprised." McKellar's voice resounded across the canyon.

Parnell looked around, estimating whether he could make it to the nearest boulder. The only object in close proximity was a scrawny cactus. "What brings you to Utah, Ollie?"

"You really have to ask that question? In case you forgot, I've got a score to settle with you, mu'fucker. You're a dead man. Me an' Palomino got our rifles on ya. When I give the command, you're a goner."

Parnell tried to figure from McKellar's voice where he was, but the cliff walls played tricks with sounds. "Christ, Ollie. This is pretty cowardly. Even for you. You're just gonna shoot a defenseless man in cold blood? Without givin' me a fair chance?"

He heard McKellar laugh. "Fair chance? It's every bit as fair as that joke of a gun duel you put me through. You humiliated me an' fucked up my hand. It's my turn to fuck *you* up."

Parnell searched his mind for an angle. After a long moment, he shouted, "Hey, Palomino. Tell your mentally challenged friend to think about things. Don't let him drag you into this. The feds are about to come down hard on this place. You kill me and both of you will spend the rest of your lives in prison."

"Nice try, Parnell," McKellar returned. "We're gonna kill you and collect the reward money for your sorry ass. The warrant states dead or alive, if'n you can trust them guvmint fuckers. Me an' Palomino can live like kings on a hundred large."

"You ever let your friend talk, Ollie?"

"Sure I do. Say hi to our soon-to-be victim, Pal."

"Hey there, dead man," came Palomino's reply from nearby.

Parnell decided to call their bluff. "Go ahead and shoot me if that's what you came to do."

"Oh, we will. You can be sure of that. But I wanna cherish this for a while. I wanna play with you a bit before the end. Y'know, like a cat plays around with the mouse before he snaps its neck and drags it off."

Parnell was about to respond when he heard running footsteps.

Indecipherable shouts.

A scream.

The night became chaos.

Gunfire erupted, booming reports that sounded like cannon fire. Parnell dove to the ground, the flashlight tumbling end over end. Shots kicked up sprays of sand around him. He heard a loud pop and felt an agonizing burn along the top of his right ear. The side of his face bloomed in an intense heat as if it had caught fire. A painful sting pinched his left side, sucking the oxygen from his lungs. Fighting the pain and gulping for air, he fired off a burst of erratic shots toward the boulders. Kept firing until he realized the effort was futile. He'd been hit. Twice.

The shooting stopped as suddenly as it had started. Parnell lay crumpled in the sand, weak, delirious, on the verge of passing out. He touched his side, his hand coming away bloody. He reached for his ear and pulled away a lump of gelatinous flesh. His face burned like the fires of hell.

He gritted his teeth, biting back the pain. Thought he heard a familiar voice increasing in volume, getting closer.

But then the voice faded and spiraled away as his world went black.

The Omniscient Scriptwriter

"**Hey, Jenn,**" **Ann said,** taking a seat next to her near the fire. "I haven't seen you at my prayer sessions the last few days. If I didn't know better, I'd swear you've been avoiding me."

Jenn caught a whiff of musky jasmine perfume. Ann's scent took her back to their carnal coupling, the erotic memory bringing heat to her cheeks.

She raised her mug of beer, acknowledging her. "I haven't been dodging you," she lied. "I've been spending a lot of time with Cale. Been belowground, reading, too, digging into Weasel's amazing library."

"Yes, Greg does have an interesting stockpile of books."

Jenn sensed Ann studying her and it made her uncomfortable. She did her best to ignore her, keeping her focus on the activity in the yard. A handful of breezers spread out around the fire, finishing dinner. Chef Alice was cleaning up around her cooking pit. Radboy Stindahl worked on his skateboard moves. The Johnstons were going over song arrangements. Broadway Bling and Hopeful Harvey Henshaw engaged in a heated political debate. She took a swig of her beer while Ann continued to fixate on her. Elaine had left not five minutes ago. *Has Ann been watching me to time her move? Has she been waiting for her chance to get me alone?*

When she couldn't stand the silent examination anymore, she turned to Ann. "Why do you keep staring at me?"

"Because astonishing beauty holds me spellbound," Ann said without hesitation.

Jenn wished she could fly far away from here. "Oh, *please*. I'm a long way from beautiful," she said, not able to meet Ann's gaze.

"You are to me, Jenn. And you are to Cale Turnipseed, too."

Is she jealous of Cale? Is that even possible?

The alcohol Jenn had consumed emboldened her. She turned to Ann, keeping her voice low. "How come you never put a move on me when I first arrived at Shangri-La? When you let me stay with you at your place? You had a lot of chances."

"I wanted to, Jenn. Oh, how I wanted to. Such a temptation.

But I never, as you say, *put moves* on people. God writes the script and I follow it to the letter."

Jenn couldn't hold Ann's arresting, mesmerizing stare. She looked away. "So you and me? We weren't in God's play at first?"

Ann laughed. "Oh, we were definitely in His play. Just not in the way I would have written it."

"So when did the script change?"

"The script didn't change. I couldn't control my impulses and went against God's will. It was a moment of extreme weakness for me. I find you ravishingly beautiful in so many ways, Jenn, and I'm painfully human. Can you ever forgive me?"

Jenn eyed the other breezers sitting around the fire, worried they might be picking up on this awkward conversation. Satisfied that no one was paying them any attention, she turned back to Ann. The melancholy in her expression almost broke her heart. Jenn had gone out of her way to avoid this woman the past week, and she felt pangs of guilt. Ann was truly a good person. Open and honest to a fault. She loved Jenn, but Jenn could never reciprocate the kind of love Ann wanted.

"Oh, dear," Ann said. "I've embarrassed you. I'm so sorry."

"No, it's okay, really. I was the one who initiated things, if I remember correctly. You've been so good to me. I appreciate your kindness."

Ann covered Jenn's free hand with hers. "Look, I fully realize your heart belongs to Cale. *That's* God's will. His script. The Lord has spoken to me. He says you and Cale belong together. There's nothing I can do—or *should* do—to change that."

The sadness in her lovely eyes overwhelmed Jenn, and she started to cry.

"Hey, there's no need for tears, my sweets. Rejoice in the divine miracle that brought you and Cale together."

"But what about you?"

"Oh, I suppose one day the right script will come along for me," she said with a despondent smile. "I'll be fine as long as I have friends like you." She reached out her right hand. "Friends?"

Jenn set her beer down and shook. "Absolutely. Friends forever, Ann."

Their handshake turned into a long, warm hug, the two of them clutching each other in the light of the fire.

A commotion near the yard entrance interrupted their hug. Jenn heard one of the teenage girls scream. Saw her fellow hobos rushing toward whatever it was.

"What's going on?" she asked Ann, fearful they were under attack again and knowing Cale was on security detail.

"I don't know." Ann stood. "Let's go check it out."

They fast-walked past the conveyance crane and the two rock crushers, a limping Ann doing her best to keep up with Jenn. They wove their way between the big haul truck and the mining excavator, catching up with the small group that had gathered. Jenn stopped abruptly, disbelieving the scene in front of her. Poppy leaned against Cale, his face and side drenched in blood. So much blood. Cale looked exhausted. Poppy looked dead.

Jenn thought she would lose it.

"Is he alive?" Ann shouted, moving closer.

"Barely," Cale answered. "He's in shock."

Ann's nursing instincts took over and she moved in to help.

Jenn found herself in the middle of mass hysteria. Lots of jostling and confusion. Shouts of "What happened?" and "Is he gonna make it?" She tried to calm herself. Attempted to keep her rioting emotions under control. Struggled to make sense of this alarming scene.

She observed the grisly proceedings, unable to move. What the hell had happened? An hour ago Poppy had been here with them, listening to the music and eating his dinner. *Has Poppy's long stretch of good luck finally come to an end? Oh, please, please, please let him be okay!*

Greg Bethea came up behind her. "Hey, Jenn," he said, touching her arm. "What's going on?"

"Oh God, Weasel. Poppy's been hurt bad," she said, nodding at Cale who was doing his best to walk her father into the yard.

Weasel quickly jumped into action, recruiting Javion Wheeler to help him carry Poppy.

"Get him to the headframe, fellas," Ann yelled out. "I've got medical supplies there."

The going was difficult, but Cale, Weasel, and Flywheel got Poppy situated in the headframe. Ann went to work on her new patient while the men, huffing and puffing from the exertion, left her to tend to her nursing duties.

Jenn ran to Cale and threw her arms around him. "Are you all right?"

"I guess."

"What happened?"

"I need to sit for a spell, Jenn," he said, fatigue sapping his words.

She helped him to a tiered rock formation where he could sit with his back against a smooth sandstone facing. The blood covering his jacket and pants appeared black as oil in the moonlight.

"Are you okay?" she said, plopping down next to him, the metallic stench of fresh blood overpowering. "Have you been shot?"

"I didn't get hit. All this is from Derek."

Jenn's hopes were floundering. "Damn, Cale. What the hell happened?"

He was in a daze, his words slurred and breathless as he recounted what had transpired out in the night desert. "Your father paid me a visit. We talked for a while and then he told me he was goin' for a walk. I thought he might've meant a walk down the railhead tracks. Or maybe a trek close to the Hyacinth perimeter. But no. He wanted to hike out into the desert. Said he wanted to go out to the shrink's airplane. I thought it was a bad idea, but you know your dad, Jenn. I asked if he wanted me to go with him and he said no. Told me he needed to be alone to clear his head. He wanted me to stay put, continue my watch on the rail spur and the entrance."

"But you didn't stay put," Jenn said.

"No. I wasn't about to let him wander across the desert at night. I felt compelled to keep an eye on him, even if that meant abandoning my post. I was worried he might break an ankle or disturb a nest of rattlers, get bit and die out there before anyone would be able to find him. But I never in a million years expected him to run into Ollie McKellar and that Indian friend of his."

"Ollie?"

"Yeah. McKellar wanted revenge for that one-sided gun duel at Shangri-La. They were able to get a few shots off on your dad before I silenced 'em. Two things saved me out there, Jenn—the moonlight and Ollie's habit of runnin' his mouth. Gave me the light and the time I needed."

Jenn felt something shift inside her. "You, um—Ollie and Palomino?"

"Yep, I did. Got 'em both."

"Wow," she said, trying to comprehend what he had just been through. "But how could those two have known Poppy would be out there this time of night?"

"My guess is they've been here, camping out, biding their time, watchin' and waitin'. They knew it would be suicide trying to storm the entrance, especially if they saw what we did to Marquez and his crew. Just wish I could've stopped 'em before they did any damage. They messed up Derek pretty bad."

"How bad? Do you know?"

"I don't. I got him back here quick as possible. Ann will let us know about his condition soon."

"Well, thank God you were there. Can you imagine if you hadn't followed him?"

"I'd rather not. C'mon," he said, getting to his feet and taking her by the hand. "Let's go find Elaine."

Prairie Dogs and Bible Lessons

DEREK SHOT? THE NEWS SHOCKED ELAINE. He'd made it back from the perilous Vegas trip unscathed only to be shot here at the mines? By Ollie McKellar no less? She had a hard time wrapping her head around it.

She quickly followed Cale and Jenn to the headframe.

Javion Wheeler stood in front of the closed door, keeping the curious at bay and giving Ann Finnegan the privacy she needed to tend to Parnell.

"What's the prognosis, Fly?" she asked.

A gust of desert wind stirred Javion's bushy 'fro. "Derek's had a rough night, Elaine. Best to let Ann give you the particulars."

He pushed the door open and she entered first, Cale and Jenn entering behind. The small room was toasty-warm, heated by a portable propane heater glowing orange in the corner. Two battery-powered lanterns provided bright-white light. A pungent, vinegary odor—rubbing alcohol, iodine, and hydrogen peroxide—mingled with sweat and desperation. Derek lay along the far wall, splayed out on an air mattress. Blood-soaked gauze covered the right side of his face. A heavy bandage wrap swathed the left side of his abdomen. Ann sat perched on a wooden stool beside him, a weary frown hardening her face.

Elaine couldn't move. Couldn't speak.

Ann stood and greeted them. "He's in pain, but he's going to be okay." She washed her hands in a bucket sitting atop the old mineshaft hoist encasement. "He lost most of his right ear and a lot of blood. I did what I could with a needle and thread. Sewed up what's left of his ear, got the bleeding down to a light seepage. There's always the possibility of infection setting in. I'm going to need a lot more peroxide and antibacterial ointment. More gauze and tape."

"I'll go into Kanab tomorrow morning when the stores open," Cale volunteered.

"What about his side?" Jenn asked.

"He got lucky there. The shot just grazed him. It was a bleeder, but it clotted up fast. Nowhere near as serious as his ear. He's a lucky man. If either of those bullets struck an inch or two to the left or right, we wouldn't be having this conversation."

Elaine let out a gasp.

Parnell gawped at her, his mouth slanted in a painful grin. "Aw, come on, Lainey," he uttered. "I'm not *that* ugly, am I?"

She went to him, took his hand. He looked absolutely horrific. She tried to keep the distress she felt out of her voice. "How're you feeling, babe?"

"Nothin' I can't handle, E," he mumbled, setting his jaw firmly. "The good doctor here loaded me up with Darvocet. Ain't she great?"

Elaine wanted to weep. Seeing him in this compromised condition punched a hole in her heart. She could see the immense pain lurking behind his cloudy eyes. He was trying his best to present a strong front, but she knew better. *What is it about men and their misguided sense of machismo?*

"Cale told me what happened," she said.

"Yeah. T-Seed is a great man. A true patriot. A goddamned hero! He saved my life . . ." His words came out loopy and slurred due to the pain meds. "First time I've ever been happy that someone disobeyed my orders." With great effort, he lifted his head from the mattress and looked at Cale. "I didn't get a chance to tell you before, but I will now. Thank you, Cale Turnipseed, for what you did out there tonight. I owe you my life."

Cale shuffled nervously and muttered, "Don't be ridiculous. Just get yourself well. We need you."

"Look, I know you're hurting, Derek," Elaine said, "but—"

"I'm not *that* bad off. I'll be back in the saddle tomorrow."

"You won't be mounting any horses tomorrow," Ann said.

"We'll see about that, Nurse Annie."

Elaine said, "I have to ask. What in the world were you doing wandering alone out in the desert after sundown? I wondered where you disappeared to after dinner. I was worried."

"No need for you to worry, Lainey."

"Apparently there was."

"Where's the problem? We got rid of two bad dudes. That's a victory to my way of thinkin'."

Parnell's obstinacy had long been a flashpoint with her. She pulled her hand from his and backed up a step. "Where's the *problem?* The problem is you almost died, Derek. And your recklessness could have cost Cale his life, too . . ."

"Elaine," Ann interjected, "I don't think you should—"

"No, Ann," she said, waving her off with the flick of her hand. "He needs to hear this." She turned back to Parnell. "You made a bad decision tonight and it cost you dearly. Cost *us* dearly. You see it as a victory. I see it as tragic. You . . . You . . ."

She felt her emotions rising. She knew what she wanted to say, but couldn't go on. He looked so pathetic lying there, this man she loved in spite of his many flaws, this man of strength and determination cut down by a pair of close-call bullets. Life was so excruciatingly fragile. He could very easily be dead right now. But he was still here with them, and though she wanted to lambast him for his stupidity and virile arrogance, she couldn't do it. Oh how tangled and twisted her emotions were at this moment.

"You okay, Elaine?" Ann asked.

"Not really," she said, her tears building to a climax she could no longer hold back. The dam broke and the waterworks flowed, soaking her eyepatch and wetting her face. She tried to talk, but was too shaky to formulate words.

"Here, Elaine," Ann said, taking her gently by the arm and guiding her to the stool. "Have a seat. Relax. This has been a lot for you to take in."

Elaine snuffed back the tears, accepted a bottle of water and a towel from Ann. She wiped her face with the towel, took several sips of water. "I'm so embarrassed," she said when she regained her composure.

"Don't be," Jenn said, coming to her and rubbing her back. "We're all with you."

"Thanks, Jenn. You're sweet to say that." Elaine returned her attention to Derek. "Listen, babe, I love you so much it makes me crazy. But I'm seriously pissed at you. You ran off and left me without a clue. *Again.* That's always been your way. But tonight? Well, you outdid yourself tonight. That's all I'll say."

"Look, I realize I screwed up, Lainey. I wish I could take back tonight and have a do-over. I'm sorry, E. It was selfish of me."

Did she just hear those words trip off Derek's tongue? Elaine could count on one hand the number of times Parnell had apologized to her. Her spirits lifted. She leaned over and planted a quick kiss on his cheek.

"God, I hate seeing you like this," she said. "Hasn't this been enough of a wakeup call for you? Can't we just take off and leave this madness behind us, Derek? If we leave now we could be home in a couple of days."

"Home? You mean Costa Rica?"

"Yeah. Costa Rica. Where our house is. Where our life is. Where we're safe. Home certainly isn't here in this dusty coal mine living underground like scared prairie dogs, waiting for the next attack. I wanna go home. I've had enough of this."

"Listen to her, Poppy," Jenn said. "She's talkin' sense. We all wanna get out of here."

"I just have to get Blanton Miles. Then we can go."

Elaine shook her head. "Forget him, Derek. He doesn't matter. Let's go home and get married. Let's have the wedding we talked about."

"You guys are getting hitched?" Jenn exclaimed in surprise.

"Well," Elaine said, looking at Parnell, gauging his reaction, "we talked about it, yeah."

"Hey, that's great news," Jenn said, taking Elaine in her arms. "I'm so happy for you guys. When? Where?"

"Not so fast," Parnell said, cutting the celebration short. "I've got things to finish up here. Three criminals in lockup and another to bring in."

"You're really going to kill those men?" Ann asked him.

"Damn straight I am. They've got it comin'."

"Hasn't there already been enough killing, Poppy?" Jenn said, pulling out of Elaine's embrace. "Let's just load up the vehicles and get gone."

"The vehicles? You mean Dobkin's limo? The jeep? The remaining rental that's already a week overdue?"

"Yeah."

"Think about it, Jenn. We wouldn't get fifty miles before we'd be pulled over and arrested. No, when we leave, it'll be by train."

Jenn made a flabbergasted sound with her lips.

"Look, no one has to stay here, Jenn. People are free to leave whenever they want. I've made that clear to everyone we've brought here."

Ann said, "Does that apply to the three men you have locked up?"

"Absolutely not. They're prisoners."

"They're also human beings. They are God's children, Derek, just like you."

"I'm *nothing* like them. The things those three scumbags have done . . . well, they're despicable. Blanton Miles, too. It's their time to die."

"Says who? You?"

"It's what karma dictates."

"Karma?" Ann said, pausing for effect. "I've heard you throw that word around a lot. I don't think you fully grasp the concept of it."

"Of course I do."

"No, you don't, Derek. You define karma based on your own myopic view. You're only applying it to those who have wronged you. What about your victims? How do you think they see *your* karma?"

"I don't think they see much of anything. They're dead."

"Their bodies might be dead, but their souls live on. Do you ever think about your own karma?"

"What're you tryin' to tell me, Annie?"

"I'm saying that with the kind of life you've led, your karma is tarnished. In the Bible, Matthew states: 'They who live violently will be more likely to come to a violent end.' Elaine is right. What happened to you out in the desert tonight should be a big wakeup call for you. God was with you out there. It's God's will that you survived."

Parnell laughed, a sarcastic snort. "There you go with your big black book of fairy tales again."

Ann refused to back down. "God has given you a second chance, Derek. You should try to do some good with it. To put it in your terms, upgrade your own karma."

"God is a myth, Annie. The Bible is a long-winded fable written by a bunch of ancient suck-ups."

Ann shook her head in disgust. "I feel for you, Derek. There's so much you don't understand. You condemn things you know nothing about. You remember when we first met?"

"Yeah. When you fixed up my busted hand in Albuquerque, then followed me to Winslow."

"That's right. And on that boxcar ride, I quoted some scripture that you challenged. You remember that?"

"Yeah. What about it?"

"You thought it was the Lord's Prayer I was reciting—you know, 'The Lord is my shepherd; I shall not want . . .' It wasn't. It was the Twenty-Third Psalm. King David's words. Three different times you called it the Lord's Prayer. I never corrected you. But now that you're back to trashing the Bible again, well . . ."

"A tad bit self-righteous, aren't you, Annie? You're just like all the rest of the Bible thumpers who spout passages written eons ago to justify their actions."

Elaine was becoming more uncomfortable with the exchange. "I don't think you're being fair, Derek," she said. "Ann is only trying to help you."

"I truly am," Ann said. "Ever since our first meeting you've made it clear you never liked me, Derek. I understand that. We're very different people. We're from different generations and much different backgrounds. In spite of all that, I've always liked you. I've always looked behind that macho mask you wear. I see the good in you, even though you have a tendency to push that side of you away. I'm just trying to help. There's still time to help yourself. There's still time to experience God's graciousness."

"It's a little late for that, isn't it, Annie?"

"It's never too late in God's eyes. Don't crucify me, but I'm going to lay another piece of scripture on you."

Parnell heaved a deep sigh.

"Just hear me out," Ann said. "Luke wrote: 'Judge not, and you will not be judged; condemn not, and you will not be condemned; forgive, and you will be forgiven; give, and it will be given to you.' "

"Are you sayin' what I think you're sayin'? That I should forgive my prisoners?"

"Yes. Forgive them and let them go. Then you and Elaine can enjoy the rest of your lives together."

"Good advice," Elaine said. "Please listen to her, Derek."

Everyone looked to Parnell, who seemed to be seriously mulling over the prospect. Then he said, "You had me goin' there for a minute, Annie. However, there's no way in hell I'm letting those three go, let alone forgive them."

Miles From Nowhere

THE NEXT DAY PARNELL WAS UP AND AROUND, much to the dismay of Ann Finnegan, who loudly expressed her concerns. Surely the crude stitching she'd done on his ear would pull out and restart the bleeding. He needed his rest, she harped. Needed to get his strength back. But he wouldn't hear it. He couldn't allow himself to spend the day lounging on an air mattress boo-hooing over his damaged ear. He had things to do. Important things, like retrieving the remainder of his cash from the vault room beneath the headroom floor and checking out the hidden escape tunnel.

Eight years ago, on his second trip here, he'd discovered a tunnel that started at the southernmost end of the mining yard and ran under the railhead a half mile before coming up in the desert, near where the rail spur met the main north-south Union Pacific line. He'd stumbled on it quite by accident. The entrance had been well camouflaged behind a jagged rock outcropping in the least traveled section of the yard. The opening was small, appearing at first glance to be a fox den. His curiosity led him to shove a couple of boulders aside. What had looked like a fox lair opened up into the gaping mouth of a substantial cave. The wall structure, with its heavy wooden support beams and handful of tools scattered throughout, told him it had originally served as a mineshaft. Closer inspection revealed the vein had failed to produce coal, and the miners had abandoned it. But who had engineered the long tunnel system? What was it for? Parnell had hiked it trying to figure it out. Approximately seven feet high in most sections and ten feet across, its rock walls had smooth aquifer striations, suggesting it had initially been carved out by a forceful underground spring over the millennia. Some sections, however, showed chisel chinks and sandblast patterns. Humans at work. A drug cartel transportation route? Was the long meandering tunnel engineered by drug merchants who had worked this area before the coal company moved in? Very possible, but he couldn't find any hard proof of that.

He needed to get out of the headframe and take care of business. But he had to shake loose of Annie first. He suggested a long walk and fresh air would do her good. He'd be fine without her for a while, he assured her. But she wouldn't budge from her mother hen protectiveness. A good nurse didn't leave her patient, she said. His kind and gentle approach having failed, he decided to switch to insult mode, bombarding her with impudent, acerbic remarks, a ploy that worked quickly. She didn't get flustered or angry; she simply left the headframe saying, "Your rudeness is very unbecoming, Derek."

He was finally alone. Carefully, he rose from the air mattress and dragged the stool over to the double cellar doors. He sat with a loud sigh, gave himself a moment before leaning over to work the combination lock. The tumblers clicked and he yanked the lock open. Grabbed the wrought-iron handles and pulled the heavy double doors open, the effort draining him. He shined his flashlight into the vault room opening and took a deep breath before lowering himself. His injuries screamed with each step down the steep wooden ladder. A dull, itchy pain throbbed in his right side. His ear and left cheek were on fire, burning like someone was holding an industrial-strength steam iron against the side of his face. His head pounded. His heart thundered. He opened both safes, and as he emptied out his remaining cash, he thought about the friends he'd left behind at Shangri-La. They deserved this money. At least most of it. He hoped to get it to them after reeling in Blanton Miles tomorrow.

Getting his satchel of cash back up the ladder posed an even bigger challenge than going down. He came back up into the headframe, exhausted. Dizzy. Nauseated. *Did I really lose that much blood?* He shook his head, clearing his wooziness but sending throbbing, stinging agony to his ear. A roaring buzz filled his head. His side ached. He felt like returning to the air mattress.

You've got to pull yourself together, dude.

After several deep breaths, he willed himself to carry on. He gritted his teeth. He was hurting, but glad he'd shunned Annie's offer of more pain meds. He needed a clear head and a surplus of strength to get things done.

He hugged the satchel to his good side and left the headframe, walking out into a blazingly bright afternoon. The light stung his eyes and the heat slapped him in the face as he ambled through the yard. His damaged ear and the heavy gauze covering the wound threw his equilibrium off and he did his best to keep his balance. He ran into several breezers—Harvey Henshaw, Broadway Bling, Chef Alice—each asking him how he was feeling, each of them mentioning how good it was to see him up and about. He could tell from their shocked, forced reactions that he must look a total wreck. Buttonhead Murphy even offered him peyote buttons he'd recently harvested. Told him the shit would grow him a new ear and kick the ass out of the pain. Said Parnell wouldn't have to worry about his footing because he would literally float on this stuff. Parnell thanked him, told him he'd take a rain check and moved on before Buttonhead could get further into his patented motor-mouth routine.

He slowly made his way to the escape tunnel shaft at the southern end of the yard. It was a bit of a hike and he labored along. He'd only been out there once this trip (to leave high-powered flashlights in the entrance) and he wanted to explore the long meandering tunnel to ensure it was clear and safe before taking Lainey and Jenn down there.

He staggered along, keeping a low profile, walking behind a low sandstone bluff to avoid running into anyone else. His thoughts turned to Ann Finnegan, a.k.a., Nurse Annie, Doctor Finnegan, Reverend Ann. The first time he'd met her—at that little doc-in-the-box clinic she worked at in Albuquerque—she rubbed him the wrong way. She had been brash and sassy, an immature girl trapped in a job she hated. She was eager to break out of her confining Albuquerque working life to discover the big world. She thought he was her ticket out. But he wasn't. Not even close. He was a jaded rail-warrior hobo trying to deal with the shitstorm life had rained down on him. He and Annie were oil and water. Polar opposites. He was old enough to be her father and her persistence in wanting to travel with him—a complete stranger dropping in off the street to have his damaged hand tended to—had struck him as odd and anxiously frantic. She was desperate to escape her dreary work routine, he got that. But good jobs like hers were impossible to come by. The Second Great Depression had blown the bottom out of the economy. Yet Annie wanted to throw it all away to ride the rails. With him leading the way, no less. She thought his life was glamorous. Crazy-ass girl. Parnell tried to set her straight, but she refused to listen.

So she'd followed him to the Albuquerque rail yards and snuck on the boxcar bound for Flagstaff. The boxcar where he slept. The train was rolling when he awoke to find her there, sharing his space. He'd been furious with her, made more so when she revealed her sanctimonious Bible-thumper side. He couldn't wait to get rid of her. So he'd jumped off in Winslow and took her to Shangri-La, where he'd left her in the care of Weasel Bethea before rolling on to Flagstaff to see Elaine.

Sure, Annie's lecturing and holier-than-thou evangelizing irritated him. She could be a self-righteous pain in the ass, a bit self-serving. But he had to admit, she had changed in the three-plus years they'd been apart. She was a mature woman now. More poised and controlled. No longer the naive country girl with wanderlust shining in her large owlish eyes. Dare he think it, but he was beginning to appreciate the woman. Maybe he even liked her. She had been good to Jenn. And Annie had done wonders in lifting the emotional spirits of the Shangri-La folks. She had become the hobo community's shining light, keeping his fellow breezers hopeful and healthy.

Annie Finnegan was a good person. But she could push things to the extreme. There was that absurdity she had proposed. Forgive his prisoners and set them free? Preposterous! He had worked too hard and risked too much to let John Dobkin go. He had him right where he wanted him. The man deserved to die a horrible death. The psychiatrist and his pilot buddy had to go, too. When Elaine told him what they had put her through, he'd wanted to personally castrate them both.

And then there was that analogy Annie brought up yesterday, about God being the all-seeing, all-knowing scriptwriter. He'd mulled that one over a lot. It made some kind of crazy sense. Fate and destiny and karma didn't just happen randomly. He'd never really believed that. Someone, some *thing*, had to be responsible for putting it all together. For organizing it. Was it possible there actually was a god who wrote the scripts for every human being traipsing this planet? An omnipotent, omniscient deity who controlled all thoughts and actions? Did prayer give believers a direct line to such a god?

Wow, that deadly encounter with Ollie McKellar has really driven you to the edge, Derek old chap.

Yes, his close brush with death had certainly shaken him up. It had upset Elaine, too. He'd worried her once again. Made her cry. He'd felt enormous guilt watching her come apart yesterday. He'd been embarrassed, struck mute as she broke down and sobbed. *Why oh why do I keep hurting her?*

Good thing she didn't know about the shootout in Dobkin's penthouse hallway. Elaine would have had a coronary.

He finally arrived at the circle of boulders that hid the cave entrance. The walk had drained him. He had a hard time catching his breath. His legs were concrete-heavy and spastic. A rivulet of sweat trickled down his back. He took a seat on a shelf of rock in the shade, set the satchel down next to him. Looked out across the mining yard. Became transfixed on the long black stretch limousine parked near mineshaft #3, the sunlight reflecting off its tinted windows.

A humming buzz came from inside the satchel. At first the sound confused him, but then he remembered he'd dumped Marquez's phone there after their call with Blanton Miles. He dug deep, beneath the cash, retrieved the still-buzzing phone. Checked the display:

CALLER UNKNOWN ...

Parnell almost answered it by reflex, but then realized he couldn't. The shrink was supposed to have this phone.

He remained seated, studying the phone in his hand. Thirty seconds later, it dinged. The caller had left a message. Parnell went to the cell's voicemail.

"Hello, boss. Well I guess I can't really call you boss anymore, can I? Your old friend Blanton here. Long time no hear, buddy. Guess we've both been busy, huh? Anyway, I know you have Conquistador's phone. You really should get your own. Mobile phone packages are reasonable these days. Even for lowlife hobos. We have to talk. Call me at this number. Immediately."

The message clicked off.

Hearing Blanton Miles' carefully controlled voice again got his stomach acid churning. Memories of their working relationship came rushing back. The way the son of a bitch had deceived him for years, Parnell under the distinct impression Miles was working for him when in reality Miles had been playing him while taking orders from Dobkin. Miles keeping up the ruse that Parnell was overseeing his own company—Locomotion Enterprises—when in fact it was operating as a money-laundering tax shelter for Dobkin.

He sat, staring at the phone. Considered what to do. After thinking it through, he decided the best thing was to take the phone back to Marquez, and have him return Miles' call. He was about to shove the shrink's cell back in the satchel when it buzzed again. He deliberated a few seconds, then decided to answer, save himself a long walk.

"Hello?" he said, putting it on speakerphone.

"You don't sound anything like Conquistador," Miles said in a taunting tone. "More like King Midas. At least the guy who used to be King Midas."

Parnell didn't know how to respond, or if he should.

"Don't be shy, Derek. I know you want to talk to me."

Talking wasn't exactly what Parnell had in mind for Blanton Miles.

"C'mon, boss, let's have a phone chat. It'll be just like old times. We can relive our glory days when I served as your loyal Chief Operations Officer."

Parnell listened to Miles laughing on the other end and it sent his blood pressure soaring. Despite his better judgment, he spoke. "We'll be able to chat plenty tomorrow, Miles. Or should I call you PuppetMaster?"

"Good one, Derek. I think you've been reading too many spy novels."

"So, does this call mean you aren't planning to meet with Doctor Marquez tomorrow."

"You're very astute, Derek. I'm not coming anywhere near that coal mine. No need to now. You've done my dirty work for me. The three marks I needed to eliminate are there with you and I know you're planning to kill them, if you haven't already. That was a nice piece of work you did at Dobkin's Henderson estate. A grenade bombing? Spectacular! I loved it. It really made a statement . . ."

"This is why you called? To admire my skill in apprehending your boss?"

"Partly. But mostly I called to thank you. In your usual haste to take care of business, you've wrapped everything up for me and put a pretty bow on it. I didn't have to lift a finger, other than keep tabs on you. I thank you from the bottom of my heart."

Parnell's anger was boiling over but he knew he couldn't lose it here. "How did you know I had Marquez's phone?"

A short blast of a chuckle, then, "You're a tough hombre, Derek, but you've always been a little naive. That phone call the other day? When you had Conquistador call me?"

"What about it?"

"First of all, he has never put me on speakerphone before. That was my first tipoff. Speakerphones are verboten in Dobkin's organization. Then there was the conversation itself. I don't know if you remember many specifics of that discussion, but the doctor used code words to let me know the situation."

"Why would he help you? You wanted to kill him."

"I didn't want to snuff the guy. *Dobkin* wanted him dead, not me."

Parnell thought about that. "So Marquez, knowing I already had Dobkin, thought that if he helped you, you'd come to his rescue."

"Exactly."

"But you're not, are you? You're throwing him under the bus."

"As I said before, Derek. You're very astute."

"And you're a steaming pile of shit, Miles!"

"Aw, is that any way to talk to a man who is doing you a favor?"

"A favor? Is that what you call this?"

"Yes. This is a courtesy call. I'm saving you a lot of time and effort. I'll even go so far as to say I'm saving your life."

"How do you figure?"

"I'm giving you a heads-up. Letting you know that the second in command in Dobkin's firm is unleashing the hellhounds. They're out for blood after the killing and destruction at the chief's mansion."

"Hellhounds?"

"Yeah. Dobkin's chopper squadron. They should be flying in sometime in the next twelve hours. They have search and destroy orders. They'll turn the Hyacinth mines to rubble. They're taking no prisoners."

"What about Dobkin?"

"What about him?"

"Don't they want to rescue their commander-in-chief?"

"I reported you'd already killed him."

"Why would you do that?"

Miles sighed deeply. "Do I really need to explain that to you?"

No, Parnell didn't need an explanation. He sat there, flabbergasted, thinking that once again Blanton Miles had all the angles figured. The man had always been a shrewd and cunning operator, able to plot and plan eight to ten moves in advance. Always able to cover his own ass no matter how impossible the situation. A heavy depression began to set in as Parnell realized he wasn't going to get him. He felt hope and possibility slipping through his hands. Once again, Blanton Miles would escape justice. There would be one critical empty seat on the Rolling Inferno.

"You still there, Derek?"

"Unfortunately, yeah."

"Look, I know this is difficult, but my advice to you is to take care of Dobkin and the other two if you haven't already, then get far away from those mines. Run like hell. Those guys in Dobkin's chopper detail are pretty committed, if you know what I mean."

Parnell did know. He flashed back to three years ago, when they were on the run, fleeing the Liberty Dogs' compound in Colorado. The Dobkin corporate helicopter tracking them, sharpshooters aboard. Them exchanging fire with the chopper from the train on the trestle over the Yampa River. The explosive end to that harrowing chase.

"You hear me, Derek?"

"Yeah, I heard you."

"I think you owe me a big thank you."

Parnell's anger bubbled up into his throat. "You're a delusional scumbag, Miles."

"That's some gratitude. I give you a heads-up warning of what's coming your way . . . provide you a chance to get out. I give you the time you need to stamp out Dobkin and the psycho twins and you call me delusional? A scumbag?"

"If the shoe fits—"

"I didn't have to do this, Derek. I could have left it alone . . . let you and all your hobo hillbillies go down in a sea of blood. But I figure I owe you something after all you've done for me through the years. And—true confession time—I feel a tad remorseful about the way we ran you out of the country."

"You're incapable of feeling much of anything, Miles. You're a fucking sociopath."

"Wow. That's harsh."

"Well, if you're lookin' for thanks from me, I think I'll save it for when I catch up with you in person."

"You'll never find me, Derek."

"Oh, but I will. Marquez knows where you're at."

Another gruff laugh. "That's hilarious. Conquistador doesn't even know what country I'm in. He's just trying to save his own ass. Can't you see that?"

"I'll get you, Miles, if it's the last thing I do."

"We all have our hopes and dreams, don't we? I've enjoyed our relationship over the years, but now it's time to say our goodbyes. Heed my advice. Get out of Hyacinth now, while you still can. Goodbye, Derek. And good luck."

The call disconnected and Parnell was left staring at the display. He'd been squeezed by Blanton Miles once again. He'd also been played by Antonio Marquez. Seething, he tossed the phone in the satchel. Started back to the main section of the mines.

Time to get family and friends to safety.

Time for the Rolling Inferno to make its first and last fiery run.

Evacuation Strategy

JENN WAS IN HER BELOWGROUND GROTTO, sharing a joint with Cale and Elaine. Mellowing out. Doing her damnedest to keep the conversation clear of their precarious situation.

And then, without warning, Poppy burst in, frantic, sweaty, shouting that they needed to get everyone together topside. Something big going on.

His sudden appearance in the subterranean chambers shocked them. Poppy was supposed to be up in the headframe, under Ann's care, resting. But here he was, two levels underground, exhausted, dazed, in pain. His wounded ear was bleeding, the gauze bandages stained a deep wine-red. Jenn tried to get him to sit down, to relax, but he was hyper and fidgety. She suggested getting Ann to look at his ear and change out the bandages, but he resisted. They had to move quickly, he said. Big trouble was on the way.

"What is it, Poppy?" she asked, her ganja-fueled anxiety spiking. It took a lot to unnerve her father like this.

"I'll fill you in topside," he said brusquely, moving quickly, leaving them behind.

They rounded up everyone and gathered in the yard. Jenn listened to Poppy deliver the distressing news in an urgent, no-nonsense tone. He'd heard from Blanton Miles. An attack was coming within the next twelve hours. A serious attack, led by Dobkin's helicopter crew. He knew them to be hard core mercenaries as he'd tangled with them during his escape from the States three years ago. He urged folks to leave as quickly as possible.

Jenn heard cries of alarm all around her.

"Can't we just give John Dobkin back to them?" Chef Alice yelled out.

"Doesn't work that way, Alley Cat," Parnell said. "They're not comin' here to negotiate."

Weasel spoke up. "So then this Miles guy didn't take the bait from our flyboys?"

"No, he didn't. Blanton Miles is too sharp for that. Nothin' gets past him. It also didn't help that our psychiatrist tipped him off during our phone call."

"Marquez? You're kidding."

"Wish I was. The shrink played us."

Weasel grimaced. "I find it odd that this Miles guy would forewarn you of an attack."

"We have a long history, Greg. He said he felt like he owed me. He's an odd duck and I don't trust him, but I know him well enough to know he's being truthful to a certain degree. They're comin' for us. And I don't think we have anywhere near twelve hours to evacuate. So chop-chop, my friends. Time's a wastin'."

They had three working vehicles, he told them. Unfortunately, the jeep, the rental Toyota, and Dobkin's stretch limo wouldn't accommodate all of them. He suggested letting the women and older men go by car and the rest hop the next Union Pacific freighter, which was scheduled to come through around eight-thirty.

"Where will we go?" the teenage girl known as Lilac asked.

"Head for Winslow. Take back roads and stay off the interstates. You might get stopped, but that'll be better than staying here."

"Winslow?" Broadway Bling said. "You mean Shangri-La?"

"Yeah."

"But I thought Uncle Sam was about to level it. Isn't that why you brought us here?"

All heads turned to Parnell. "At last report the feds hadn't shown up," he said. "It's a safe haven for now. But those who think Shangri-La isn't safe can head further east. There're some friendly hobo camps I know of near Amarillo and Oklahoma City. I'll give you names. They'll take you in without a hassle."

"What are *you* gonna do, Derek?" Fingers Johnston bellowed.

"I'll remain here until I'm sure everybody has gotten out safely. Then I'll be hoppin' the next train, headin' to Winslow. Got some business to take care of there."

Ann Finnegan objected. "You're in no condition to be doing sprint-and-grabs, Derek. You need to go in one of the cars."

"I know you're lookin' out for me, Annie, but I'm okay. I'm here until the bitter end. This is all happening because of me. This is my responsibility."

Jenn felt her world slipping away. The apocalypse she had feared since they arrived here was coming and Poppy was acting like General Patton, old Blood and Guts himself.

"Don't be ridiculous, Poppy," she called out. "This isn't on you alone. You're wounded. You should go in the limousine with Ann. There's plenty of room for you to stretch out."

"Listen to Jennifer, Derek," Elaine added. "Let's leave right now."

"We'll go after I dispose of Dobkin and friends. And only after I'm sure everybody is out safely. That's final. Now let's get a move on, people."

There was a momentary pause as the breezers let it all sink in. Then, noisily, desperately, they broke into small groups to make their getaway plans. Passengers for the three vehicles and their destinations were decided quickly. The limo was going to Winslow while the jeep and rental Camry would try their luck further east in Texas and Oklahoma. A few—Weasel, Flywheel, Ann Finnegan, Harvey Henshaw, and Cale—volunteered to stay behind with Parnell, Elaine, and Jenn. They'd be the ones hopping the train at eight-thirty, God willing. Jenn hoped and prayed that the Union Pacific freighter came through tonight. If not . . . well, she didn't want to think about that.

While the first-departing breezers cleaned out their underground living spaces and stowed their meager belongings in vehicles, Poppy took her and Elaine out to what he described as his underground escape route. He led them inside the cave entrance, shined his flashlight into the long, dark tunnel that he said extended a half mile and came up near the main north-south tracks where they'd hook the freighter.

"There's no need to hike the tunnel now," he told them. "I just wanted to show you where this was. In case we get separated later."

Jenn couldn't see his face, but he sounded completely exhausted. "You're scaring me, Poppy."

"We need to be prepared, Jenny. They're comin' by air. This'll give us a concealed way out."

Jenn's throat tightened up. Her hands were clammy. She felt lightheaded. She wished they'd stayed at Shangri-La. Wished they'd never come to this wretched, godforsaken place.

Elaine said, "Let's get back, Derek. You're not well and this cave is giving me the creeps."

"I'm fine, E. And this tunnel system will end up saving us." He shined his flash down on an aluminum tool box near the cave opening. "My last trip into Kanab, I bought half a dozen high-powered flashlights. Strongest LED light you can buy. Forty times stronger than a regular flash. They're right here. We'll need them. That tunnel is so dark you can't even see your hand in front of your face."

"You've walked it before?" Jenn asked, staring uncertainly into the pitch-black void.

"Yeah. Two or three times."

"I don't know, babe," Elaine said. "I'm worried about you. Are you sure you're up to hiking this tunnel? You sure you can handle a sprint-and-grab? Because Cale and I just went through a near disastrous train-grab with Ann, and I don't think—"

"I can hop a train in my sleep, Lainey," he said forcefully. "Don't worry about me. I'll be fine. I really wish you and Jenn and Annie would take my advice and take the limo to Winslow. Annie especially worries me. How's she gonna catch a moving train with that bum knee of hers?"

Elaine blew air through her lips in frustration. "Somebody's gotta look after you, tough guy," she said with an edge. "Let's get back. I want to say a few goodbyes before everybody hits the road."

"Yeah, let's go" he agreed. "I have three executions to oversee."

A chill ran through Jenn.

God help us all.

Fire in the Hole

ELAINE WAS ALONE WITH PARNELL inside the entrance to mineshaft #2. She watched him stagger alongside the Rolling Inferno, pouring gasoline over the wooden coaster cars from a tin can. He was on edge, his motions agitated. His pain was palpable, cringing every time he swung the gas can.

This was perhaps her last chance to talk him out of it. "You're actually going through with this, Derek?"

He shook the last drops from the can and tossed the empty container aside, where it clanked against the rails. "For the last time, *yes,* I'm doin' this." He put a hand on the lead car to steady himself. "I built this coaster for a reason. I'm gonna see it through."

Elaine shook her head in disbelief. *How ludicrous is this?* Derek looked like a walking-talking corpse. His skin had a sickly grayish tinge to it. Blood seeped through his bandages. He'd been weakened, taken down a couple of notches, and was doing his best to show a strong face. But while his show of strength might have convinced some of the others, it didn't fool her. She knew him too well.

This could have been so different. Should have been different. They should be back in Costa Rica, relaxing in their Caribbean stilt house. They should be sharing a joint while listening to steel-drum music plink over the rhythmic swish of waves lapping the beach.

She had spent the past three hours debating whether to leave him behind with his insane execution fantasies. Should she stay or should she go? An hour ago she watched the first two groups of breezers leave, eight of them packed into the jeep and rental car, headed for Texas and Oklahoma. She wanted so much to be riding in one of those vehicles. The black stretch limousine was still here, but they were almost loaded up and ready to leave for Winslow.

She made one last feeble attempt to get through to him. "C'mon, Derek. Let's just cut our losses and join them in the limo. Let's take the money to our Shangri-La friends like you said you wanted to. Then we'll be free of this nightmare."

"You know my thoughts on this, E. You, Jenn, and Annie go

in the limo and I'll catch up with you later."

"No—no," she heard herself respond. "I traveled halfway around the world to be with you. I'm not letting you out of my sight again." A conflicting voice in her head badgered her, *You are a crazy woman. Time for you to leave this guy behind. Think of yourself for once.*

Parnell said, "Well then, I wish at least Annie would take the limo. Her knee isn't healed yet. She has trouble with the sprint-and-grab, even with two good knees."

Elaine couldn't hold back from correcting him. "That again? *You're* the one who's going to need help hooking that freighter, old man. Not Ann."

"I've never needed anybody's help hoppin' a train!" he said, angrily.

"You will this time," she said, baiting him. "I might have to call on Captain Turnipseed to save your aging ass."

"You think so, huh?" he said, going to her and pulling her into his arms, kissing her neck. "I'll be fine, E. We'll be on that Union freighter tonight, free and easy."

"I'll feel better when we're far away from this place."

He smiled at her, then kissed her. "Not much longer now, sweets," he said.

She leaned into him, raking her hands down his back, careful as she kissed him to stay clear of his wounds. Parnell's condition turned the kiss into an awkward ballet. Elaine teetered in his shaky embrace, wondering whether she was doing the right thing. *Am I enabling him? Should I be more forceful?*

Parnell grasped her elbow and began to lead her out of the mineshaft. "It's time to get this done. I'll go get Weasel and Flywheel and we'll round up our inmates."

His voice was weak and hoarse. He appeared incapable of walking ten feet. Elaine told him she'd do the roundup, that he should sit for a spell and rest. He offered scant resistance, which told her that he wasn't his usual ornery self. He was fading. She had to get him out of Hyacinth soon.

She walked out into the bright yard, luxuriating in the fresh air. The gasoline stench inside the mineshaft had become suffocating, and the clean desert air revitalized her. She hurried to find Weasel and Flywheel.

Fifteen minutes later the captives were strapped in, Dobkin sitting alone in the lead car, Marquez and Diego side-by-side in the second car. Parnell stood in front of the coaster, straddling the tracks, clicking one of Chef Alice's butane fire-starter wands. Elaine, Weasel, Flywheel, and Ann stood on either side of the gasoline-drenched cars.

"What the hell is this?" Dobkin said to Parnell. "You're sending us on an amusement park ride?"

"Trust me, Dobkin, it won't be amusing."

Dobkin did a once-over scan of Parnell. "You look worse off than me. What happened? You get your hair cut by a sadistic barber?"

"It's none of your concern," Parnell replied. "Now if it will please the court, the jury has reached a verdict on the three criminal offenders being tried today—"

"Jury? What fucking jury?" Dobkin boomed. He turned around as much as his restraints would allow and looked at Antonio Marquez. "Our coal mining hobo thinks this is a trial."

Marquez said, "Yes. He's obviously suffering from some type of delusional psychotic episode. I believe the man needs proper medication."

Parnell scowled at them. "I'm not the psycho here!" He clicked the fire-starter wand and stared at the dancing flame. "Any more outbursts and I'll light up the Inferno, let my coaster take you down where you belong. Now, if the court pleases, we will proceed with the sentencing phase . . ."

Muttered grumbles came from the captives, who twisted and turned in their seats trying to bust free.

". . . Today the Parnell justice system is sentencing John Dobkin to death by roller coaster for his continued crimes against humanity—"

"Death by *roller coaster?*" Dobkin erupted. "Is this a joke, Parnell?"

"No joke. Now shut the fuck up! I'll have the bailiff work you over if I hear another chirp outta you."

Bailiff? Elaine thought. *Don't make this into a big production, Derek. Let's just get this done and get gone.*

"My people are going to crush you," Dobkin threatened.

"That line is getting old," Parnell said, continuing to flick the butane wand. "It's been a few days and still no sign of anyone comin' for you. Maybe your loyal peeps aren't so loyal after all."

"They'll be here. Trust me."

"Looks like they're gonna be late to the party. Too bad for

you."

"What about us?" Antonio Marquez said. "Kill us and you lose your one chance at getting Blanton Miles."

"That ploy doesn't hold water anymore, Doctor Strangelove. I had a chat with Miles on your phone a while ago. He confirmed that you're full of shit."

"You believe *him*? You're taking the word of a career criminal over that of a respected, board-certified psychiatrist?"

"Respected? Anyone who respects you is crazy. Or ignorant."

Marquez refused to go quietly. "What did we do to deserve a death sentence? I was trying to help you out."

"You're no saint, Marquez. Now for the last time, shut your face. This is my court and I'll tell you when you can speak. So, let's get to the misdeeds of our primary death row offender, John Dobkin. Mister Dobkin's crimes include, but are not limited to, illegal prostitution, human trafficking, murder for hire, conspiracy to murder, money laundering, kidnapping, extortion, blackmail, false imprisonment, racketeering, perjury . . . Jesus, I could go on for days laying out this offender's sheet."

"You make me sound so accomplished," Dobkin said coolly. "Maybe I'll hire you on as my publicist."

Parnell uttered a hollow laugh. "You still don't get it, do you? Your hiring days are over, Dobkin. You're about to *die*. You'd best save your money for bribing Saint Peter at the pearly gates."

That brought a headshake and an eye roll from Ann.

Elaine studied the men in the killer coaster. Dobkin looked farcical in his soiled, wrinkled robe, the knot on his forehead swollen to scary proportions. Marquez and Diego wore looks of absolute terror. They squirmed in their seats, trying to break free of their restraints. But John Dobkin showed no fear. He sat straight and tall, confronting Parnell with his unwavering stare. A slight smile tugged at his lips, a smile that dared Parnell to take action. *How can this man remain so calm when he's facing execution? Do sociopaths view themselves through the same contemptuous eyes they scrutinize their marks?*

Parnell continued. "And as for the alleged well-respected Doctor Antonio Marquez and his ace pilot Diego, your crimes include the murder of one Lloyd Oshkosh Moss, kidnapping across state lines and federal jurisdictions, false imprisonment, aggravated assault, attempted rape . . . I'm sure I could find a few other shocking charges with a little digging."

"But we didn't kill anybody," Diego complained. "There was no rape either."

"I said *attempted* rape, moron," Parnell said, giving Elaine a quick glance, "which, in this case, is just as bad as actual rape."

Elaine didn't like the direction of this conversation. "Let's just get this over with, Derek."

"Good idea, yeah. Grab me that torch over there, will you, Greg?"

Weasel retrieved a two-by-four with one end wrapped tightly in burlap.

Ann spoke up. "I want to say a prayer for these men before you do it, Derek."

"A prayer? Wouldn't do any good, Annie. These guys are spawns of Satan."

"I don't care," Ann said, moving to stand in front of the coaster with Parnell, clutching her Bible to her chest. "If you really must do this, then I cannot in good conscience sit back and let these human souls pass without a word from God."

"All right," Parnell said with reluctance. "But hurry it up."

Before delivering her parting words, Ann asked if any of the three men wanted to confess their sins. She was answered by mumbles of "Like hell!" and "We haven't done anything that needs confessing."

"Okay then," she said, flustered. She opened her Bible to a marked passage and began reading, not getting far before being cut off by the squawking walkie-talkie.

Cale's voice. "We've got problems, Derek. Helicopters are headed this way. Four of them in formation. Approaching fast."

Parnell cursed and took the torch with him to pick up the talkie. "Can you see any markings, Cale?"

"No. They're too far away."

"You said four choppers, correct?"

"Roger that. Total of four whirlybirds. You want me to fire on them?"

"No, hold off. I'll be up there pronto. Have you radioed Henshaw yet?"

"No."

"Let Harvey know. Tell him to take appropriate cover. Is Jennifer up there with you?"

"Yes."

"Can you hear me, Jenny?"

"Yeah, I can."

"Listen, I want you to get down off that ridge. Go grab your stuff and hit the escape tunnel. Time for us to move out. Okay?"

"What about Cale?"

"He'll be fine, sweetheart. I'll be with him. We'll meet up with you later in the tunnel. Just go. Now!"

Parnell switched off the talkie.

Dobkin started clapping slowly, mockingly. "I told you they'd come for me. They'll show no mercy. You're a dead man, Parnell."

"Yeah? Well, you won't be around to see it," Parnell said, igniting the torch with the fire-starter wand. The smoky stink of burnt burlap filled the mine entrance, bringing about fits of coughing and cussing. He took the burning torch to the last cart, touched it to the wood. The cart caught fire with a sizzling *whoosh*, and he had to back up to keep from getting burned. Extending his arm, he ran the torch around the sides of the remaining cars, Marquez and Diego squirming and screaming for help as the fire encircled them. Parnell then went to the console and flipped the switch. The Rolling Inferno jerked forward with a loud screech and a thump, beginning its trip down the tracks.

Parnell's roller coaster plunged into the depths, the squeaking wheels and terrified screams gobbled up by the hundred-foot drops through dark caverns. The strong reek of gasoline and charred wood hung in the air.

Parnell barked orders. "Okay, let's move it. Quickly. Once that coaster hits those methane pockets there's gonna be one hell of an explosion. C'mon, hurry!"

They scrambled out of mineshaft #2. Once out in the yard, Weasel said, "Where's this escape tunnel you told Jenn about?"

Parnell looked at Elaine. "Lainey, show Greg and Fly and Annie the escape route," he commanded as he made his way to the ridge lookout shack.

"No," Elaine said, struggling to keep up with him. "I'm going with you. I meant what I said, Derek. I'm not leaving you."

"Jesus, E," he said over his shoulder. "I'm trying to protect you. Can't you see that?"

"I do, and I appreciate it, but—"

Her words were cut off by a trio of deafening explosions, three concussive blasts coming in quick succession, so powerful they knocked Elaine to the turf. Stunned by the blasts, she looked up from her sprawled position in the sand and saw the mineshaft entrance had caved in. Nothing but rocks and dust and support timbers where just a few minutes before there had been a wide access. They had come close to being buried alive.

She experienced an intense unreality, a surreal haze saturating everything, giving the scene a dreamlike quality. *How is it that our lives have become this unhinged?*

She lifted her head to see Derek awkwardly climbing the ladder up to the guard tower on the ridge. Weasel and Flywheel stood below waiting to follow him up.

She felt a tug at her sleeve. A female voice filtered through the post-blast ringing in her ears. "Are you okay?" Ann had crawled up next to her.

"I think so. Are you?"

Ann shook her head. "Are any of us?"

Dirty Birds

PARNELL FELT WEAK AND SHAKY on the climb. Couldn't catch his breath. The pulse of helicopter rotors beat the air in the distance, cracking like drum rimshots.

He stopped to rest, doing a quick scan of the yard below. Mineshaft #2 was completely obliterated. He allowed himself a faint smile; John Dobkin was finally dead and buried.

"We nailed the son of a bitch, Greg," he said gleefully as Weasel joined him up top.

"That we did," Weasel said, frowning as he watched the approaching aircraft. "But it looks like it might be payback time."

"You and Javion don't need to stay," Parnell said as Flywheel joined them. "I can handle this myself."

"Like hell," Flywheel said. "It ain't in my DNA to cut and run. I'm with you all the way, bro."

"Javion's right," Weasel said. "We're your posse. We're with you until the job is done."

"The job *is* done, Greg," Parnell said. "No need to stick it out here with me."

A questioning look passed between Weasel and Flywheel.

"We're staying," Weasel said.

Parnell eyed the oncoming choppers. "Okay then. Let's go relieve Cale."

He turned in the direction of the lookout shack, but halted as he saw movement below. Thirty yards from the mineshaft cave-in, partially hidden in the shadows of the big earth mover, Annie Finnegan helped Elaine to her feet. A wave of guilt washed over him. *Nice going, Derek. Really good work looking out for your better half.*

"Everyone all right down there?" He worried that Elaine might have been hurt in the blast.

Ann waved up to him from where she kneeled. "We'll make it. Just a bit dazed."

"You okay, E? You need my help?"

Elaine's voice carried on the breeze. "I'm taking Ann to the escape tunnel and then I'm coming back."

"No, you're not. Stay in the tunnel and I'll meet you. I want you where it's safe."

"No, Derek. I'm coming back for you and that's final."

Stubborn-assed woman! So exasperating! He watched her and Ann rush through the yard. No time for arguments.

Parnell led Weasel and Flywheel around the solar panel grid to the lookout post. His ear wound burned something fierce. His head throbbed. He looked west, squinting into the late-afternoon sun, seeing four black dots flickering in the desert heat, lined up in a precise four-across flying formation. Cale was crouched behind the plywood barrier, peering at the oncoming aircraft through high magnification binoculars.

"How far away are they, Cale?" Parnell said, entering the shack. Weasel and Flywheel jammed in behind him.

"Three miles, maybe four," Cale mumbled. "I think they mean business." He handed him the binocs. "Here, have a look."

Parnell glassed the horizon. Four large choppers, none having identifying markings. The two helicopters on the inside of the formation were bigger than the two on the flanks. *Two transport choppers and two gunships?*

Cale said, "You think they're coming for Dobkin?"

"Maybe. I have a sinking feeling they know he's already dead."

"How would they know that? It just happened."

"You'd be amazed at how sophisticated Dobkin's communication network is."

"No disrespect intended, Derek, but do you think this is a good idea? Us perched up here like sitting ducks?"

"We're only stayin' long enough to be sure everyone gets out safely."

"I thought everyone had left already."

"No. The limo's still here," he said, continuing to scope the horizon. "Jenny went to the tunnel, right?"

"Yeah. Shouldn't we be headed there, too?"

Parnell lowered the binoculars, doing his best to hide the tremors in his hands. "You go on, Cale. We'll handle this. You should be with Jenny. She needs you right now."

Cale looked at him doubtfully. "You sure? You won't call me a coward for backing out?"

"I would *never* call you a coward. The absolute best thing you can do for me right now is to go be with my daughter."

"Okay," Cale said. "Be safe, guys."

The three of them said their farewells to T-Seed. When he was gone, Parnell checked out the weaponry that surrounded them. Two high-powered automatic rifles with long-range scopes. The M-16 grenade rifle. The SA-7 surface-to-air missile launcher. He said, "Looks like we have plenty of firepower to mess 'em up good. Grab a rifle, gentlemen. We'll give 'em a welcoming party they won't soon forget."

Parnell loaded one of the five-foot-long missiles into the SA-7 and strapped it on, then activated the power supply to the missile electronics. Weasel and Flywheel set up on either side of him with the Bushmaster assault carbines, each loaded with 30-round clips. Parnell aimed the SA-7 launch tube in the direction of the fast-approaching chopper fleet. He peered through the iron sights.

"That thing looks evil," Flywheel said. "Does it work?"

"We'll soon find out," he said, adjusting the angle of the tube. "No way to test it, but my weapons guy tells me these babies can take down large aircraft from four miles away."

Flywheel eyed the horizon. "I hope the dude knows what he's talkin' about."

The chopper squadron flew in low over the desert basin. The downdraft from the four choppers kicked up sand and tumbleweeds along the desert floor.

"Time to let them have it?" Weasel said.

"Not yet. Let's see what they're up to first."

One of the gunships broke formation and circled Marquez's plane. The other attack chopper flew east, toward the Hyacinth entrance where Harvey Henshaw was stationed. The two transport choppers continued flying directly at them.

"Who are they, Derek?" Weasel asked.

"Can't tell. The two smaller choppers look like they're from Dobkin's fleet, but the transports look more like U.S. military. They've scrubbed all identification."

Parnell heard something then, over the punctuating thumps of rotor blades. An extended low-pitched moan followed by three clipped screeches. An owl? *Oh shit no, not an owl! Not now!* He heard it again, and pulled his head back from the sights. Looked around in confusion.

"You guys hear an owl hooting?"

"An owl?" Weasel said, his quizzical look and surprised tone implying the absurdity of it.

Parnell looked to Flywheel for an answer, but Javion only stared at him with genuine concern.

That's it, then, he reasoned. *I've gone over the edge. I'm going batshit crazy!*

A loud explosion in the canyon reclaimed their attention. Parnell picked up the binoculars and had a look. The first gunship had bombed Marquez's airplane. One wing was gone. The windows were blown out. Flames engulfed the fuselage. Plumes of smoke escaped from underneath the charred engine cowling.

"Holy shit!" Weasel howled. "They just annihilated the shrink's plane. They've got bazookas!"

"Muthafucker!" Flywheel exclaimed.

Then a second explosion as the fuel tanks went up with a deafening *whoomph.*

Another commotion to the east. Parnell turned to see the limo leaving the mines, kicking up a trail of dust as it traversed the gravel road leading out to the interstate. The second gunship was in hot pursuit, drawing a bead on the Lincoln like a raptor hunting its prey. *Oh, Christ, no!* He tried to remember who had elected to take the limo to Winslow. Couldn't recall.

He saw it all unfold as if it was happening in slow motion. The attack copter pulled in low over the racing limo, the gunner crouching in the open bay, leveling the bazooka, taking aim. The first shot missed, blowing a large pothole in the road behind the limo. The second shot didn't miss. The limo blew apart into a million pieces of fiery metal and glass. The chopper veered off, leaving a trail of smoking wreckage behind.

Parnell couldn't harness his anger. "You fucking spineless bastards!" he shouted, swinging the launch tube around and aiming it at the tail section of the retreating aircraft. He pulled the trigger on the grip stock and waited for the seeker electronics to lock in on the target. An eternal five seconds later, a green light illuminated in the sight mechanism followed by a constant buzzing sound. One second after that, the missile left the tube, the recoil making him stumble, the rear-tube exhaust running a spray of intense heat across his back. The missile whooshed out over the desert gorge, its fins sparkling in the fading sunlight. It followed the chopper in a straight line, increasing in speed as it soared, quickly catching it from behind and lighting up the desert in a monumental explosion as it connected.

"Hot damn, that thing *is* evil," Flywheel shouted, giving

Parnell a high-five.

"One down, three to go," Parnell shouted, quickly loading a second missile into the tube. He was stunned and a bit terrified at the SA-7's immense destructive power. The heat-seeking, lock-on-target technology was amazing. *What a weapon! Buster was right. You hardly even have to aim the thing.* "They know we're here now, gentlemen," he said. "Go ahead and open fire."

The lookout shack erupted in a cacophony of noise as Greg Bethea and Javion Wheeler began shooting. The two transport choppers flew straight at them, coming in low over the ridge, machine-gunners strafing the rocky surface. Shots clanked against the shack's aluminum roof and pocked the plywood walls. Weasel and Flywheel fired and ducked repeatedly. One of Weasel's shots caught a shooter in the chest. The gunner fell from the open cargo bay, flipping end-over-end down to the desert floor. The second transport helicopter went for the power grid. Parnell heard the sickening crunch of solar glass shattering, and knew from the severity of it that his treasured power grid had been knocked out.

The two transport choppers swung back out over the desert and circled the ridge while the remaining gunship came directly at them. *Too close for another missile.* Parnell unhooked from the SA-7 and set it aside, picked up the M-16 grenade launcher. If he missed from up here, the grenade cartridge would fall to the desert floor before detonating, and not blow back on them.

He took aim through the launcher sights. Waited. A hundred yards out, the helicopter banked into a wide turn and flew along the rim to give the gunners a direct line of sight. Weasel and Flywheel opened fire. Parnell visually estimated how far in front of the aircraft he needed to aim to bring it down. Adjusted his aim accordingly. Let the grenade launcher rip. The projectile left the chamber with a metallic *clang*, ascending toward its target in a long, looping arc. At first it looked as though his shot would sail low and miss. But the grenade pack had just enough velocity to strike the landing skids. The dusky skies lit up as the chopper exploded in a tremendous ball of fire and smoke, the sound of the hit reverberating through the canyon. The shack walls trembled. The burning chopper pinwheeled round and round down to the desert floor where it crashed with a muffled thump.

The transport helicopters came at them with a vengeance, four machine-gunners laying down a barrage of bullets so thick they couldn't return fire. The assault was fierce. Shots pelted the earth around them, kicking up rock chips and dust. The small shack's walls and support beams splintered under the onslaught. The three of them stayed low as the two remaining choppers hovered along the rim of the ridge and laid down a continuous blanket of gunfire.

Suddenly Weasel dropped his rifle and screamed, "Damn, I've been hit!"

Parnell crawled to him. Greg Bethea had taken two slugs, one under his right collarbone, the other in his throat. Blood gushed from his neck at an alarming rate. His breathing was ragged and bubbly. One look at the neck wound and Parnell knew it was a lost cause.

Weasel opened his mouth and tried to say something to him. His words came out in a hoarse whisper. Parnell had to lean over and put his good ear next to Weasel's mouth in order to hear him.

"We had a good run, didn't we, partner?" Bethea uttered, grimacing in pain. "Never thought I'd be . . . hoppin' the westbound . . . this way . . ."

The bullet had punctured Weasel's jugular. No way possible to stop the bleeding. Of all the horrible luck, Weasel had to catch a bullet in his neck. "You're fine, Greg," he lied, feeling the need to console his friend in his final moments. "Here, stretch out. Make yourself comfortable. We'll be out of this mess soon."

Parnell saw the fear and uncertainty in Greg Bethea's dying eyes, and a great sadness overcame him. Sadness coupled with a white-hot anger. He picked up Weasel's carbine and joined Flywheel in defending their position, firing a burst that took out another gunner. Incoming fire remained heavy. When Parnell went to load another clip, he saw Weasel staring sightlessly at the roof of the shack.

Greg Bethea was dead.

"He's gone, Fly."

"Goddamn, man! It ain't right."

One of the transports circled the ridge and made a calculated approach that told Parnell they were going to attempt a landing.

"It's getting' too hot in the kitchen, Fly. Time for us to hightail it outta here. You first. I'll cover you. I'll meet you down below and we'll head to the tunnel, meet up with the others."

"Gotchya," Flywheel muttered before slipping out the back of the shot-up shack and running in a crouch under cover of a rocky ledge that led to the ladder.

Parnell fired off a few final rounds, then bolted from the

shack, following Flywheel's route under the protective shelf of rock. Across the way, on the far side of the ridge, the big transport chopper came in for a bumpy touchdown. A half-dozen soldiers hit the ground running, dressed out in helmet-to-boots desert camouflage.

Army National Guard.

Are they working with Dobkin's syndicate? Or is this the feds' Operation Vagabond in action?

He dashed for the ladder under heavy gunfire, grabbed the top rung and swung himself up. He caught a glimpse of Flywheel below, standing with his Bushmaster at the ready.

Parnell was about to descend when a spray of bullets peppered his chest, knocking him off the ladder. He fell, flopping over the ladder rungs like a rag doll, landing fifteen feet down at Flywheel's feet.

The last things he remembered before losing consciousness were the extreme burning that spread across his chest like molten lava and Flywheel coming to his aid.

Parnell's Westbound Whistle Stop

ELAINE LEFT ANN AT THE ESCAPE TUNNEL and started back on the gravel path leading to the mines. Rapid bursts of machine-gun fire came from the ridge.

She stopped. Heard a far-off explosion.

Shouts.

More clattering gunfire.

Worry and fear consumed her. Just the three of them up there in that flimsy shack, defending the ridge. By the sounds of it, they were greatly outnumbered.

Her emotions were all tangled up. One minute she thought: *Dear God, please keep my Derek safe.* Followed by: *Why did I ever fall in love with such a lunatic?*

She picked up her pace, albeit tentatively, knowing the little pistol she gripped tightly in her right hand wouldn't do much against a horde of attackers armed with semiautomatic weapons. She entered the mining yard. Stopped. Listened to the intense gunfire, the thumping clank of rotor blades, the high whine of helicopter engines. Decided that despite the potential for disaster she had no choice but to push forward.

It was her beloved Derek up there taking the heat.

Oh, please let him be okay!

She followed the path, coming to the sharp bend that wound around the yard. A hundred yards away, under cover of a rocky ledge near the ladder, Flywheel crouched beside a prone body. Soldiers dressed in camouflage fatigues and combat helmets fired down on him from atop the ridge. One attacker tried to come down the ladder. Elaine watched Flywheel step out and nail him in the back with a well placed rifle shot. The soldier's helmet flew off as he fell from the ladder, his body bouncing down the rocky hillside into the yard. Flywheel quickly kicked the ladder away and retreated back under the ledge.

Uniformed soldiers and not private mercenaries? What gives?

She moved closer. Realized with a shudder that Derek was the man Flywheel tended to. She saw the white bandage covering his right ear, the familiar T-shirt with the words **JUSTICE IS A LOADED SIX-SHOOTER** emblazoned over a graphic of a long-barreled revolver. His favorite shirt.

Had he been shot? Did he fall?

Flywheel talked to him, all the while keeping an eye on the ridge above.

Elaine threw caution to the wind and broke into a run, a raucous scream bursting from her lungs. "DEREK! Oh, Jesus, I'm coming, babe!"

The gunners on the ridge opened fire again and she halted, ducked behind a boulder. It took every ounce of her toughness and resolve to wait them out. When they finally pulled back to reload she ran up under the outcropping and dropped to her knees.

Derek had already lost a lot of blood. She felt for his pulse. Faint and erratic. His eyes were open, but they were murky, halfway focused on something only he could see.

She freaked.

"Derek, it's me, baby," she said, her mind in utter chaos. "Stay with me. I'm here for you."

He mumbled something unintelligible.

Flywheel spoke to her. "You shouldn't be here, Elaine. He's messed up bad. Now you're in danger, too."

Javion's lecturing pissed her off, considering the situation. She ignored him, electing instead to try to get through to Derek. "What happened, babe?"

Parnell's eyes cleared slightly and he looked up at her from where he lay, seeming to take a minute before he recognized her. "Bad," he croaked, pausing, licking his lips. "Took a few . . . in the . . . chest . . ."

He shivered noticeably. Had trouble getting enough air into his lungs to push his words out and articulate his thoughts. Couldn't shape his mouth to enunciate properly. Kept frantically licking his lips. Severe dehydration. So much blood.

He was fading fast.

NO! Please don't take him from me!

She grabbed his hand and squeezed, shocked at his weak grip.

". . . I . . . I just wanna say . . ."

"Don't talk, Derek," she said. Sweat slicked his pain-contorted face. She wished she had a bottle of water for him. "Save your strength. We'll get you out of here soon, love. Just hang on."

Flywheel gave her a disparaging glance, as if to say *Don't count on it.*

Derek grimaced in pain as he struggled to sit up. "No, I hafta say something . . ." he said with a strained effort. He blew out his breath and lay back, frustrated by his failed attempt to rise. She watched him trying to compose himself. A long minute passed before he was able to continue. "I love you, Lainey . . . with every . . . ounce . . . of my being. I . . . I always have . . ." He paused again, another bolt of pain twisting up his face.

This was like a sucker punch she didn't see coming. She was going to lose him. The one and only true love of her life. They had been soul mates, if there was such a thing (Derek always made fun of her when she used that term). The realization left her woozy, on the verge of fainting. There was no way they were going to get him to the tunnel, let alone get him on a moving train. What she had feared for years was finally happening. Her Derek was going to die in a senseless gunfight. She tried to hide her panic. Attempted to conceal her swirling emotions—anger, loss, sympathy, injustice. She reached down, swept her hand across his fevered brow, trying to relax him. "I love you, too, Derek," she told him, her words sounding thin and sad to her ears.

Clearly stressed, he spoke again, so softly she had to lean in closer to hear him. "Some day . . . when it's your turn to ride the westbound . . . I'm sure . . . I'll see you . . . again . . . at my whistle stop. So . . . sorry . . . karma is . . ."

He never finished the thought. It was as if a switch had been thrown; he jerked several times in the spasms of an intense seizure and died.

Elaine lost it. She fell on top of him and let out a caterwauling wail. "NOOOOHH, NO, NO! IT CAN'T BE! NOT NOW!"

The shooting started up again from up on the ridge, sprays of bullets showering the rocky overhang. Flywheel tried to separate Elaine from Parnell, telling her they needed to make a break for it before they became victims, too. But she clung tightly to Derek's body, refusing to let go, sobbing uncontrollably.

"I know this is difficult, Elaine, but we have to clear out."

"No! I'm not leaving him, Javion," she said, her shoulders shaking. "I can't leave him here like this. I'm staying."

"Ain't no way Derek would've wanted that. Don't make this more difficult than it already is."

Elaine hated Javion Wheeler in that moment. She felt as if her insides had been scooped out and slopped across the rocky ledge. She was empty. Depleted. Her reason for living was suddenly gone. A deep, dark hole had been punched in her psyche. *How will I ever make it without him?*

Another barrage of shots rained down on the ledge, then stopped. Flywheel tugged at her shoulders, trying to separate her from Parnell's body. She grabbed handfuls of his shirt and hung on with a strength and desperation that startled her. But Javion Wheeler was too strong for her, and with a heave-ho, he yanked her upright and out from under the overhang.

Flywheel's youthful strength allowed him to half-carry/half-drag Elaine down the path with his left arm while firing off defensive cover shots with his right. She twisted and kicked and screamed all the way. When they stepped inside the escape tunnel entrance, Flywheel let her go and dropped to the ground, exhausted. Elaine stood there, bewildered, disoriented, her cheeks slicked with tears. Everything seemed so unreal. So terrifyingly harsh and ugly.

She brought her hands up to her face, saw the ragged strips of Derek's bloodied shirt in each hand.

It was all she had left of him.

She leaned against the cave wall and cried.

She listened to Flywheel's heavy breathing, thinking, *I have never felt so all alone.*

She had the shakes. Felt cold and beat down. A large part of her had died up on that ledge along with Derek.

Flywheel came to her, placed a hand under her chin and lifted her face to him. "Sorry about havin' to do that to you."

She looked at him, his wild 'fro framing his dark face in the dim light. She wanted to thank him for saving her, but could not find the words in her jumbled mind. Instead she said, "Greg Bethea is gone too, isn't he?"

"Yeah," he said, shaking his head sadly. "I'm so very sorry for your loss, Elaine. Sorry for everything that's happened."

"I know this might sound weird, but will you hold me, Javion?"

"Sure." Flywheel threw his arms around her. "Doesn't sound the least bit weird to me," he said, clenching her tightly.

She felt safe and protected in Javion's muscular embrace. They stood there, still as statues, mute as church mice, holding each other, two survivors of a very black day giving each other the strength to continue.

Shortly, Flywheel stepped away from her and said, "The shooting stopped. They'll be here soon." He handed her one of the high-powered flashlights that Derek had bought for escape purposes. "We'll need these to get down the tunnel. C'mon, the others are waiting. We got us a train to catch."

The Last Train to Winslow

THE TEMPERATURE DROPPED with the setting sun. The survivors huddled in the tunnel exit, half a mile out in the desert. Six cold, disheveled, emotionally drained souls, peering out from under a grouping of saguaro cactus: Jenn, Cale, Elaine, Flywheel, Ann Finnegan, Harvey Henshaw. Communications were limited to facial expressions and hand signals.

The gravity of the day's events devastated Jenn. Poppy dead? Greg Bethea too? Didn't seem possible. Two of the toughest, most fearless men she knew were gone in a flash of gunfire. According to Flywheel, they had taken the westbound within minutes of each other. Jenn had been out here an eternal two hours, contemplating that sad reality. Too much time to think. Far too much time waiting on a train she feared might not show. The southbound freighter from Provo ran on a scattershot schedule. If the train didn't come through tonight they could all be dead by morning. That sobering realization dragged her down further.

She watched Hyacinth burn. The shooting had stopped, but she heard the shouts of gunmen. A large helicopter circled the mines. She was well aware that, should they be discovered, the big copter could finish them off with a well-placed explosive. Flywheel said the attackers used bazookas to bomb their 'bo friends who were trying to flee in Dobkin's limo. She shivered at the thought.

Her concerns about the train vanished when, at 8:50, the hoped-for Union Pacific freighter rumbled into view. Relief swept through the cactus bunker. Harvey Henshaw applauded. Ann gave thanks to the Lord. The six of them crossed the rails and lay low, beneath the gravel berm, on the far side of the track bed.

As per usual, the Union Pacific slowed to half speed to negotiate the eastward curve around Coughlin Butte. This sprint-and-grab should have been a slam dunk, but Elaine—who normally hopped moving trains with the speed and agility of a gold-medal high jumper—wasn't into it. Clearly, she was devastated over Poppy's death. She was in a trance. She remained silent, but her stunned, hopeless expression said it all. She was despondent, not the least bit interested in going to Winslow. She wanted to stay with Derek. Without Derek, her life was finished. Jenn certainly understood her fragile state of mind, but they had to get on that train. All six of them. Jenn knew Elaine well, and feared she might be tempted to throw herself under the freighter's wheels and end it all. She asked Cale and Flywheel to stay with her, and they did so dutifully. As the twin locomotives thundered past, Cale and Javion got to their feet, pulled Elaine up by her elbows and got her moving. As the first open boxcar came into view, they loped beside her and, at the precise moment, grabbed hold of her arms and heaved her up and on before catching on themselves.

All six aboard and accounted for.

They were on their way, rolling southward, toward the Arizona state line and ultimately Winslow. It comforted Jenn somewhat. *Tougher to hit a moving target.* Through the open boxcar doors she watched the orange glow from the Hyacinth fires light up the darkening skies. A column of smoke spiraled from the top of the ridge like a gray arthritic finger pointing to the heavens. She wouldn't miss this place, this lonely, desolate plot of rock and sandstone and miles of underground passageways. Wouldn't miss living like scared groundhogs. She was ecstatic to be saying goodbye to this arid stretch of Utah desert that had become a graveyard for so many—Poppy, Greg Bethea, Oshkosh Moss . . . quite a few of her new breezer friends as well.

Her heart was heavy, her emotions frayed. The scenario she had feared for so long had finally happened—Poppy, dead and gone. She hurt, almost as much as Elaine, but she knew Poppy would want her to stand tall and take charge in his absence. She had to summon the strength to carry on. It was difficult, this trying to appear strong in the aftermath of tragedy. She'd had far too much practice at it. She'd lost Lulu Solton three years ago. More recently, Russell Holt. Now Poppy. Three people she loved, each one suffering a brutally violent end. Three spirit-crushing losses. Too much heartache for a 22-year-old woman to endure.

Am I a jinx? Am I the reason they're dead?

This was the burning concern that haunted her. And now that Cale was in her life, those questions became more front and center. *Is it possible I'm a danger to him? Is Cale safe with me?* Jenn lay back in his arms and Cale pulled her in, kissed the back of her neck. She smiled uneasily, thankful for the dim interior that masked her apprehension.

The train rounded the bend and picked up speed. Hyacinth disappeared behind Coughlin Butte. The mood in the boxcar was solemn, morose.

Four hours to Winslow.

The swaying railcar made her sleepy. She snuggled closer to Cale and hugged Poppy's money satchel to her chest. He'd entrusted her with it last night. Told her if anything happened to him, she was to deliver the cash to their Shangri-La friends. Sadly, it turned out to be his last request. *Did he know somehow that today would be his dying day?* He had risked his life for her, not once, but twice. She couldn't escape her guilty feelings. It was her fault Poppy had been killed. If she had never made that call for help to him in the middle of the night, he would probably still be alive and well in Costa Rica, making love to Elaine every night. She would deliver the cash. Jenn owed him that. She owed him her life, if she was being honest.

How will I ever be able to repay him?

They had been in transit thirty minutes when it started to rain, tentatively at first, raindrops plinking the roof, then erupting into a full-scale downpour. Jagged flashes of lightning slashed across the night sky. Harvey Henshaw and Flywheel moved back away from the open doors to avoid getting drenched. The torrent intensified. Walls of water obscured their view of the passing countryside. The rain drummed the roof in a pounding, angry deluge as the train roared onward. *God is crying down on us. We have disappointed Him.*

She looked at Ann, who was propped up against the far wall and doing her best to console Elaine. Elaine, however, wasn't paying her much attention. She was obsessed with the shreds of Poppy's T-shirt. Despite coaxing from Ann, she refused to let go of the precious rags, repeatedly bringing her hands to her face and rubbing the bloody cotton scraps against her cheeks.

Jenn watched Elaine go through her obsessive ritual. It made her sad. A little embarrassed. Like spying on someone performing an intimate, private act. She looked away, wishing she knew some magical way to pull her out of her funk. Unfortunately, Jenn had learned the fresh wounds of tragedy healed only with the passage of time.

The downpour stopped twenty minutes later. Jenn breathed in the rain-soaked air. She loved the bleached smell of sage and creosote bush after a desert rain. The scent had a calming effect on her, something she very much needed right now.

The remainder of the trip passed quietly, the only sounds the creak and clatter of the rocking boxcar and the train whistle that blew furiously as they approached gated crossings. They arrived at Winslow Yards a little past one in the morning. Cautious, ever on the lookout for railroad bulls, they left the train and trooped through the switching yard, darting between decoupled railcars. Jenn felt sluggish and stiff after the ride on the freighter. Her legs refused to cooperate as she navigated the tangle of crisscrossing tracks. Cale helped her along, keeping her from tripping and falling on her face.

They regrouped at the head of the hiking trail leading into Homolovi State Park. They slogged along the trail, six scruffy refugees headed for the promised land. Beams from their high-powered flashlights sliced through the opaque night, providing shaky illumination along the dark trail. Tiny vapor clouds escaped their mouths as they walked. Jenn's fingers and feet were numb. Behind her she heard Elaine sobbing and sniffling, Ann at her side, uttering constant reassurances.

The trail opened up into a wide stretch of desert hardpan that led to the floodplain aqueduct—the big steel pipe that was the south entrance to Shangri-La. The Little Colorado rushed and gurgled on the other side of the tree line. The leaves of the cottonwoods and aspens hissed softly in the night breeze.

Cale noticed it first as they neared the large conduit. "What the hell?" he said, stopping, directing his flashlight at the drainage pipe. "The signs are all gone."

Every one of the tin hobo glyphs that had marked this camp entrance for years had been removed. The big steel spillway looked naked without the breezer signage. Jenn noticed something else. The light on the far side of the pipe—the Shangri-La village grounds—looked different from here. Far brighter than it should be for this time of night. And then she heard faint noises in the distance. The growling sounds of gas generators and heavy machinery. She caught a whiff of something smoky and putrefying. *Burnt hair?* A bead of worry worked its way up her spine. She looked at Cale questioningly. *Something is very wrong here.*

Guardedly, they approached the aqueduct entrance. Cale shined his flash into the dark void, pushed his rifle out in front of him as he entered the pipe. Jenn followed close behind, the others falling in behind. They shuffled through the silty sediment that covered the floor. Jenn kept her eyes down, worried about snakes and poisonous lizards. Poppy had told her tales of his hobo friends who'd had the misfortune of stumbling upon four-foot western diamondbacks and plump Gila monsters nesting here. Upsetting a slumbering venomous reptile was the last thing they needed right now.

They hiked on, Jenn thankful not to encounter any reptilian creatures. They turned the corner leading to the exit and stopped. Bright light streamed through the opening. The sound of groaning motors and rasping chainsaws was louder here, the burnt hair smell much stronger.

"What's going on?" she asked Cale, fear thinning her voice.

Flywheel answered for him. "I think we're too late."

She turned to Javion. "Too late for what?"

"I hope I'm wrong, but I think maybe our Shangri-La brothers and sisters got stomped on, same as us."

"Well," Cale said, examining the magazine on his rifle, "only one way to find out. Everybody check your ammo. No telling what we'll be walking into."

Harvey Henshaw said, "You sure we wanna do this, T-Seed? We can always head back."

"Back where?" Cale replied.

"He's right, Harv," Jenn said. "I assure you we'll only be here long enough for me to deliver Poppy's money." She held up the satchel. "Fifty grand is sure to do a lot of good for our friends."

Ann said, "True, but I don't think your father would want you to do this if it puts you in danger, Jenn."

"*Danger?* You think Poppy didn't face much worse coming to my rescue? I'm a Parnell, damn it! I *will* deliver this cash."

Elaine spoke for the first time since they left Hyacinth. "I could have been a Parnell," she said, so faintly that Cale asked her to repeat it, which she did in a slightly louder voice.

Everyone stopped what they were doing and stared at her. Elaine's declaration was the saddest thing Jenn had ever heard.

Ann said to Elaine, "You've always been a Parnell to me."

This started Elaine crying again and Ann realized her mistake. She apologized profusely, telling Elaine she was only trying to lift her spirits.

"Look," Cale said, "How about if Jenn and I head out? Anybody who doesn't want to go can stay here."

"We shouldn't split up," Flywheel said. "We need to stick

together . . . strength in numbers, ya know."

"Javion's right," Jenn said. "We should all go together. Can you make it, Elaine?"

Elaine huddled with Ann in whispered conversation. Finally Ann said, "We're good. We'll follow you."

Flywheel said to them, "You ladies still against carrying a weapon?"

"Guns," Ann said, spitting out the word as if it was poison. "They bring nothing but trouble, Javion."

"I'm just sayin' . . . sometimes they *prevent* trouble, too."

The group left the pipe, walking out into the long fallow field that served as the Shangri-La shooting range. They tramped fifty yards in darkness to the shooting stations.

Arriving first, Cale stopped and said softly, "What the hell?"

The wooden structures that framed each shooting bay were gone. Nothing left but four rutted, barren patches of earth where Jenn had stood with Weasel, Billy the Kid, and Flywheel when going through firearms training.

"Freaky," Jenn whispered.

They moved out to where the targets should be. Jenn couldn't believe it. Every one of the "most hated" celebrity targets had been hauled away along with the supporting hay bales. Nothing but an empty field now.

They walked through a small grove of pinyon pine, stopping just inside the tree line to view the Shangri-La spread from atop the knoll. Banks of lights running on gas-powered generators lined each side of the camp. The entire area had been leveled. All the tents and shacks and lean-tos had been flattened. A couple of men in hardhats hurled pieces of wood and junk into a large bin. A bulldozer worked the far end, demolishing Ann's mini-mansion, the dwelling Poppy had maligned as "Big Rock Candy Mountain." Ann's prized brushed-copper roof now sat on a flatbed truck, glowing under the lights.

The breeze shifted, returning the putrid burnt hair smell.

Jenn heard movement behind them, from back in the trees. Cale heard it, too, and swung his rifle around in the direction of the noise.

"T-Seed? Flywheel?"

Three scruffy men came out from hiding. The man doing the questioning looked familiar to Jenn, but she couldn't be sure.

"Well I'll be damned," Cale said, smiling, lowering his rifle and going to the man who had spoken, hugging him affectionately. "How the hell are you, Moons?"

"I've been better." He nodded at the decimated hobo village. "How'd you escape this horrid scene?"

"We've been gone a few weeks. Just got back. What happened down there, Moons?"

Jenn learned that Franklin Mooney—'bo handle Moons—was one of Cale's closest Shangri-La friends. Moons and his two buddies (known in the breezer community as Stinger and Tex) had lucked into part-time employment in New Mexico six months ago, working as ranch hands near Santa Fe. They had returned to Shangri-La two days ago, just in time to catch the feds in action.

"Musta been a hunnerd of 'em," Moons explained. "Seemed that way, anyway. Soldiers, they were. U.S. Army reserves. Helicopters flyin' ever which way. Gunfire. Bombs goin' off. Chaos everywhere. Me and Sting and Tex sat up here and watched our friends gunned down in cold blood. We heard the screams, the cries for help. It was a fuckin' holocaust! I'll never forget it as long as I live."

"These are dark times," Tex added.

Operation Vagabond, Jenn thought.

Flywheel said, "You just sat there and watched the slaughter? You didn't go after 'em?"

Stinger said, "You're kidding, right? It would've been suicide, Fly. Like huntin' grizzly bears with peashooters."

"Yeah," Moons agreed. "Just too many of 'em. Too much firepower. We'd heard rumors in Santa Fe the past month about some government domestic military operation playin' hardball with hobo squatters. Then earlier this week we heard more about it, and that they were going to be hitting camps in Arizona soon. We cut our employment short to get back here, but we were too late. Fuckin' pricks!"

"Did they kill everybody?" Jenn asked, astounded by this latest setback.

"They came in like gangbusters and bombed the shit out of the place," Moons explained. "Gunned down our friends like they were goin' after rabid dogs. When the smoke cleared and the survivors surrendered, they rounded them up and hauled them off. Not sure where they were taken, but we think they'll deport illegals and jail the rest for trespassing and vagrancy."

"Sweet Jesus," Cale said, shaking his head. "Any idea how

many survivors there were?"

"We don't know," Tex said. "All I know for sure is I lost my wife and son."

All eyes turned to the man named Tex, whose craggy face drooped forlornly.

Jenn ran her fingers over the soft calfskin of the satchel, thinking about the cash it held. Surely these men could use it to get a new start somewhere. But so could Javion, Harvey, and Ann. She knew Poppy had left a pile of cash at the Costa Rican beach house and that Elaine still had money from her modeling and artist days. She and Cale had the money that Poppy had given them. They were all set. They didn't need this cash and Poppy did want her to give the money to deserving Shangri-La breezers.

She made a quick executive decision.

She would divide it up between six of them. She did the math in her head. It came to a little over eight thousand apiece, a huge amount for hobos accustomed to surviving on next to nothing.

She announced her intentions and dispersed the money amid appreciative, though surprised, gratitude.

"I guess we should be getting out of here," Moons said, looking back out at the Shangri-La grounds that had become a ghost camp. "Nothin' left for us here."

Elaine spoke in a frail voice. "I want to go home."

"Where?" Jenn asked. "Costa Rica?"

"No. My house in Flagstaff."

"Are you sure?" Jenn said, knowing Elaine was still on the FBI's Most Wanted List.

"I've never been more sure of anything in my life."

Part 5:
Aftermath

FIVE YEARS LATER

The Little Train Conductor
The Queen of Flagstaff
King of the Hobos

The Little Train Conductor

JENN SMILED AS SHE WATCHED her husband playing with Mason. Today was their son's third birthday. Cale's world revolved around the boy and little Mason absolutely adored his father, his tiny blue eyes twinkling with unmasked adoration every time he looked at Cale. Mason was the center of their universe, a magnificent gift from God. After two heartbreaking miscarriages, Jenn had finally delivered a healthy baby boy three years ago today at Flagstaff Medical Center. Mason Gregory Turnipseed—seven pounds, seven ounces of bawling, giggling wonder.

They had celebrated his birthday earlier today with Mason's Godmother Ann and a group of kids from the neighborhood. A house full of shrieking, hyperactive preschoolers and their mothers with a couple of uncomfortable dads trying to make themselves useful. Cake and ice cream and a huge stack of wrapped gifts, many of them needlessly expensive, Jenn felt. But Mason hadn't been interested in any of it. Jenn had barely cut the cake when he started in with his "Twains, twains!" demand. Ever since his grandma Elaine had given him the model train set last week as an early birthday present, it was all the boy could think about. His sole focus the past week was *"Granny Ewaine's twains."* Mason's train obsession was cute at first, giving her and Cale a few laughs. But today, with the birthday revelers present, Mason's obsession with the train set bordered on rudeness. The child turned his nose up at all gifts not related to the model trains. Jenn and Cale apologized repeatedly to the other parents for their son's behavior, but the guests understood. Typical three-year-old behavior, they said.

Now they were in the rec room, Cale and Mason down on the floor playing with the model trains that were once Poppy's pride and joy. After Elaine brought the train set over last week, Cale worked well into the night to get it set up and running. When Mason woke up the next morning and saw the impressive display spread over the rec room floor, his face lit up and he'd let out a shriek of joy. And the setup *was* quite impressive. Papier-mâché mountains, bridges, tunnels, lakes and streams, an alpine village, an intricately detailed railroad depot. Mason was hooked. He couldn't get enough of the miniature train cars squeaking and clacking over the extensive network of tracks.

She and Cale had decided earlier this year that Mason's third birthday would involve a train theme. It seemed appropriate on several levels. They had lived the hobo life that revolved around railroads. It seemed a good way to honor Poppy's memory, and Elaine wanted to find a good home for the miniature trains. Too many painful memories in that Lionel set for her to keep in her guest bedroom, where it had been through most of her and Poppy's ten-year relationship.

Mason did love a couple of the gifts he received. His godmother Ann gave him a navy blue conductor hat with the words **MASON THE TRAIN CONDUCTOR** embroidered in white above the shiny patent leather bill. Mason's Aunt Gina and Uncle Frank sent him their gift from Boston, a darling little denim railroad engineer costume, replete with striped overalls, matching hat, and red neckerchief. Mason wore the outfit now but had replaced the engineer's hat with Ann's conductor hat. Jenn had never seen anything so adorable. She could envision Poppy looking down on this scene, grinning from ear to ear.

Cale's boisterous laugh pulled her out of her reflections.

"You gotta ease up on the throttle, Mister Conductor," he said, retrieving the little locomotive that had derailed for the umpteenth time. "That's what happens when you go too fast on those turns, Mase." Patiently, he set the locomotive back on the tracks and recoupled it to the line of railcars.

Mason was oblivious to Cale's words. He held the remote control in his hands shouting *choo-choo!* over and over, giggling with delight as he ratcheted up the speed, his excitement causing his conductor hat to slip down over his eyes.

Jenn sat back on the sofa and beamed. She was tired but happy. Watching the two men in her life playing with Poppy's trains filled her with a contentment she'd long thought wasn't possible. She was blessed with a devoted husband, a healthy happy child, and a group of close friends that included godmother Ann Finnegan, Harvey Henshaw and his new wife Gloria, and several neighbors in their subdivision. Elaine lived close, north of Flagstaff near Humphreys Peak, fifteen miles away. Jenn and Cale had lucked into a foreclosure deal on this nice three-bedroom house in the Aspen Trails neighborhood shortly before Mason was born. Their den walls were lined with bookshelves overflowing with the novels and biographies she liked to read. Cale had converted the garage into his workshop where he built shelving units and furniture.

Life was good, there was no denying that. Her world had improved immensely since that dreadful day five years ago. Sights and sounds of that last day at the Hyacinth mines would forever haunt her—helicopters, bombs, automatic rifle fire, death and destruction, the long ride in the dark of night to Winslow on the rattling UP freighter. Thankfully, her nightmares had ceased. She and Cale had helped each other exorcise their demons. Professional counseling also helped. But most of Jenn's anxiety and depression faded away after Mason arrived.

The world outside their windows also looked much brighter these days. A new president and his administration had changed the political landscape in Washington D.C., slowly rebuilding America from the ground up. A New Deal type of legislation had been pushed through that put millions of Americans back to work, rebuilding roads and bridges and working on other key construction and conservation ventures. Cale and Harvey Henshaw were both beneficiaries of the new federal plan, working on Arizona state projects the past couple of years. The Supreme Court had found the violent and murderous tactics taken by the Operation Vagabond task force to be unconstitutional and criminal, which led to the roundup and imprisonment of many key participants. The Internal Revenue Service also put a plan in place that pardoned all tax evaders, so that Cale and others like him could pay their taxes on a penalty-free payment system without facing prison time. There was new hope and prosperity in the States that was infectious and beautiful. Still a long way to go to bring America back to the top of the global heap, but things were looking up.

Of course, both she and Cale lived with the fear that they would be pinned for the murders they'd committed. Jenn knew there was no statute of limitations on murder, Poppy had told her that many times. But it seemed after five years they might be safe. The killings they had done had taken place in remote locations, and much of the evidence had been destroyed by subsequent events. Besides which, the U.S. Department of Justice had their hands full prosecuting those responsible for the Operation Vagabond debacle.

Jenn stood, feeling a tiny kick in her belly. If all went well, Mason would have a baby sister in another five months.

She went to where Cale was sprawled on the floor. "I think I'll go give Elaine a call," she said. "Let her know how things went. You need anything?"

"Look, Mommy, look!" Mason shouted. "Choo-choo!"

"Yes I see, darling," she said, ruffling her son's hair and exchanging smiles with Cale.

Cale said, "Give Elaine my love."

"I will. So you don't need anything, then?"

"No, I'm good. Got everything I need right here."

Jenn leaned over and kissed the top of his head. She left the rec room knowing exactly what he meant.

The Queen of Flagstaff

ELAINE DISCONNECTED WITH JENN. She was happy to hear her grandson was enjoying the model train set and that his birthday party had been a success. She apologized for not being there, but Jenn understood. This was a special day for Elaine, a day of remembrance. Today marked the fifth anniversary of that terrible night at the Utah mines and Derek's death. She still couldn't quite rationalize that little Mason Turnipseed had come into the world the same day Derek Parnell had left it. Sure, it was three years after Derek's demise. But on the same exact calendar day?

Coincidence? Derek always claimed there was no such thing.

Karma? Definitely.

Some strange and beautiful metaphysical power had been at work, for sure.

As Ann Finnegan would say: The Lord gave and the Lord taketh away.

It had taken Elaine some time after Mason's birth to feel comfortable in her role as a grandmother. A thirty-nine-years-young grandma? There was no actual bloodline there, of course, but she loved Jenn as she would her own flesh-and-blood daughter, and she cherished Mason as if he was her genetic grandson. Her heart soared every time little Mase smiled at her with those shining blue eyes and called her Granny Ewaine in his high-pitched toddler voice. How could she not respond to that? How could she not love him with all her heart? And within a few months, there would be a second little Turnipseed. A girl. Elaine couldn't wait to spoil her rotten.

She took her phone with her to the kitchen where Raff was finishing his supper.

"Everything okay, honey?" he asked, dabbing his mouth with a napkin and pushing back from the table.

"Yeah. Things are good. Mason had fun at his party. Jenn says hi."

He came to her, placed his hands on her hips and kissed her. Stepped back and searched her face. "You know you're the most beautiful woman on the planet, right?"

"Oh stop it, Raff," she said, playfully slapping at his arm.

"I mean it. You are. Would my gorgeous lady like coffee? I'm making some."

"Sure. Please."

She sat at the table and watched him measure out the coffee, pour it into the filter and place it in the Cuisinart. He set the carafe on the burner and started the brewing process.

Elaine met and fell in love with Rafferty Blaylock just after Mason was born. She had been through a couple of difficult years after Derek's death, years of intense psychotherapy and self-examination coupled with a few sticky legal issues. During that time, as a cathartic part of her therapy, she got back into her painting, which led to several local gallery exhibitions. On what turned out to be a very special night at one of her showings at West of the Moon Gallery in downtown Flagstaff, Raff walked through the doors and into her heart. She remembered his approach like it was yesterday. He was a few years older than her, nicely dressed in a pinstriped, three-piece suit. Pleasant, natural smile. Angular face with a strong, cleft chin and thin, straight nose. Full head of striking silver hair. Hazel eyes that shined with curiosity and intelligence. No ring on his finger. He told her he'd seen her event advertised on the gallery website and just had to make the trip from Tucson to check it out. Said he was an amateur painter himself, but not very good. She liked his self deprecating nature. Wasn't full of himself like a lot of the men who hit on her. He showered her with so many compliments it embarrassed her, then scared her, she thinking he might be a well-heeled stalker. But as the night wore on, she came to understand he was sincere in his praise. He seemed to have an intuitive grasp of painting and they talked shop during lulls in viewings. He told her he was drawn to her *'My Life with Derek'* painting. It spoke to him, he'd said. *Stirred* him. So much movement and color and emotion on a single canvas. It captured perfectly the random chaos of this life, he'd told her. He wanted to know all about her inspiration for it. Wanted to know about Derek. Elaine remembered wondering how anyone could be so enthralled by that painting. She considered it to be one of her lesser works, and had brought it to this showing only because she needed one more piece to fill her space.

Raff purchased the "Life" painting and two of her other canvases that night. He stayed in Flagstaff for the next week. Elaine saw him every night. During the day he worked on his laptop and made phone calls from his hotel room. He was a financial consultant, helping people get back on their feet after the nation came out of the long Second Great Depression. By day, Elaine painted in her home studio, trying to focus on a new triptych of the Grand Canyon, but thoughts of the silver-haired handsome man who'd suddenly burst into her life kept intruding on her focus. They were together every night, dining at Brix Restaurant and Josephine's. Afterward they went to Firecreek Coffee for dessert and acoustic music or the Museum Club for drinks and dancing. Raff was charming and eloquent. Sincere. She grew to trust him almost immediately. She told him about Derek, keeping the more lurid details to herself. He told her all about his late wife, Francine, who'd been killed four years earlier in a car accident.

Elaine decided to take the plunge on their third date. She invited him back to her house and they'd slept together. Raff had been here ever since, except when he went back to Tucson to rent out his house. Three months after that first night of intimacy, they were married in a civil ceremony in the rear garden of her home, surrounded by desert marigolds and purple aster, the breathtaking San Francisco Peaks providing a scenic backdrop. It had been a torrid, whirlwind romance, a dizzying affair. And now, more than two years later, Elaine was blissfully happy to be Elaine Leibrandt Blaylock. *Mrs.* Rafferty Blaylock.

She reveled in the domestic tranquility Raff brought to her life. He gave her an inner peace she had never known. And she, with her artsy, bohemian side, was good for him. She helped to loosen up the rigid businessman persona he'd hidden behind early on. She'd opened him up, even getting him to dress in jeans and smoke weed with her on occasion. He refused to do peyote buttons with her, but she respected that. They were good together. Balanced each other out.

"Here you are, my sweetness," Raff said, setting a cup of coffee in front of her and taking a seat next to her. "You sure you're all right? You're a million miles away, baby."

"I'm fine, hon," she said, smiling at him, taking a sip. "Just thinking."

"About Derek?"

He had accompanied her this afternoon to Citizens Cemetery in South Flagstaff to visit Derek's grave. They had stood together in front of Derek's gravestone, Raff's arm wrapped around her, his concern obvious. But she made it through just fine. She didn't get emotional or weepy the way she had in past visits. She'd managed to place the bouquet of red roses and white carnations at the base of the marker and tell him she loved him and missed him without going off the deep end. Raff had stood back, respectful, giving her space and privacy.

"Well, yeah," she said. I was thinking about him some. But mostly I've been thinking about us, Raff. The way we met. How great it is being with you . . . being your wife." She took another sip of coffee. "I guess visiting Derek's grave brings out the sentimental side of me."

"I like that side," he said, rubbing her shoulder. "I like *all* your sides, Laine."

She laughed. "You're such a dirty old man."

He leaned in and kissed her. "You're complaining?"

"No, I'm complimenting."

"You going to write in your journal tonight?"

"Yes. I've got to get an entry in."

She'd started keeping a journal soon after Derek's funeral, mostly at the behest of her first therapist. It was indeed a therapeutic exercise, writing down her feelings and detailing what she could remember of her and Derek's adventures. The journal had turned into a pile of notebooks over the years, with many of the entries reading like an ode to tragic lost love. There were even tear stains on some of the early pages. She left nothing out. She started out writing in it daily, but she had slowed down the past couple of years to maybe once a week. But on this day each year—this iconic date that marked both Derek's death and Mason's birth—she wrote a passage, without fail.

She'd told Raff about the journal and even shared some of her entries with him, at least the ones pertaining to Derek (she would never show him some of her entries about him, they were so wild). She'd been reluctant to share information about Derek at first, thinking she would be violating his memory. But after she started reading pages to Raff, she realized it was a beneficial exercise that brought them closer together.

Her phone buzzed, startling both of them. Elaine checked the display. "Oh my God! It's Javion."

She answered. "Well if it isn't the long lost Flywheel."

"Hey, Elaine. How've you been?"

"Great. How about you?"

"I'm chillin'. Philly's been great to me. Picked up steady work on a road crew, me an' a buncha my bros. Been livin' in a nice singles apartment complex."

"That's wonderful, Javion. Long time no hear . . . not since just after my wedding, I believe. To what do I owe this honor?"

"Sorry about bein' a bad correspondent, Elaine. Have you heard the news?"

"What news?" she said, holding the phone tight against her ear and giving Raff a nervous glance.

"About that douchebag, Blanton Miles? The bastard Derek wanted to snuff?"

"No, I haven't heard anything. What about him?"

"He was murdered, execution style. Shot in the back of the head in L.A. It's all over the Internet an' TV news. Happened yesterday."

"Jesus! Who did it?"

"Unknown assailants. A professional hit. Looks like Derek finally got what he wanted."

Yeah, five years too late, she thought. "Well, I guess that's a good thing, Javion."

She'd left that violent world behind five years ago and had written it off as a tarnished part of her past. This talk about a professional hit felt alien to her. Stirred up ugly memories. Shook her.

"You still there, Elaine?"

"Yeah, I'm here. Thanks for letting me know about it. I'll check it out."

"Oh, and Elaine? Congrats on your federal pardon."

"I thought you already knew about that."

"No. Somehow I missed that newsflash. Jenn told me. I just got off the phone with her."

"Ah. Well, that's kind of old news now. How do you think I've been able to stay here in Flagstaff?"

"I dunno. I figured somethin' like that had gone down with the feds. Just wanted to say I'm happy for you, even if I'm late with it."

"Thanks, Javion. I appreciate it."

Four and a half years ago, in a blatantly political move, the outgoing administration's President had pardoned Elaine and twenty-seven others convicted of various felonies. The Attorney General, after reviewing Elaine's case, decided that all evidence against her was circumstantial and based on hearsay. All charges were expunged from her record and she was once again a free woman.

"Well, gotta run, Elaine. You've got my number. Give me a ring sometime."

"Will do. And if you're ever out West—"

"Won't be happenin'. I've had an ass-full of that part of the country. Philadelphia's my home now. I'm done wanderin'."

"I understand, Javion. Good talking with you. Be well."

"You, too."

She disconnected.

"You okay, Laine?" Raff said, eyeing her with concern. "You look a bit undone."

"Grab your computer, Raff."

"Why? What's up?"

"Please. Just get your laptop."

He got up from the table and left the kitchen. Returned a minute later. Flipped up the lid of his laptop, slid it in front of her.

She did a search on Blanton Miles. Several hundred hits came up. She selected the Associated Press feed dated yesterday.

Dobkin International Services CEO Murdered
Sept. 23 – AP Wire Services, Los Angeles

Blanton P. Miles, the newly elected Chief Executive Officer of Dobkin International Services, was discovered face down in a ditch along Mulholland Drive by LAPD homicide detectives working out of the Hollywood Division. Captain Vincent Borrowitz says Miles was shot twice in the back of the head in what appears to be a professional gangland slaying. A longtime high-ranking company executive suspects the hit was an inside job. There has been much turmoil among the upper management ranks at Dobkin International since the founder, John Dobkin, was found murdered in Utah five years ago. The source goes on to say there could be as many as twenty-five suspects in the shooting as many have pushed to take control of the company over the past four years. Blanton Miles is survived by . . .

Elaine closed the article and shut the laptop, pushed back from the table. "Oh my God. How weird is this, Raff? If I didn't know better, I'd think Derek got him from heaven."

"You're tired, Laine," Raff said, empathy in his tone. He slid the laptop away from her. "You've had a long, trying day and you need to stay off the computer. What say we hit the hay early? I'll show you just how much I love you."

"You're sweet, hon. But I really have to write my journal entry. After you get done with me, I won't be good for much else."

"Fair enough," he said, his male pride shining through. "How about we meet in one hour. Our bedroom. I'll roll us up a joint and then we'll get down on it."

"No."

"No?"

She stood and started walking out of the kitchen. "I'll do the rolling. Your joints are like toothpicks, Raff."

"Fine, then. You do the rolling. We'll get wasted on one of your patented fatties. Is it a date?"

She turned back to him. "Absolutely. I'm gonna rock your world, Raff."

King of the Hobos

ELAINE SAT ON THE LOVESEAT IN HER STUDIO and opened her journal to a fresh page. She gazed out the picture window at the sun setting over snowcapped Humphreys Peak, collecting her thoughts. And then she put pen to paper.

> September 24
>
> Dear Journal:
>
> Today marks the five-year anniversary of Derek's death (and my grandson Mason's third birthday). I wrote in these pages last year about the strangeness in the way those two events line up. Mason's Godmother, Ann Finnegan, claims God is a master scriptwriter who delivers these timelines. I'm beginning to believe there is some truth to that, especially since I learned tonight that Blanton Miles — Derek's old nemesis — was found murdered yesterday. All of this can't be random. There has to be a higher power at work . . . a master scriptwriter. He delivered one hell of a script to this family. It would make a great TV movie of the week if it weren't so sad. I know I probably wouldn't watch it.
>
> So, Journal, as I've done the past four years on this date, I visited Derek's grave today. For the first time in I don't know how long I handled it well. I think I might finally be getting over Derek and all those awful things I went through with him. That certainly doesn't mean I don't still love him and miss him terribly. I do. My heart aches for him quite often, in fact. It just means that I'm getting better myself. It's evidence of my personal healing. Of course, my husband has been very instrumental in my recovery. Without Raff, I don't know where I'd be. He is so sweet and caring. Very affectionate and always there for me. This is not a slight

against Derek. They are (were?) two very dissimilar men, each with their own unique qualities. I love (loved?) them both in wildly different ways, and they both have loved me in passionately diverse ways. Some women never meet the right guy. I've been lucky to have met the right man twice. My relationship with Derek was wild and reckless and adventurous. Just like him. My time with Rafferty has been quiet, stable, domesticated . . . wonderful. Two different men, two contrasting experiences. Complete and total love in both cases.

Anyway, at the risk of repeating some of my entry from last year on this date, I want to lay out what I think Derek Parnell's legacy truly is. I have a gut feeling (one of Derek's favorite sayings) that this might be the last time I write about him in these pages. So here goes . . .

Derek Parnell was many things. He had a chameleon-like personality. To many, he was a feared vigilante, a purveyor of justice who didn't think twice about offing someone if he felt their crime was serious enough. He couldn't stand phony, bullshitting people and rip-off artists . . . people who took advantage of the down-and-outers. His enemies called him The Man with Tombstone Eyes. I believe he had close to 20 kills in his lifetime, and it was only his resourcefulness and elusiveness that kept him out of prison. There is no doubt he was haunted by his own unique demons. But Derek also had a softer side that he showed to me often. That was especially true during most of the three years we lived in Costa Rica. And he was completely dedicated to his daughter Jennifer. He searched for her for seven long years, never giving up the hunt, even when folks were telling him she was probably dead. But he never stopped believing, and his persistence finally paid off when he found her in the Colorado Rockies. He risked his life for her on numerous occasions. I was always impressed with his steadfast commitment to Jennifer, even when it took him away from me. I'm quite sure I don't have what it takes to spend seven long years pursuing someone I wasn't sure was still alive. But he did, and I admire that strength of character he possessed. And though he and Jenn had their ups and downs, it was obvious to me that he loved her and was completely dedicated to her.

And let's not forget that Derek could have lived the high life if he wasn't so committed to helping his breezer friends at Shangri-La and other major hobo camps. He had lots of money, but felt as if he didn't deserve it. He masqueraded as a hobo, riding the rails and sleeping in the woods, making the rounds of hobo villages and handing out cash to those he felt were deserving. All this while searching for his daughter. He quickly grew to legendary status, the breezer community giving him the ultimate 'bo handle of King Midas, a tag he grew to despise. I also admired this trait in him, this selfless generosity he had.

So, Journal, in closing I'll just say that Derek Parnell was a complex, highly intelligent man with a quick temper and a trigger finger to match. He was detached in many ways, a true loner who always traveled his own path. Lone Wolf was the code name Dobkin's syndicate gave him, and it fit. But even with all his flaws, for the better part of a decade, I loved him with all my being. God knows I'm quite imperfect myself. I'm not judging him, mind you. Just telling it like it is. I think probably the best moniker I can use to describe Derek Parnell is that he was King of the Hobos.

Now if you'll excuse me, I need to sign off and go show my husband how much I love him. Here I come, Raff!

Acknowledgements

No writer is an island. No novel is a singular effort. I had a lot of help in giving birth to this one, and I would like to thank the following for their support.

First, my wife, Cheryl, an award-winning technical writer and editor extraordinaire. She also keeps the household running, giving me the freedom to spend hours each day living in my fictional worlds.

Carole Mauge-Lewis, an artist with a special vision into my stories, who delivered another terrific cover, her third for me. This one depicts the badlands of southern Utah wonderfully as well as the dark mood of the novel. Thanks, Carole.

The following folks were immensely helpful in shaping the early chapters . . .

Jim Butorac, Chuck Clark, Angela Durden, Shane Etter, Jennie Helderman, Erika Passantino, Roy Richardson, Jedwin Smith, Fred Whitson.

A very special thanks goes to my friend, Cale Turnipseed, for allowing me to use his name for one of my main characters. Smile on, Cale. You're a literary star!

And finally, I want to thank my loyal readers, for, without you, there would be no books. I greatly appreciate your continued support.

Jeff Dennis
Loganville, Georgia
July 4, 2017

About the Author

JEFF DENNIS lives in Loganville, Georgia with his wife, Cheryl, and a roomful of guitars. *HOBO JINGO* is his fourth novel, and fifth work of fiction. You can read more about him on his website at www.jeffdennisauthor.com.